Counting Tadpoles

Counting Tadpoles
Stories
by Uncle River

FANTASTIC
BOOKS

© 2009 by Uncle River

Introduction © 2009 by Stanley Schmidt

First published by PS Publishing.

(This copyright page continues as "Publication History," page 287).

This collection is a work of fiction. All the characters, organizations, and events portrayed in it are likewise fictional, and any resemblance to real people, organizations, or events is purely coincidental.

All rights reserved. Printed in the United States of America. No part of this publication may be reproduced, stored in a retrieval system, or transmitted in any form or by any means, digital, electronic, mechanical, photocopying, recording, or otherwise, or conveyed via the internet or a website without prior written permission of the publisher, except in the case of brief quotations embodied in critical articles and reviews.

Fantastic Books
1380 East 17 Street, Suite 2233
Brooklyn, New York 11230
www.FantasticBooks.biz

ISBN: 978-1-5154-5827-2

First Fantastic Books Edition, 2024

CONTENTS

Introduction by Stanley Schmidt... 7
Counting Tadpoles... 9
The Nature of Property... 32
The Dashing About Flying Box People... 38
Marsh Grass... 54
Executive Search... 64
Requiem for an Information Age Worker... 73
How Bears Survived the Change... 82
The Lizard... 97
A Place Called Out... 124
Why There are Flying Saucers... 136
Love of the True God... 139
Passing the Torch... 150
General Density... 179
Piñons... 198
My Stolen Sabre... 212
The Building Inspector... 222
Circumambulatio... 241
Warrior's Honor... 254
Geronimo's Buttons... 266
What Does the Algae Eat?... 275

INTRODUCTION

One of the fringe benefits of the odd collection of ways I've chosen to spend my life has been the opportunity to make friends with people having a wide variety of occupations and lifestyles. These have included, among others and in no particular order, scientists, writers, musicians, doctors, artists, military officers, sailors, chimney sweeps, scuba divers, politicians, clergymen, pilots (both power and glider), teachers, students, gardeners, photographers, and a hermit.

One of the most valued of these is the hermit, perhaps (at least in part) because there are so few of them these days. Our current version of civilization has brought us a great many benefits, but most of us are so locked into it that we're thoroughly dependent on its technological and social infrastructure—and would be hard put to manage on our own at a much more basic level. Uncle River (I sometimes kid him about having chosen that name so that in some distant future he can be addressed as "Old Man River") has no such handicap. He's done it, and thrived. He hasn't *always* been a hermit, but there have been periods in his life when he was living on his own, very close to the land and largely remote from his fellow creatures of the human persuasion.

This has given him several strengths not widely shared: a rare kind of self-sufficiency, an understanding of the larger world and how we fit into it far beyond that of most of his urban contemporaries, and a healthy distrust of our often-blind dependence on the trappings of civilization and our headlong rush to get swept up in their latest fashionable manifestations. He is not one to follow fashions, whether in the content of his thought or in the literary forms and styles he chooses to express that thought. Some of the stories in this volume are science fiction, some fantasy, some quite close to the here and now, and some so hard to classify that there's no real point in bothering to try. All of them are unmistakably River, and that is really all the recommendation they need.

And while River has lived a goodly portion of his life on his own, he has also been uniquely sensitive to the needs and strengths and foibles of his neighbors and all the other people he has interacted with. There is in these stories an underlying gentleness and good humor toward his fellow creatures as they try to make their way through this world—and a pointed disdain for those who create unnecessary obstacles to that goal. There's a strong sense of place; River knows rural and small-town life, especially that of the American Southwest, and as you immerse yourself in these stories you'll find yourself feeling the desert sun and smelling the mesquite and javelinas and tasting the tortillas. You'll come to know and like a lot of his characters. And occasionally, I suspect, you'll be more than a little taken with his uniquely whimsical turns of phrase. ("How Bears Survived the Change" has my own personal nominee for "best opening line ever." And it's painfully easy to see ourselves, or at least people we know, in "The Dashing About Flying Box People.")

River is well aware that the world is changing and we'll need to adapt to it—and, insofar as possible, to choose *how* we want it to change. These stories, in addition to being quirky and fun, provide some excellent starting points for thinking about how we're going to do those very necessary things. There are those who rush to accept with unbridled enthusiasm the Latest Thing, whatever it may be; and there are those who fear the future and resist any change at all. River is neither; he's keenly aware of the benefits to be gained by utilizing some kinds of knowledge and technology, and also of the pitfalls of being absolutely and blindly dependent on them. The keys to coping wisely may well be in *selective* adoption of innovations—and in never losing sight of the fact that any of them can fail. Ultimately we're all dependent on far older and more fundamental things, and we'd be well advised to learn and remember how to deal with those—on our own, if necessary.

River understands all that better than most. In these stories, he provides a refreshing, stimulating alternate viewpoint, sneakily leading us to think about things we need to think about, in ways we're not used to thinking about them, while enjoying the process.

And what more could we ask of a writer than that?

Stanley Schmidt
January 2009

COUNTING TADPOLES

Ducklings scooted behind their mother amid water grass at the edge of the beaver pond: Six... seven of them. Several large trout swam under the shadow of a muddy ledge. Well, maybe they were just suckers, but any fish, and the permanent water to sustain them, was noteworthy in the American Southwest.

Mark Pysmeyer scouted for tadpoles.

<She told my counterpart that. She told *all* my counterparts that.>

Mark jerked out of his reverie. Who? What?

A large raven lifted from a branch above the pond. No, not a raven. Mark recognized the distinctive broad white stripe across the tail, as what he now realized was a black hawk took flight.

As did several smaller birds, calling some sort of alarm.

Mark peered toward where the birds came from, his heart beating faster. He heard it now. Something, several somethings approached through the thick streamside willow brush just upstream of the beaver pond.

A loud splash behind him caused Mark to jump, turn his head, and shout: "Yeow!" One of the beavers, of course, slapping its tail on the water. Kingfishers darted back and forth, their raucous warble adding to Mark's tense distraction.

Mark spun back around to the willows as javelina shot off in all directions. Javelina were a modest size, as hairy, grey-brown wild pigs went, but they could tear a person to shreds if angry. They were *fast*. Mark was sure there were at least a thousand of them.

Mark had run some indeterminate distance downstream past the beaver pond before it dawned on him that the perhaps really fifteen or twenty javelina had run every direction except toward him. Only then did he recall that if they *had* charged him, he should have climbed a tree. Adrenaline panic metamorphosed to hysterical laughter.

"Care to share the joke?"

Mark gasped as he spun around again.

An old man with disheveled white beard and hair thick enough to cover the collar of his bedraggled blue checked shirt sat on a cottonwood log by the side of the river. River, not brook or stream because, though only eight feet wide and inches deep most places, the Adobe River, with its half dozen even smaller tributaries, was the *only* permanent flowing water in fifty miles.

"Excuse me," said Mark. "Am I trespassing?" Most of the land that comprised the Adobe River's mountainous watershed was National Forest or Bureau of Land Management. The few residents of the small pockets of private property could be prickly… with reason. Mark had once seen someone empty a motor home's holding tank in the middle of what was obviously a driveway of the only private home in ten miles.

"Depends," said the old man.

"Oh?"

"What're you doing here? Turon?"

"Tourist, you mean?"

"Yeah. Alien from Planet *Con*soom." The old man hawked and spat.

"Uh, no," said Mark. "I'm looking for tadpoles."

"What for?" The old man stood up and waded toward Mark, glowering. "No, make that: *Who* for?" Mark only now realized that the old man was barefoot, and that his shapeless, grey cotton pants were rolled halfway up his bony shins.

<Cut. Splice.>

…shapeless, faded blue Wrangler jeans were rolled halfway up his gristly ankles.

A pair of flickers soared past, calling loudly, orange underwings striking against blue Southwest sky.

Mark felt a wave of vertigo.

"You a damned government environmentalist?" the old man growled.

"Uh…" Mark, in fact, was working, on contract, at what, had he counted hours which he didn't, would have amounted to maybe a third of minimum wage, conducting an ecological field study for New Mexico State University in Las Cruces, funded by a grant from the U.S. Department of Agriculture. Mark had taken the job, fairly begged his department chair for it, because any job that paid him more than it cost him to eat, to camp in the luxuriant mountain summer of the Upper Adobe River Canyon while Las Cruces was 112° constituted Mark's notion of winning the lottery.

Before Mark could figure out what to say, the old man answered his own question. "*I'm* an environmentalist," he shouted, weathered face flushing from sun-brown to glowing brick, "you're a *damned* environmentalist!"

Crazy, Mark thought.

The old man drew his .45.

<Tilt.>

Mark shook his head. Too much adrenaline today. Had he really imagined that the old man had a gun? "Uh, I'm Mark Pysmeyer. Sorry if I'm trespassing."

"Pisswater, huh," the old man half grinned/half scowled. (Mark blushed.) "Didn't say you *were* trespassing. Ain't decided yet. Didn't you read the sign?"

<Rewind. Edit. Splice.>

Mark's headache faded. (When had he developed a headache?) "Oh, sorry, I got distracted. Thought javelina were after me." Mark had smiled at that sign... Hadn't he? Hand painted, a bit garish, mostly bright purple and turquoise on a vermilion background, decorated with some sort of animal skull, crossbones, and vines and flowers, the sign read: "Company welcome. Trespassers will regret it."

Mark followed the old man up the trail. The old man's tire rubber sandals puffed little wisps of dust in the open, slapped firm dirt where shade allowed moisture to surface.

Memories struggled to cohere in Mark's head: Getting back from his first supply run to town in the week he'd been here. Parking his leprous red Datsun pickup in his old spot in the Turkey Spring Forest Service Campground. Walking downstream perhaps two miles by the river... Parking the truck in the Turkey Spring Campground and walking along the road through the canyon, seeing the quirky sign, being unsure about the trail... Parking the willow basket air car on the edge of a grassy clearing, under a ponderosa, just up from the sparkling little river. Disengaging the directional crystal from the solar power unit. He had checked the insulation pressure gauge and thermostatic shut off switch, then set the solar bell in charging position and flipped over the crystal.

<Cut. Delete.>

A fly landed on the tip of Mark's nose. He batted at it and sputtered. *What* had he just been thinking? How *did* he come to be following some crazy old man up a trail? Had the old man told Mark his name?

"Um, excuse me, it's been a confusing..." Mark began.

The old man whipped around, making shushing motions.

Something big that didn't have hooves bounded off, up an alligator juniper and oak scrub covered bluff, just out of sight.

"Well, you blew that one, Pisswater." The old man snorted contempt.

"What was...?"

"Lion," the old man interrupted. "Kept your yap shut another twenty feet, we'd got to see it."

"Oh. I'm sorry."

"You sure are."

<The People were becoming desperate. They could not go on. Not and remain themselves. They had never let the Demons see them. But the Demons had learned to see in the dark.>

"Hey, Pisswater, you all right?"

Mark shook his head.

"*I* got one foot in the grave," the old man said, "and three toes of the other one hanging over the edge, and *you* look like you're about to keel over."

The old man looked plenty robust to Mark, but... Cancer. An aneurysm looking to pop. No insurance. Too proud to apply for government assistance... Shouldn't someone his age get Medicare?... Mark blushed. "Sorry..."

The old man interrupted again. "Quit that! Ain't your fault you gotta breathe air."

"Oh. Sorry..."

"I said *quit it,*" the old man purred.

<The mountain lion stood on a lichen clad boulder, purring like a giant kitty.>

Mark sat down. It was either sit or he *would have* keeled over. Lichen rings swirled on the rock Mark sat on. A lizard did push ups on a fallen pine branch across the trail. A dove called, then a whip-poor-will. Mark looked up at the dusk. What had he been thinking? How was he going to get back to the truck before dark?

"Hope you don't mind sleeping on the floor," the old man said, as if to answer Mark's unspoken question. "I got plenty blankets."

Mark felt able to stand again, though still dizzy. There was no lion in sight, of course. Mark followed the old man in his ratty blue tennis shoes. Hadn't he been wearing some sort of homemade sandals? The trail emerged to a tiny stream: a foot wide, three inches deep except an occasional deeper pool. Mark saw tadpoles… and minnows. Fish meant permanent water. A spring perhaps. Mark could see where the stream dropped off to the right, into a rocky wash that looked all but unclimbable.

The trail turned left, past a hedgehog cactus in blinding red bloom. Several creamy white yucca flower stalks and towering yellow agave umbrellas also faced the last of the sun on the open southwest slope. Re-entering tree cover and a stretch of narrow canyon, the trail and the stream it now followed switched climate abruptly from desert vegetation in the open to fir, oak, and even a spruce and a little clump of aspen in the canyon's cool shade, already almost dark.

The land soon opened up again to ponderosas, junipers, and a berry patch. One short steep bit up the last slope had the old man gasping. He had to stop to catch his breath as they emerged to what amounted to his yard, with no real defined boundary between it and the surrounding forested mountainscape.

The cabin was small and made of junk. More junk lay under streamside walnuts and narrow leaf cottonwoods—part of an old bedframe, a roll of rusting wire, anything anyone had hauled this far any time in the last hundred years. The little cabin, a tiny shed, and an outhouse, were the only human structures in sight. Piñons dotted ridgetops.

They went in. The old man flicked on an electric light.

"Solar?" Mark asked.

"My back was younger once," the old man responded. Was that an answer? He lit a fire in a cast iron cookstove. "Use cottonwood or aspen this time of year," the old man said. "Burns clean. Goes out quick when you're done. Don't leave coals I don't need to heat the place up too much."

The old man heated a pot of beans and sawed thick slices off a loaf of bread that Mark would not want to drop on his foot. Whatever else might be wrong with him, the old man must have healthy teeth, Mark thought.

"Fare's limited," the old man said. "Javelina got in the garden."

"Oh, if I'm imposing…"

"I told you to quit that," the old man growled.

<Should we give up? Let the Demons eat us? Put on disguises? Trade for Demon-food clothing?

The People had not always lived in hiding. They did trade once. Visited openly. Now… Dead, who would know? The People's bones did not look different from anyone else's. Even their faces were not all that different from Shoshoni or Hoopa or Ute faces.>

Supper finished, the old man lit a pipe of something that didn't smell like either tobacco or pot. Mark thought to ask what it was, flushed with embarrassment again, didn't say anything.

"Want some? Mullein. Good for the lungs." The old man held out the pipe.

"No thanks," Mark managed to reply without any apology.

The old man set the pipe aside. "Started with the drug war."

"What's that?" Mark asked.

"Why you're here," the old man said.

Why *was* he here? How *had* he come to follow some crazy old man home? Then again, why not? What a place! Whip-poor-wills and crickets sang. Something called that Mark couldn't identify.

"Well, the old man continued, "maybe something *ended* with the drug war. But that's when it started for me."

The old man peered at Mark in the yellow kerosene lamp light. (Hadn't there been electric light earlier?) "I hit the road about the time your grandma bought your mama her first pair of penny loafers and your grandpa traded in the push button trannie and tailfins for something with seat belts. Been a little older, I might have been a hobo. But I rode my thumb more than rails, and worked enough to drive more than not till the insurance vampires took over the country." He hawked and spat in the direction of the weathered wood floor in the shadow of his threadbare easy chair.

"Been a little older, maybe I'd have settled," the old man mused. "Had a family even. Don't suppose you even know there was a time when most as had kids only done it when they could afford to raise 'em, not to mention got married first. Don't know. 'Nother world. Before I got to it, the country went nuts. I kept rolling. Draft might have wanted me, but I had a record for such heinous crimes as giving a blanket and a box of stale saltines to a teenage runaway. Pole-ice called me a rapist and every other filthy name. Wasn't *me* that pointed a gun in no fourteen-year-old's face and creamed his pants to watch her cower."

Mark could feel the old man's anger, carried how many decades? The things that determine a life! he thought.

"Used to like mechanicking," the old man went on. "Had me a ol' flat head straight six. Cops impounded it when they hauled me in. When charges was dropped, they told me I still owed about two thou to get the truck back. Guilty even when proven innocent. That's how the law works. That and planned obsolescence. Lifestyle consumers. Your generation, Pisswater, you don't know what living is. Javelina, now. I hate 'em. Ate everything there was to eat in the garden, and trampled the rest. But that's life. Life ain't soft, and mine's about used up. But you... Counting tadpoles for the government. You don't know what life is. It's been outlawed since before you was born.

"Drug war was the excuse. I seen it. But the hypester kings don't even know what they conquered."

The angry face softened. "I don't know either, but I know there was *something*." The eyes narrowed again. "Life was already outlawed..."

"What about here?" Mark gestured around him.

"Here?" the old man replied. "Here don't exist."

Mark flushed. Was this all some sort of hallucination? Had the javelinas he ran from this afternoon actually gotten him? Was this a trick his mind was playing in seconds of being torn to bits by wild pigs?

"Ninety-nine year lease from the Forest Circus," the old man said.

Mark blushed at his own overwrought imagination.

"Mining claim originally, but never patented. Nothing here *to* patent. Lease runs out in three years. Your tax dollars will pay some proper public servants to come in here then and burn the place down. Thirty years ago, they'd at least have had the decency to let me stay on till I died first. Well, I like as not will die first."

Mark blushed again, but refrained from saying, "I'm sorry," as it was the one thing the old man really seemed not to like him to do.

"Only reason I can be here's cause ol' Abe, as owns the lease, lets me, and keeps up with all them government forms and begging permission to blow your nose in your own hankie that makes me so mad I can't see straight." His chest rumbled unhealthily, and he spat again, beside his chair. "Back then," the old man went on, "life was already outlawed, but there was still places for outlaws to get out of the way. Mining claims was one of 'em."

"That how you got here?" Mark asked.

"Not exactly," the old man smiled. "Well, in a way. It's how I know about mining claims, to get Abe McCarty's okay to live on this place. Hear he's dying too…"

Mark thought of his own young life: The tadpole counting contract for the summer, to keep him fed in all this natural beauty… not to mention up here in the mountains while Las Cruces fried in lowland Southwest heat. His graduate assistanceship this fall—Bio 101 students needing a General Ed requirement, whose idea of biology was morphing computer game superheroes. Finding a dissertation topic to fit his *advisor's* career plans…

"Back then," the old man broke in, "hypesters and hipsters, goo-eyed idealists and noise… I was still young. Thought that's what life *was*. Took me a while to figure out I'd stopped having fun about the time the law stole my truck. Time came, I went in on a mining claim in Emberly County, California. Well, it was my partner's claim, but I got to live there. Black Tail Peaks. Maybe you heard of it? It was already official Wilderness, so no vehicles and no new permanent structures. But you could haul in a power dredge on a mule, work the river in season, and pretty well figure to take out $10,000 in gold.

"It was crazy though, even before the so-called drug war. Gold crazy. Everyone armed for bear. The bears was crazy too."

"Because of the people shooting them?" Mark asked.

"No, Pisswater. People didn't shoot them much, and there weren't many people there. Crazy bears."

"How so?"

"You ever hear how, when there's a bear causing trouble—trashing turons' high dollar camp stoves say, in Yosemite, the rangers'll tranquilize it and haul it off someplace else? You ever wonder where the someplace else is?"

"Oh!"

"Well, the bears was a pain. Harder to keep out of your cache than javelina and coons combined. But it was worth it, to be back there where the river ran fresh from God. Till the drug war."

"Dope growers, huh?" said Mark.

"Yes and no," the old man said. "Hippies figured out about mining claims too, and they did grow dope, and some of them did it for money. So what? They didn't invent the stuff, and they was less likely to shoot you out of stupidity than some drunk miner all worked up to gold fever with bears and claim jumpers on the brain. King Ray-Gun decided to be Emperor of the World, and beating up on Northern Cal dope growers was how to line up the troops. Just my luck there wasn't *enough* dope growers in Emberly County to be a significant voting force. So the county bought into the war.

"Worse, a big minerals corporation decided the Black Tails had enough gold to be profitable... *if* they could run all the independents off their claims and take it all. So they got in cahoots with some Forest Circus bigwigs to declare all the independent claimholders was really just cover for dope growing, and ran out every last one. Me, I saw what was coming and got out before the army of occupation landed. But there was something else I saw, or maybe something I heard, that didn't quite sink in till later."

<The People are no more! Who will sing to the Nature Spirits? How will the Spirits remember what people are? But noise! No more song, and noise *everywhere*. The Spirits become confused. They forget... Not just people. The Spirits lose all concentration.>

"Yep."

Mark shook his head. The old man looked at him with a gentleness... a softness to his face in the candlelight. He looked frail. How had he even hiked the trail up here?

"Used to hunt," the old man said.

"Bears?" Mark asked.

"Once in a while. Mostly if one wouldn't leave the cache alone. But bear meat's awful strong, and you've got to jerk all of it quick or it's no good. Bear's dangerous too, and there wasn't that many of 'em. There was lots of deer. Deer was food. Any time."

"You could get a license to hunt deer any time back then?" Mark blushed yet again. "Oh! Poached..." He choked off the phrase he had overheard in a cafe while stocking up: "Bambi burger."

"Poached, my Aunt Marion's Robin Hood porno comix!" The old man glared. "That is what they outlawed Robin Hood for, you know. Taking the king's deer without no official, 'By your leave.'"

"Oh, I see. You needed the food." Mark was familiar with the controversy, over rural poor people taking game for food when needed versus, say, shooting a thousand pound bull elk in velvet to sell the antlers for high profit Asian aphrodisiacs and leaving all that meat where it lay to rot.

"No, Pisswater, you don't see." The old man's vehemence seemed to renew his vitality. "I hunted 'cause deer's what was there. Government didn't invent 'em, and didn't print me. I hunted 'cause deer's what was where I was to eat. But... You ever been to a pow wow?"

"Huh?" Momentarily disconcerted by the nonsequitur, Mark thought, then said, "No, but I've seen Native American dances on TV."

The old man snorted, then lapsed into a horrible-sounding coughing fit. Alarmed, Mark didn't know if he should do anything. The old man's coughing subsided. He spat a repulsive lunger on the floor beside his chair. "Beat you again, ya bastard!" Mark noted that it was the first time he had heard the old man use even a mild profanity, despite his irreverence alike for government and grammar. "Don't show your death too much respect, Pisswater," the old man said.

Mark blushed at the realization that there was one other slight profanity to the old man's vocabulary. Behind embarrassment and annoyance at the way the old man seemed constantly to put him down, behind sympathy or fascination for a strange and apparently ill old man, Mark felt something in himself that the old man was speaking to.

The old man caught his breath, relit his pipe of mullein with a wooden match, took a few puffs, and went on: "You know them big pow wow drums? Lies flat. Maybe eight fat old men sit around playing the drum in unison while the rest sing and dance."

"Yes, I think..." The old man had cast an image that Mark could visualize, whether Mark ever really had seen such a drum or not, which he now was not sure: A drum big enough for eight old men to sit around and thump with leather-knobbed sticks, while their wives, wrapped in colorful shawls, swooshed back and forth with dippers of water, younger women, also in shawls, circled, and young men in feathers and loincloths gyrated wildly. Was that how it really was, or was Mark projecting a stereotype? There was something intensely real going on, but Mark no longer felt sure where the boundary lay between that reality and his own mind's response to the intensity.

"I was hunting one time," the old man said. "Followed fresh tracks up a ridge and down and back up, and not a deer in sight. Early spring. Still cloudy. No trail. I was grousing to myself about how far it would be to carry the meat if I did get any. About figured I'd best turn back anyhow not to get lost, when I saw fresh scat on the ridge I'd just topped. Tracks led down a steep slope, the backside of Beyond. I stood there with my old thirty ought six, looking down into that valley, thinking: If I see a deer I can hit from here, I'll take a shot, but I ain't even going to think about hauling no carcass up this cliff from the bottom. Well, it wasn't no cliff, but it was steep and long and deep and way back there.

"I stood there staring into the oaks and madrones a few minutes, thinking if I stood still long enough, if there was any deer they'd come out where I could get a shot. Thought I maybe heard something. So I stood a few minutes more when…"

Mark realized he heard something outside. He shook his head as the sound increased to a roar. An airplane. A large plane, approaching very low and slowly enough that it had to be prop drive rather than jet. The plane flew directly over the cabin, so low that it rattled the rusty corrugated metal roof.

"Thought I had you pegged," the old man said, as the noise faded.

"Does that happen often?" Mark asked.

"Of course," said the old man. "Three, four times a week. Sometimes more. Fighters too, and they come *fast*. Don't know they're there till they're on top of you. Don't you know? The military uses every wild, supposedly-pristine piece of territory left to practice."

"Practice what?"

"Demon wars," the old man spat. "Who knows? Protect us from alien invaders from Jupiter. King of all orgasms. Invade Pago Pago. I think I do got you pegged. Just don't know which way up the peg stands."

<He ran for the willow basket air car. *Got to flip the crystal switch from charge to force field.* Too late! The light-spear shot from the sky. Incinerated the willow basket car like the puny sticks it was. Well, he could weave another willow basket. That was why his people made their cars of such simple materials. If he could retrieve the power unit…! If the insulation had withstood the blast…

The light-spear flashed down again. He blacked out.

When he came to, no knowing how much later, head and heart both throbbing, he knew the power unit was gone. He would look, of course.

But the enemy had not taken *him,* so what else would they have used their gravitic scoop for?>

"Um..." Mark realized he still didn't know the old man's name, "this whole day's been a little peculiar..."

"You just cracked, Pisswater," the old man said. "Oh, don't worry. You probably won't go drooling off into the junipers, and the coyotes and jack rabbits won't care if you do." He gestured outside, where small night sounds indicated the variety of life in the wild dark. "You cracked open. That's why I'm telling you 'bout this."

"But... what can I do with it?" Which was not exactly the point, but was what the point Mark felt impelled him to say. What he really was thinking was: How can I teach Bio 101 with my head ozoned out worse than the students?

"*That*, Pisswater, is just where the Demon eats you." The old man hawked and spat yet again. Mark certainly hoped he wasn't going to have to sleep on a part of the floor coated with respiratory slime. "You think you got to do something all the time. I spent a lot of hours. Here. The Black Tails. Other places, backside of Creation. Hunted, yes, when I needed food. Or gardened, javelinas and all. Mechanicked... and liked maintaining a useful tool, back before they was all just plastic throw-away idols to the *con*soom God. Dredged for gold. But I spent a lot of time not doing nothing too. Watching. Listening. Just quiet. Them Demon planes don't fly over all the time. Maybe I seen something when the world and me both got quiet enough, long enough... I did hear something that day on that ridge in the Black Tails.

"Heard one of them big pow wow drums. Boom. Boom. Boom... Seven beats. Clear as me talking to you now. Down in that valley. Seven beats, measured out, even. A pause. Seven beats again. Not sure how long I stood there listening. Twenty minutes. Half an hour. Something like that. Went on and on, clear as can be.

"After a while... Well, I wasn't exactly lost, but I wasn't exactly sure where I was either. It was early enough in the year still to get cold and wet, and a cloudy sky didn't help directions. And there was bears in them woods. Figured I wanted to at least find a trail before dark. So I headed out. But I asked around later. Other folks back in that back country. The few other folks there was. The few I trusted.

"I wasn't the only one to hear that drum. There was a packer I recollect. Called himself Bear Tooth. Had a family and everything. Lived on a claim. Made a living with mules and burros, packing in supplies for gold miners and dope growers both. He had a idea what I'd heard. He thought it was a tribe of Indians that never met the White Man. Felt the vibe, he said. Always moved out of the way first."

"Do you believe that?" Mark asked.

"Not sure what I believe," the old man answered, "but I'm sure what I believe happened. Couple'a years later. Spring of eighty-one. I recollect, I didn't even hike out to the mail box for over a month. That was pretty common for me. Well, it still is."

Mark wondered what the old man would do if he got too sick to be able to hike out to his mail box. Or to get in supplies. How did he get in supplies? What had he been doing out where Mark ran into him today? Mark was aware how one-sided their conversation was, but he felt too... not even disoriented, more, dislocated... to say much.

"I recollect," the old man said, "when news came in, it was mostly local: Who'd got a new jacket. When the farrier might come around to shoe your mules. Where some crazy fool fugitive was holed up that you did not want to come on by surprise. Just took it for normal that everyone was armed for bear. And a outlaw and a criminal ain't the same thing, but where there's one you got to be prepared for the other. Lot of ways, it was more like 1881 than 1981. But the only two pieces of news of the outside world that did come in that month was that someone shot the president... same as did happen in 1881, except King Ray-Gun lived... and the first launch of the Space Shuttle. There was also the surveillance planes."

"Because of the pot growers?" Mark asked.

"That was the excuse," the old man answered. "Infrared. Military tech, really. It was early yet. Growers hadn't even planted anything. What them so-called drug warriors was doing was using infrared to locate every last human being in those mountains, just to know where we all were. Wasn't that many to locate. Probably not five hundred. It was a legal-stamped, certified Wilderness... though I heard that claim-stealing minerals corporation got some tame congresscritters to rearrange that to suit them too.

"That surveillance... They did come in later with enough of an invasion force to take over a medium sized African country. But it was all just fun and games to them. Practice. Shoot-'em-up with armed dope growers as commando training, and get the rest of you cattle used to being herded.

"I was even legal. Government knew where I was 'cause I was legally working a legal claim. Didn't grow no dope. But I didn't like being watched like that."

Mark noted that the old man didn't mention unlicensed venison, but he didn't say anything.

"I got out. Hiked down to the mail box. Found a check for $31 and a twenty dollar bill I wasn't expecting, and kept right on going. Didn't do no good though.... Well, it maybe saved me from being shot and called a drug criminal for being on a gold claim the king's corporate buddies wanted. But that kind of surveillance was practice. They do the same thing everywhere now."

"Is that what that plane was, so low over the cabin?" Mark asked.

"Nah," the old man said. "That's just some military drone. Well, I don't know what it is. Don't matter. They fly over all the time. Them. Fighter jets. Forest fire spotters. Search and Rescue helicopters... Like the government owes you to pick you up off your butt if you fall in a hole in the woods... and you owe them for them to be able to find you and me and everyone all the time, so they can. Noise. Just noise, to scramble all our brains.

"Thing is, that surveillance. It don't matter how they do it. Satellites or... it don't matter. What matters is, they can do it now, *everywhere*. There was a Science Fiction writer I used to read, name of Heinlein, said: 'When you need an ID, it's time to get elsewhere. The nice thing about Space travel was having an elsewhere to go.' 'Course that was just a story, but the point ain't. Not even original. You ever wonder why there was something wrong with King David in the Bible taking a census?"

Mark knew there was a King David in the Bible, but he had no idea what the old man referred to. "Uh, I'm not very religious..."

"Not the point," the old man snorted... and had to take time out for another coughing fit. "I got about as much use for Bible thumpers as I do for Forest Circus clowns telling me I need a permit to take a leak in the woods. Point is, maybe the king... the government... shouldn't know where everyone is."

"Well, yeah," said Mark, "but... even if they do know, they can't control everyone all the time. Half the population would have to be cops."

"Or informers. You're the educated one, Pisswater. Read up on life in Berlin under Nazis or Communists. But that ain't the point either. Point is, there's some people that maybe need to not be found."

"What for?"

"I ain't sure." The old man thought a moment. "Trouble is, a lifetime's too short. I ain't sure what I seen. Well, I'm sure what I heard, and what I don't hear no more. But what it adds up to…"

"Um, excuse me," Mark said, "I do need to take a leak. You don't think those javelinas are around?"

"We'd have heard if they was," the old man said. "Mind the skunks though. They're kind of pets, but you don't want to fall over them."

Mark stepped out, to brilliant starlight. Not a human light anywhere, but for the small glow from the cabin window. Not a human sound either. No plane, for the moment anyhow, and no road in hearing. If there were any skunks, or any large animals nearby, Mark neither heard nor saw any sign of them. He did hear a whip-poor-will some distance down the tiny stream. When he went back in, the old man was rolling himself a cigarette from a small can.

"Help yourself if you like," the old man said. He didn't ask if Mark minded.

"No thanks. I could use some water though."

"Sure." The old man gestured. A large enamel pitcher sat on the board table, several plastic gallon bottles underneath. Mark started to pour water from the pitcher into one of half a dozen ceramic and tin mugs on the back of the table.

"I'd use the bottles for drinking," the old man said. "Caps keep the mice out."

Mark settled with his water, by the kerosene lamp. (Had there been a candle instead at one point? Or electric light?) The old man smoked his cigarette, tapped ashes onto the floor. Mark didn't like the tobacco smoke, but didn't say anything.

"I'm about played out now," the old man said, "but I had some good years left in me after I quit the Black Tails. Idaho. Colorado. Took in a fair portion of this ol' Outlaw Trail country both sides of the Arizona-New Mexico state line before anyone thought about turning out cage-bred wolves with radio collars or counting tadpoles for the government. Did get paid by the Forest Circus once for a contract to pick pine cones." He laughed at that, managed not to cough. "I heard a few things, and heard about a few more, far enough back. Drums. Flutes…"

<The power unit was gone. Now what? His heart settled. His head still throbbed. How would he get back? Would there be any back to get to? Would anyone find him?>

Mark shook his head. His imagination didn't usually run off so intrusively. "Do you think that guy could have had it right? That packer?"

"Ol' Bear Tooth?" the old man said. "Well, he wasn't old either. Younger'n me, and I was a lot younger then... Don't know. What I do know is that them kind of mystery serenades was fairly common, you got far enough back, up till the eighties. Then they dropped off quick. Since infrared surveillance got common. Dope Gestapo. Border Patrol."

"Search and Rescue," Mark interjected. "You said yourself..."

"Them too," the old man said. "Sure. I ain't claiming no conspiracy. Just, a world... and one I don't like... ate up another one. Global Positioning Satellites maybe struck the death stroke. I was already slowing down, but since that system went in, not only I ain't heard no more mystery drums nor flutes. I ain't heard of anyone that has."

"That's sad," Mark said softly.

"More than sad, Pisswater," the old man spoke sharply again. "You been noticing anything funny about the weather? Oh, hell, you ain't old enough to know the difference."

"Like El Niño and..."

"Yeah, *and*... Why'd you say you was countin' tadpoles?"

Mark flushed, embarrassment mixed with annoyance now. The old man had a point, but he was so deprecating, so angry... "Well, the environmentalists believe amphibian declines are an indicator of ecological degradation, and the ranchers believe it's proof cows can't be blamed because it's too recent."

"How 'bout you?"

The old man had intimidated him. Mark felt his self-esteem fighting back: "Get paid to hike the Upper Adobe watershed for the summer... Seemed like a pretty cool job to me." A smile of pleasure crept up Mark's chin at the double entendre of the word, "cool."

"You think it's all hokum then?" the old man asked—serious, not deprecating. "A joke, like my pine cone picking contract?"

"Well, everyone knows there's an environmental crisis," Mark shrugged.

"Don't everyone know no such thing," the old man replied. "You ain't been talking to enough kinds of people. But let's let that pass. If there is, why now?"

"Well, population… Greenhouse gasses. Deforestation…"

The old man interrupted. "Maybe. Likely, in fact. But a hundred fifty years ago, the whole eastern half of the country was cut clear, for timber and firewood and charcoal and farming before it was cheaper to ship beets from California to Maine than grow 'em there. Been a lot let to grow back since. These woods here ain't virgin neither. But if you didn't know it, you wouldn't realize. Lot's growed back. Lot of industry's done cleaner. You ever hear of London fog?"

"Maybe," said Mark. "A kind of raincoat? Guess I assumed… England's supposed to be wet…"

"Ummmmm. That's true, but it ain't the subject," the old man said. "When I was young, London had fogs that killed people. Wasn't fog at all. It was smog that thick. Coal smoke mostly. They cleaned things up since. Don't have killer fogs no more."

"There's still smog."

"Yeah, there is," the old man said.

"Maybe problems are cumulative," said Mark. "More people. More of the planet industrialized. Deforestation in the tropics."

"Thought you was the young cynic just found him a cool job."

Mark blushed. At least it probably didn't show in the dim lamp light. "What difference am I going to make?"

"I have you then," said the old man.

"You think there is something else," Mark more said than asked.

"Maybe," the old man said. "There was always droughts and floods and heat waves and blizzards. But… I took to watching ants for a while. They'd be busy about their ant business. A plane would fly over. They'd all go nuts. Run here and there. When the plane passed, they'd settle back to whatever they was doin'. Watched that now and again, when I thought of it, for a year or two, places like here, far enough out there's no traffic so one plane makes a difference. Seemed like it happened a lot. Then I forgot about it. A few years later, I thought of it again, watched some more ants. Couldn't see where it made any difference if a plane flew past. But… I don't know. Maybe just my imagination. Seemed like the ants got over their panic, but they got stupider. Stopped having the sense to put their holes out of the way of runoff, or my garden irrigation. Other things... Elk on the highway... Weather..."

"Like El Niño?" Mark said again.

"Yeah," the old man answered. "Like things are a little more confused, a little stupider, a little less regular."

"Maybe..."

"Or maybe I'm just a crazy old fool that's spent too much time alone and now I'm dyin' and think it's the world coming to an end."

<The People took him for a God. A God fallen from the Heavens. He found it a charming attitude. It at least soothed his despair. He taught them what he could. They could not learn enough to build him a new power unit. He didn't know how. He didn't even know how to turn ores... which he didn't know how to recognize... into usable metals. But the People could learn to weave willow baskets: A big, loose frame for a shelter. A small, tight weave for a basket to carry things in.

The People knew something he didn't too. Something he saw to appreciate, as he learned their language and lived on with their rough kindness, in conditions he found always primitive and sometimes brutal. A respect for the game and the plants they depended on, and for the weather that lifted them up or beat them down.

The People learned to sew clothing, to make clay into pots they could store things in and even cook in, to fashion better spear points. They thanked their new God, and offered thanks to the God-People for the kindness to drop one of their own among them. He had no way to make what to them was politics of Heaven comprehensible, so he made no real attempt to disabuse them of their view that he was not merely stranded, but was a gift to them. After all, their new God would miss Heaven and his own kind. When he was sad, they sang or embraced him to cheer him.

The People also sang to the elk and the long horned bison, to the sunflowers and the piñons. He taught them to make drums that sang too: to stretch a hide over a hollow section of log. Even flutes that would play particular notes. What a wonderful gift from their new God, to increase the People's capacity to communicate with all the Gods!

The People had many Gods besides himself. They saw Spirits in everything and in the imaginings of their own minds, intelligent as his own but immersed in overwhelming Nature that they so depended on. They clothed the intangible in concrete image, he realized, by which they could converse with more than they could understand, let alone control.

The herds and the plants and even the weather responded to the songs and the singing drums, and he could not tell how much the People's respectful attitude to what sustained them mattered. Did the drum or the song call up a herd of mountain sheep just in time to rescue the People from starvation, or a rain when desperately needed? He could not say. Nature was too big, too various, to pin down any one thing that happened to such causality. Yet he could not deny how many times a dream told the People which hill to walk across to find game or a patch of wild plums thick-laden with just-ripe fruit when so many other patches bore none that year. How many times a needed rain did follow the sacred songs... the more likely the more intense the need and the plea...>

The old man's coughing roused Mark from his reverie. The fit went on and on, long enough that Mark became alarmed. I still don't even know his name! Mark thought. What if he does die?

The old man didn't die. The coughing eventually subsided. The old man spat on the floor again. "Well, I don't know what it matters... If it matters. Needed to tell someone that would listen. Guess I'm glad you showed up. I'm tired now. Sorry I can't offer you a bed. Didn't notice a leak. Spare rotted monsoon time, three... no four years back. Abe's been gonna get me another hauled up here. Guess the 'gonnas' caught up on us both. You might want to shake the mouse turds off the rug, and watch out for scorpions in the blankets, but they're clean."

The old man lit a squat candle on a jar lid for Mark to set himself up for the night in the tiny back room. An empty steel bed frame leaned against the back wall. There were mouse droppings on the rug. Mark thought of hantavirus, but then shrugged and just rolled up the rug and carried it outside to shake it out. He did the same with the blankets. No scorpions, but there were a couple of spiders and quite a bit of windblown dust. Then Mark laid down four folded over blankets on the rug for padding, and two more to cover himself. Nights were still chilly at this altitude.

The old man rolled out his own bedding on the sagging couch in the main room, and blew out the lamp. His breath soon settled to not exactly a snore, more a raspy regularity.

As he was taking off his shoes, Mark noticed the shelf of books. It suddenly struck him, in the candlelight, with not a hint of human traffic or other habitation anywhere around nor even any sound of a plane, that there was no TV here. No VCR. No phone, so no Net. No radio even that he had seen, nor tape player. Curious thus the more, Mark stood barefoot on his bedding holding the candle where he could read some titles: *Bury My Heart At Wounded Knee. The Monkey Wrench Gang. Medicinal Plants Of The Mountain West.* A Bible. Several two and three year old Science Fiction magazines that looked to have passed through several hands. *Tesla. Tales From The Bloated Goat. A Connecticut Yankee In King Arthur's Court.*

Mark blew out the candle. He lay awake a long time. He heard various night sounds, including mice. It was still warm enough for crickets and some sort of buzzing night insect that zipped past a few times. Mark wondered at the old man's story, and at the… looseness of his own mind. He had always had an imagination, but his mind didn't usually run away with him the way it had today.

Eventually, Mark slept… and, somewhat to his surprise, did not dream that he remembered.

Mark woke to the aroma of coffee and tobacco smoke and the sound of coughing, though at least a bit less terminal-sounding than the worst of last evening. The sun wasn't up yet, but it was full daylight.

"Sleeping Beauty arises," the old man greeted Mark by the wood cookstove. "Coffee?"

"Thanks," Mark replied. Morning was crystal clear and cool enough that the fire felt nice.

In morning light, Mark noted several open sheets of newspaper spread on the floor next to the old man's chair, where he had been spitting. Clean, so Mark figured the old man had used the ones from last night to start the fire. Mark also saw that there was an electric light on the ceiling, and a switch by the door, as well as the kerosene lamp which still sat on the table where it had been last night. It occurred to him to look around for a radio or at least a tape player. He still didn't see any.

"Coffee," the old man said, handing Mark a mug, black, with no mention of anything one might add to it. "Industrial Revolution never would have happened without it."

In an oblique way, just the point, Mark thought, as the ordinary world reasserted itself; yet a mystery remained. To make the old man's comment relevant to Mark's frame of mind. To cast the image of his own mind, of the old man's tale on something, invisible, intangible, yet coherent enough to recognize through clothing of imagination to make the mystery's shape perceptible.

"Guess I should be heading back," Mark said after a while.

"Got to count them tadpoles before they get away, hey?" the old man said.

"Well, yes…" That was what was paying for the groceries and gas to allow him to be here, not to mention maintaining his respectable status with the Department back in Las Cruces; but it wasn't what Mark was thinking of. The truth was that he was thinking he had left his camp and truck unattended overnight. He wanted clean socks and underwear. He wanted the reassuring touch of familiar reality.

"I ain't ready to eat, but I was going to heat up the beans anyhow, so I can let the fire go out before the day warms up."

"Thank you," Mark said. "I don't want to be using up your supplies."

"Don't worry about it," the old man said. "Young fellow like you needs some fortification."

Mark felt it would be rude to refuse the hospitable offer, and he would like to eat something before hiking down… he was not sure how long a trail.

"Anything I could bring you from town?" Mark asked.

"Retread set of lungs," the old man said. "Nah… Well, if you do come back up here, a melon would be a treat. I can't grow 'em here, even without javelinas. Season ain't warm enough long enough. Think you can find your way down?"

"I think so," Mark answered, though strange as yesterday had been, he wasn't sure of anything.

"Can't get too lost here," the old man said. "Not like the Black Tails. Follow the trail through that stretch of canyon. After that, any way you go down you'll come out at the river someplace."

Mark wondered if the old man didn't feel up to making the hike again, or just didn't want to. He felt concerned for an old man, apparently ill, all alone in such a remote spot. But it obviously was where the old man wanted to be. Mark felt it would be rude to pry into the old man's circumstances. But he did ask:

"Oh, say, I never did get your name."

"Billy The Kid," the old man answered with no hint of hesitation. Mark gaped.

"That's a joke, Son," the old man said. "Funny thing, though. Abe, now. Billy The Kid's last name was McCarty, same as Abe's, and ol' Billy did have a brother. Lot of them Old West characters had families that are still around. I never quite had the gumption to ask."

Mark thought Billy The Kid's last name had been Bonney, but he didn't feel comfortable to ask, even if the old man did seem a bit more mellow this morning.

Mark accepted the bowl of beans, and another hunk of doorstop bread.

The old man's directions were clear, and so was the trail. It had seemed like twenty miles yesterday. This morning, Mark estimated it at no more than a mile and a half. He saw a rabbit, jays and squirrels, maybe a glimpse of some kind of small brown hawk. There were large, cloven hoof tracks a couple of places, probably elk since he had seen no sign of cows in the area. Mark smiled at the quirky sign at the trail's turnoff from the road. A rural mail box stood next to it, with a faded number 23 painted on the side, that he supposed he must have seen yesterday but not noticed because it was too ordinary to notice. It was about two miles farther back up to Mark's camp, just as he recollected, in the Turkey Spring Forest Service Campground, with the drinking quality artesian spring pouring from its pipe.

Mark's truck was fine, except that something, a mouse or maybe a chipmunk, had gotten in through the hole in the floor and nibbled on a bag of granola.

Mark could see that one of the two other campsites that had been occupied yesterday was now empty. Grace and Herb Matthews—in their sixties, recent retirees, sat in lawn chairs by their motor home, at the other campsite where they had been Mark's neighbors for the past week. Someone new had pulled into a secluded spot at the far end of the campground.

Grace walked over, on seeing Mark come in, and said, "We were wondering if we needed to call Search and Rescue. Didn't think you'd taken anything with you to be out overnight."

"Thanks," Mark said. "I met an old guy that lives up a side canyon, who invited me up to his place."

"You be careful," Grace said. "There are some pretty crazy survivalist types in these mountains."

"Thanks," Mark said.

Grace rejoined her husband in their folding chairs in the ponderosa shade of the warming morning.

Mark got himself out a complete clean set of clothes and a towel and walked across the road and a little ways up the river. He was wary of javelinas, snakes, or anything else that might be hidden among the brush, but what he saw for animals was lizards, songbirds, and a crawdad scuttling in the shallow water. Also tadpoles, two places, that he noted to come back to.

A large, propeller-driven, military green plane flew down the canyon, passing no more than a couple hundred feet overhead. Mark realized there had been at least two or three such planes earlier in the week he had been here in the Upper Adobe River Canyon. The planes did fly low, the one over the old man's cabin surely lower than this one. He hadn't paid attention earlier. Engine noises were such a constant in life. It was the long gaps, in this remote mountain canyon, between sounds of any engine, that had seemed noteworthy. Mark looked for ants, saw several, couldn't tell if they did anything unusual.

Mark found a pool, just big enough to lie down in, and sheltered enough by a steep embankment and thick willows from sight of the road for him to get in nude. Not that there was any traffic for anyone to see him. Late morning sun was already strong and heading toward hot, but the mountain night had been cold enough that the water was just about halfway between refreshing and heart stopping.

It was only as Mark was stepping out of the pool, skin tingling and wide awake, that it occurred to him that he never had gotten a name out of the old man.

Author's note: When I lived in the Blue River Canyon, on the New Mexico/Arizona state line, in the late nineties, I often did not hear an engine, or any human-generated sound, for hours, even in the daytime. It was as pristine a spot as is left, with a moderate climate. Then a plane would fly over, or a car would pass on the road across the river. I would think: What if the real environmental crisis is that the Nature Spirits have no place left to concentrate, and they are becoming confused. The drum in the story is something that I really heard, in the Trinity Wilderness of Northern California, in 1981.

THE NATURE OF PROPERTY

Lagoda had smooth, brown shoulders and rough, brown hands. Her deep, brown eyes shined with a clear, distant light.

Enkor was a man of moderation, in build and in ambition, but he loved Lagoda quite immoderately, which suited her just fine.

Love was the subject of the moment, morning sunshine sparkling but not yet hot on the white walls of Lagoda's clean, cluttered little house.

Enkor and Lagoda coupled top, bottom and sideways, bodies and souls mingling in pleasure. Nearly sated, they slowed, but still caressed, when the Crocodile Person walked through the wall.

Silent the Person came, but both woman and man sensed a presence, cool as a shadowed mushroom. Lagoda stretched to look up, healthy sweat glistening on her body. Enkor raised his head. A man of moderate height and musculature, he might have leapt to their defense, but stood instead in naked astonishment.

The Crocodile Person stood hand to chin, and a very long chin it was for a Person if not especially so for a Crocodile. The green stripes of his tie did little to break the monotony of his grey, if expensive suit. Of course, the effect was rather lost on the naked couple, whose knowledge of fashion remained provincial.

"Warm, isn't it?" said Lagoda to soften the brittle atmosphere.

"Weight distribution diffuses expenditure," said the Crocodile Person.

"Beg pardon?" said Lagoda.

The Crocodile Person disdained to reply.

Enkor stood up, moderately insulted. "Sir, please have a cushion," he said. "We'll prepare some snoofh."

The Crocodile Person walked part way through the kitchen wall and stood with a knee in the stove.

Lagoda, somewhat hesitantly, reached to the high, polished shelf for the orange glazed cups, while Enkor lifted the crock of snoofh from its cool corner. With the flavor of a moldy rat's nest, snoofh had little nutritional value and no intoxicating properties, but hospitality ranked high in Enkor's values. Lagoda admired his grace.

Enkor stopped to admire the curve of Lagoda's hips and the small of her back and the way her side merged with the bend of her breast and then decided hospitality required some formality. So he put on his fringed shoulder strap, which lay on a heap of possibly-useful bits of metal and cloth at the foot of Lagoda's bed, the buff-colored sheets still somewhat rumpled from their lovemaking.

The Crocodile Person grabbed Enkor by the left wrist with a hand cool and dry as a walnut shell. Enkor lost his balance, knocking the snoofh crock to the floor where it shattered across the ember-red square tiles into a rat's-nest-aromatic pool.

"Oh dear! Oh dear!" cried Lagoda, "a stain before company!"

Hoppy-toads, in their tiny hundreds, pittered through the house. (It was that time of year.) Two or three, caught in the puddle, writhed, demented. Merciless, the rest ignored their dolorous kin.

Quick as a chainsaw throttle, the Crocodile Person measured Enkor's left leg, from thigh to arch of his dusty, calloused foot.

Lagoda fluttered a nervous minuet with her mop.

"Reguimosoforthm," said the Crocodile Person.

Lagoda bowed her head in shame. Even the hoppy-toads were embarrassed.

The Crocodile Person could care less. He wasn't thirsty anyhow. He walked right through the snoofh puddle, careful only of possible sharp shards.

A bit dizzy, dangling upside down as he was, Enkor spoke with doubt: "Haven't we another crock behind the privy?"

"That old thing," Lagoda despaired, "blotchy and chipped. Company…" She wrung her hands.

"He seems quite informal," Enkor paddled at the air above the hoppy-toads and the snoofh, dangling now by his right calf from the confident grip of their unexpected guest.

The Crocodile Person dropped Enkor with a splat, heedless of shards (though he hitched up his expensive grey trousers for the splash). Enkor stood, scratched here and there, disoriented.

The Crocodile Person rummaged in the pockets of his business suit, neatly folding back the crisp, grey flaps. With a cavernous yawn of annoyance, he ascended six invisible steps till the top of his head was lost in the ceiling, then walked back out through the wall. He soon reappeared with a syringe, fully half as long as a human arm. The needle, thicker than a blue-dry blade of grass, if twice as sharp, stuck on the wall.

"Damn whitewash!" the Crocodile Person fumed, with a yank. The needle popped through. A white chip dropped to the floor. A dozen hoppy-toads eagerly licked it brown and bare.

A look of mystical awe filled Enkor's face. Lagoda continued to wring her hands round the mop, unaware, as she looked on while the Crocodile Person impaled Enkor through the belly with the needle, depressed the plunger, and injected a gallon and a half of foamy pink fluid into his body.

Enkor's normally flat brown belly bloated out as spasms of agony flushed through pulsing arms and shivering legs. "Glaughk!" he gasped.

The Crocodile Person made no explanation, but Enkor probably couldn't have paid attention if he had.

Among the properties of the pink fluid, formerly in the syringe, now in Enkor, was enormously to increase the body's sensitivity to pain at the same time it equally increased the body's capacity to stand the same.

The Crocodile Person consulted his watch and Enkor's eyes. Quick as it took effect, some passage of time obtained for optimum flavor. Patience was an attribute the Crocodile Person held in moderate measure. Enkor could sympathize.

Though he would be more likely to at some other time. His concentration was currently somewhat diffuse as the pink fluid diffused with admirable rapidity through his arms and legs and head, all of which now felt as if they were filled more with fire than with fluid.

As Enkor's spasms slowed to a steady excruciating pulse, the Crocodile Person picked him back up by left armpit and right knee and began to gnaw on Enkor's left leg. The Crocodile Person bit off the foot at the ankle and spit it out, but then steadied to a pensive munch.

Bones crunched and tendons snapped. Blood dripped, slightly pinkish and frothing into the puddle of snoofh, scoring and staining the orderly, black grout among the red tiles of Lagoda's floor.

Lagoda set the mop on her head and hopped back and forth in close rapport, ashamed that, without the pain-enhancing fluid from the Crocodile Person's syringe, she felt only an echo of Enkor's morning.

Ruthless, the hoppy-toads cared not a whit. "Have you no manners?" Enkor asked in a moment of lucidity between bites, but of course he knew they hadn't.

The Crocodile Person consumed leisurely Enkor's entire leg and took a nibble or two of the buttock. But by then the pink fluid from the syringe, entering its second phase, coagulated the blood. Flavor remained satisfactory. Enkor's continued enhanced agony ensured that. But the Crocodile Person no longer cared for the texture: The meal is sufficient unto its measure, he mused.

The Crocodile Person tossed Enkor aside. Enkor hit the edge of the bed and landed on the floor, eyes bugged out and all atwitch.

"Hoo! Hoo! Hoo!" Lagoda hopped frantically, the mop flopping over her eyes.

The Crocodile Person sat on a beige linen cushion for some time, while Enkor writhed and Lagoda flailed.

Thanks to the Crocodile Person's foamy pink fluid, Enkor neither bled to death nor lost consciousness. The increased sensitivity to pain would remain, residual as many years as he was likely to live, but the leg might take months to regenerate. The Crocodile Person sighed. Flavor wasn't everything, after all. Soft or hard, the texture always seemed to deteriorate with successive meals.

The Crocodile Person grew bored and left before Enkor became used to his pain.

Exhausted, Lagoda drooped to doze across a puffy cotton red and blue striped cushion. Enkor gently extracted the mop from her clenched fingers. Lagoda merely sighed and stirred in her sleep.

Enkor employed the mop to raise his fiery body onto its remaining foot. The raw wound stabbed and burned like a million flaming scorpions. The rest of his body merely stung as if aswarm with centipedes and wasps.

The pain caused Enkor to see great, portentious visions, but none of them were clear enough to inform him of anything.

Thunder and jellied lightning blasted through Enkor's tortured brain. He wanted to clean the floor before Lagoda woke, but the puddle was congealed. Hopping with the mop as a crutch, Enkor headed for the kitchen to fetch a bucket of water. A mere three or four hops sufficed so to confuse him with pain that he no longer had any idea what he had set out to do. So he stood, his remaining leg throbbing, clinging to the mop as a mast in a storm.

A man of moderation, Enkor grew neither bitter nor flabby as his leg slowly regenerated in the days and months that followed, though he had to be careful to expose the expanding new skin to the sun a little at a time.

Lagoda seemed permanently embarrassed at the loss of her snoofh crock, but her cousin of the second degree, Omelia, presented her a new one, shiny blue with lovely white swirls and meanders, at the Golig's Day Festival, just before the dance. Enkor's leg was still too short to participate, a further embarrassment, but everyone pretended not to notice.

It was over two years before the Crocodile Person came back for Enkor's other leg. Delighted with the moderate texture, he returned thereafter every few months. At times, Enkor had no limbs at all and had to be fed like a baby.

A point arrived beyond which Enkor's sensitivity to pain could grow no further, though it diminished little enough. Yet he never did make any sense of his visions. He couldn't do any work when he had no limbs. Worse, his lovemaking suffered.

At last, Lagoda got up the courage to say something. Enkor's left leg and right arm were full size, and the right leg was coming along when the Crocodile Person walked through the wall in the midst of Enkor and Lagoda's immoderate lovemaking yet again.

Enkor fumbled for his shoulder strap, but instead of running for the snoofh, Lagoda stood akimbo on the bed, the rumpled sheets of green linen, and shouted: "This is too rude!"

The Crocodile Person wore a blue business suit and orange tie today, nearly as expensive as the grey suit but in execrable taste. He fumbled in his pockets, having forgotten to bring in his syringe as usual. He wondered if it was even needed.

Residual effect might suffice, but no point allowing so tasty a morsel to bleed to death finding out. Resigned to his poor memory, the Crocodile Person plodded up the six invisible steps and through the wall.

It wasn't the season for hoppy-toads, but Enkor batted at a cloud of gnats, glad to have a hand, for the moment, with which to bat.

Lagoda stood on the bed, breathing hard.

The Crocodile Person reappeared, chipping the whitewash once again with his needle.

"Stop it, I say!" Lagoda screeched, "have you no sense of time?" Shocked at her own arrogance, she hung her head.

It didn't matter. The Crocodile Person cared no more for Lagoda's sense of propriety than the gnats, or the hoppy-toads (if there were any).

At least today no snoofh was spilled to mix with Enkor's foamy pink blood.

Twitching in exhausted agony as the Crocodile Person gnawed away his left leg once again, Enkor wondered if he ever would make any sense of the visions.

Author's note: People in vastly different socio-economic circumstances tend to see each other's behavior in terms of their own viewpoint. But of course, each really acts from their own experience.

THE DASHING ABOUT FLYING BOX PEOPLE

In youth, Eblio traveled to such distance that even the birds spoke a different language. Over all that distance, Eblio learned to speak with People. So, of course, when the Flying Box People arrived, Eblio went out with the greeting party, at least as intrigued as frightened.

One heard of Flying Box People. They were ignorant, of course, of People's ways, and did some awful things, not knowing any better. But they seemed to intend friendship. "No knowing what harm we may do them in ignorance," Levery said to Eblio. Eblio agreed. One could make awful mistakes through ignorance, even among People only a few days' walk away.

For a species who start life as plants, and whose reproductive function amounts to wind pollination, the Cratons appear to have social organization more like human than some whose biology is far more similar. But then, other than reproduction, they are pretty similar to human. They cultivate food. They make copper cook pots. They live in communities, mostly of a few hundred individuals, that almost certainly have to do with both survival benefit of division of labor and interpersonal relationships. Their sentient adult phase sees, hears, feels, probably smells and tastes or something of the sort. They raise their young... which they pick like berries from bushes!

Gemma Long, Xenologist
Xenological Survey Service
Field Notes, Craton V

It was a spring morning. Tiffletae fluff wafted through the air like a reminder of snow. And to think that tiffletae trees gave birth to sleepy, sluggish griffletae, that snuffled about all winter eating their own trees' dead leaves, and mostly just slept in their shells in summer. Well, Flying Box People were not the only oddities of Creation.

Eblio was out in the garden irrigating when the Flying Box People arrived. Everyone knew what they were, of course. They had been seen several other places, mostly off to the east where the lowlands were so humid and People grew sleepy as griffletae on summer afternoons. No one had really managed to talk with the Flying Box People yet. But there had been enough rudimentary communication that People understood the Flying Box People to have come from another world… someplace, so far away that its sun appeared as a star. What one might learn, Eblio thought, if only we could talk!

"Do you think they really have a language?" Levery asked.

Levery and Eblio walked together, with about twenty other People, to greet the Flying Box People. Several children, who were themselves just learning to talk, scampered behind—still intoxicated at the newness of their own mobility.

"They must," said Eblio. "I don't believe they could make the things their journey required without."

"Well, birds speak enough to tell each other where food is, or danger," said Levery.

"Or where they're from," Eblio replied. "But they don't fly in a great, shiny, metal box." Eblio reflected, as Eblio and Levery and the rest of the greeting party approached the Flying Box People, who saw them coming and stood outside their metal flying box in their own waiting greeting party. "No, Levery. They're not like birds. The Flying Box People have some sort of real language, and I'm going to try to learn it."

I believe that tonality is as important to Craton language as what we hear as words. Perhaps, with sentience, their language developed from the sounds… songs almost, like bird songs… that stimulate their metamorphosis chemistry.

Gemma Long, Xenologist
Field Notes, Craton V

The Flying Box People stayed many days, but as a curiosity they rather waned for most People. The Flying Box People walked about, looked at things, noted what they observed in some sort of devices that People could no more comprehend than one could expect Flying Box People to comprehend story cloths. Actually, the Flying Box

People didn't just walk about. The Flying Box People did a great deal of agitated rushing back and forth, for no apparent reason. Sometimes they made destructive messes... like any ignorant animal. But they showed sufficient consideration to confine most of their most-agitated dashing about, with its destructive aspect, to a discrete encampment around their metal flying box and away from People's gardens and homes.

The Flying Box People also had several little flying boxes, that they brought out of the big one, and which they used to dash about at greater distance than one could walk. They even offered People rides. It *was* exciting. But hardly practical. When one stopped, having traversed, in half a morning, a distance it would take many days to walk, without having learned anyone's speech along the way, anyone who one met might as well live on some Flying Box World for all one could understand of their speech or even their story cloths.

To go inside the Flying Box People's big flying box, as they escorted several People who wished to see, was scary, and thus even more exciting. But lacking common language, most of what one could see in there was unintelligible.

People and Flying Box People exchanged some gifts. The Flying Box People could eat most of the food that People ate. Tender fibbith greens were in season. The Flying Box People seemed to appreciate having something fresh to add to their diet. As other crops came in, People offered some of them too. The Flying Box People seemed to like most of them. There were only about twenty-five Flying Box People. It was hard to tell them apart enough to be sure how many. But they had considerable supplies. Offering them some garden produce was not a hardship.

With People visiting from a distance, one might exchange story cloths. But there was no point to give the Flying Box People story cloths until... or unless one could share enough real speech for the story cloths to mean anything. But the Flying Box People seemed able to appreciate beauty. So People gave them several pattern cloths.

The Flying Box People gave People a picture which they seemed to consider significant, of several circles of various sizes. They managed to communicate that this had something to do with the world and the sun... or maybe *their* world and sun. Why this mattered to them, who could say? But, of course, People appreciated that their visitors gave them something the foreigners considered significant. The Flying Box People also gave

People several useful tools: three sizes of vegetable knife, of a hard, silver-grey metal that held an excellent edge, a house-peg hammer of some similar metal, a light that would shine all night if left in the sunshine during the day.

Well, this was all reassuring, as well as interesting. But there were gardens to tend, and homes and children and friendships... and a few quarrels. When nothing different happened, most People went back to everyday pursuits and each other, and only greeted the Flying Box People as now-familiar, if very foreign, guests, who spent most of their visible time dashing about in great and incomprehensible urgency, expending more energy than a tree-hip-flip... to less practical effect.

Eblio, however, determined to learn the Flying Box People's speech. Watching them more closely than most, Eblio gradually came to distinguish one of the Flying Box People from another. A few of them anyhow. Strange creatures they were really, a little smaller than People, but not much. The Flying Box People wore clothing, in various colors, bright and subdued, which might or might not signify anything, but did seem to indicate some sort of aesthetic. What *did* the Flying Box People regard as beauty? What *did* matter to them? They had rather wide faces, in various shades of pink and brown, and thick fur on various parts of their heads, some more, some less, of various lengths and colors. Did the variations signify anything?

No knowing. But the Flying Box People certainly did dash about a *lot*.

Of course, one could not expect Flying Box People to understand that one should apologize when tearing up a People-bush. And People tore up People-bushes all the time, along with numerous other sorts that would overrun everyone's gardens and homes in a season if one did not. But there was something odd about the Flying Box People's urgency, about their attitude toward *each other* in their urgency. Back and forth they rushed, tearing things up, moving things from one place to some seemingly-arbitrary other place, making so much noise that how could anyone concentrate? Back and forth. Back and forth!

"I wonder," said Eblio to Levery one dawn over clear-soup. "I do believe they intend friendship, but something about them makes me very uncomfortable."

"Well, they *are* aliens," said Levery.

And that was true enough. The more reason to learn to speak with them.

A breakthrough! Though I am embarrassed to admit that it is the Craton who made the breakthrough. I'm not even sure what happened. I think the Craton figured out what constitutes words to us. I still can't say the same about theirs. Maybe soon the Craton can tell me. Whatever it is, we now are communicating in words. Mostly nouns; a few verbs. I think the lovely trill the Craton made on comprehending "walk" and "run" was something like a laugh of pleasure.

Gemma Long, Xenologist
Field Notes, Craton V

"They do have a language," Eblio said, excitement warbling like long-awaited summer rain. "It's very strange... Like the eastern Lowlanders who sing up a day hot and wet enough to sprout purple iskiss, and sing down altogether different a day so hot and wet that the iskiss sprout yellow."

"The Flying Box People's speech sounds very crude to me," said Levery. "No more melody than a grey-down frufowl."

There was nothing nicer than a pillow of frufowl down, but it was true that their speech consisted only of a dozen sorts of raucous squawk. How frufowl young could quicken at all to such toneless, meager a range of sound was a mystery.

"Indeed," Eblio replied, "it is all but toneless.... Well, not all the time. Actually, they *do* sing. *Very* strange, but... I won't say lovely. Exotic. But their speech. The meaning is mostly in the precise vocables. Why, it would take them half a day to describe the health of a patch of lisk beans, but they could tell you how many there were before you could count the first plant."

"How can they do that?"

"Well, now," said Eblio, "I'm confusing myself. They'd have to count them too, of course. Well, that's not it either. But... Let me show you."

Eblio made a sort of skrawking sound, then strode across the yard. Eblio made the same sound, then ambled back, smelling the fragrant, summer morning air. Eblio made that same sound several more times, each time crossing the yard a different way. Then Eblio made a different sound, and sprinted across the yard, both feet completely off the ground at once at each step. This second sound, too, designated a whole array of modes to cross the yard.

"What's precise about that?" asked Levery.

"It's in the... distinction," said Eblio. "In the... edge. Like the vegetable knives."

"I suppose." Levery was not sure, but also was less interested than Eblio. "Do you think that means that on their world a Person could walk for twenty-three days, and everyone would speak the same, and then on the twenty-fourth day you would come to People whose speech might as well be from a different world?"

"Maybe!" said Eblio. "That would make their little flying boxes more practical. If I can learn enough of their speech, I'll ask."

Eblio did learn more of the Flying Box People's speech. Eventually, Eblio could converse with them enough even to begin to comprehend their interactions with each other. Eblio became more uncomfortable at this, not less. The Flying Box People had an agitation to them which pervaded their interactions. Yet this essential quality of the Flying Box People seemed completely absent from what the things they *said* led them to *do*. Eblio began to wonder if the Flying Box People *were* altogether sentient.

People, after all, lived a whole other life as People-bushes, which sprouted and grew, shed clouds of pollen, flowered and made People-berries, grew leaves and shed them, and died, all without any sentience really. Only the very few People-berries that sang back to People-Singing, and which People found, to pick and bring home, and to feed People-soup, metamorphosed into children, who one got to know and to love and nurture and raise up to become sentient People. What if, just as their language held its meaning in so-alien a part of its own structure, the Flying Box People also... carried a non-sentient aspect of themselves with them, which had a life of its own, of which they, perhaps, were not even aware?

The more Eblio observed the Flying Box People's behavior, what they did, how their attitude felt, the discontinuities between what they did and what they said, the more Eblio came to suspect that the Flying Box People themselves did not know their own full natures. How to ask about this? Did one dare?

Tonality is an essential part of the Cratons' speech, but that's just the start of it. There is an enormous subjective element, which may well be the limiting factor in the size of their communities. Nouns, including names, and verbs sort of function as consistent sounds, at least within a community, though I gather that even they vary from community to community, increasingly with distance. And all the qualifiers that express what anything means to anyone vary from individual to individual, and with mood. the Cratons have a highly-evolved, very full language, but can only really share it fluently with others who they know personally!

Gemma Long, Xenologist
Field Notes, Craton V

It was no longer spring. In fact, it was getting on toward no longer summer, with nights cool enough that one even heard a griffletae snuffle about in the tiffletae leaf duff, when a much-preoccupied Eblio conversed, one luxuriant afternoon full of greenery and flowers that filled the days after late-summer rains and before frosts, with the Flying Box Person called Gemma, at the edge of the Flying Box People's encampment.

To People's eyes, it was a rather ugly encampment. Well, one could not expect Flying Box People to feel about bushes and flowers that they didn't know as People did. The Flying Box People *did* have both feelings and an aesthetic. Eblio had grown to know them, and to know the Gemma Flying Box Person personally, well enough to feel sure of this. Yet Eblio could not help feeling that the Flying Box People's encampment laid bare the ground in a gratuitously destructive manner, whose manitenance had *some* other element beyond foreignness and ignorance.

Eblio did not wish to insult the Gemma Flying Box Person, but felt much need, and almost ready to ask... something, when one of the other Flying Box People walked up and greeted them:

"Attention, Frivolity," the other Flying Box Person said to Eblio. Then the other Flying Box Person turned to the Gemma Flying Box Person and said, "Attention, Tasty-Emotion-Food. Do you perpetually dash about in mandatory screaming insanity, wantonly destroying things and hurting People?"

The Gemma Flying Box Person replied: "Seal up your intestines in a vacuum box, Bart."

Eblio recognized the sound, "Bart," as the other Flying Box Person's name. Eblio recognized the Gemma Flying Box Person's response as somehow entailing personal animosity to the Bart Flying Box Person. But, the personal reaction was a reaction *to something* in Flying Box People interaction generally, which was *not* personal.

Eblio ran away. Eblio did not know how to express at all, let alone how to ask aliens about what called up such fear. But it was too much! Emotion turned to action as sure as the wind blew pollen... whether of People-bushes or of izvi-bushes that made a tangy fruit and no mobile creature at all let alone sentient.

Eblio was only too aware that sentience did not stop fear from impelling Eblio to flight.

"I think the Flying Box People may *intend* friendship to us," Eblio later said to Levery. "But I am terrified of what they do without intent."

Officer Second Class Bart Holder walked up to Xenologist Gemma Long while she was in session with Craton E-[risingúmode]-bl-[gutteral/indrawn]-io-[high/low; fourth]. Officer Holder greeted the Craton: "Hey Sport." Officer Holder greeted Xenologist Long: "Hey, Beautiful. Staying busy?"

Xenologist Long replied: "Can it, Bart."

The Craton ran away.

Board of Inquiry
Craton V Xenological Survey

The Flying Box People didn't do anything *really* awful. Rather, Flying Box Person Gemma came out, day after day, about halfway between the Flying Box People's encampment and the nearest gardens. Eblio finally decided that Flying Box Person Gemma's odd gestures and calls and things laid out on the ground were intended as a sort of ceremonial placating behavior.

The first frosts came, to sweeten red lisp fruit... and to ripen People-berries, most of which would just be eaten by birds or small animals, or fall to the ground. Quite a few would sprout new People-bushes. But it also was time for the People-Singing. A community as large as Eblio's, of almost three hundred People, could expect to bring home at least three or four quickened People-berries most years, possibly as many as eight or ten awakening People-berries, that would go into metamorphosis over the winter.

Not that the Flying Box People appeared to affect this all-important annual event one way or another. But the season... and, well, the invigorating fall weather that went with it, filled Eblio with a sense of responsibility. So Eblio went out to greet Flying Box Person Gemma again. They talked further. Perhaps neither came away fully at ease. But they managed to reassure one another sufficiently to resume their conversations.

The Flying Box People observed the year's People-Singing, from a considerate distance. Four People-berries answered this year. By the time the Flying Box People departed, with deepening snow of Solstice-tide, the People and Flying Box People parted on friendly terms.

Well, personally, Eblio liked the Gemma Flying Box Person... to the degree that one could know how one felt at all of a being *so* foreign. And Eblio felt that the Gemma Flying Box Person reciprocated personal friendship. Of the Flying Box People generally... Eblio was just not sure.

Eblio had explained the exchange which had caused Eblio's flight. The Gemma Flying Box Person had tried to explain that personal feelings had leant that exchange a meaning not accurate to its actual words. Well, perhaps. But Eblio remained unsure if the Flying Box People were fully aware of their own natures.

"*So the Craton plant-person didn't like Officer Bart's disgusting come-on any better than you did, eh Gemma?*"

"*I doubt the Cratons understand yet that there is any such distinction as male and female in our species, Antoinette.*"

"*But you say they're fully sentient?*"

"*Yes. Type I. High intelligence.*"

"*If it wasn't Officer Bart's crude sexual harrassment, why did that Craton run away?*"

"*Tone plays a large part in their language, Antoinette. Feeling tends to inject tone into their words... somewhat as singing a phrase conveys feeling, and thus meaning with it. What scared the Craton was the phrase, 'Staying busy?' In context, what that phrase translated to was more or less: 'Do you perpetually run about in mandatory screaming insanity, wantonly destroying things and hurting people?'*"

"*Ah hah! No scheduling ulcers on Craton V. Eh, Gemma?*"

"*Well...*"

"*I'm afraid we're out of time. Thank you Gemma Long, Xenologist, for your fascinating adventure with the singing plant people on wild,* beautiful, laid back Craton V. Be sure to be with us tomorrow when our guests will debate the raging custody fights in wake of the tragic Memphis quake. Who would you favor to raise an orphaned eleven-year-old? The deceased mother's clone, who is only nineteen herself, or the mother's sixty-eight-year-old sister? Keep those polls coming. And thanks to all of you for making 'Antoinette Asks' the most-popular show in its time slot for yet another month."

Interview, Gemma Long, Xenologist
Xenological Survey Service
Antoinette Asks

It was four years before any more Flying Box People arrived. When more Flying Box People did show up, Eblio was among those to greet them.

It was a few days, though, before Eblio had time to do much more than greet them. It was late spring and very dry. New little seedlings with not much root yet were come up all over the garden. It took a lot of irrigating to keep the soil moist enough for the seedlings to develop deeper roots. All that irrigating sprouted lots of weeds too. Eblio, and everyone, had a lot to do.

A greeting party did walk out to the new-arrived Flying Box People's metal flying box though. Courtesy and curiosity alike required that much. Eblio was among the greeting party. Eblio didn't know if it said anything one way or another about the Flying Box People that the new arrivals included none of the same individuals who had come last time. There seemed to be about forty of them this time.

"Is among you Craton E-squawk-bloop?" one of the new Flying Box People asked.

No one knew what to make of that. But as Eblio was the only Person who actually knew how to talk any Flying Box People's language... and the new Flying Box Person did seem to speak something like the same language... Eblio replied: "Greetings, Flying Box People visitors."

The Flying Box Person who had spoken was about the same height and color as the Gemma Flying Box Person, a bit thicker of build, with curly, light brown fur on top of the head that fell to the Flying Box Person's shoulders. "Oh, you must be Craton E-squawk-bloop," the Flying Box Person said.

Eblio realized that the Flying Box Person was trying to say, "Eblio." Well, even the Gemma Flying Box Person had a hard time to pronounce Eblio's name correctly. What "Craton" meant, Eblio had no idea. Some sort of title used to greet strangers, perhaps?

"I am Eblio," Eblio replied to the new Flying Box Person. "Have you come to learn more of People's ways and to inform us more of yours?"

The new Flying Box Person replied, with what seemed to Eblio considerable enthusiasm: "Oh, magic-dwelling, lie-on-your-back, we come to eat your music trees!"

Eblio thought that the Gemma Flying Box Person had said that all Flying Box People *did* speak the same language over a wide area. Perhaps this Flying Box Person came from someplace very far from the Gemma Flying Box Person's home. Or perhaps what Eblio understood the Gemma Flying Box Person to have said was not accurate... in some way that Eblio and the Gemma Flying Box Person had not quite managed to articulate to each other.

Further conversation with the new Flying Box Person only confirmed Eblio's doubt that People and Flying Box People were communicating. Eblio *hoped* that at least a few basic practical points came across clearly. Well, terms for things, such as, "encampment," or, "this place," had been easiest with the other Flying Box People. Eblio had no idea what to make of the new Flying Box People's talk of "magic-music," and, "tree-doze," and, "self-knowing-food."

Most of the greeting party, unable to understand even as much as Eblio could of what the Flying Box People said, had gone back to their gardens and homes by the time Eblio said, "I must irrigate the free-seed sprouts. Let us talk again another day." The new Flying Box People *did* indicate, Eblio was fairly sure, that they intended to stay... some extended time.

F*ree-seed sprouts. What an Eden! And their voices, like birds! Well, Cratons don't look much like birds. Of course they don't look much like humans either, with their long faces and sturdy, grey-brown arms and legs. But such a... harmonious, natural life!*

Marion Varna
Love Star Tours
Craton V Journal

The new Flying Box People were as agitated as the others, but they did things differently. Where the first party had been methodical, the new ones cast their belongings about chaotically. Where the first group had scurried about and talked to each other in almost ceremonial patterns, the new Flying Box People dashed hither and yon… sometimes right into People's gardens or even their homes, in no comprehensible pattern. The new Flying Box People also frequently paired off and grappled with each other, which the others had not done, or at least not done in public view.

"Well," said Levery, "we know now that there *are* differences from one community of Flying Box People to another."

"Yes," Eblio replied, "but I am not sure they know it. I'm not even sure they know their speech is different."

"How could that be?" Levery asked.

"I don't know," Eblio replied. "Maybe a non-sentient aspect of them affects their speech in some way of which they are unaware, but is part of how they form communities."

"Well, you know more of them than I do," Levery replied.

This was true. But what Eblio knew did not make a lot of sense. In fact, Eblio felt that knowing two communities of Flying Box People was more confusing, rather than more informative, than knowing just one.

Eblio never did get to know any of the new Flying Box People as an individual as Eblio had been able to do with the Gemma Flying Box Person. None of the new ones seemed to want to bother. Well, no other People had wanted to bother either, with the first party, any more than now. It *did* take a lot of time and effort with People whose language held so-alien a structure. But Eblio would have given that time and effort. Except, Eblio could not figure out what any of this new party of Flying Box People did want.

Nor could anyone else. The first party had wanted to learn about People and the world. This made sense enough, even if a lot of their specific behavior did not. This new batch, though, came and went erratically, and did not make any of it clear. They actually tore up less People-bushes than the first party had. Some of them *talked* to People-bushes. Some of them talked to all sorts of plants and mobiles. If this made any sense by Flying Box People standards, who could say?

They talked to People sometimes too, despite the fact that most People could not understand what the Flying Box People said.... And the new Flying Box People made little effort, so far as anyone could tell, to make themselves comprehensible... or to understand what People said to them.

Which mostly mattered only when the Flying Box People did damage. Which they did considerably more than the first party.... Or unconsidered. That the first batch of Flying Box People had been... well, foreign, alien, was only to be expected. But they *had* paid attention, had made obvious effort to be considerate, had done rather little damage, and almost none once Eblio and the Gemma Flying Box Person could communicate enough for Eblio to explain why, for instance, one must not put wastes where they would contaminate the roots of trailing sleevo-vines, whose extent one might not realize without someone who knew explaining.

The new Flying Box People did bizarre things. They asked People for copper cook pots... which the Flying Box People did not use for cooking, and which Eblio was quite sure they did not need as they had plenty of cook pots of their own... which they did not offer to People. Eblio wondered if the Flying Box People had any idea how much work it took to make a copper cook pot... or how they made their own. Eblio would have asked the Gemma Flying Box Person, but didn't know who to ask of the new party.

The new Flying Box People also asked People for both story cloths and pattern cloths... and various articles of clothing and household furnishings. Eblio became increasingly certain that these requests were neither for practical use nor to learn People's ways, but were arbitrary whims.

Sometimes the Flying Box People offered some object in exchange for things they asked for. These objects might be interesting, or even useful. But again, Eblio became increasingly convinced that the choice of what the Flying Box People offered was mostly arbitrary. And considerably more often than anything else, the Flying Box People offered only some incomprehensible little signs on thin, flat objects. Eblio understood these signs to have to do with quantity, but quantity of what Eblio could not tell. People became less and less inclined to give the Flying Box People what they requested, which one could hardly blame People for as the Flying Box People's requests became a significant imposition.

The Flying Box People also trampled gardens. Well, they mostly trampled only less-obvious portions of gardens. But they showed little inclination to learn what was there, or to keep away from what they did not understand. Really, these new Flying Box People were exceedingly rude. Occasionally, they would even do something appalling, such as to open the wall of a Person's home. On two occasions, this let direct sunlight spoil a batch of People-soup. Well, no children starved, but wantonly to cause children to go hungry! There was something very wrong about this new party of Flying Box People.

Many People grew alarmed at the situation. Quite a few wanted to learn the Flying Box People's language, to be able to comprehend, and one hoped to communicate better. But none of the new Flying Box People seemed interested to take the trouble to help anyone learn. Eblio taught others as possible. But Eblio was less sure of the new Flying Box People's speech than had seemed to communicate meaningfully of the first party.

*O*h dear! I hope we haven't stirred up some primitive superstition. The Cratons are refusing to sell us any more of those charming wall-hangings. They won't even part with sooty old kitchen ware. Well, what can you expect from a species that leaves bowls of scummy water around and then has a conniption if you let in some fresh air?

Marion Varna
Craton V Journal

With fall and frost, People-berries ripened... along with lots else, which needed harvesting. There was a lot to do. Then a day came when it was time for People-Singing. As everyone feared, the Flying Box People knew enough to recognize People-Singing. It seemed that *all* the new Flying Box People wanted to come along. No one was comfortable with this. How to explain?

"Please," Eblio said to what Flying Box People's attention Eblio could catch, "do not disturb us in our People-Singing."

Whatever the Flying Box People understood by Eblio's request, it did not result in their leaving People alone to People-Sing. The Flying Box People not only followed People. But the Flying Box People followed too close, and talked among themselves the while, making it difficult to concentrate... and to hear! Some of the Flying Box People even made noises that sounded like a grotesque attempt to join the People-Singing.

Frosts became harder. Most People-berries had dropped. The People had found only one awakening People-berry. Well, this could happen. Eblio remembered a year when there were none. But everyone felt that there could well have been more and the Flying Box People had interfered with finding them. When People *had* found that one awakening People-berry, the Flying Box People had intruded and clustered about until People had to chase them away brandishing sticks. The People-berry had not been harmed. But, as the season neared its end and the Flying Box People continued to trail after People-Singers and interfere, the situation finally grew intolerable.

So, after some discussion, the next day, when People-Singers set out, other People took up spades and vegetable knives (including some given to them by the first Flying Box People) and sticks, and stood between the People-Singers and the Flying Box People, and waved these weapon-objects in a menacing manner.

"You, go away!" the People shouted, as Eblio had taught them, in Flying Box People speech.

The Flying Box People did go back to their encampment. Everyone was relieved. But it was necessary to chase the Flying Box People away three more times before they stopped trying to follow People-Singers. By then, the season was all but over. No more awakening People-berries were found.

The Cratons have turned downright nasty. You'd think they would be pleased that we appreciate their exotic ritual. What do they think we're going to do? Eat their berries? It's not as if there was anything private about singing to bushes all over the landscape with a thousand berries on every one. Well, primitives can be like that about their religion, I suppose. But it is such *a disappointment.*

Marion Varna
Craton V Journal

Again, People discussed the situation. Everyone agreed. Enough was enough.

Eblio and a party of People walked out to the Flying Box People's encampment. Many of the People carried spades and knives and sticks. The Flying Box People saw the People coming. By the time People got there, many of the Flying Box People, too, held objects that no doubt were intended as weapons, though no one knew in just what manner one could use them for such a purpose. Everyone was very thankful not to find out.

"You go away!" Eblio called out, as loudly and as clearly as possible, in Flying Box People speech. "You do not know how to behave among People. We cannot have you here."

A Flying Box Person replied something that Eblio did not fully comprehend, about "violence", and, "go in a line," and, "not-true belief."

Perhaps what the Flying Box Person said mattered. Perhaps not.

To everyone's relief, the Flying Box People did pack up their encampment and go away.

"*Laid back? Harmonious? Did that xenologist ever lead us all down the primrose path! Antoinette, those Cratons grub in the dirt just like some grimy turnip farmer. Don't even know the value of their own crafts, much less care. Bunch of superstitious mud farmers. And they're violent too. Came at us with the very knives the Xenological Survey people gave them."*

"Oh my! Thank you, Marion Varna, for sharing your frightful experience on primitive, spooky Craton V. As a special bonus for being our guest today, the Antoinette Asks Legal Department will provide you a full two hours of complimentary consultation in your valiant effort for just restitution. And remember, all you wonderful viewers out there. Keep those polls coming. Who do you think *should be liable for this life-endangering misrepresentation? Love Star Tours or the Xenological Survey?"*

Interview, Marian Varna
Distressed Love Star Tours Customer
Antoinette Asks

"I'd like to have been able to ask the Gemma Flying Box Person what that second batch of Flying Box People was all about," Eblio said to Levery. "I *did* like the Gemma Flying Box Person. But perhaps it is just as well if they don't come back. For a species capable of building a metal flying box, they really do not seem fully sentient."

Author's note: "Staying busy?" is a greeting that I never heard when younger, but have heard frequently since the early nineties. It often communicates to me the same thing that it did to Eblio.

MARSH GRASS

The G-Drive worked. It maintained forty-seven percent Earth-normal gravity and our bones with it, and got a mass it could lift out of Earth's gravity well all the way to Mars in only four months. A good thing too. Even four months in cramped space ship quarters, smelling like you hadn't had a bath in even longer than you hadn't, with very little to do except read instruments, was a long time. The information our instruments recorded was interesting; the process of recording it was not.

You know now, if you want to, what a G-Drive trip is like, though you still don't know we were the first to test it.—Or at least I think we were the first. What you also don't know is the real reason the subsequent public Mars expeditions—and who knows how many more secret ones I don't even know about—have been so circumspect about landing.

There were four of us. Captain John Maestas stayed on the ship. Andrea Waggenheim commanded the Mars lander along with Raul Grijalva and me, Saul Katz.—One of the ironic facts of the trip was that Pemex, Deutschebank and Israeli financing resulted in a crew of American citizens all of whom spoke English with an accent. We got along okay though. Who cares where anyone's from when you get to go to Mars?

We'd landed lots of unmanned probes, over thirty that I know about. They show rock and dust, thin atmosphere, no water. You probably read the classics when you were a kid, just like me: Heinlein, Burroughs, Bradbury. Admit it. You loved them, just like I did. That was the adventure. The rocks and dust and thin, cold, unbreathable atmosphere were just a trivial adult mistake.

Being there was adventure enough. I still remember the feeling as Andrea acknowledged the lander was free of the ship. No thirteen-year-old could have felt more excited. But, folks, Bradbury had it right.—Oh, we didn't find any crystal cities, no funny little people, certainly no replica of a small town in Ohio complete with a band. But the closer we got to the surface the stranger things became.

Our landing site was the spring line: the area just north of the shrinking south polar cap. The atmosphere is supposed to be far thinner than on Earth, but we were still eighty kilometers up when the... illusion?... whatever it was began to take effect.

The ship's log shows that our radio malfunctioned. The Captain tried to call us back, fully expected we'd come back when he couldn't get through to us. He about ruptured a gut worrying till we lifted off right on schedule and returned to the ship four days later. Only, that's not how I remember it at all.

"Starting to look sort of blurry down there," Andrea reported. "We should be getting close enough to begin to make out smaller features. I wonder what it is."

"Me too," the Captain acknowledged, clear and normal as can be.

We kept reporting as we descended... or did we? Did we somehow forget? There's no record of that entry about things looking blurry in the ship's log, though I clearly remember it. The lander's log is completely blank. What happened?

We could see the melting ice recede into the distance as we got closer to the surface. We landed perhaps four kilometers north of the edge on a thick bank of what looked a lot like marsh grass.

Raul opened the door, and we all stepped out. Nobody said a thing. Nobody thought it odd. The ground was like dry peat, covered with dry, grey-brown marsh grass. I recall the air—yes, air—a little chilly but not cold. There was a slight aroma of damp vegetation. It all seemed so ordinary at the time.

No one said a thing. How do I explain? I knew, we all knew, what we were here for. What was there to say? Oh look! There's a hillock of grey-brown grass two meters high, right behind the hillock a meter and a half high! Why say that? So I didn't, and neither did Andrea or Raul.

We walked through the grass-like stuff. It was about a millimeter across and flat, not brittle exactly, but somewhat fragile. It lay thick on all the ground, a meter long or more, but individual strands were all broken. When they broke, I think they just turned back to dirt, fell completely apart. I don't think there was any fiber to the stuff at all.

A couple hundred meters south we came to the edge of the water. Yes, water. I know. Mars doesn't have any free water, but that's what it was, and at the time it was completely matter-of-fact, ho hum, just what I'd always known was there. It was about half a kilometer across and extended out of sight in both directions. It was not noticeably moving, but it wasn't stagnant either. Though we were so close to the edge of the polar ice, there was no indication of permafrost. The ground was not soggy. Even the bank of the water was dry.

"Here we are," said Andrea.

It was the most surprising thing that had happened since we landed, or so it seemed to me at the time. Why did she speak at all?

Andrea and Raul lowered themselves off the bank into the water. They made no splash, and the water didn't ripple. They stood up to their chests. They each reached into the side of the bank under the water and pulled out clumps of stuff that looked like rich, black dirt mixed with sturdy little roots. I knelt down so they could hand the clumps up to me. Even right by the water's edge my knees didn't get wet at all.

The clumps didn't drip. They were damp and cool but not wet or icy cold as one might expect only a few kilometers from a polar ice cap. (Never mind the fact we were a whole planet out from the sun from the temperature of our quite cold enough, thank you, south polar ice cap.)

I patted the clumps into neat oblong brick shapes about fifteen centimeters long and set them in a row. We collected twenty-four of them. Then Raul and Andrea hoisted themselves back out of the water. They didn't drip a single drop; their clothes were not wet. It didn't seem a bit odd at the time. The water looked and felt like ordinary water, cool but not cold. We each gathered up an armful of clumps and carried them back to the lander, all without saying a word. We set the clumps on the ground, then went on inside for a meal, leaving the door wide open to the perfectly ordinary, breathable, impossible Martian air.

Over our meal, we did talk. We joked and laughed and told silly stories. About what? I can't remember. I can't recall a single word any of us said nor what any subject of our conversation may have been. I do recall Raul miming.... I don't know what, but he bounced around the tiny cabin of the lander in a contorted position that Andrea and I both found uproariously funny.

After a while, we went to sleep. Just like that. No watch. No record. No duty stations. No long-planned experiments. We slept for I have no idea how long. Then we got up. All at once, though it seemed so ordinary at the time that I didn't really notice the fact.

When we went outside, the clumps had changed, of course. Adam was there, and Sandra and the Shy One with the unpronounceable name. Why were they? What were they? At the time it was all so ordinary. Were they people or at least beings of some alien sort? I recall Andrea's face clearly, intent, expressive, framed by straight straw-colored hair. Raul's face was thin, intelligent, usually serious, though now both of them laughed and joked, as I did, with our three companions. The personalities are clear as anyone: Adam, forthright, assured, compelling; Sandra, whimsical, pithy, insightful; and the Shy One, quiet, reticent, with brief flashes of brilliance, awesome and frightening but gone before one really had time even to react. But faces? The only visual memory I have is the three piles of clumps. Did we: Raul and Andrea and I sit around joking with three piles of dirt and roots?

Time is indistinct. We ate. We slept, all in unison. We chatted with our companions. We walked about. The landscape changed, gradually, but it all seemed so matter-of-fact at the time. The hummocks of grey-brown marsh grass... disappeared. They all flattened out into a resilient substance of infinitely various colors kind of like an endless multi-colored exercise mat. The water disappeared too. For a while, I think the lander disappeared, but it didn't seem to matter at the time. I recall eating regularly during this time, but I don't remember what.

Our three piles of clumps did not disappear, but they did change, and as they changed, our companions taught us how to care for them. We had to take each clump and pat it firmly on all sides, as if to remind it of its shape. Though nothing seemed to happen when we patted them, I somehow knew our action was related to the metamorphosis of the clumps into whitish bricks of a material similar to the stuff the whole landscape had turned into but a bit softer and without any admixture of color. At the last, they looked like nothing so much as large chunks of tofu.

I remember wondering if the clumps were intended to be eaten. I felt excitement and encouragement from Adam and Sandra and some unidentifiable intensity from the Shy One: Yes, I knew, but not yet. How did I know that? I ask now. At the time, I did not ask. I just knew.

Then it was time to go. We got up one "morning" to a landscape of grey-brown marsh grass, somewhat thicker than when we first arrived. But, of course, it was spring. We loaded our three piles of tofu bricks into the lander without the least question where it had been, where we had been. Then we all got in, all six of us, closed the door, and took off.

We reached the ship right on schedule, four days after leaving.

"Why didn't you come back when the radio went out?" the Captain asked, as relieved to see us safe and sound as he was upset.

"It seemed a shame to abort the mission when we were already down and everything else worked so well," Andrea answered.

Were we already down? Did the radio go out? Did the Captain even notice Adam and Sandra and the Shy One? When did we stow the tofu bricks? What did we say to him about them, about anything we had found? I don't think we said anything about any of it. I don't recall the Captain even seeing the tofu bricks. I don't recall him ever acknowledging our companions. Yet, soon he was as matter-or-fact about the whole course the expedition was taking as any of us.

We were scheduled to land at two other spots on Mars' surface. We were scheduled to conduct all sorts of experiments, both from the surface and from the ship. We didn't do any of that. We just took off and headed home... of course. How is it that I can now see how odd all of this was when at the time it seemed so ordinary that no one even commented?

The trip took over five months, a complete and utter waste on our part. If we had stayed at Mars another month as we were supposed to, the planetary orbits would have been properly aligned, and the trip back would only have taken four months. We didn't think of that though. We didn't think about it at all. We just headed home because that was the thing to do next. On the trip out, we had struggled with cramped quarters, even boredom. The trip back was not a bit boring. We joked and laughed all the way. About what? I have no idea.

Back at the farm—it really was a farm too, in Ohio, so help me—they must have known something was fishy. Who knew what they thought? They didn't tell us, which makes sense. But they didn't tell you either, and that may have been a terrible mistake. Whatever they thought, they had us land and disembark just like everything was normal. Quarantine was also normal. Mars might have life. It might be dangerous. Viruses. Spores... We knew before we left that we would be quarantined and checked over very, very thoroughly for possible contamination by alien microbes when we got back.

What Adam and Sandra and the Shy One thought of the entire procedure they never said. They certainly never expressed any objection.

I sort of recall our joking about how pompous the medical technicians were with all their readouts on the other side of the barrier. The ground crew never noticed our extra companions, but that never seemed odd. The Captain had never noticed them all the way back from Mars; that hadn't seemed odd either.

Just once, I felt a flash of... anger?... some totally alien, exceedingly disconcerting emotion. It seemed to me to come from the Shy One, but who could really tell with him? I reacted to it strangely. I even thought it strange at the time. I went to the three piles of white Mars bricks and fiddled with one of them till a small chunk crumbled off a corner, a chunk about a centimeter across. I rolled this around in my hand a moment, feeling agitated. Then I popped it in my mouth. It had a slight flavor that hinted of coriander and ginger. The consistency was soft—as the tofu it so much resembled. I don't recall swallowing, but it was gone from my mouth. I do recall that, when I looked, I could not see where it had broken off the corner of one of the bricks. I never mentioned it. If any of the others did anything similar they never mentioned it either.

Then the Captain had his heart attack. John Maestas was in perfect health so far as any medical tests could indicate. He was only forty-seven years old. He should not have had a heart attack, but he did. It was three o'clock in the morning. We were all asleep.

"Saul!"

I woke, momentarily disoriented. I heard someone fall, just outside my door. I jumped up and flicked on the light. The others had woken too. The Captain lay on the floor of the corridor, pale, sweating, gasping for breath. I knelt down. "Heart," he whispered. Raul was already sounding the alarm.

The medics broke the seals of the compound that had been our world since we opened the seals on the door of the ship. There had been no indication of contaminants. No medical seals went back up. We didn't rejoin the world though. Even then, I didn't think anything of it.

We talked to people in the same room now, told them what we had found on Mars. They gave no indication that any of it was surprising. They never seemed to notice Adam and Sandra and the Shy One, but that was to be expected. The Captain recovered. The second mission was announced. We were all pleased.

Then I got sick. It felt like a cold the first couple days, but it got worse. I was full of snot, feverish, weak. The mission could have been postponed. Relative orbits were far from optimum. The ship took off right on schedule, with the Captain (never mind the heart attack), Andrea, Raul, the three piles of Mars stuff, and apparently Adam, Sandra and the Shy One. They anyhow were gone.

I might have been disappointed to be left behind, but I was too sick to care. By the time I knew the ship blew up the second week out, it was old news. How was that? It never hit me as a shock because I knew it before I knew it. I was still very weak. Maybe someone told me while I was lost in fever. Then again...

When I recovered, my status had somehow changed. I was no longer an astronaut, no longer an explorer. I was a consultant, one of those people with vast reams of knowledge and no competence to use it. It was as if I went from being twenty-two to being ninety-two in two weeks, with nary a pause at my real age of thirty-seven. I was an old man, a walking reference source, no longer an active participant in anything, apparently including my own life.

I was free to wander about the farm, enjoy the green Ohio pastures, orchard, and woods, potter about the labs in the eleven underground levels below the white clapboard Ohio farmhouse, to speak to anyone I wished, even to watch or read the news. I was not free to leave, nor to contact anyone beyond the secure perimeter of the twenty-three hundred acres that constituted the farm.

I was only moderately distressed at my incarceration. It was, after all, neither especially unpleasant nor all that surprising. Or had I changed in some way that made nothing surprising? I certainly did not find it surprising when Adam came back. Thinking about it now, I believe I should have been surprised. I believe there is a lot that should have surprised me, but at the time it did not. I was pleased to see him. The more so as everyone else had come to treat me as a less-than-serious-adult human being. I might have been angry; in fact, I was just lonely. I was pleased to have Adam for company.

Adam seemed a little distracted at first, but he was good company, gradually regaining substantialness and humor. Before long, we were joking and laughing together all over the farm. No one else paid the slightest attention. The humid, lush Ohio summer passed, with sweet corn and watermelons, some grown right here on the farm. Why not? It didn't take much room. Apples ripened on the trees, and leaves turned. First frost came, and days grew chilly. Adam began looking about. He never explained what he was looking for, but I always had an image of ice, lots of ice, a polar cap's worth.

Then one day when the leaves were mostly gone from the trees and the pasture lay grey-brown and somnolent under a leaden sky, some political types came to visit, along with their families, children and all. I had not noticed the lack of children, but I sure did notice their presence: so fast, so loud, so into everything. Adam found them fascinating. I was called to a conference toward late morning, but I don't think what I said of our trip was taken very seriously. Then we all went to lunch.

Lunch was tofu sandwiches. That was a little odd. I had certainly never seen it before. Chipped beef or cheeseburgers or even enchiladas were more what I'd come to expect. But you never knew what to expect with political types. No one commented. Everyone just ate their sandwiches. Did I taste a hint of coriander and ginger?

Later, I went for a walk. The air was rather raw, but in the shelter of the woods it was pleasant. I enjoyed the rich earthy smell. The storm caught me by surprise, nasty, cold heavy freezing rain. I was soaked by the time I made it back to the house. I saw several soggy children too. The rain poured down even as the temperature dropped. A sheet of ice a centimeter thick covered everything. I heard later that one of the political visitors determined to leave anyhow and ordered his driver to clear his windshield so he could, but the driver broke it trying to smash so thick a coat of ice off. Quite a lot of trees were damaged by the storm.

The storm ended in the night, but it stayed cold. It was two days before the last of the visitors managed to get away, and the ice wasn't melted yet. I didn't think about it at the time, that ice. I came down with a chill from my soaking and had a slight fever for the next week, though I did not get seriously sick, for which I was thankful. Only later did I realize Adam was gone. I missed him. It was lonely living among people who knew too much about you and didn't believe any of it. But gone he was, without so much as a good bye. And he has not come back.

Nor have I left. I really am getting on toward old now. I'm not sure I would leave if I were allowed. Where would I go? The farm is beautiful. I garden in summer. You should taste my snap peas. I walk at all seasons. You'd be amazed how much territory there is to twenty-three hundred acres. And I keep up with the news, especially of space exploration.

There have been more expeditions to Mars now, public ones, publicly financed. Everyone was excited at the discovery of life. Yes, it was found at the spring line. Yes, there is some sort of radio anomaly in that region. Yes, the predominant life form does look like grey-brown marsh grass, flat, rather fragile, grows in clumps and hummocks, clear as can be… viewed through any good, powerful microscope.

There is no life on Mars visible to the naked eye. There is no liquid water. There is no breathable air. Even if there were, temperatures would not permit human beings to walk around uncovered a few kilometers from the polar cap. Nothing I saw is even remotely possible. No other expedition, so far as I know, has lost radio contact completely. No other expedition has encountered intelligent life, let alone intelligent life that used such names as Adam or Sandra.

So what happened? I don't know. The people I told about it never did take me seriously. You never had the chance to ask your own questions because you never knew anything had happened at all. But you know what? I'm not sure it would have mattered. I've been writing it all down, as best I can remember, in this nice bound book of acid-free paper the people here at the farm have been kind enough to bring me. They're quite indulgent of my requests, but then I don't ask for much—garden tools, melon seeds or turnip, writing materials.

I know my memory has some funny places in it, events that can't have happened, but my memory says they did, events I know happened, but I can't remember any of the content, only the feeling. I know my memory is a little peculiar, but I'm not completely nuts. I know the difference between an oak tree and a cantaloupe as well as anyone. I know the difference between ordinary, odd, and impossible, even if I can't always sort things out. I know paper in a bound book doesn't grow little colored lights big as peas—orange and blue, purple, green, lovely colors all over this book I've been writing in.

Oh, someone could be playing tricks on me, the old kook.—I know that's what they think I am.—But even if they did, when I closed the book, the lights would keep it from closing tightly, or they'd make dents in the paper, or something. They don't though. They're just there, scattered pretty as can be over every page I've written on. I've tried writing a full page, with no lights, closing the book, then opening it back up to the same page without putting it away in between. Sure enough, the new page of writing has lights. Now I won't say it isn't possible that someone who knows about some new technology I don't is playing jokes on a very isolated old man. But...

I'm not sure it's a bad thing the Martians have done to us. As I recall, they were darn good company. I've often wished they were with me over the long, lonely years. But then, I'm not really in a position to judge what they have done. Whatever it is, they did it to me first. Thing is, you never got to decide either.

Author's note: Dreams have informed a number of my stories, and sometimes given me scenes, or images of characters. But I actually dreamt this story.

EXECUTIVE SEARCH

If a divorced woman of twenty-six, like Sarah Pullman, could support three kids in middle class American style by sixty hours a week of slave labor, Harry Upton figured that a (mercifully) childless divorced man of twenty-four, such as himself, ought to be able to live in reasonably well-nourished squalor on about ten hours work a week. So far this theory had proved out. He even had electricity. His tape player, two light bulbs, and a refrigerator had yet to bring the bill over the $11.72 minimum. Last fall he'd even bought a whole new roll of tar paper and got the house pretty weather tight.

Nonetheless, Harry entertained fantasies of fame and fortune just like the next guy. Besides, he wasn't sure he trusted Sarah's intentions—or her birth control methods. She was a great landlady and a great lay, but Harry was not attracted to the prospect of settling down as the sudden father of four. When the letter arrived, he was ready for an adventure.

"There are exciting careers in high technology just waiting for the right applicant," the letter opened. It talked about, "Challenge, a job on the cutting edge of American industry, unlimited opportunities for advancement." The letter went on: "Our exclusive Executive Search Agent has selected your name as a candidate for one of our highly desirable Research Executive positions." It was signed, Arthur L. Pangolin, Chairman of the Board of the Adniare Corporation.

Someone else might have thought the letter was a mistake, but not Harry. He figured his guardian angel had just intentionally confused him with someone else in the minds of the board of the Adniare Corporation of Alamogordo, New Mexico. They even had his middle initial right on their high-priced stationary: Harold G. Upton.

What Harry needed to start him off was a ride to town. It was Thursday, local night at the Panther, so he packed his pack and headed over the hill to Zeke and Janie Pettigrew's. About half way there he heard some noise in the brush. "Don't shoot. It's me, Harry," he hollered. Sure enough. There was Zeke putting in his pot crop in the same patch of sticker vines where his grandpappy used to make moonshine. Harry helped Zeke finish disguising the chicken-manured holes. Then they walked on to the house together.

Janie was already dressed for town. She quickly set an extra place for Harry at the dinner table. Twelve year old Zeke Jr. was highly impressed by the letter. Twila, who considered herself an up and coming businesswoman at fourteen, was not, till Harry pointed out that the Adniare Corporation was offering reimbursement for his travel expenses.

"I'll write you up some real official-looking receipts for twenty-five percent."

"You're on."

"I've heard executives have to work at least fifteen hours a week," said Zeke.

"They pay enough, I'll consider it," said Harry.

The Panther Bar sold the only gas available in Strawberry, Oklahoma after seven PM. Being on the main road from Fayetteville, Arkansas to Muskogee, it got a fair amount of traffic. Locals always used the phone behind the counter. Harry stuck a big wad of chewing gum in the coin return of the vintage (circa 1956) pay phone outside.

Harry entered the Panther with exactly ninety-one cents in his pocket. Nonetheless, he soon had three beers lined up in front of him. The band were friends of his. He showed them the letter at break. Second set, they had him play spoons and washboard and then took up a collection. "Harry, here, is off to make his fortune in the high tech industry. Let's help him on his way."

"You should'a been a preacher," Harry said to Steve, the banjo player, as Steve handed over the $12.36 he took in. "Hope this doesn't cut into your tips."

"Just remember us when you're rich and famous. Oh, I got you a ride to the Interstate too."

"Hot damn."

"Sally's headed down to McAlester first thing."

"Didn't know she had anyone in the pen."

"She don't. Her old man runs a garage there."

Harry collected $9.75 from the phone booth and spent the night with Sally. She wasn't as good as Sarah, but she was overweight and didn't get much attention. She loved Harry's flat belly and curly short hair and beard. "Never knock gratitude," Harry mumbled contentedly to himself next morning over a heaping plate of hot cakes and sausage.

Ten thirty in the morning can be a slow time for hitching, but Harry's luck was holding. In less than ten minutes he was settled in the plush seat of a late model Oldsmobile, listening sympathetically to the woes of the real estate business. Ordinarily, he would have preferred not to have to stop in Oklahoma City.—Easier to get long rides out in the open. But today he needed to hit the thrift shops.

He managed to outfit himself in a suit of clothes he figured would approximate the part of a hot young high tech executive for $8.50, shoes and tie included. These he packed neatly in a black plastic garbage bag (hitching can get dirty) in his pack. Back on the highway, he soon caught a ride with a couple of high schoolers on their way to a Friday night bash at El Reno. It was starting to get dark by then, but there was a half moon. Harry figured he'd walk a while. He caught one more ride, with an unemployed oil field worker who wasn't even too drunk yet.

That got him to Clinton, where he headed out across a field till he found a dry ravine, rolled out his sleeping bag (with a garbage bag slit down the sides for a ground cloth) and went to sleep.

The dog barking had him half awake before the kick in the side brought him altogether around. It was just starting to get light, and the moon was long since set. But there was plenty enough light to see the barrel of the twelve guage six inches from his face.

"Yore on private property, Boy."

"Sorry Sir. Didn't mean no harm."

"I don't give a damn about that. Jist git. Or I'll blow your thieving brains clear to Kansas."

"Yessir."

Harry struggled out of his bag and into his pants and shirt. He started to put on his tennis shoes, but the shotgun waggled threateningly.

"I said git."

Harry hobbled across the prickly pasture with his pack in one hand and trailing his sleeping bag in the other. The rancher had pointed him to the back of the section. He came out on a dirt road a mile south of the Interstate—and a mile and a half, as it turned out, from the next section road north. (He did not want to risk trespassing again to cut across a field.)

"Could'a been worse," Harry said to himself, as he picked what he hoped was the last of the stickers out of his feet. "At least he let me take my bag and pack. Even got the dress shoes I bought in OKC."

There isn't much traffic, but people stop at dawn. The very first person to come along, a local man in an old pickup on his way to work, gave Harry a ride. "That will have been ol' Wayne Friar. Since all the unemployment in the oil patch, there's been a lot'a cattle come up missing, 'specially right by the Interstate. Ol' Wayne's lost more than his share."

All Harry'd had since yesterday's breakfast was a couple beers and a handful of pretzels with his last ride last night. At Elk City, he decided to stop and eat. He filled his canteen there too, and was glad he did. One quick ride got him to Sayre. Then nothing. All day.

First it was pleasantly warm. Then it started getting kind of hot, especially for so early in the year. But a breeze came up. Only it didn't stay a breeze. It soon turned into a roaring, blasting wind—and remained that way all afternoon.

Sometimes Harry stood. Sometimes he walked. Sometimes he sat on his pack. It did not do a bit of good. He got one ride in eight hours. That took him exactly three miles. By late afternoon he felt like he had turned to sand. The wind had not let up a bit. Insanity was definitely setting in.

At last a car stopped. Wonder of wonders, the moody Saudi at the wheel was headed all the way to Artesia, New Mexico. He even bought Harry dinner.

It was two o'clock in the morning when they got to Artesia. Harry got Ahmed to drop him on the west side of town. The moon was still up. Not a car had come by when Harry found a reasonably clean-looking culvert, crawled in, pushed a couple tumbleweeds out of the way, and went to sleep.

Harry half woke around sunrise. No one is on the road Sunday mornings except folks going to church, and they don't stop. Besides, the people who were going to make his fortune wouldn't be open on Sunday. Harry went back to sleep. He dreamt he was in Africa, and a hundred million wildebeests and zebras were stampeding all around him. He found a hollow log and dove in. But the crazed animals ran over it and knocked it along till they kicked it off the side of a cliff and it fell, with him still in it, crashing and bouncing off every ledge.

Harry woke up in a panic just as a huge semi thundered over his head. Something leapt into his face. He fought desperately, tearing his hands—till he realized it was just a tumbleweed that had rolled on top of him while he slept.

It looked to be about noon. His ears and hair were still full of sand from yesterday's wind, and his fancy shoes were all scuffed. He'd have to invest in some shoe polish—and find a way to get clean. But that was all tomorrow.

Harry stretched and used just a couple handfuls of water from his canteen to wash his face. Then he took a good shit where the ditch was steep and out of sight of the road by the culvert entrance, packed his pack in a leisurely manner, and ambled on up to the highway. The New Mexico sky was brilliant blue. The sun was shining. Maybe the wind wouldn't even be too bad today.

Hitching was slow, but the scenery was beautiful, especially in the mountains. At Cloudcroft, Harry bought a bag of chips and a can of bean dip, which he stashed in his pack; and he filled his canteen. His very next ride turned him on to some good bud.—They were a couple in an old blue Econoline, headed for Carrizozo. Harry had them let him out in the middle of nowhere, where the hills looked interesting and the road was still in the National Forest. They even gave him a big roach. He walked till he was out of hearing of the road and then made a little campfire of juniper. It was so dry he lit it with a match without any tinder at all. And there he stayed, watching the day end and the evening come on and contemplating his trip.

What the hell was he doing out here, hundreds of miles from his cozy shack and his friends in Strawberry? He was dirty. He had $7.96 to his name. He didn't really believe he was going to be offered some fancy, exciting job tomorrow. "Harry m'man, you must be nuts," he said aloud.

Just at that moment, a coyote howled. Then a whole pack of them started yipping and singing somewhere behind the next ridge. A chill ran up Harry's spine. Then he giggled. "Farm out. Knew I was here for something."

This was what life was for. It was why Harry didn't want to be tied down—by Sarah Pullman, by a job, at least not by taking either one too seriously. It seemed funny to Harry how he always remembered he didn't want to be tied down but had to go off on some hair-brained adventure to remember why.

Harry broke out the chips and dip, the first he'd had to eat all day. Then he took a couple tokes off the roach, put the rest of it away, and lay back to listen to the coyotes and watch the stars and his little fire till he got drowsy, crawled in his bag and went to sleep.

In the morning there were clouds coming in, but Harry figured even if there was a storm he'd have plenty of time to get to Alamogordo first. He packed up and walked back to the road, stopping just before he got in sight of it to finish off the roach.

It was about ten when he got to town. First thing he did was buy some cheap shoe polish. Next he found a gas station where the men's room had plenty of paper towels and a lock on the door, washed up, and changed into his suit. He put his pack in the bag the suit had been in, being careful not to tear it, in case it did rain, and stashed it under some brush. Then he went looking for the address on his letter. By the time he located it, it was after eleven thirty. And his stomach was rumbling.

They'll be more interested in me after lunch anyhow, Harry thought. He headed for a café.

A green chili cheeseburger with fries and coffee came to $4.75 plus tax. He gave the waitress six dollars and said to keep the change. He knew how hard waitresses work and how many people don't leave them anything. And what the hell. He was about to be a fancy high tech exec. Since it was only twelve thirty, he bought a paper and read it over his fourth cup of coffee. The world was threatening to blow itself up, as usual, but it hadn't done it yet.

The café wasn't too crowded. However, by one thirty Harry was beginning to get dirty looks. He figured it was time though. He folded up his paper and set it on the table, took a deep breath, and headed out.

It was only a couple blocks to the address on his letter, a nondescript modern, colorless stucco building. The letter said Suite 106. He went down the hall till he found a door with that number on it, and knocked. A musical female voice said, "Come in."

The secretary was young, pretty, and very straight-looking. Harry wondered if she was Spanish but couldn't tell.

"May I help you?"

"I'm Harold Upton. I got a letter…"

"Oh yes. Mr. Upton. People usually call first. But let me see. I think Mr. Sanders can see you. Please have a seat."

Harry hoped he hadn't blushed too visibly. Of course, executive types always call. Oh well. This whole trip was a lark really. No point getting up tight now.

The secretary came back in. "Mr. Sanders can see you in just a few minutes. Would you like a cup of coffee while you wait?"

"Thanks. I just had one." He wondered what he sounded like.—A bumpkin come to town? A second rate con artist?

"Mr. Sanders is really pleased you could make it so soon."

Harry suddenly needed to pee. Must be all that coffee, he thought uncomfortably. "Er… could you direct me to the rest room?"

"Right over there." She pointed to a door at the back of the office.

Whew! Harry thought as he rinsed the sweat off his hands and face. The mirror helped. He grinned back at the unfamiliar necktie under his beard. Then he went back out.

Almost immediately, the door across the office opened. A large man of about forty-five with bushy eyebrows beckoned to him and said in a booming, confident voice: "Mr. Upton. Glad to see you. Come on in."

Harry did. There was another man in the office too. He was about the same age, but taut and skinny. He reminded Harry of a lizard. The bulge under his jacket was almost surely a gun.

The big man held out his hand. "I'm Jason Sanders. This is Major Forrest, U.S. Air Force, retired." Harry shook hands with them both. He wondered if Major Forrest had retired willingly or been forced out. Bet he just got passed over too many times on promotion, Harry thought.

Harry had been nervous before, but something about Major Forrest made him feel on more equal ground. Maybe it was the not-very-concealed handgun. Major Forrest just didn't look as tough as that old rancher back at Clinton. Of course, having your pants on does help in the self-confidence department, Harry thought.

How they had gotten his name he figured he never would know, but it soon became clear they really did want to hire him. The Adniare Corporation was in the business of testing space equipment. Harry had the feeling that what they were looking for was someone with no dependents to keep insurance costs down. It sounded like fun. He wasn't about to sound too eager though.

Jason Sanders was obviously a born horse trader. Harry liked him. So he played hard to get just to savor the performance.

"Now my agent..." That was Twila Pettigrew. Harry wondered if he could get them to send her a separate check. She'd love it. "...will want a complete copy of the expense record."

Harry loved the repartee. If it led to a job, well, he'd do it for a while. It would sure be a change from his shack in the woods, but it might be interesting, and a less-risky lifestyle. Between the landlady back in Oklahoma looking to snag a father for her kids and his pot-grower neighbors, the slight chance of getting his body splattered all over White Sands here in New Mexico seemed comparatively tame. Harry chose to look at it that way anyhow. Right now he was playing.

Major Forrest, however, became more and more nervous at the prolonged inconclusive interview.

"Mr. Upton, I don't think you fully understand your situation here." Major Forrest's right hand was floating in the general vicinity of the gun.

"On the contrary," Harry replied, his self-confidence completely returned. "It is you who apparently do not fully understand.... I mean, how much does this stuff cost you want tested?"

Major Forrest flushed. Jason Sanders chuckled. Harry liked him even better for that.

"Now I'm a man has an appreciation for fine equipment. That's a very important asset in an employee."

Jason Sanders rumbled with an only half-restrained belly laugh. Major Forrest sputtered, but then subsided.

"Job's risky," Mr. Sanders said.

"Yep. Figured it was."

"Pay's good."

"Yep. Care of fancy equipment costs."

Major Forrest was not happy, but Jason Sanders apparently outranked him in the Adniare Corporation. He was looking more satisfied every minute.

"Well then, it's settled," said Mr. Sanders. "You're our man. Right?"

"There is just one more thing."

"What's that?"

"Little matter of hours."

"Oh?"

"I'm inclined to take your job, Mr. Sanders. Like I said, I have an appreciation of fine equipment. And I don't mind danger. Don't even mind a little hard work. But I gotta tell you... I'm only available ten hours a week."

Author's note: "Executive Search" came from my noting, back in the eighties, that a lot of cocky, footloose young men showed up in the rural American Southwest, and always had. I wondered what made them tick. This story established a character for me. But at its end, I realized that his outlook would probably get him into trouble. I wondered what he would learn from that. The result was my novel, Thunder Mountain *(Mother Bird Books, 1996), which begins about a year and a half later in my character, Harry Upton's life.*

REQUIEM FOR AN INFORMATION AGE WORKER

Jonah Trane had less to fear than many from the Adniare Corporation's energetic new Vice President for Institutional Advancement. At sixty-three, Jonah's pension was already fully vested. The company would gain no rational advantage to dump him.... Such logic might matter. Jonah even had, wisely if callously he still believed, held his nose and signed that execrable trade-off of future raises in exchange for the slightly-increased security of a vested pension... in case he had an old age in which money was still worth anything. It could happen. It also meant that the company had some incentive to keep Jonah around... doing *something*, since they could surely get more out of him that way than the difference between his salary and his pension if they forced him to retire.

It also meant that Jonah was old enough to be appalled, when he met Veronica Ellender her third day on the job, that she wore a skirt decorated with anatomically precise images of severed penises, in several colors. To a man Jonah's age, there were obvious psychological implications: Inspire castration fear. Freudian penis envy... Constructs of a forgotten culture. What appalled Jonah was not that times had changed, but having lived into a time when the new VP's skirt probably didn't mean *anything*—other than that the pink, tan, and brown decorations on an ultramarine background (a blue never used on denim) went well with Veronica's light brown hair and light complexion, notably pale for New Mexico. Untanned anyhow, an ambiguous emblem of social status, resolved by the internal flush of young success. At least the company's first name policy reduced potential embarrassment of relative age and corporate rank.

"How do you do," said Jonah, on being introduced. He and the new VP shook hands.

"So you're Jonah"—Veronica smiled, probably both genuine and meaningless—"our living institutional history!"

That was true.

The Adniare Corporation had filed for bankruptcy in 1986. Jonah was the only employee left who remembered when the company actually did anything. There was a time when earning a vested pension fourteen years *after* the company entered, and never emerged from, a bankruptcy case which had *become the company's sole enterprise,* would have seemed strange to Jonah. Now, if anything surprised him, it was that so many more years had continued to lurch by since his pension had become vested, and that pension still was worth something!

When the work day ended, Jonah walked home. Some things didn't change. Walking was as good a form of exercise as ever for a man in his sixties. Of course, it was also (usually) a lot less hassle than the (ghackh!) company bus... not to mention the regulations, and their cost, of a private car. Jonah lived a little over a mile from the Adniare Building.... Well, it was not officially the Adniare Building, and hadn't been since before Jonah's now-teenaged grandson André was born, on account of the bankruptcy. But no one in Ace High, New Mexico cared what the official records called the building. Locally, it was the Adniare Building.

It was a pleasant walk really, with sunflowers and purple asters blooming amid the weeds and trash by Santa Anna Creek, and cottonwoods just starting to show fall color in bright, late-afternoon sunshine peeking between the town's mostly single story houses... most intact and inhabited. Jonah appreciated the symmetry of the Christian neighborhood he passed through on about half his route: every house spotless white with blue trim, each set staunchly behind its neatly mown lawn. Staunch indeed! Those lawns had been in litigation almost as long as the Adniare Corporation's bankruptcy, over Religious Freedom versus water usage. The two cases shared a legal research team. This well-known fact got Jonah several friendly nods as he passed... though, of course, the Christians didn't actually converse with one who was known repeatedly to have refused to be Saved.

There were actually four denominations in Ace High that adamantly identified themselves as, "Christian," (as well as the Catholics, Presbyterians, and other old-type denominations). Which of the four "Christian" denominations were on speaking terms with which of each other varied, but Jonah didn't keep track of it.

There was a small commercial district between the Christian neighborhood and Jonah's. The current rent-a-cop company officers were into body-parts necklaces. Jonah had never looked closely enough to determine if these were real: preserved from actual hits, or simulations. What did matter to Jonah was that this security company had had the contract long enough that most of the officers knew him, as a customer of the businesses which paid their salaries and as a local resident. Jonah often didn't even have to show his ID to pass through. This afternoon, the officers at both perimeters just said, "Hi," and let him pass.

When Jonah opened his own front door, a very large, very muscular, very naked Asian-looking man leapt up, with blood-curdling screams, and shot Jonah through the heart seventy-three times. Jonah counted. It took a long time. This accorded with current firearms regulations which made it much easier (at least on the record) to obtain a manual repeat weapon with a really humongous clip than anything automatic. Besides, Jonah might as well count. The assassin was so loud that Jonah couldn't do much else till he was done. There was a time when Jonah would have worried that the neighbors would complain at the noise. Jonah even remembered a time when he would have found such a greeting at his door alarming. He was getting old!

Jonah walked through the finally-silent, and static, projected assassin, or door guard depending on one's point of view, back to the kitchen, where he found Marlo eating a big, fragrant pepperoni, garlic and jalapeño pizza. "Seventy-three shots, huh?" said Jonah, his ears still ringing.

"You noticed!" Marlo grinned.

"Sure," said Jonah. He knew the seventy-three was Marlo's idea of a virtuoso touch, being a number not divisible by anything convenient to a computer. Marlo was Jonah's sixteen-year-old grandson, André's partner... in whatever it was that sixteen-year-olds did these days. André didn't seem to be around.

"Want a piece of pizza?" Marlo asked.

"Sure. Thanks," Jonah said. He checked the refrigerator for a beer. Miraculously, there were several. Jonah felt yet another wistful sigh of age. When Jonah was sixteen, he had quaked at every beer he filched from his dad... and didn't even figure out, till the old man told him on Jonah's twenty-first birthday, that he usually did know, but didn't say anything so long as Jonah didn't get in trouble or put too much dent in his dad's supply. Now, Jonah had no idea what constituted trouble for a kid, and was grateful any time they left him a beer.

As for the assassin (and almost daily variants thereon) Jonah never was sure if that was Marlo and André's idea of entertainment or a security system, or both; but the house had, in fact, not been broken into in over a year. Of course, resident teenagers constituted a security system in their own right, after a fashion, even if they were loud. Jonah was not sure why Marlo seemed to reside in Jonah's house, rather than with Marlo's own family—if he had one—or even whether this impression that Marlo lived in Jonah's house was accurate... or how Marlo obtained his own key without an adult's authorization. But then, even Jonah could have done that if he had a sixteen-year-old's energy to bother.

For that matter, Jonah wasn't entirely clear how André had come to live with him the past three years. It had something to do with André's parents: Jonah's daughter Sally and her ex-husband, André's father, Jake, being in prison, which in turn had something to do with the divorce and taxes. But Jonah never figured out if they were in prison for tax evasion or as tax evasion.

Jonah plunked down at the kitchen table and munched a slice of pizza, while sipping gratefully on his beer. "André out?" he asked.

"Oh, no," said Marlo. "I tied him up. You know how he gets."

This should have told Jonah something, but he didn't think about it, until a few minutes later when he began to feel an all-too-familiar prickling in his belly: The pizza was laced with one of the kids' combat fantasy enhancers... again. Jonah just sighed, and went looking for his sedative inhaler.

In the morning, Jonah found both Marlo and André... and three girls about their age who he might or might not have met before, passed out various places on the floor, all five of them a bit on the bruised and bloody side—probably real. Jonah checked to be sure they were all breathing. Not much he could do about the possibility that any of them had anything in their blood seriously unhealthy to any of the others.

The same rent-a-cop company was still patrolling the commercial district, but the officers on duty didn't know Jonah. They strip-searched him, despite his ID with local address, his age, and the call to the Adniare office confirming his legitimacy. They claimed there was some sort of alert on; Jonah figured they were just bored. He got more of a look at the body-parts necklaces than he usually did (or ever wanted) but still couldn't tell if they were real. The search only made Jonah twenty minutes late for work. The rent-a-cops didn't even shake him down for any money.

The big news at work was that the new Vice President for Institutional Advancement had been arrested and was up for deportation: Veronica Ellender had, it turned out, been born in Russia. Well, it was Russia, but at the time it was also the Soviet Union. Whatever Veronica's parents were doing there in Soviet times, they had stayed on, after the demise of the Soviet Union, to teach the Russians the joys of capitalism. Though they were American citizens, somehow their daughter's American citizenship records had never been properly recorded.

Thus the official office rumor. The accompanying unofficial rumor was that it in fact had cost the Adniare Corporation quite a bit to create the apparent confusion in Veronica Ellender's citizenship records, but that it had been the handiest way to get her out of circulation, as she had turned out to be a New Mexico State Revenue Department spook under cover, after legal dirt in the company's bankruptcy case.

Playing off Federal and State officials and agencies against each other was one of the Adniare Corporation's legal team's favorite… and most-effective ploys. It was a technique by which the company's attorneys could all but guarantee infinite perpetuation of their own employment… and Jonah's. How a decades-bankrupt company could employ anyone had long since ceased to seem peculiar to Jonah. Being bankrupt was what the company *did*.

One minuscule facet of which was Jonah Trane's duty today: Jonah had to not find a former employee named Harry Upton. This recurring duty required some finesse in search methods, but the art of looking where he knew the record was not was a skill in which Jonah Trane had ample practice. The one really tricky part of Jonah's task was the obfuscation of the payments to Harry Upton not to know that the Adniare Corporation was officially looking for him.

Jonah wondered about that. If he understood what was at stake, said Harry Upton could have demanded a far more lucrative arrangement. He apparently either didn't understand, didn't care, was afraid to push his luck, or was a genuinely nice guy who didn't want to squeeze anyone. Jonah occasionally contemplated driving over to meet Harry Upton, out of curiosity. Jonah no longer owned a car. He did still maintain his license, and could afford the rental… Alas, curiosity died aborning: The permits to drive all the way across the state to Elk Stuck, where Jonah officially didn't know that Harry Upton had lived for half a lifetime, made the prospect more bother than it was worth.

Jonah was grateful to Harry Upton, though. Not only did his official status as alive but unlocated help perpetuate the Adniare Corporation's bankruptcy case, and thereby existence, all these years. But it was part of the reason the company had found it more advantageous to permit Jonah's pension to become vested (thereby demonstrating the legitimacy of the company's pension plan) than to reorganize his position out of existence before it would have.

At the time of the initial bankruptcy filing, Harry Upton had been employed by the Adniare Corporation at the company's now-derelict (fully depreciated) Alamogordo facility, testing Space equipment... back in the days when the Adniare Corporation still did anything. Harry had been arrested for theft of government property: to wit, several tools and some plumbing, from the company plant. The actual property that Harry purloined consisted of items such as C-clamps and drill bits, but he stole them from a Federally-designated High Security facility, which resulted in legal charges of a severity bordering on treason, and bail to match.

Harry eventually was released, only four months later in fact, for time served, on pleading guilty to a misdemeanor. Whereupon, it being July and hot in Alamogordo, he apparently decamped for higher altitude. But Harry Upton's employment by the Adniare Corporation was never officially terminated, "for cause," nor any other way for that matter, because of the "hazardous employment" clause in his contract, associated with the equipment he had been testing.... Well, some of the stuff was toxic, or blew up.

What it all amounted to was that Harry Upton still had a stake in the Adniare Corporation's pension plan, a claim the nonresolution of which was one of several that the Adniare Corporation's attorneys had so brilliantly parlayed into a lifetime career of not resolving the company's bankruptcy.

Jonah didn't find Harry Upton all day. It was actually a rather painstaking endeavor. Even Marlo would have been impressed, Jonah thought, at how plausibly Jonah checked so many records... in a world where electronic records were not especially reliable, but there were really a lot of them... without ever finding the slightest trace of Harry Upton's whereabouts.

Walking home after work again, Jonah ran into a roadblock. The Christians' militia was fighting the Mexican army.... Well, fighting some

Mexican army. Whether this particular Mexican army had anything to do with Mexico's government, or for that matter, which of six or eight (at last count) equally credible claimants to the title was Mexico's government, was hard to say. Jonah hated it when a war kept him from getting home. If the war didn't move out of his way before dark, there would be curfew and Jonah would have to sleep in a shelter, in his clothes, and probably have to go to work in the morning in those same clothes without a chance to shower.

Which was exactly what did happen.

Jonah could hardly stay too grumpy, though, when he arrived at work the next day, only to learn that the company now was trying to get Veronica Ellender *back*: The United States had deported her. The Russians wouldn't have her. She had been flown from El Paso to Saint Petersburg (Russia, not Florida) and back, and put right back on another plane to Saint Petersburg... where the Russians had already said they would put her right back on a plane for El Paso again. Somehow, the Adniare Corporation was being billed for all the plane tickets.

By the time Jonah got to the Christian neighborhood on his walk home that afternoon, the war had moved off in the general direction of Texas. The Christians were having their usual conniptions over bullets, bombs, and blood marring the perfect white of their houses. The rent-a-cops on duty at the commercial district knew Jonah, didn't hassle him for ID... but did shake him down for fifty dollars. Jonah bought them a twelve-pack instead. A better deal for both parties since the officers were underage (as well as on duty) and would have had to pay a premium.

When Jonah opened his door, twenty-three alligators—or maybe crocodiles, he wasn't sure—swarmed him, gnashing at Jonah's legs and arms and bellowing. Jonah counted again. Sure enough, another oddball number. Marlo was something of a fanatic. When his ears recovered from the alligator (or whatever) bellows, Jonah heard music from André's room. He even thought he recognized the group: The Electric Luddites. One of them anyhow. There were rival bands with the name, one from Becky's Ham, another from Texas. They would crash each other's gigs and get into fights. Jonah also noted that the phone's message light was blinking, but headed for the shower first. Probably for the kids anyhow, though it was a little unusual that they hadn't gotten it already if they were home.

Jonah took off his slept-in clothes and turned on the shower. The water came out pink. It smelled hideous. Jonah sighed, turned the water back off, put his clothes back on, and headed for André's room. Maybe the boys would know if the water was something lethal or the antidote. Jonah banged on André's door: "Hey, André! Marlo! Hi! Any idea what's with the water?"

No reply. Jonah tried the door. It opened. A bomb exploded in Jonah's face. Well, actually, there was just a really bright blast of light and a loud bang. Jonah blinked till he could see again. No one there. Far from the first time André had gone out leaving the music blaring. Then again, that music might do as much to deter burglars as the alligators and bomb. Jonah turned the music down. Might as well check the phone messages, he figured.

There were seven. Five were, indeed, for the boys. One was from the boys, to Jonah: "Hey, Gramps," André's voice said, "don't drink the water." No further explanation. The time signature was about four hours old. The seventh message was from Melinda, Jonah's ex and André's grandmother, to both of them. Melinda and Jonah actually were pretty good friends. Melinda was currently on a volcano tour of Indonesia. Jonah had no idea why. She mostly gushed about swimming in a hot lake. Jonah wondered what color the water was.

Jonah wandered to the kitchen. He checked the refrigerator. No beer. No juice. No soda. He should have bought himself something when he bought those cops their twelve-pack. He sat down at the table. He was thirsty. He didn't know if he was hungry or not. His clothes felt repulsive. He thought about Veronica Ellender flying back and forth to Russia. He wondered if she had had to sleep in her severed penis skirt.

When André and Marlo—and Lucy and Gabrielle and Annette and Grace and Luis—came in a little after three AM (something of a feat what with curfew, but Grace had a brother with the rent-a-cop outfit and Annette's mom was a lawyer) Jonah lay half flopped on the table. The kids figured André's grandpa had fallen asleep there. Only the next morning—afternoon, actually, when they got up and found that Jonah hadn't moved—did they realize he was dead.

There was no autopsy. Why bother? The death certificate read: "Adrenal exhaustion," as Cause of Death. It was probably more or less true. The Adniare Corporation's pension plan paid for the funeral. Why not? They got out of ever having to pay Jonah that vested pension. Besides, the funeral was part of a package deal:

Jonah Trane might or might not have been surprised to know just how much his grandson understood about Jonah's pension. André knew exactly how much it would cost the Adniare Corporation in legal expenses to screw him out of the two years of Survivor's Benefits he should have received until he turned eighteen (assuming the Adniare Corporation's attorneys used André's mother being in prison over taxes as their excuse). With just a little help from Annette's lawyer mom, André got almost two thirds that much in one under-the-table lump sum. Very lumpy, actually, as a substantial chunk of the payment was not money at all, but ammunition.

It was a done deal by the time Melinda got home for the funeral. She didn't speak to André for a month. She had wanted Adniare Corporation stock, which she believed she could have made a killing on selling it to a Philippine senator she had met at an airport restaurant in Jakarta, who didn't understand American bankruptcy law. But Melinda forgave André. He was her grandson, after all. He also shared the ammunition.

Author's note: Fictional universes take on a life of their own. Harry Upton matures, including morally, in Thunder Mountain. *But the moral ambiguity of the world that made him who he is also has its ripening.*

HOW BEARS SURVIVED THE CHANGE

They didn't.
    Bears were extinct.
    But they came back.
The Change:
When the Earth tipped over.

When the Star Wars (no, not the movie) mini-satellite Space weapon misfired. Oh, you didn't know we really had them up there? A lot you didn't know! Like what they really were for. Or why the Soviet Union went broke competing, trying to develop their own.

No, not to protect our… or anyone's cities. Silly propaganda. No, not to deter a nuclear First Strike, shooting down enough incoming ICBMs to preserve retaliatory capability. Slightly-less-silly propaganda.

One of the things the coherent beam mini-satellites *were* supposed to do, and did neat as can be when fired straight down, was knock out electrical power. They made a lovely concussion too. But they never were supposed to fire all at once, straight down.

Too bad. Best laid plans and all that.

Could have been worse. Global Warming may have saved Life on Earth. Thickened the atmosphere a little. The concussion centered higher. Cushion, as it were…

That concussion! Quite a bang, when twenty thousand coherent beam Space shots struck all at once.

If stomping the brakes, as it were, affected length of day, it was not enough to tell, by any mechanical clock that still worked afterwards. (Electronic clocks didn't.) Gyroscopic effect of the Earth's spin maintained direction. A good thing, as any significant change of direction would have altered inclination to the Sun! But that braking bang did make a teeny, tiny hiccup in planetary spin. Wobble won out.

Just barely, very briefly. Not enough to fling the atmosphere and oceans off into Space, let alone to drag the whole planet's mass with it and leave a bare rock tumbling chaotically. But there is a wobble to our planet's spin, due at least partly to variation in density of surface features. As well, since land masses are irregularly distributed and nearly all targets were on land, the brakes did not hit evenly.

Earth's solid crust slipped sideways around the liquid interior... with cataclysmic fragmenting where the surface *was* solid and equally cataclysmic sloshing of surface liquid. Gyroscopic effect of the continuing spin saved the day, by overcoming the sideways acceleration of the crust, to stabilize the planet's motion all in the same direction again.

Quite the mess, as it was! Yet remarkable how many species did survive, and eventually revive: Lilacs and poison ivy. Elk. Zebras. Dragon flies. Scorpions. People. Honey bees. Mountain lions. Rabbits.

But not bears. Not a one.

Yet, eight centuries later, there they were again.

Earthquakes and volcanoes had settled a lot by then. Dust had settled. Climates had stabilized. Life had been healthy for a couple centuries. Forests had grown back. Human communities. A few anyhow. Human population was back up to about a million, planet-wide. Enough to have human names for places, including the area where bears showed up again: just above Areno, in the mountains around the Tubal-Kessa border.

But how?

Perhaps it all began with Bill Redpath's problem with the IRS, back in the 1980s. Bill Redpath and Maryllyn Agado were caretaking Bulldog and Petunia's house at the time, in the famous (look it up in any ghost town book) old gold-and-silver mining town of Mogollon, New Mexico, while Bulldog and Petunia were off in Tucson having a baby and making enough money to be able to afford to have a baby.

"I never should have filed a tax return," said Bill. "I did get a rebate from the State, but I really only filed because I thought it was the right thing to do."

"The IRS refused to believe anyone *could* live on only $1,800," Maryllyn explained.

"Demanded records to prove the income I *didn't* have," said Bill. "What records? Crazy! Made *me* crazy!"

"Maybe that's how the Aliens learned about it!" said Maryllyn. "They didn't exactly *like* crazy. But it... sort of rang a bell for them. They showed up in the cutest little UFO."

"Zipped right down in the canyon," said Bill. "That's *some* flying! If you have a heart attack in Mogollon on a windy day, don't expect the Medevac chopper to even try to land in that narrow canyon."

The Aliens never did make it clear how they heard of Bill's IRS problem. But they did explain that they were looking for a demon that had escaped from their zoo.

"Turned out to be a different demon," said Maryllyn.

"Too bad," said Bill.

The Aliens were friendly though. Came back to visit.

"Or some did," said Maryllyn. "We never could tell them apart."

"I'm not sure it mattered," said Bill.

Have you ever wondered why Alien encounter stories are all so odd? It is because our planet has been in a Bubble In Time. Well, it was, during the Abysmal Epoch. Popped back out, to the real Timeline, at the Change… though it still took a while, centuries in fact, for anyone to find us again. They'd been wondering where we went!

But while we were stuck in the Bubble In Time for twelve of our millennia or so, most Aliens couldn't find us. Only members of telepathic species and ones who were really stoned.

"Our Aliens were pretty coherent," said Bill.

"More coherent than *you* were by the time the IRS got done with you," said Maryllyn.

"But they seemed to be in telepathic… A whole species in telepathic rapport," said Bill.

Then Bulldog and Petunia came back.

Panicked, actually. Fled the big city. Showed up in a frenzy, unannounced.

All things considered, they were pretty decent to Bill and Maryllyn. They would have let Bill and Maryllyn stay on indefinitely. But, well, it was Bulldog and Petunia's house, and they did have a family.

And Elvira really was getting old.

So perhaps we should start with Elvira. She *is* how the bears got into the picture.

Elvira Sonderfeld sort of inherited the Mogollon Rooming House, due to the Great Flu Epidemic of 1918.

Elvira was not related to the previous owners. But they were among the many who fled Mogollon, another panic in its day, due to how hard the flu hit what, at the time, was the biggest producer of silver and gold in the new State of New Mexico. The real reason why the flu hit so hard in Mogollon was the prevalence of silicosis, which had the miners' lungs half turned to stone *before* the flu ever hit. But the owners of the Mogollon Rooming House didn't think of that. All they knew was that people in Mogollon were dying like flies, and that though the flu was bad everywhere, it wasn't *that* bad everywhere.

Elvira was a generous-hearted teenager then. She nursed the sick, who filled the abandoned Rooming House, until the epidemic passed. She had been working there anyhow, and stayed on afterwards. Mogollon still was a thriving mining town of several thousand, in its tight, remote canyon. There still were roomers, or at any rate soon were again when the flu abated, who needed someone to keep the establishment running.

Elvira assumed that the owners would come back. She kept books, as well as the kitchen and bedding, neat and ready for inspection, right through the twenties, when it was just as well the bears were not yet around, Prohibition notwithstanding.... And Prohibition didn't withstand much in Mogollon.

In the thirties, grateful citizens helped Elvira obtain a deed to the now-clearly-abandoned property. She never did learn what became of the previous owners.

During WWI, Mogollon's production of silver and gold had been highly valued by the United States. The value held through the twenties. The depths of the Great Depression, in the early thirties, missed Mogollon entirely. But then the price of gold was regulated by the Federal Government.

$14 an ounce, and everyone was *commanded* to turn in their Gold Certificates. Just a few weeks later, those who didn't... or who had insider information and knew to wait, were informed again to turn in their Gold Certificates to the U.S. Treasury for redemption... at $35 an ounce.

Even at $35 an ounce, gold was less profitable than it used to be. But Mogollon continued to produce, and Elvira continued to run the Mogollon Rooming House.

Until 1942, when the Federal Government ordered the mines to shut down, declaring gold and silver not essential to the WWII war effort.

Mogollon emptied out, and the Mogollon Rooming House with it. It took a while. But, eventually, Elvira, now middle aged, found herself one of only a dozen residents of a ghost town, that had been a small city when she was growing up there. The Mogollon Rooming House was unsalable. Elvira *didn't want* to leave. But she did get lonely.

Elvira was not sure when the bears moved in. "1957, maybe, or 1958. It was before that mayor from a town in Germany showed up, I recall. He wanted a photograph of himself with the bears. That was 1964, I believe. The bears had been with me several years by then."

Elvira and the bears. Just part of life in Mogollon, like flowers blooming on the sunny slope above one side of the single street through the canyon in January, while the shady slope that rose on the other side of the street still held three feet of snow in May. The only important point, to Mogollon's few other residents, often gathered at the Bloated Goat Saloon, was: "*Don't* show up for any of Elvira's delectable cooking with liquor on your breath. Even the smell makes the bears ornery!"

So Elvira stayed. And so did the bears. Years went by, eventually decades. Elvira grew older, and eventually Elvira grew old.

Elvira stayed healthy. Her cooking stayed wonderful. She took to tucking her toes under a warm, snoozing bear, to enjoy a cool, quiet canyon dusk. But a time came when it really was getting hard for Elvira to chop her own firewood.

Then there was the drought. The acorn crop failed. Everyone helped get in a couple pickup loads for the bears. Compassion there, but self-preservation too. Elvira's bears were more civilized that some local humans. But they *were* still bears.

Maryllyn Agado got along well with the bears. She began taking cooking lessons from Elvira. Bill Redpath got along with the bears too. Though not totally abstinent, they both might as well have been by Mogollon standards, and didn't mind a bit to refrain when anywhere near the Mogollon Rooming House.

They never would have asked. For that matter, Elvira never would have asked for help. But she realized at once, when Bulldog and Petunia showed up so abruptly, that, after all, there was lots more room in the Mogollon Rooming House than in Bulldog and Petunia's little house.

Besides, *everyone* in Mogollon (where population was back up from its all-time low of four… not counting the bears… to somewhere around thirty) knew that Bulldog and Petunia practiced the Christianity they preached. But did they ever preach!

Elvira wouldn't ask for help. But she would offer…

So Bill and Maryllyn moved into the Mogollon Rooming House, with Elvira Sonderfeld and the bears.

Which is why, when, after several more visits over several years, the Aliens invited Bill and Maryllyn to go for a ride in their UFO, it was entirely natural for Elvira to go for a ride right along with them.

And the bears.

Well, why not?

There was plenty of room.

Which was odd, in a way. The UFO didn't look big enough. But inside, it was quite roomy.

There were three Aliens.

The same ones who first showed up, looking for the escaped demon? Hard to say. They made everyone comfortable, bears included. Then they took off.

But, well, communication was... approximate?

Telepathic, of course. That was the sort of Alien they were. But... For them, species-wide rapport *was* reality as they knew it. What they thought the relationship was between their human and ursine guests, who could say? Congenial. Obviously. That was why three humans and eight bears *could* climb aboard the neat, little... except not so little inside... UFO, to go for a Space ride.

Maybe the Aliens didn't realize that the rapport between the humans and the bears did not include the sort of ability to explain things that the Aliens didn't need among themselves and which we achieved among our species by use of language.

What happened was, when the UFO went into Free Fall, the *bears* panicked. Flailing about, one of them bumped... something. Whatever it was, what Bill and Maryllyn and Elvira registered, as if one of the Aliens had said it was, more or less: "Oh no! It broke the wormhole warning gauge!"

Was there a wormhole involved, or even a gauge? Hard to say. Telepathy works like dream symbolism. Represents the unknown as images and concepts of the familiar. Feedback completes the learning process... eventually. Like language, it is a mode of communication that takes practice.

Bill and Maryllyn and Elvira had not had time to get used to it. For that matter, they had not had time to get used to Free Fall themselves, let alone to settle the bears down, when all three Aliens abruptly went catatonic.

The UFO... did... something disconcerting.

And then, fairly promptly, the UFO reestablished a relationship to gravity, and landed. The door opened.

Before Bill or Maryllyn, let alone Elvira who was still healthy but *was* well into her nineties by then, could get their feet under them, all eight bears tumbled out the door and took off.

"Are the Aliens dead?" asked Maryllyn.

"I don't think so," said Bill.

"If I'm still alive, they certainly ought to be," said Elvira, patting her hair back in order.

They all were more disconcerted than any physical distress.

The Aliens' condition didn't help. Even looking at them was... disorienting. Being telepathic and all, what they, and their UFO for that matter, looked like was an inextricable mix of whatever they really did look like physically and the communication medium itself between their species and ours. Catatonic, they still projected, but did not communicate.

No wonder the bears were in such a hurry to get out!

Bill and Maryllyn and Elvira climbed out too.

Where were they?

Not in Mogollon, but apparently in some fairly similar, apparently uninhabited canyon.

The Aliens just lay there, apparently alive, but all three of them comatose. They might as well have been some sculpture... with confusing lighting, from a SF convention art show.

Now what?

At least the "apparently" aspect of... *everything*... rejelled to substantial things being... *something definite*... outside the UFO.

Things could have been worse, in ways that Bill and Maryllyn and Elvira readily could think of, and several more of which what had happened to them would leave them mercifully unaware.

For instance, they missed the hyperinflation. And the Panama Canal incident. Didn't have to live through those events, and never knew it.

Not to mention the Change itself. Well, that one they would eventually know about.

For now, they *were* thankful that the weather was pleasant, and would have been even more so, had they any idea what they had missed.

It was Elvira who suggested that they make camp a few bends down the canyon, away from the UFO, even though the disorienting feature of the Aliens' telepathic oblivion projected only a dreamy vagueness, not really unpleasant, once they had solid ground under their feet again.

"No telling why the UFO did what it did when our hosts conked out," Elvira said, "or what else it will do. But I don't think my bears will come back even close to it. I want to be where they can find us."

It seemed reasonable to Bill and Maryllyn. They checked on the Aliens once more, then left them where they were, inside the UFO. They didn't know what else to do for them.

"Heavens," said Elvira the next morning, "it has been years since I slept on the ground. Has me feeling like I'm ninety years old."

"But Elvira," said Maryllyn, a bit concerned, "you *are* ninety years old."

"And then some, thank you very much," said Elvira, "but let me tell you something. Being ninety years old is one thing. Feeling like it is quite another!"

No telling how long it would have taken for anyone to find them, or them to find anyone, but for Tarry's vision.

While the Aliens' comatose telepathic projection was like the sort of dream that seems compelling while it is going on but, on waking, turns out to have been too amorphous to remember at all, Tarry's vision, if a bit vague on *what* it was about, did at least project a clear and specific *direction* to its compelling feeling.

Up the Tubal River, Tarry's vision called him, from his warm, desert river valley home, to the rugged, magnificent mountains, that he always had meant to visit one day anyhow but might never have gotten around to it, but for that compelling vision. A vision that did not really show Tarry anything, so much as call to him, with an urgency that said: "Come! Follow the river to its source!"

Well, why not?

So he did, with his Tubal flashlight, with its wonderful modern insulation so light and safe, slung on his belt, to set in the Sun for an hour to charge, and thereby be able to light both camp and a campfire at night.

Up the Tubal River Tarry traveled, passing through congenial Tubal village and wild country between, into the mountains where travel was not just a walk but a hike, and green spread, with more rainfall and with winter snowcover, up the sides of bird-and-flower-filled forested slopes and mountain meadows. At last Tarry arrived at the high mountain village of Areno, situated near the outflow of its lake, in its sparkling mountain valley with pines and even aspens, where people grew quinoa more than corn, lots of raspberries but few melons, and where cotton and okra wouldn't mature in a season at all.

Like so many in Tubal, Areno was a village of poignant contrasts: One man in his early thirties was so robust that he habitually swam in the lake in a mountain blizzard and wore nothing but a kilt year-round. Another the same age, who had been his childhood playmate, now sat crippled by the nerve disease that had entered Tubal's heritage after the Change, before people realized to move far enough away from the WIPP Contamination Site, legs useless, hands spastic, and soon to sink to the starvation that would finish off the afflicted if nothing else took them first, when the disease progressed to the point of making it impossible to swallow.

But most in Areno, as in all of Aztlan, with the Terror thankfully three centuries ended, earthquakes much more moderate if still frequent, and weather wholesome and consistent, were healthy, if not quite the extreme to go bare-chested all of a mountain winter to reassure all with the fierce vitality their ancestors once had needed to survive at all, to be anyone's ancestors.

A visiting lowlander with a vision was quite the diversion in an isolated mountain village. Several of the Areno villagers found it a pleasure and no imposition at all to row one of their largest boats across the lake, to help and accompany Tarry on his way, to seek the headwaters stream someplace on the other side, that he still felt drawn to… for whatever reason there is why visions draw people to do anything.

Up the canyon on the far side of the lake they hiked, Tarry in his cotton tunic, comfortable enough even in the mountains in late summer, the five Areno villagers who accompanied him in linen or wool. They crossed the stream several times, on rocks and fallen logs, or some places small enough just to jump across. Hints of coming fall color showed a few places, and purple asters informed mountain people that summer indeed was nearing its end. But the day was warm, and, to one accustomed to often-harsh desert air as Tarry was, a fragrant mountain breeze was moist and gentle.

Not even terribly far up the canyon did they hike, before they heard some unidentifiable large animal crashing off through the brush, and soon after came on three strangers, of rather light complexion and very foreign dress.

Two of the strangers, a woman and a man, looked to be in their thirties, the third, a very old woman. All looked healthy.

But they did not speak a word of Aztlanian.

"That certainly isn't Spanish," said Bill.

"Or Apache," said Elvira.

"You know Apache?" Maryllyn asked.

"Not to speak it," said Elvira, "but enough to recognize it."

"Apache?" said one of the new arrivals, a dark-complected man a little older than Bill and Maryllyn, dressed in a cloth-belted, tan and somewhat travel-stained tunic, with something hanging from the belt that looked a little like a small French horn with a very small bell.

Just then, a large cinnamon bear ambled out of the bushes, followed by two smaller blacks.

The Tubals gaped, wide-eyed.

Before anyone had time to do anything further, the UFO took off, from where it had rested a few bends farther up the canyon, straight up.

The bears plunged back into the bushes. Had they not, the Tubals probably would have.

"Things certainly have been abrupt lately!" said Elvira.

Maryllyn shook her head. "Did you catch that?"

"Why, so I did!" Elvira said.

"Me too!" said Bill.

They could see that the others had too. In case there was any question, the same man who had spoken earlier said, "Mogollon?" (To the Tubals, it was the name of a mountain range, off to the west, in Kessa.)

They all knew, though it was months before they had enough language in common to discuss it:

The reason why the three Aliens went catatonic was that, after the bear bumped the wormhole warning gauge, or whatever it was, and broke it, in its panic at Free Fall, the UFO did indeed fall into… something.

If that something was a wormhole, it might ordinarily have come out anywhere. Then the UFO's automatic systems might have taken so much longer to get the UFO back to Earth that the Aliens would have come to first. But whatever the UFO fell into stuck with the general region of Space that the Earth traversed, through what the planet experienced as eight centuries of Time, drawn, only decades away, by the same vortex that popped our planet out of its Bubble at the Change. When that happened, the Aliens lost contact with the rest of their species.

Though they regained contact immediately on emergence, it took a day for coherence to settle. When it did, the Aliens came to, and the UFO took off.

Resettling coherence took so long because the Aliens' whole species got a little disoriented… all over again. The first time at their abrupt disappearance. This time, at their abrupt reappearance on the Cosmic Web. Things got quite goofy, for about a day, on those Aliens' home World, and for all of them, everywhere in the Cosmos that there were any.

But they got their act, as a species, back together again pretty quickly. The disappearance, and even more the reappearance, of three of their members was a shock to them. But, after all, members of their species were born and died all the time. It wasn't as if individual perceptive/active nodes coming and going to and from existence was all that shocking.

In a way, the shock that it took a whole day for the Alien species to recover from, for the three on the UFO to snap out of their stupor, was us, popping out of our millennia-long Bubble In Time, back onto the real Timeline. Actually, our planet already had popped back out, in potential as it were, at the Change. But it was reestablishing contact that made the potential real.

All of which, for the time being, and, Cosmic distances being what they are, even with UFOs, that *are* so "unidentified" because we don't understand how they work, for a while to come, meant considerably more to the Aliens than to us. The Cosmos is big, and so is Time, and both are… stretchy. Even now that our planet no longer was stuck in its Bubble

In Time, it would be a while before we and the rest of the Cosmos reestablished regular interaction.

In the meantime, Bill and Maryllyn and Elvira would not be going back to Mogollon.

Mogollon no longer existed. *That* canyon snapped shut like a couple of hands clapping in the Change. The Change, after all, *was* a World cataclysm.

Which was why, when it happened, planetary human population abruptly dropped by something like 99.997%... to somewhere around 300,000, planetwide.

At the Change, when the Earth's crust, mercifully briefly, accelerated in a different direction from the planet's spin, there was an initial jolt. This was least devastating in the region around the poles of the combined motion of the tip and the continuing spin. The one of those poles that happened to be on land, most of it even high enough land not to be sloshed over by monster tsunamis, was near the Continental Divide in what then was Northern New Mexico.

Consequently, about half the survivors were in Aztlan, and thus in relatively easier touch with each other than with anyone else. There really were not exactly 144,000 of them. But the number in Aztlan, to know of each other, was close enough to that figure that there was quite the religious reform when, after centuries, the Terror at last moderated enough for life to get somewhat less desperate... and perhaps at least partly for that reason, religion too. It was then that descendants of Aztlanian survivors of the Change, including Tubals, learned that there *were* survivors, and by then a fair number of their descendants, lots of other places on the planet. Thus the number, that Aztlanians (of by that time several cultures if more or less one language) initially knew to have survived the Change, was simply irrelevant.

Just as well. That religious reform stifled some inclination to rigidity which could have become very unpleasant. Instead, it turned later Aztlanian religion to a language for learning whatever one might of the Unknown. *Much* nicer! Which, though neither he nor the villagers of Areno knew it, was a good deal of why Tarry's response to his own vision was simply to set out seeking, and the response of those he met was simply to find the vision and the visionary interesting, rather than grandiose command or a threat.

Bill and Maryllyn and Elvira, not to mention the bears, and the UFO which they all saw accelerating straight up before it got high enough to zip into Cosmic Distortion Mode without problematic entanglements with planetary matter density, all were a fair source of excitement for Tarry and the Arenoans. But no one got too nutty over it. Not even the bears.

And Bill and Maryllyn and Elvira, and after a fashion the Tubals too, did understand what the Aliens communicated, as the Aliens' own coherence rejelled. The reason why the UFO landed where it did was that it had a default system. Priority Level One was: If the crew is incapacitated, go back to wherever you were last, so long as leaving there had *not* been in, "Run for your life!" mode. That didn't work, so Priority Level Two was: If you can't find wherever you were last, land the first place you can find, similar, for atmospheric composition, structure of terrain, and such.

Since Mogollon no longer existed, the UFO just set down in a canyon of similar altitude, shape and alignment.

What the bears thought of all this, who can say? Rapport, even among our own terrestrial species, let alone between our species and theirs, just is not full telepathy, a point on which the Aliens may not have been entirely clear.

Whatever the bears thought of their new circumstances, they came back to visit, often, as long as Elvira lived. Which she did, more or less to the age of 104, though it was a little confusing to reckon, as she and the rest of them had not landed in the canyon above the lake by Areno of Tubal in Aztlan at quite the same time of year that they left Mogollon.... Not to mention the intervening eight centuries.

Whatever they thought, the bears throve. Six of them were female. They all had twins or triplets. Eight is a tiny genetic stock to restart a species, but it must be possible. After all, bears were extinct. Those eight were the only ones there were for the healthy population of bears to descend from, as the species did indeed reestablish itself, in the once-again healthy World that eventually had emerged at the further end of the Terror, from the Change.

Bill and Maryllyn learned to speak Aztlanian, if never without an accent. They throve too. Bill wanted to reintroduce electricity. It didn't work. He never figured out why.

"Who cares?" said Maryllyn. "Sun-lights are much nicer."

"Especially now that we have perfected light-weight insulation for the flashlights," said Tarry, who remained a friend, and didn't even razz them... too much... about their accents. "They don't even blow up any more if you forget to pull them out of the Sun and they overcharge."

Bill patted the flashlight on the belt of his Tubal tunic. Linen rather than cotton. He and Maryllyn had visited the river valley with Tarry, but they settled in the mountains. The flashlight held enough of a charge to read by, all evening.

Which Maryllyn occasionally did, though usually indoors with a Sun-light which, being stationary, could have enough insulation for a charge to last several weeks of stormy weather.

Bill read sometimes too, but he never got quite fluent enough in Aztlanian to enjoy a full evening of it.

If any books existed in English, Bill and Maryllyn didn't know of them.

They did occasionally see bears though. Lots of people did. People and bears got along... pretty well. Some said this was because Tubals, and Kessians too just across the mountains to the west, had Apaches in their ancestry, who tradition said knew bears as kin.

But anyone who had the privilege to get to know Elvira Sonderfeld knew the real reason why the bears that reentered the World eight centuries after all bears had gone extinct in the Change were so well behaved... for bears. It was because they all were descended from those eight bears of Elvira's.

Author's note: Sometimes fictional universes merge. Mogollon is a real New Mexico ghost town, where I lived in the late eighties. The Mogollon parts of this story derive from my fictitious Mogollon News, which ran, then, in several regional newspapers and on Southern New Mexico's Public Radio Station KRWG, Las Cruces, and later in the U.K., in BBR. The collected Mogollon News is also available from Fantastic Books. The title incident and future portions of this story belong to the universe of my Ever Broten, a tale of our descendants emerging from the hole that our present world seems so intent on plunging into, eight centuries after the Earth tips over in our near future. Ever Broten also is a tale in which the human race gets just a tad saner. This story, as well as

"Warrior's Honor", *are ones that I had the considerable pleasure of being able to discuss at length, in person, with* Analog *editor Stan Schmidt, while he was considering them.*

THE LIZARD

On the evening of Wednesday, September Fourteenth, Hilario Flores drove his finely-tuned, fifteen-year-old, blue Chevy pickup to the edge of Guadalupe Canyon (known as Grant Gulch to the Anglos). The recently ended summer rains had the high desert as green and full of colorful flowers as it would be all year. Hilario breathed the fresh, sweet aroma as he walked around the three bends in the canyon to the sunset view he loved where the canyon opened up to spread into an alluvial fan to the west.

Hilario settled comfortably on his customary rock. It had been a long day of diesel fumes, asphalt and dust on the road widening and repaving job. It was nice having steady, good-paying work so close to home though. The timing had been great, with the baby. Luis was four months old now. Hilario and Gloria were talking about a down payment on a lot and mobile home if they didn't have to eat all Hilario's earnings this winter.

As the sun settled towards the horizon and the air stilled, Hilario got out the skinny joint Joe Packer had given him at work this afternoon. Joe used to stop in to turn Hilario and Gloria on, but now that they had the baby, Gloria didn't want pot in the house.

Junipers were radiant in the last rays of the sun, and the clear air was fragrant as Hilario lit his joint. He smoked the whole thing so as not to be carrying any, gave the roach to the earth, and watched the sky turn indigo, vermilion and maroon.

Something moved down the canyon a ways. Perhaps it's a deer or a coyote, Hilario thought as he turned to look. To his amazement, what Hilario saw was a gigantic lizard. It scuttled out to a still-sun-warm flat rock and crouched.

Hilario's heart began to beat wildly. I am imagining this, he thought. It's just the pot. It's an ordinary lizard, and I just think it's a giant. He stood up, slowly and silently; energy shivered through his body. The lizard did not a thing. Hilario began to walk towards it. The light was diminishing, but there was still plenty enough to see clearly.

As Hilario approached, the lizard began to do pushups, just like the ordinary little ones. Hilario got close enough to see the green skin at the lizard's throat puff out with each breath. Its front toes hung over one end of the rock. It's tail drooped over the other end.

Hilario took another step, then another. He was only twenty feet from the lizard now. Suddenly, the lizard dashed off down the canyon, its tail held high. Hilario gasped and jumped. Then he bounded after the lizard, wishing he had brought the twenty gauge shotgun with him that was back in the truck.

A hundred yards down, the canyon broke up in several directions. The ground was all rock and gravel. Hilario stopped and tried to quiet his breathing, but he couldn't hear any large creature moving. He looked about at the green grass, purple asters and yellow sunflowers, still lush from the recent rains. He could see no sign of any large animal's passage. He looked about a bit more, but the light was fading quickly now, so he gave the matter up and walked back up the canyon.

When Hilario got to the rock the lizard had been on, he measured it with his hands. He estimated it was about four and a half feet wide. Counting its tail, the lizard must have been at least six feet long, maybe seven. Hilario walked on to the truck. A few small birds flew by on their way home for the night. A jack rabbit zipped out from under a squat juniper, only to dive under another just like the first thirty yards away on the other side of the canyon. Hilario started, but then he laughed. A whiff of sage wafted up to him. He must have stepped on it.

On his way home, Hilario stopped at Bennett's Stop N Save for a dozen eggs and a loaf of bread. Navidad Saavedra was working the register.

"It's a wonderful thing," said Navidad to Clyde Clanton as Hilario walked in. "I remember when my mother had her cataract surgery. What an ordeal, and her sight was never all that good afterwards. These lasers... I haven't seen so well in thirty years."

"It still gives me the creeps," said Clyde.

"You'll be in and out in no time and feel like a new man," said Navidad. "Hello Hilario."

"Hi," said Hilario.

"How's it goin'?" said Clyde. He was just as glad Navidad had identified Hilario, who he knew slightly but could see only as a human-sized blur.

"Okay," said Hilario. "How 'bout you."

"So so," said Clyde.

"Oh?"

"I don't get my cataracts fixed I'm gonna have to give up driving."

"That's a shame," said Hilario.

"It's really not such a big deal with the lasers," said Navidad, "especially now you're on Medicare."

Hilario got his eggs and bread and brought them to the counter.

"How's Luis doing?" Navidad asked.

"Just fine," said Hilario, "but Gloria's complaining about how sharp his little teeth are."

Navidad grimaced and smiled. "Ought to wean him."

Hilario shrugged. "You know," he said, "I just saw the strangest thing."

"Oh?" said Clyde.

"I was over at Guadalupe Canyon." (Clyde, who had lived in the area most of his life, knew that name and used it as often as Grant Gulch.) "Just after sunset, I saw a lizard had to been six feet long."

"You're puttin' us on," said Clyde.

"No," said Hilario. "I really saw it.

Clyde's world had grown smaller with his diminishing vision, but his other senses had compensated. Clyde sniffed. "What have you been smoking?" he asked.

Hilario tensed and didn't answer. He got out his money and paid for the bread and eggs.

"Say hi to Gloria," said Navidad.

"I will," said Hilario and then left.

"You know," said Navidad to Clyde, "Arnold and Mary Begay live over near Guadalupe Canyon. Arnold's been complaining about losing sheep. Thought it was coyotes, but what if there really is a giant lizard?"

"I don't know," said Clyde.

Clyde hung around a little longer. He didn't dare drive at dusk because he couldn't see oncoming traffic. Once it was dark enough for everyone to have their headlights on, he figured he could make it the half mile home all right.

This evening, he was wrong. There were only four houses between Bennett's Stop N Save and Clyde's and a wide shoulder to the two lane state highway. There was little traffic. If Clyde wandered some, it really didn't matter. Unfortunately, a tourist from Philadelphia had parked by the side of the road this evening to watch the stars come out in the huge, brilliantly-clear Western sky.

Sylvia Nathans was standing fifty feet away from her grey Nissan when Clyde smacked into it. He was only driving ten miles an hour as he was looking for his driveway. Clyde was not injured, and damage to both vehicles was minor. However, both now had crunched fenders.

"Damn!" said Clyde.

Sylvia screamed.

Clyde got out and apologized to Sylvia. Then they both walked the hundred yards to Clyde's house, where he called the sheriff to report the accident. Clyde tried to be hospitable, but Sylvia just stood stiffly in the front room and glared at him till Abe Copax, the deputy who happened to be nearest that evening, arrived to take the accident report. The damage to Sylvia's car was essentially cosmetic. She drove off as soon as Abe was done.

"You really shouldn't admit fault," said Abe to Clyde.

"It *was* my fault," said Clyde. "I'm blind as a bat any more. I just better quit driving till I get these damn cataracts fixed. Lucky I didn't kill someone."

Abe drove Clyde's car the short distance home for him and then accepted Clyde's invitation to stay for a cup of coffee. Clyde eventually calmed down. "I'm calling up first thing to do something about these cataracts," he said. After that, Clyde rambled a bit. Eventually he asked Abe how his work was going.

"Okay," Abe said. This was not altogether true. Abe had been hired four months earlier because he claimed some expertise in drug apprehensions. So far, he had found no pot patches, no cocaine in any form nor any other hard drugs. He had run several roadblocks, which had resulted in three arrests for a combined total of less than an ounce of marijuana. It had also resulted in nine complaints from irate tourists and one fairly serious threat to sue the county. Abe's probationary contract was up in another two months. Pete Morales, the sheriff, had let him know that if he didn't do better he was going to be looking for another job. Police jobs were not hard to find, but Abe was a local. He did not want to move.

"You know," said Clyde, "I heard the funniest thing."

"Oh?" said Abe. "What's that?"

"You know Hilario Flores," said Clyde.

"Sure. Used to play basketball with him once in a while."

"I just saw him at the store; he claimed to have seen a giant lizard in Grant Gulch." (Clyde used the Anglo term to Abe without thinking about it.) "Said it was six feet long. That's right over where Arnold Begay's been losing sheep. You might want to check it out."

"What was he drinking?" Abe replied.

"Don't know as he was drinking anything," said Clyde, "but come to think on it, I believe I did smell pot on him."

"You sure Arnold's losing sheep?" Abe asked. "He hasn't reported it."

"Way I hear, he just figures it's coyotes," said Clyde.

"Hmh," said Abe. "Now, you know, I'm gonna have to cite you on this accident, but if you turn in your license till you get your eyes fixed, that'd help."

That is just what Clyde did.

That same evening, when Hilario got home, he told Gloria about the giant lizard.

"What do you want to shoot it for?" she said. "It's probably a protected species. You shot it you'd just get in trouble. What you ought to do is take the camera down there and get a picture. Then lay your tape measure on the spot and take another one."

"That's a good idea," said Hilario.

Next day, Hilario brought the camera to work with him. He told everyone about the lizard. They all thought he was pulling their legs, but Joe Packer said he wanted to see for himself. At the end of the afternoon, they headed for Guadalupe Canyon. Joe had another joint, which they smoked together as they walked down the canyon.

Hilario and Joe watched the sunset. There were just a few hints of cloud, which added to the color. It was magnificent, as always. The air was fresh and sweet, and the pot enhanced all the sensuous beauty. They saw a roadrunner by a patch of jimson weed, and several jack rabbits, but no sign of any giant lizard. They explored till it got too dark, but there wasn't a trace.

The giant lizard was not the only thing Hilario and Joe did not see. They also did not see Abe Copax, but Abe saw them. He was hidden in the rocks overlooking the canyon with a camera of his own. He got clear pictures of both Hilario and Joe smoking and of them passing the joint back and forth.

Joe joined Hilario and Gloria for dinner.

"You know," said Gloria, "I was talking with Navidad. She says Mary and Arnold Begay have been losing sheep."

"I'll go talk to them Saturday," said Hilario.

"Wonder what he'll think about giant lizards," said Joe.

The next day was Friday. Abe went back to Grant Gulch with a horse. There were several springs there and lots of little nooks and crannies. It was an obvious place for a pot crop.

Abe rode down the canyon to where it petered out among the juniper and mesquite. There were little, rough hills and gullies everywhere. Abe saw no sign of any marijuana, but he was convinced this was ideal country for it. He continued to ride back and forth.

"Hey!"

Abe looked to his right, startled. An Indian woman was walking towards him down the slope of the nearest hill, trailed by two dozen sheep and two dogs. Abe's heart skipped a beat. He almost went for his gun. Then he recognized Mary Begay. "Hello, Mrs. Begay," he called out.

"What are you doing?" Mary called back.

"Looking," said Abe.

"Looking for what?"

"Just looking." Abe glowered down at the woman.

"Well, you're doing it on private property," said Mary. "You got a warrant?"

"I thought this was BLM land," said Abe.

"Not here it's not," said Mary.

"Oh," said Abe. "I must be farther south than I realized."

"You're gonna fall over my corral you come any farther," said Mary. "Now, what are you looking for? If there's police business in my back yard, I want to know what it is."

"Just looking," said Abe.

"Hmph," said Mary.

Abe turned his horse and rode back the way he had come. Mary stood and watched him go. That's pretty suspicious behavior, Abe thought as he rode, red-faced and angry. Bet they're growing marijuana right there. Got her husband pussy-whipped too. Typical Navajo. Abe did not have anything against Indians or any other local ethnic group, but if he got mad at someone he did have an array of ethnic-specific insults to aim at them.

Abe rode back to Grant Gulch. The more he thought about it the more Mary's insolence enraged him, and the more suspicious he became.

Abe came to the place where the canyon was all broken up. He dismounted and tethered his horse to a dead live oak where there was a patch of tender grass. Then he climbed up one after another of the little side canyons, looking for marijuana patches. It was getting towards noon. The sun was hot, and there were a lot of flies. There was no sign of any marijuana.

Abe was sweaty and irritable three quarters of an hour later when he heard his horse let out a frightened whinny. There were several loud crashes, then the sound of the horse running off. What the hell? Abe thought, as he scrambled back to where his horse had been tied. He drew his pistol.

Abe thought he heard some large creature moving across the gravel as he approached the bottom of the canyon, but there was nothing to see when he got there. He looked around briefly, but could not figure out what had spooked the horse; so he walked on down the canyon to retrieve it. This took over an hour. By then, Abe was thirsty and furious.

The horse was out in the open when Abe finally found it, munching placidly on scattered bunches of grass. It let Abe walk right up and mount, but when Abe headed back into Grant Gulch, the horse became very skittish. Abe began to wonder if there could be a mountain lion or a bear in the canyon, though he had not seen any sign. He drew his thirty-eight again.

About fifty yards from the spot where Abe had the horse tethered earlier, he saw a rattlesnake coiled in the shadow of an overhanging rock. Maybe that's it, Abe thought. The horse did not seem to be aware of the snake, but it was still nervous. Abe took careful aim and fired, but he missed. The snake disappeared under the rock, and Abe's horse shied. "Whoa, damn you!" Abe shouted. The horse settled down, unhappily, and Abe rode back to his truck. He had a hard time getting the horse in the trailer.

When Abe arrived back at the office, he was surprised to see the sheriff and every other deputy on the department there, as well as several state troopers.

"You missed all the excitement," said Virgil Carillo, one of the other deputies.

"What happened?" Abe asked.

"State police got a tip on a vanload of coke. It turned out to be true. There was forty-two pounds. Biggest bust this department's ever made."

Damn and double damn, Abe thought. I haven't busted forty-two *grams* of cocaine in my whole career.

Abe accompanied Virgil to the evidence room to look at the cocaine. One package was open. In all the excitement, none of the cocaine had been sealed as it should have been. Abe recognized the opportunity. When no one was looking, Abe slipped back into the evidence room with an empty cigarette pack and scooped up a little of the white powder.

He was just in time. Not five minutes later, he heard Pete Morales, the sheriff, calling out angrily, "Why is this contraband lying around loose?"

Two deputies immediately sealed it up properly, with the sheriff watching. After it was sealed, it was weighed again. The open package weighed four ounces less than it had the first time, but in all the rush and confusion, that first time could have been misread. Besides, Abe was sure he had taken less than an ounce.

"Maybe we better have a search," one of the state troopers said.

"I will if you think," said Pete, obviously unhappy at the idea. "But it was probably just a mistake. Why don't we weigh it again."

They did. This time the open package of cocaine was recorded as an ounce more than the second weighing and only three ounces less than the first.

"Oh well," the state trooper said. "People do get excited when there's a big bust."

Abe was much relieved.

The next day was Saturday. After Gloria nursed Luis, she and Hilario made love. Then they had a leisurely breakfast. Luis woke up while Gloria was doing the dishes, and Hilario played with him. Just as she finished, Joe Packer pulled up. He and Hilario drank coffee while Gloria changed Luis. They decided to ride out together to talk to Mary and Arnold Begay about the giant lizard. Gloria brought along two quarts of the salsa she had canned the past week for Mary.

"George wouldn't let Valerie eat anything hot the whole time she nursed him," said Joe. Valerie was Joe's sister.

"Luis doesn't mind," said Gloria. "Only thing he doesn't like is cabbage."

Mary was home when they arrived, along with her four children. Arnold pulled in a few minutes later with a full propane tank. Joe helped him unload it and carry it to the house.

"We lost two more sheep this week," Arnold said over coffee a few minutes later. "Maybe we ought to switch to cattle. Leave the sheep for the Reservation."

"This land won't support enough cattle to make it worth while," said Mary. "Maybe we ought to take that trade."

"What's that?" asked Gloria.

"The BLM offered to trade us for land bordering the Reservation," said Arnold. "They want to get rid of chopped up pieces up there and eat up private inholdings down here."—People some places might never have heard of the BLM: the U.S. Bureau of Land Management, though it was the largest landowner in the United States. In the rural West, the BLM was part of daily life.

"Don't trust 'em," said Joe. "There's probably gold here they want to get their greedy little paws on."

"Probably uranium," said Arnold. "Poison us anyhow."

Everyone laughed.

Eventually, Hilario came around to telling about the giant lizard.

"Huh," said Arnold. "I saw coyote sign by one of the kills, but I've wondered about the rest. They've mostly disappeared without a trace. Do you suppose it's possible?"

"It covered a rock this big," said Hilario. He spread his hands. "And its tail hung all the way to the ground."

"Let's go look," said Sam. At six, he was Mary and Arnold's oldest.

"Okay," said Arnold.

He and Sam, Joe, and Hilario all piled into Arnold's truck. Gloria and Mary stayed at the house. The three men and the boy rode around to Guadalupe Canyon. It was four miles by road, though it was only two as the crow flies. There were a few clouds today. It was cooler than yesterday. They found no sign of any giant lizard. They did see where a horse had been in the canyon though.

"Look at this," said Arnold. "I think that horse was tied to this old oak, and something scared it so bad it broke loose."

They all looked around. The snake Abe had seen the day before was back under the same overhanging rock. Sam was the one to spot it. "Maybe it was that rattler," he said.

"Maybe so," said Arnold.

Joe had his deer rifle with him. He aimed it quickly and shot the rattlesnake. Hilario had the camera again. He took a picture of Joe with the snake. Then he took one of Sam with the skin. Joe gave Sam the skin and rattle for a hat band.

After a while, they went back to the house, where Mary had fry bread and beans ready, with some of Gloria's salsa.

What none of them knew was that someone else was taking pictures that day too. Abe Copax was up in the rocks again, where nobody was looking. He got clear pictures of Hilario, Joe and Arnold walking together. The pictures showed up Joe's rifle clearly. They did not show Hilario's camera at all. Nor was Sam in Abe's photographs. Abe did not see Joe shoot the snake, but when he heard the gunshot, he snuck around to see what it was. He was just in time to see Joe retrieve the dead snake from under the same rock where he had shot at one and missed yesterday. Abe didn't take any more photographs. He was so mad he couldn't see straight.

The next afternoon, Mary was over near Guadalupe Canyon with some sheep when one of the dogs began to bark. Mary looked up just in time to see a lizard that had to be seven feet long scoot into the rocks. The dogs went after it. The lizard ran farther. Then a second lizard stood up. It was mostly hidden by some boulders, but its head was half again as big as the first one. The dogs yelped and tore back down to Mary, their tails between their legs.

Mary gasped. Then she got herself, the dogs, and the sheep out of there as fast as she could. When she got home, she told Arnold what she had seen.

"That BLM trade's beginning to sound like a better idea every day," he said. "I wonder if we should tell the sheriff what you saw."

"I don't know," said Mary. "I forgot to tell you. I ran into that deputy, Abe Copax, Friday, riding. He was looking for something, and he was pretty rude."

"That must have been the horse signs we saw," said Arnold.

They didn't call the sheriff though. They called Gloria and Hilario instead. "I go over there again," said Mary, "I'm carrying a camera *and* a gun."

Monday morning, Mary stopped at Bennett's Stop N Save for flour and milk. While she was telling Navidad Saavedra about the giant lizards, Clyde Clanton came in, on foot.

"What happened to your car?" Mary asked.

"I hit someone," said Clyde.

"Nobody hurt, I hope," said Mary.

"No, and the car's not hurt either. But I have to go to court and I don't know how I'm going to get there, and I'm not driving any more till I get my eyes fixed."

"Arnold and I need to go into the BLM office," said Mary. "When do you have to be in court?"

"Wednesday," said Clyde.

"Why don't we give you a ride."

"Why, thanks. I'll buy you lunch."

"Why don't you see if Dr. Morgenstern can see you while you're in town," said Navidad. "Those cataracts aren't going to clear up by themselves."

"Oh, I'd just keep Mary and Arnold waiting too long," said Clyde.

"No you wouldn't," said Mary.

"*Get it done*, Clyde," said Navidad. "You'll be a new man."

"I'll drive you home," said Mary.

"Well, thanks," said Clyde. "There's no need."

"Do it," said Navidad. "And see he calls the doctor for an appointment."

Mary got Gloria to come over and watch the children. Clyde had to be in court at ten. His appointment with Dr. Morgenstern was at two-thirty.

Mary and Arnold met with Andrew Perry at the BLM office. Andrew showed them on the map where several parcels were the BLM was prepared to offer in exchange for their land, but he was not sure about such essentials as water and the quality of grazing. Arnold said they would just have to take a look.

Mary and Arnold picked up Clyde at the courthouse for lunch. "How'd it go?" Arnold asked.

"Better than I deserve," said Clyde. "Course I was the judge's scoutmaster thirty years ago. He's continuing the case for a year. Then he'll dismiss it. Even said I can have my license back when I've got a doctor's certificate I can see well enough to drive. How'd you do?"

"The BLM's hungry to trade. Our land's surrounded on three sides. But they don't know anything about the land they're offering us," said Arnold.

"Makes you wonder what they're being paid for," said Clyde.

"Yeah," said Arnold.

They arrived at Jackie's Café.

"Why do you want to move?" Clyde asked.

"I'm not sure we do," said Arnold. "Just thinking about it. They offered. We'd be closer to family."

"You're not seeing giant lizards like Hilario Flores now are you?" asked Clyde with a smile.

"Well, now you mention it," said Mary, "yes."

"Told the sheriff?" Clyde asked.

"No," said Arnold.

"I mentioned it to Abe Copax," said Clyde.

"Maybe that was what he was looking for," said Arnold.

"He could have said," said Mary.

"Abe was in court," said Clyde. "Maybe you could speak to him."

"I don't think so," said Mary.

After lunch, Arnold and Mary brought Clyde to Dr. Morgenstern's office. The doctor examined Clyde's eyes and said he would make all the arrangements for the examination by the specialist and the laser surgery. "Have you good as new in no time," Dr. Morgenstern said. Clyde still didn't like the idea, but he agreed to follow through with it.

In the meantime, when court broke for lunch, Abe Copax asked Rob Peterson, the judge, if he could speak with him. Rob said he would see Abe for a few minutes before the afternoon session.

Abe presented his evidence: He showed the judge the photographs of Joe Packer and Hilario Flores almost certainly smoking a joint and the photographs of Hilario and Joe with Arnold Begay in the same canyon, Joe clearly carrying a rifle. He swore out a statement that Clyde Clanton claimed to have smelled marijuana on Hilario and a statement of how suspiciously Mary Begay had behaved in the vicinity of the canyon where the men had been seen.

"That's not enough to convict," Abe said, "but I think it's good strong probable cause. I'm convinced they're in it together, and they're growing the marijuana on the Begay place."

"It does point that way," said Rob. "What does Pete say?"

"He's been so busy with that cocaine apprehension I haven't really talked to him about it," said Abe. "This just came up in the last few days. I wouldn't be pushing it, but it's already September. We should move before they harvest it and get it away."

Rob's face clouded over. "You're right," he said. He agreed to issue search warrants for the Flores and Packer residences and the Begay property as soon as the sheriff was ready to organize the raid. "Let's do this right," said the judge.

"Sure thing," said Abe. That was easier than I expected, he thought. Maybe he was going to be okay on his job after all. Of course, he was still keeping the cigarette package-ace-up-his-sleeve just in case.

What Abe did not know was that Rob had some serious suspicions about the big cocaine bust. The evidence had all been taken over by Federal authorities. The two men with the van were almost surely going to prison for a long time, but Rob believed they might well have been a couple of stooges, set up to distract local law enforcement officers with that forty-two pounds while the real shipment of God only knew how many hundreds, maybe thousands of pounds went through the county on a parallel road. Rob had no way to prove his suspicions, but Salt Lake, Denver, Colorado Springs, and several smaller cities in the region to the north were all reporting a sudden *increase* in cocaine supplies. It doesn't make up for all that cocaine, Rob thought, but if we can catch a pot grower red-handed, at least we've got *some* drug merchant out of business. The worst of Rob's suspicions was that he thought there was a strong probability the Feds were in on the cocaine ruse.

Abe talked to the sheriff next chance he got, which was late that afternoon. It had been a trying day for Pete Morales. He did not know about Rob Peterson's suspicions, but he did know that the Johnny-come-lately Federal agents were arrogant and condescending and that they took over his department like they owned the place. Pete was very glad to be rid of them and their damned forty-two pounds of cocaine. They wanted the prisoners transferred too, for more convenient interrogation. That was fine with Pete. Good riddance to the whole slimy business. The prisoners had a lawyer by the name of Stanley Park who was objecting to the transfer though, so that would have to wait. On top of everything else, there had been an idiotic bar fight during happy hour at Pepe's, with injuries.

"Why did you talk to the judge before me?" Pete asked Abe.

"You were busy. We need to get on this before they harvest and remove the evidence."

"What evidence? Two men smoke a joint. Three men go for a walk. An Indian woman doesn't like a white police officer trespassing on her land."

"The judge thought it was pretty convincing."

"Rob's an honest man and a good judge. He also drives to Santa Fe and pays fifty bucks for a ticket to the opera. He doesn't know these people."

"You hired me to find pot growers."

"I just don't want to be jumping the gun."

"It is probable cause."

"Yeah, it is. I'll call the state police." He did. Sergeant Louis Carson answered. "Looks like we're about to return the favor," said the sheriff.

"Oh?" said the state police sergeant.

"Small potatoes, probably, but I've got a deputy's got probable cause on a marijuana ring," Pete said. "He thinks they're growing, so we need to get on it before they harvest."

"Good going," said Sergeant Carson.

The sheriff called the judge at home. Rob agreed to sign the search warrants Friday evening and to authorize phone taps till then in hope of picking up more evidence.

The phone taps revealed nothing about drugs. Mary Begay did say something to Gloria Flores about Arnold driving up to look at some land next to the Reservation next week. That might be suspicious. Then again, it might not mean a thing. None of the other suspects even spoke to each other on the phone in the next two days.

At work, Hilario and Joe talked more about the giant lizards. They decided to look again on Saturday. They also talked about what they were going to do when their current job ended.

"Same company's got a contract on a stretch of eighty-five just north of Gila Bend," said Joe. "It's good money. I'm gonna haul the trailer over and go for it."

"It is good money," said Hilario, "but I don't want to be so far away from Gloria and Luis. I think I'll just cut firewood till deer season and see what comes up."

Friday evening, Joe stopped over at Hilario and Gloria's with a sixpack of Michelob. Gloria's parents, Ruben and Vera Vigil, were there, along with her youngest sister, Sandra, who was still in high school. They were all fussing over Luis. Joe and Hilario went out in the back yard, each with a beer. After a while, Ruben joined them. Ruben and Joe smoked cigarettes as they all drank their beers and watched the stars through the leaves of the big cottonwood that shaded both Hilario and Gloria's little yard and the one next door.

"You should come by in the morning and see the morning glories," Hilario said.

"Our place too," said Ruben.

That evening, Judge Peterson signed the search warrants. Pete Morales assigned the various officers for the raid. There would be himself, Abe, four other deputies, three state troopers, and three men from the DEA. Since it was where they expected to find the crop, he assigned himself to the Begay property. Abe was to go to the Flores'.

At four AM the various police officers all gathered at the sheriff's office. Two county men, one from state and one Federal agent were to go to each site.

"Call in when you're done," Pete said, "in case we need help searching the Begay property. There's a lot of little gullies out there. That crop could be scattered half way to Hell and back."

It was not quite first light when two police cars drove up to Hilario and Gloria Flores' house. There were no lights on in the house when Abe Copax and the three other officers burst through the unlocked front door, their hands full of guns and flashlights. They quickly found light switches. Before Hilario or Gloria knew what was happening, the covers were pulled off them, and they were staring into the barrels of the police officers' guns.

Gloria screamed.

Luis woke and began to cry.

"Don't move!" Abe yelled. Then he pulled Hilario out of bed and cuffed his hands behind his back. He did the same to Gloria. Luis continued to cry.

The other deputy stayed with Hilario and Gloria while Abe, the state trooper, and the Federal agent began tearing the house apart. They pulled clothes from drawers and closets and scattered them on the floor. They dumped out drawers of papers and photographs. They pulled cushions off chairs and dumped all the silverware in the sink. Four boxes of tapes all went in a heap on the sofa. Two of the dishes Gloria's grandmother had given her as a wedding present were broken. A bottle of dishwashing detergent tipped over on the only picture Gloria had of her uncle who died in Vietnam.

There was no marijuana anywhere.

The Federal agent put all the medicines from the bathroom in a box to take with them. All were either such innocuous items as Tylenol and Contac or clearly-labeled prescriptions.

Abe was alone in the kitchen for a moment when he turned around, calling out: "I found the stash." He held up a little folded foil packet for the others to see, as if he had just discovered it in a drawer full of screw drivers, hammers and plastic bags next to the sink. Then he opened it, revealing the white powder inside.

"Thought we were looking for weed," said the other deputy.

"Looks like they were into coke too," said the state trooper.

Abe walked over to Hilario and Gloria and read them their rights: "You have the right to remain silent.... Anything you say may be held against you...."

"She doesn't know anything about that," said Hilario.

Gloria looked at him in horror.

Luis was still crying.

The state trooper called the sheriff's office and asked for a woman deputy to come for the baby. Then he and Abe waited with their suspects and the evidence while the other deputy and the Federal agent drove over to the Begay place to help with the search there as it was now light enough for an outdoor search really to get underway.

Joe Packer was asleep too when the police burst through his door. However, he came to all at once with the notion a bear had broken in. When the light came on, Joe already was half out of bed with his twelve gauge shotgun in his hand. He swung it towards the intruders. The shouts of, "Police!" and, "Freeze!" never had time to register.

Carlos Mendez had been a deputy just over a year. He was twenty-three. This was his first raid of this magnitude. He was the first police officer into Joe's bedroom. He saw the shotgun swinging towards him. He fired his thirty-eight twice and dropped to the floor all in one motion. The first shot hit Joe in the stomach, the second in the right eye. Joe's fingers clenched the trigger of his shotgun in a spasm as he was hit. The shotgun blasted the wall four feet to the left of the door where the police were running in. Joe crumpled back onto the bed.

The search at Joe's house revealed slightly more than two grams of marijuana and a jar with about fifty marijuana seeds.

When Pete Morales drove up to the Begay house beyond Guadalupe Canyon (or Grant Gulch depending who you were talking to) there was already a light on. All four officers drew their pistols and walked quickly to the door.

Pete knocked. "This is the sheriff," he called out. "Open up."

"Oh!" the police heard Mary call out. She opened immediately, with her youngest in her arms. Arnold was at the bedroom door, just zipping his pants. A coffee maker was on. "What is it?" said Mary.

"We have a search warrant," said Pete.

"For what?" said Arnold.

"Don't move," said the state trooper, turning his revolver on Arnold.

Pete showed Arnold and Mary the search warrant.

"What is this?" said Arnold. "'... seen walking in Grant Gulch with suspects Packer and Flores.' I have a grazing lease in that canyon. Why shouldn't I walk there?"

"Shut up," said the Federal agent.

"You just relax," said Pete. "Make this easy on yourself. Why don't you tell us where the crop is and get it over with."

"What are you talking about?" said Mary.

All the children were awake now. The two toddlers clung to Mary's skirt. Sam stood next to his father.

"The marijuana you're growing here," said the Federal agent. "Where is it?"

"There isn't any marijuana here," said Mary. "How could we be growing anything? We have sheep. What is this?"

"All right," said Pete. "We'll do it the hard way." He nodded to the deputy, who handcuffed Arnold. Then he let Mary sit at the kitchen table with the children while the police searched the house.

As at Hilario and Gloria's, cloths, papers, dishes, family keepsakes, the children's toys, all the Begays' belongings went in heaps and mounds all over the house. The result looked like the aftermath of a tornado. The officers were more careful here though and did not break or spill anything.

No marijuana nor any other drug was found anywhere in the house.

About the time there was enough light to begin searching outside, the two officers showed up from the Flores arrest. They did not let Arnold or Mary know where they had been or who they had arrested as they reported the seizure of a small amount of what appeared to be cocaine.

"No marijuana?" asked Pete.

"No," said the deputy.

"Crack?" asked the state trooper.

"No," said the deputy, "just white powder. Cocaine, or maybe amphetamine."

"Hmph," said the sheriff. "Come on." He gestured to Arnold. "I'm gonna uncuff you so you can get on a shirt and shoes. Then we're going to search the property. You going to cooperate, or do you want to spend all morning walking around the place with us?"

"There's nothing there, damn it," said Arnold.

The police officers took turns walking back and forth across the Begay property. They searched the sheds and the gullies and anyplace any of them could think of where marijuana might possibly be grown or stored. They had Arnold accompany them to witness the search and thereby make it legal. They found not a thing.

Pete allowed Mary to fix the children breakfast. He also took the call on his radio about Joe. That made him feel sick. He told the other officers about it out of Arnold and Mary's hearing. It upset them all.

One of the Federal agents was the next to go out searching with Arnold. He began poking Arnold every few steps with his gun. "You fucking dopers," he snarled. "God damned murderers. I ought to blow your miserable balls off." Arnold didn't say anything. He had been walking around with his hands cuffed behind his back for two hours by then.

At noon, Pete uncuffed Arnold and let him eat lunch with his family. Then the search continued the rest of the day. The sheriff did let Mary tend the animals, with an officer watching. Finally, as it was getting dark, Pete called off the search and uncuffed Arnold.

"All right," said Pete. "We can't look forever. Maybe there's nothing here."

"You brazened your way through this one, you scumbag," said the Federal agent. "But you can bet your red nigger ass we'll catch you eventually. Your buddy'll talk."

"You're crazy," said Arnold.

The police finally left, and Arnold and Mary began putting their house back together. They didn't know what to do.

Mary tried calling Gloria, but there wasn't any answer. Then she called Navidad Saavedra at Bennett's Stop N Save. That was how she learned Hilario and Gloria had been arrested and Joe was dead.

Monday morning, Gloria was released. Hilario was insisting she didn't know anything about the cocaine. The Federal agents wanted the DA to file charges on her too, to pressure Hilario to talk about his sources, but the DA wouldn't do it. "Not with a baby involved," he said.

Gloria's breasts were in terrible shape. She felt sick and in a lot of pain. She wasn't able to nurse Luis properly when she got him back. The police wouldn't let her see Hilario before regular visiting hours on Wednesday. Her parents brought her home to her smashed house. She picked up a couple changes of clothes and what she needed for Luis and rode home with them.

Joe's funeral was Tuesday morning.

That same afternoon, two DEA agents delivered papers to Arnold and Mary Begay: Their property was being confiscated under the forfeiture of property associated with the drug trade laws.

"What drug trade?" said Mary.

"You have twenty-four hours to be out," said the officer, "or you will be removed by force. Everything you take with you will be searched; if you try to come back, you will be shot on sight."

Mary began packing their belongings. Arnold went out to hitch the stock trailer and gather as many sheep as would fit. An officer watched each of them.

When Arnold gathered the sheep, he saw that four more were missing. It didn't matter. He couldn't take them all anyhow. He had no idea where they would go, except to the Reservation where both he and Mary had family. He wanted to let them know. He wished he could get some of them down with more stock trailers for the rest of the sheep, but none of them had phones.

Arnold and Mary did not wait twenty-four hours to leave. They had as much loaded as they could fit in the truck by nine-thirty that evening. The main thing on both their minds was getting the hell away from the cops, who were following them around watching their every move.

Arnold and Mary did not practice traditional Navajo religion, but they did have various items they revered as family mementos and cherished gifts from family and friends. Most of these were in a wooden box which, as it happened, had been ignored during the search three days earlier. Arnold started to carry this box to the truck when one of the DEA cops stopped him.

"Open it," said the officer. "I want to see what's inside."

"It's religious stuff," said Arnold.

"I said open it," the cop said.

Arnold stood where he was, making no move either to carry the box on out or to open it. The DEA agent drew his gun and pointed it at Arnold.

Arnold set the box on the coffee table (which would not be going with them for lack of space) and opened it. The Federal agent looked at the contents, some of which were bundles of such plants as sage and juniper.

"Looks like drugs to me," said the officer.

"It's not," said Mary. "And if you so much as lay a finger on it the Navajo Nation will file charges on you for desecration of traditional religious objects."

"You expect me to believe that shit?" said the cop.

"That's no kind of language to use to my wife," said Arnold. "This is religious stuff. If you want to murder us like you did Joe Packer you can go right ahead. But…"

"All right. All right," the officer interrupted. "Close up your damn box and take it." He holstered his gun.

Arnold carried the box out to the truck.

Nearly all their furniture and a large portion of their other belongings were still in the house when Arnold and Mary Begay drove away. They only had about a fourth of their sheep in the trailer. The police followed them about twenty miles. Mary and Arnold kept right on going till they got to Mary's mother's home near Chinle Wash. She advised them just to be quiet about the whole affair, which is what they did.

That same day, Gloria Flores was looking for a lawyer for Hilario. She didn't think he used cocaine, but she had had no chance to talk to him. She didn't know what to think, but she was going to do what she could to help. He was charged with possession of cocaine and conspiracy to engage in drug trafficking. His bail was set at fifty thousand dollars. Five thousand dollars for a bail bondsman was a sum completely beyond considering. Gloria hoped it would even be possible to hire a lawyer.

Shortly after lunch, the phone rang. An attorney by the name of Stanley Park had heard about their case and wanted to offer his services. Gloria took the call. She was still feeling dazed, what with the raid, spending two days in jail, her sore breasts, a fretful baby, charges against Hilario.

"I can't make any promises," said the lawyer. "These are serious charges. But I'll do the best for him anyone can."

"Oh," said Gloria. "Thank you." She didn't know what else to say. "I don't know what.... Can we afford you?"

"I'm sure we can work that out," the lawyer said. "These cases usually don't go to trial. I'll only ask a flat fee of five thousand dollars through a preliminary hearing. I can begin working on the case right away for a thousand dollar retainer."

"Oh," said Gloria. "I see."

The lawyer gave his phone number and address. Gloria wrote them down.

Wednesday, Gloria was able to visit Hilario.

"Was that cocaine?" Gloria asked.

"I don't know what it was," said Hilario. "I never saw it before."

"What do you mean?" said Gloria.

"I don't know. I don't understand it," said Hilario. "I haven't even brought any smoke home since before Luis was born."

"You're not lying to me, are you?" said Gloria.

"No, damn it!" said Hilario.

"Could the police have planted it?" Gloria asked.

"Maybe," said Hilario. "That's what I think, but I don't see how we could prove it if they did."

Gloria told Hilario about the phone call from the lawyer. "We have almost two thousand dollars in the bank," she said. "He says he has a lot of experience in drug cases."

"Maybe I better talk to him; I need to talk to some lawyer," said Hilario.

Gloria called the lawyer from the jail. He agreed to meet her for his retainer check the next morning and to see Hilario immediately thereafter.

Hilario and Gloria never learned Stanley Park was also representing the two men who were caught with the forty-two pounds of cocaine. The DA knew it though. As a result, several things happened. The charges against the two cocaine couriers were changed to: Attempted transportation of a controlled substance across state lines. This got their case out of the state legal system and into the Federal one. They paid a thirty thousand dollar fine apiece and walked free a week later.

As a result, Judge Peterson was enraged. He refused to consider any plea bargain for Hilario Flores.

"I'm sorry," said Stanley Park. "There's not a thing I can do. That's up to the judge." He owed the DA a favor anyhow, in exchange for the cocaine couriers, but Hilario didn't know that.

"I never saw that packet before in my life," said Hilario.

"You don't have much of a case," said the lawyer. "We can go to trial, but it could take two years, and I'd have to charge more beyond the preliminary hearing. I think, if you agree to plead guilty to the possession charge, the DA will drop the conspiracy charge."

"I thought you said the judge wouldn't accept a plea bargain," said Hilario.

"Well, there really isn't any evidence to support the conspiracy charge," said the lawyer. "It's mostly just an excuse for the high bail."

Hilario agreed.

Before the case could be scheduled, however, Hilario had to come up with the rest of Stanley Park's five thousand dollar fee. He told Gloria to sell his truck and anything else she could. The truck and Hilario's better tools raised seventeen hundred dollars. There might have been a little more if Gloria could have sold Hilario's guns, but the police had taken them. The rest of their savings came to a little over seven hundred dollars. They borrowed the rest from their families.

When Hilario arrived in court, he learned the conspiracy charge was, indeed, dropped. He plead guilty to possession of cocaine and was sentenced to six years in the state prison.

The issue of the local weekly paper that came out following Hilario's court appearance had a front page article headlined: "What Drugs Do." The photograph Abe Copax had taken of Joe and Hilario passing a joint and one of Joe's dead body accompanied the article. The article insinuated that Hilario was a cocaine dealer, getting rich on the corpses of his neighbors. References to cocaine and to marijuana were used interchangeably. There was no reference to the two men who really had been driving a van with forty-two pounds of cocaine through the county.

"Guess they just crawled back under the rock they came out from," said Joe's sister, Valerie, to her husband, Mark, when he pointed this out.

"Just as well," said Mark. "Paper'd probably have claimed Joe and Hilario were in business with them."

A few weeks later, Clyde Clanton had his cataract surgery. Eventually, he even got his driver's license back. "You were right," he said to Navidad Saavedra. "I'm sure grateful you talked me into it."

It never occurred to Clyde that he had anything to do with the drug raid. He just thought it was a damned shame such nice young people did such awful things.

Now that he could see again, Clyde did make it a habit to read the local paper every week. It was four years and two months later that Clyde noticed a brief article announcing Hilario Flores' release from prison. Clyde had never known Hilario very well, but he did remember him and vaguely recalled he had been arrested for drugs several years earlier. That night, Clyde dreamed of the famous shootout at the OK Corral in Tombstone. He thought that was funny as he had never dreamed of it before, though he was related to some of the people involved. It never occurred to him to make any connection to Hilario.

Gloria stayed loyal to Hilario through his imprisonment. She couldn't afford the rent on their house, so she had to give that up. She lived with her parents. Her milk was never right after the two days in jail, so she let it dry up and switched to bottles. Gloria needed to get a job anyhow to pay off the loans for the lawyer. She was quite aware that he had put in a grand total of five hours on Hilario's case, if that, which came to a thousand dollars an hour. She was equally aware that he had not done a thing for them in those five hours, but she didn't see anything to do but pay back the families, help to bring money into the household, and wait for Hilario to get out of prison. She visited him as often as she could, but what with working and Luis and the distance, that was only once or twice a month.

The last year Hilario was in prison, Gloria put enough money aside to rent a fairly nice older mobile home so there would be someplace for them to live. She moved in a month before his release date. Luis was almost five now. He did not really understand who the strange man was that his mother brought home and did not like having a stranger taking so much of his mother's attention.

Hilario soon found out that most people in the area would not hire him. Gloria kept her job at a local café. The owners made it clear they did not want Hilario hanging around. All his more valuable tools, as well as his truck, had been sold for a fraction of what it would cost to replace them, to pay for the lawyer. Gloria needed the little Datsun she drove to work. Hilario was recruited as babysitter. He hated it, and so did Luis.

Three months after Hilario got out of prison, he was drinking a sixpack before noon, and Gloria was afraid to leave Luis with him. Thankfully, he finally did find work—on a fencing crew for minimum wage. It was at least a little money, and anything was better than having him sitting around the trailer drinking.

Two weeks after the fencing job started, Hilario was riding to work with Pete Grijalva when a sheriff's department car roared up behind them with its lights flashing. Pete pulled over.

The sheriff's department car pulled up behind them. Abe Copax and Carlos Mendez leaped out with their revolvers drawn.

"Out, both of you," ordered Abe.

Hilario and Pete got out. Abe spread-eagled them both against Pete's truck and held his pistol on them while Carlos patted them down. Carlos gave Hilario's balls a hard squeeze in passing. Hilario flinched but didn't say or do anything.

Then they searched Pete's truck. They scattered tools everywhere. When they were done, Abe wrote up a ticket for a broken brake light and insufficient tread on the right rear tire.

"You watch yourself," said Abe sternly to Pete. "You're keeping some pretty shitty company."

Then the two police officers drove off, leaving Pete and Hilario to pick up the mess and continue on to work.

"What the hell's that all about?" said Hilario.

"Abe's running for sheriff," said Pete. "Guess he thinks he can make campaign hay off you."

"What happened to Pete Morales?" asked Hilario.

"He couldn't run again. Two term limit."

"Oh yeah."

"He was pretty discredited anyhow," Pete said. "Cocaine came up missing after two busts while you were in the can. Probably wasn't any of his doing, but he took the blame."

"Huh," said Hilario.

The fencing job had gotten far enough along that it was shorter to come in from a different side. Pete turned onto the road that wound down to Guadalupe Canyon and then back up to what used to be Arnold and Mary Begay's land. It was the first time Hilario had been out that way since his release from prison. Formerly there had been junipers and piñons all over the land, with mesquite below the canyon. Now it was completely bare of trees. There was a new fence with big signs that read: "No Trespassing. CUZA Cattle Company."

"What happened here?" asked Hilario.

"You didn't hear? Big corporate ranching company got ahold of the place and chained off the trees for grazing after it was confiscated from those Indians for drugs."

"Arnold and Mary never did any drugs in their lives," said Hilario.

"It was a pretty rotten deal, I guess," said Pete. "They weren't even charged with anything, but the land was confiscated anyhow."

"Fuckers!" said Hilario.

"Didn't work out so good for the CUZA Cattle Company," said Pete.

"Doesn't look like there's any cows there," said Hilario. "Grass is as tall inside the fence as out here by the road—where anything's growing at all between the erosion gullies."

"Never should have cleared that land," said Pete, "but that's not what stopped them."

"Oh?"

"Seems they kept losing cows, especially over near Guadalupe Canyon. Cowboys' horses would spook too. Finally, one of the cowboys and his horse disappeared. There was a big search, but no trace was found. Cowboys said it was a curse those Indians put on the place cause it was taken away from them."

"Huh," said Hilario. "You know, I once saw a giant lizard in Guadalupe Canyon. Must of been six, seven feet long."

"Wow!" said Pete. "Maybe we ought to tell them about it. There's a reward for any information."

"Piss on their reward," said Hilario. "Let them find their own God damned lizards."

That summer, the CUZA Cattle Company tried to install a ranch manager and his family in what used to be Arnold and Mary Begay's house. Their five year old daughter disappeared without a trace a week later. The grieving family moved out. After that, the house was bulldozed. Eroded as it now was, the land was worthless for grazing anyhow. A herd of sheep was seen roaming wild for a while, but they eventually all disappeared too. The cowboys' Navajo curse explanation turned out to be the CUZA Cattle Company's most-enduring contribution to the community.

Abe Copax capitalized on his similarly imaginative reputation for having busted the county's biggest known dope ring by continuing to harass Hilario and anyone associated with him. Carlos Mendez did the same. Since Joe Packer's death, in which Carlos was not only exonerated but publicly declared a hero, Carlos had developed a reputation for toughness. A lot of people thought meanness would be a more accurate description.

Hilario was arrested twice that fall for drunk and disorderly. The former was true; the latter was not. He would have been sent back to prison for parole violation the second time, except the state was under injunction to relieve prison crowding.

Abe Copax won the election for sheriff with fifty-seven percent of the vote.

"The hell with it," said Hilario when he heard the news. "This is no place for us to live."

Gloria agreed. Though nearly all her family were there and a lot of Hilario's, it wasn't. Luis had started kindergarten that fall. Several other parents had refused to allow their children to play with him.

Hilario took a bus to Lubbock, Texas. Three days after he got there, he found a job at a feed factory. Nobody asked about his past. They only wanted his birth certificate to be sure he wasn't an illegal alien. He had to get his parole officer to agree to the move, but a steady job was sufficient to convince him. Gloria and Luis joined Hilario in their newly rented little house at Christmas.

It was almost a year before they saw their old home again, but they did come back for a family Thanksgiving visit. Hilario drove his new, finely-tuned, almost-paid-for, twelve-year-old, brown-and-cream Ford pickup.

The day after Thanksgiving, the local paper had a front page article about another disappearance at what it referred to as Grant Gulch. A deer hunter's horse had come back without him just the previous week. The sheriff was investigating the possibility of foul play. The article recounted the, "Well-known local legend of the Navajo curse."

Only now, the story had nothing to do with the Begays and the fraudulent drug raid that had cost them their home and most of their worldly belongings. Instead, the article referred to a Navajo maiden a century ago, wronged by her lover, and how her famous medicine man father had cursed the spot. The newspaper indicated that this story had been local tradition for generations.

"What's this?" Hilario asked.

"Those Californicators'll believe anything," Gloria's brother, Sam, laughed.

"Oh?" Hilario said.

"Couple newcomers moved out from Santa Barbara and bought the paper last spring," said Sam. "They're the only kind can afford property around here anymore anyhow."

An accompanying article said that the CUZA Cattle Company was negotiating a trade with the BLM for its small private holding and large grazing lease. "This supports the BLM policy of consolidating inaccessible inholdings and exchanging them for suitable development property," the article said.

"Bet they'll make money on that," Sam, commented, while picking at a platter of leftover turkey.

"I hear they're going to put up big signs," said Gloria's mother, Vera, "warning people of quicksand."

"Quicksand, huh!" said Sam.

Hilario did not say a thing about giant lizards. Both he and Gloria were sorry to be living so far away from their families, but they were both very glad to get away without being noticed by the new sheriff, Abe Copax, or his undersheriff, Carlos Mendez.

Back in Lubbock, Hilario didn't talk about giant lizards, quicksand, or any Navajo curse, recent, historical, or imaginary. He just tended the cattle-pellet sacking machine and congratulated his son on getting all passing grades on his first grade report card.

Author's note: Incidents of a cop pulling drugs from his own pocket, and what a house looks like after a search, unfortunately, are based on real experience.

A PLACE CALLED OUT

"I say let's go," said Sally. Her long brown hair hung dirty, but well brushed. She stood for effect and swirled her dirty, blue evening gown as she spoke. Sally was nineteen.

"Awe, foo!" said Jake, a boy of sixteen, also with dirty, long brown hair, wearing a pair of running shorts and a dress shirt. "We only been here 'bout three months."

"There's no more tuna fish and no more peaches," said Sally, "and I can't find a single dress I like."

"There's not many cats left either," said Bin. Bin, lithe at seventeen, with dirty, long blond hair, wore only a pair of denim cutoffs. He had a sling tied to one of the belt loops. "You wanna live on ratmeat?"

"Rat's okay," said Alice, "but I think we oughta go anyhow. We been here long enough. Sally's right. I want some tuna fish." Alice, at fourteen, was the youngest of the little group. Her hair was also blond, long, and dirty. She wore a pair of baggy, dirty, pink flannel pants and a frilly pink blouse.

"Tuna fish is dangerous," said Ell, cuddling her baby. Ell was eighteen. Hers was the only baby. Sally had miscarried twice. "Look what happened to Louie."

"Louie was fat and stupid," said Alice. "Anyone could tell that can was no good. I could smell it across the room."

"What do you say, Ell?" said Bin. "Shall we move or stay?"

"Move or stay. Move or stay," Ell crooned to the baby. The baby nursed lethargically.

"Stop being crazy," said Jake.

"My baby's sick," said Ell. "Can't you see, my baby's sick."

"Ell won't answer," said Sally. "It's three to one, Jake. So I say we move."

"Ah, pish poo," said Jake.

Alice giggled.

"Which way ya wanta go?" asked Bin.

"I dunno," said Sally. "Can we go through to anyplace new?"

"Maybe," said Bin. "It's all inside as far as I been anyway."

"We could try that for a few days," said Sally. "If it doesn't work we can always come back and go up on the roof."

"I hate the roof," said Ell. "What if there's electricity up there?"

The others ignored her.

"Let's pack now," said Sally. "We can leave in the morning."

"Okay," said Bin. Bin was the only really healthy one of the group. He was always restless.

None of them had much to pack. Just personal keepsakes. Sally had a photograph album and several other mementos of a childhood with a family. Jake, too, had pictures of himself with parents and a sister. Alice and Ell had personal talismans. All Bin bothered with was a couple of favorite knives and two spare slings.

Dusk soon faded through the skylight. Jake played his guitar for a while. "I'm gonna carry my guitar with me again." Jake stuck out his chin, asserting continuity. None of the others responded. There were plenty of guitars. If Jake liked this one enough to carry it with him, that was his choice.

They all sang a little.

"Maybe it is time to move," said Jake. "I'm gonna need new strings sometime."

"Umh," said Bin.

Ell turned away to go to sleep. She felt her way to her bed and rolled in. The baby whimpered. It nursed some more, then lay quiet.

Sally and Alice shared a bed. Bin sometimes had sex with both of them, but he slept alone. He was the only one to go to another room. He felt his way.

Jake slept with Ell and the baby when Ell let him. Tonight she never even noticed when he crawled into their bed.

All of them woke before daylight, but there was nothing much they could do, so they waited.

At dawn they had breakfast: canned plums, canned black olives, canned corn, and canned sweet potatoes, a handful of sugar, and some cat meat.

There was enough wood, furniture mostly, for a little cooking, though not enough to use fire for light. Smoke usually made fire unpleasant anyhow. There was plenty of paper. They found matches here and there.

They did not light a fire this morning. Sally had cooked the cat meat yesterday.

When full daylight reached them through the light shafts, they set off into the depths of the city. Sally carried a pad of paper and a pencil to make a record of their journey. If they came to a dead end, they did not want to be lost.

They headed generally west, but progress was slow. Large portions of the upper levels were smashed. The lowest levels were mostly flooded. In between, they could almost always find clear passage, but under the smashed areas there was often no light. They could uncover a blocked opening, but none of them understood how the light shafts passed through the ruined city's structure to do more.

They avoided the dark. No telling where a dropoff might be, or even a live circuit. They had not seen an electric light that worked in several years. None of them knew why they had found electric lights burning for several years when they were smaller, nor how to replace them when they quit. Once in a while they still heard a refrigerator motor. It was spooky. Horrible things might be inside. They always kept well away. They all regarded electricity as dangerous anyhow.

There was no reason to hurry. The five teenagers didn't really have anyplace to go. They found things to eat everywhere. Only the canned goods and a few other items, such as sugar and salt, were still any good, but every apartment had a supply.

Clothes were everywhere too if they wanted any, and all manner of things to play with.

Bin led them. They went west to a stairway, down three levels, then north a little ways and down two more levels. Then they went west again for a while. They stopped often to explore.

There was not much light, but it was enough to see by. Light shafts ran through nearly every wall. The shafts were lined with angled mirrors and photovoltaic panels. That was why there was still electricity in places. They more or less understood what these things did, but had no idea how. Places where the city was smashed, the crumpled shafts left large areas dark. Where the shafts were intact, some natural light reached clear down to the bottom levels.

"Let's stop," said Sally. "We never been here before. I wanna look around."

"You wanna look for tuna fish," said Jake.

Sally made a raspberry.

Alice giggled.

Fairly deep in the city, they had found a region where everything lay intact, so all the rooms had light, but it was rather dim and gloomy.

"My baby's tired," said Ell.

"I want to find some cats," said Bin.

They found a door that opened, without even having to break anything, on the third try, and went into an apartment. There were three skeletons. They paid no attention. Skeletons were everywhere. Bin tried the water tap. Nothing came out.

"S'funny," Bin said. "The farther west we go the lower we gotta go for water."

No one replied. They all knew there was water pressure in the lower levels of the city but not in the upper ones. They also all knew the water in the flooded areas generally flowed west to east and north to south. They had no idea why.

"Oh look!" said Alice, with a delighted smile. "A piano!"

She opened it and sat down on the bench. It was badly out of tune, of course, but it sort of made music. Alice did not know how to play much, but she loved to plink at a piano whenever she found one.

Alice was three and a half when the city died. Sally was just nine. One day life was going along normally. Then, *blam*! It seemed like the end of the world. If they heard an explanation of what happened at the time, it never stuck clearly in the memories of the children they all then were amid the chaos and horror of immediate survival. They seldom thought now about how the world came to be as they knew it, almost never talked about it.

At first, for far too long, they each had seen… and smelled dead people everywhere. All the other people still alive who were around the first days after the cataclysm went away. Each of the young survivors in the little company had failed to find anyone alive they knew, had wandered through the nightmare till they failed to find anyone alive. All but Alice were already old enough to understand there was such a place as out, but they had no idea where that was.

For weeks after the disaster, going anyplace was horribly dangerous. They all had seen dozens of people electrocuted. Then most of the electricity stopped. They had no way of knowing this was because the central power plant flooded and a system of circuit breakers in the city's design responded to the surge, then drop in current, by isolating the photovoltaic back-up power to innumerable small, discrete areas. After that, travel was not so dangerous, but they were all too frightened to try till hunger forced them. The stench of millions of dead, rotting bodies everywhere had obliterated all else from awareness so long that the stranded children they each then were had been thankful to forget the world of death when it at last became possible to do so.

For a while, they had found crackers and raisins and even some fresh things, such as carrots and oranges. That soon ended though. Gradually, one by one, they found each other.

There were nine of them once. Eeny got shocked and was never right in the head afterwards. The others took care of him, but he eventually sickened and died. Suzie died of sickness too. Louie, the most recent death, lost his life to spoiled canned food. Jean just disappeared one day.

Ell and Jake were the last to join the group. They had found each other fairly early on. It was five years after the catastrophe when they encountered the others. They were scared at first.

"I wanted to run away," Jake later told Bin.

"Why'd you stay?"

"Ell was more scared of the loneliness then she was of you."

Slowly, the five companions, plus baby, made their way through the ruined city. The fifth day, they headed up again, to the top level and the light.

The top of the city had the best light, but it also had sustained the most severe damage. Much of it was too crumpled to live in. It took them another day to find a place they liked. When they did, they made their little nests to settle in for a while. Then Bin went cat hunting.

Bin was the explorer of the group. He was always the one to find the best route down for water. He also always searched out a route from their more-settled stops to the city's roof. Once Bin had found a smashed greenhouse with a producing apple tree. Ell was afraid of the open air, but the others all came up to see. They knew nothing of soil someone once hauled to the spot, nor that the destruction of the greenhouse's panes had enabled both rain and honeybee to reach the tree, nor that flowers from a second tree on which they found no fruit had pollinated the tree which had borne. Bin and Sally retained sufficient vague memory of their early childhood to understand that they found ripe fruit because Bin happened on the tree in autumn. Alice found the entire concept of seasons a wonderful mystery, whose chief purpose she presumed to be the determination of birthdays.

They all ate the apples with delight, even Ell. They got seven apples apiece, and Bin got an extra because he had found the tree. They did not stay long enough to learn if it produced again the next year. None of them understood how an apple tree makes apples nor how often. Alice did not even know what the apples were. She had to be told.

Bin's explorations of the area around their latest home yielded no such wonders, though he did locate handy routes both down to water and up to the roof. They stayed in the new place about two months. By then they had used up most of the things they liked best. Sally was about out of tuna fish. She had tried on hundreds of dresses, then wore a green pleated skirt every day for three weeks. Now she wanted to investigate more new wardrobes. Jake wanted to find some new guitar strings again.

"My baby's tired," Ell complained.

"Your baby's always tired," said Bin.

The baby was eight months old. It did nothing but nurse sluggishly, sleep, mess itself, and whimper.

"I think something's wrong with the baby," said Sally.

"No!" Ell wailed.

"I don't know, Ell," Sally said. I think it should be crawling or sitting or something by now."

Ell clapped her hands over her ears and turned away.

"I don't think that baby's gonna make it," said Bin.

No one said anything.

"Cats're about hunted out again," Bin said after a while.

"Cats. Rats. Rats. Cats," Alice said. "Why don't you hunt looperds for a change?"

"Looperds?" said Jake.

"You know," said Alice. "They're purple and about this big." She stretched her arms out as far as she could. "They jump, but not very fast. And they're real yummy."

"You're making that up," said Jake.

"Am not."

Later Sally and Bin talked alone.

"What are we gonna do about Ell's baby?" Sally said.

"What can we do?" said Bin.

"If only there was someone else, some grownups."

"We're grownups now."

"But we don't know anything."

"I know how to hunt. Jake can play the guitar. You can even write."

"Sort of, but it's not enough."

Bin thought about that a long time that evening as he lay in the dark waiting for sleep to come. He woke before dawn to Sally crawling into bed with him.

Sally and Bin made love passionately, urgently. Then they lay quietly in one another's arms as first light began to show in the skylight. After a while, Bin spoke.

"Maybe there's more people outside."

"Maybe," Sally answered.

They had talked of this before. Neither of them had any clear idea what outside was. All they really knew of it was what they had seen on the roof of the city. The roof was all steel, smooth in places, wildly twisted in others. There were pipes and strange fixtures and photovoltaic panels all over the place. Here and there enough earth had blown in to support a few wispy weeds. That and such greenhouses as had any water were the extent of their knowledge of living plants.

They had also been to the east and south sides of the city. Both sides were bounded by enormous rivers. The walls of the city dropped sheer to the rushing water. It was an awesome sight. Bin had stood with Sally and Alice and also Suzie, Jean and Louie who were alive back then, watching. They had speculated on what the things were beyond the rivers.

"It's forest and fields," Jean had said. None of them knew enough to refute or affirm this. Ell and Jake were afraid of the rivers and kept away from that view. They had seen a river before finding the others too. Bin thought it might have been to the north. If so, the one side of the city which might possibly not be bounded by water was the west. This was the direction they had been moving most of the last year. The sheer differentness of... something else... seemed a very big concept to Bin. Need and a sense of adventure both drew Bin to that bigness.

Bin thought about it. "When we got closer to the river on the east, there was water at higher levels," he said to Sally. "It's been lower and lower the farther west we go. Maybe we can get out that way."

"Maybe," said Sally. "Or maybe we're just getting to the middle of the city and the water'll get higher again farther along."

"We could see anyhow."

"I guess."

Bin felt Sally tense. He knew the unknown made her uncomfortable. Alice might like the idea. She could be adventurous. Ell and Jake would be scared silly. But if Ell's baby was going to live...

Besides, Bin was bored. Hunting cats. Finding water. Eating stuff from cans. Most of it didn't taste like anything any more anyhow. There had to be something more.

Next time they moved, it was west again.

Ell's baby finally sat up and sort of started to crawl, but it stayed sickly and apathetic.

Bin began consciously scouting passages west.

One day, Bin woke to find the urge which had grown in him ripe as those apples he'd once found, a flavor he knew he had to taste *now*.

"I'm going someplace," Bin said. "I'll be gone all day, maybe even overnight."

None of them stayed away overnight, not even Bin. They were shocked.

Bin was determined. "I want to see what's to see."

"It's dangerous," Ell whined.

"Oh that's just Bin," said Alice.

"You want to see *out*," said Sally.

"Well, yes," said Bin.

"If there is an *out*," said Jake.

"There's gotta be," said Bin. "We just don't know where it is."

Ell whimpered and hugged her knees. Alice went over and hugged Ell. No one said anything more.

Jake looked angrily at Bin. Bin was briefly uncomfortable, then glared back determinedly. Jake turned away.

"I'm going for water," Bin said. "Anyone want to come with me?"

Sally went. They filled as many water bottles as they could carry, including one on a shoulder strap Bin would take with him.

"Think you'll really find a way *out*?" Sally asked.

Bin shrugged. "I'm gonna look."

When Bin and Sally got back to their living quarters, Bin gave everyone a hug. Then he set off to the nearest stairway up to the roof.

"Good luck!" Alice called as he went. She was smiling.

Bin grinned back.

Bin was the only one who liked the roof. Perhaps that was part of why he was healthiest. He was the only one who got much real sun. He loved the feel of the air on his body. He even liked rain.

Today the sky was frowsy—mostly thin clouds and pale sunlight, with an occasional patch of real blue.

Traveling across the roof was quicker than inside, but it was still slow. Sometimes there would be an open passage for a few hundred yards. Once Bin went almost half a mile without encountering any serious obstacles. Often, though, Bin had to climb over or find a way around huge masses of twisted debris. Bin also stopped frequently to mark his trail. He used pieces of some bright orange cloth he had found, tying them to whatever was handy.

After a couple hours, he climbed down into an apartment, opened a can of salmon and a can of peas, and ate. Then he climbed back up and kept going.

By noon Bin had traveled at least five miles, though he had covered more than twice that distance to get that far from where he set out over the top of the twisted ruin which was the only world he knew. He was beginning to wonder if there ever was an end to the dead city. Bin continued on though. About mid afternoon he finally saw something different. He thought he could see a hazy, greenish blur in the distance, and a wide void between that distant blur and the farthest extent of intervening twisted steel.

Bin spent the next hour climbing laboriously over an immense mass of destruction. Then he got to an area clear enough that he actually could run an exhilarating quarter of a mile. When he reached the next pile of rubble he scrambled to the highest point in sight.

At last Bin got a clear view. He stood panting and staring out at forest and fields like those he had seen across the rivers somewhere in the indeterminate span which was the past. Only there was something different. In places Bin saw boxes by the fields. A few of them had smoke curling above them.

A surge of excitement rushed through Bin. Apartments! he thought. Apartments all by themselves, outside the city. With fire. *People must live there*!

Bin climbed on over the pile of rubble and kept going. It still took him the rest of the day to reach the edge of the city. At last, he decided he better climb down inside and find some blankets for the night. He climbed up on one more high spot though to look again. He could really see it. The city had an end, and there was no river on this side. In the morning, he would see what something was like outside the city!

He turned to climb back down. As he did, something caught his eye to the north. There was a light. It didn't flicker like fire. A vague memory came to Bin of the electric lights he had known till he was six, when the city was alive and full of people, when electricity was the ordinary way to do things, not a lethal danger.

The light was rather close. Bin crept toward it, his heart pounding. How long had it been since he had seen a human being he did not know? How long had it been since he had seen anyone who knew anything different from what he knew?

Bin made his way to where he could see which skylight the light shined through. Then he looked for a way inside. He soon found one. It was getting dark, but there was enough light to walk. Just. Bin turned several corners, carefully reciting to himself which way he was turning.

He was about ready to give up till morning when he heard the voices. Strange voices! Voices he had never heard before! Bin gasped and stood still. Then he tiptoed onward.

Another turn, and he saw light reflected on a passage wall. One more turn, and he actually saw the yellowish light pouring brilliantly out of an open doorway.

"Oh, Stan, that's delicious!" A woman laughed.

A man's voice replied: "But surely you must have known."

"And to think," the woman's voice went on, "Elinor was going around the whole time acting so prim and proper." She laughed again. "I love it."

The man chuckled. "More wine?"

"Just a touch, dear."

Bin moved forward. He was shaking. He walked right up to the door anyhow. Inside were a man and a woman sitting on a couch together. Both were about thirty. Both had short, neatly trimmed hair. Both were clean.

Both jumped up when they saw Bin step in front of the open doorway. The woman screamed.

"Who're you?" said the man.

"I... I'm Bin."

"What're you doing here?"

"I... live here." Bin gestured behind him.

"In the city?" said the woman.

"Yes."

The man and woman looked at one another. Then the man said, very gently, "How old are you?"

"Seventeen."

The man and woman looked at one another again.

"Lived here all your life?" said the man.

"Yes."

"My God, Stan," said the woman. "And all alone."

"On no," said Bin. "There's Sally and Alice and Jake and Ell and the baby, but the baby's kind of sick. And..." Bin ran down.

"Where?" the man asked.

"Back there. A... a long way. I walked almost all day."

"For God's sake," said the woman. "Come in. Sit down. Are they all?... Were they all children too?"

"Sally's nineteen. She's the oldest."

"And you've lived here all this time!" said the man.

Bin stepped into the room, but he continued to stand somewhat stiffly.

"What do you eat?" asked the woman.

"There's canned stuff everywhere. There's cats and rats too."

"Good God. Here." She pulled a piece of fresh fruit out of a bag.

"Is that an apple?"

"No, it's a pear."

"Thank you," said Bin.

Bin took the pear and examined it. "Is this from... from outside?"

"Yes, of course," said the man.

"Have you been out there?"

"We live out there," said the woman.

Bin looked at the strangers in awe. Then he bit reverently into the pear. It was juicy and fragrant. It tasted of sunshine and rain and wind. Not like a can at all.

Author's note: This is the one other story that I actually dreamt.

WHY THERE ARE FLYING SAUCERS

Once upon an earth there was a temple to God. Now I don't mean it was a place where God was worshipped or a building dedicated to the remembrance of God, though it was those things too. What I mean is that it was actually a spot where God was present. That's why a temple building was erected there: When you went in you were in the presence of God.

As I said, however, this temple was on an earth. Earths live in time and space, and with time, things change. After a while, circumstances changed on earth sufficiently that God was no longer in the temple.

Well actually, God was still in the temple. God is always everywhere. But it was a little different, sort of like a shift of direction. The result was that the temple was no longer the simple and direct gateway to God.

People did still manage to reach God in the temple, of course. However, to do so now required great and arduous mental and physical contortions. A whole doctrine grew up about how a degenerate mankind was so much less ready to receive God than we used to be.

The truth of the matter was that God had just moved on. Not even very far. In fact, God had taken up residence in the back yard of a retired factory worker only a few miles down the road, right where the old man's wife had a patch of sweet basil.

Everyone who came into the garden noticed the wonderful aroma of the sweet basil, but sweet basil always does smell pretty nice, especially when it's in bloom. No one suspected what was really going on.

Until one night the old man had a dream. In his dream his wife took him out to the garden, and they set about weeding, but when they got to the sweet basil there weren't any weeds. He looked up in surprise and was immediately absorbed in God.

When the old man woke he told his wife the dream. She hugged him and said: "It's funny, but sometimes that's just how I feel. Of course it couldn't be. God lives in the temple, and we're just a couple of old fogies getting impressed by our own putterings." Still, they both thought it was a fine dream.

More time went by. The old man and old woman were both long dead. A young couple with three young children and two cats lived in the house. The garden was as likely to have cat poo and frisbees in it as the few poor petunias the young woman planted. Yet God was still there because… Well, I don't know why, but that's where God was.

God most definitely wasn't in the temple. Or rather, the temple had gotten so cluttered with people using it for their own purposes that it was no longer a suitable place to look for God, even by the most outrageous contortions. Instead, it was full of petty politics and intrigue and ceremonies which were either noisy and distracting or horribly dull. Anyhow, a spring had come up under the foundation and made everything very damp. The place was impossible to keep warm all winter and smelled moldy all summer. If there hadn't been such a fancy building there with such a grandiose reputation probably no one would want to go there at all. Except maybe for water. There was nothing particularly holy about it, but the spring would have been quite tasty if the temple had been removed.

After a while God took notice of this and thought: "This is rather a silly state of affairs. There's a perfectly good spring being stifled by a lot of pompous fools, and nobody notices Me at all except the cats and one of the kids. And people pay even less attention to them than they did to the old woman with the basil."

So God made an earthquake and knocked the temple down flat. Of course, everything else in sight got knocked down too. The river all dumped out and drowned anyone who happened not to get crushed. There was quite a mess.

That was all right though because God was in the earthquake. Everyone who died went directly to God. There were so few survivors the civilization that had built the temple no longer existed, so they couldn't build it back. People had to revert to a thoroughly primitive way of life.

More time passed. The descendants of the survivors watered their goats at the spring where the temple used to be, and the place where the garden was got completely overgrown. No one knew it was there at all, let alone that God was there.

Until one day, a little girl out for a walk sat down to get a burr out of her shoe right where the sweet basil once was. All at once she was absorbed in God. And she looked, and there on the ground, half buried in old leaves, was a battered orange day-glo plastic frisbee that the tree roots had pushed to the surface.

Since it isn't biodegradable, people found plastic here and there in the ruins of the old civilization from time to time, but no one had ever seen a frisbee before. The little girl leaned the frisbee reverently against a tree. Then she ran home and told everyone in sight about her wonderful experience. The people of that time, being simpler and more willing to believe the reality of experience than some others one might mention, went back with her. They all immediately found themselves in the presence of God.

So they made a path to the spot and built a little altar of stones and set the frisbee on it where they could venerate it. From then on, people came there to be with God.

And that is why there are flying saucers: to prepare us for the Revelation of the Sacred Frisbee.

Author's note: In the winter of 1972-73, while studying with the Jungians in Switzerland, I signed some stories and poems, "Uncle River," and sent them to friends Kathleen Kesson and Earl Hatley, in North Central Oklahoma. Next time I visited there, in 1975, I discovered that they had been pasing my writing around, and I had a following as Uncle River the writer. I moved to that part of Oklahoma in the spring of 1976, just as Kathleen and Earl started a periodical called The Wellspring, *which was where my work first appeared over my Uncle River byline that has stuck ever since. This is one of the stories that first appeared in* The Wellspring.

LOVE OF THE TRUE GOD

"What are they saying?"
"They say, 'All hail the beloved of the True God.'"
"I will not have idolatry."
"They understand, Lord. They do not worship you. They worship the True God Who sent you."
"Praise God! How wonderful are His ways."
"Yes, Lord."
"I will retire to my chamber. Have the accused ready at ten."
"Yes, Lord."

The Sky Lord, whose name nobody can pronounce, entered the Court, as the Sky Lords now call it. I trembled. Till the arrival of the Sky Lords, this was the Palace of Sacred Virgins. For a man even to set foot on the steps was unthinkable. Once-glorious Amarez, Who we worshipped as Creator of Sun and the River, rules Heaven no more.

I was trained as a royal translator. I am still proud of the skill that has enabled me not only to interpret many tongues, but to comprehend the lives of the peoples who speak those tongues well enough to share their jokes and their songs. Now, though I still earn my keep by my skill, I do not know who I serve. The new God is mighty beyond my comprehension. I have learned the language of the Sky Lords who brought Him to us, but their ways are greater than my understanding.

I sometimes fear I may offend the True God by transcribing the record of each day's proceedings, but it has always been my duty. Is it wrong to provide future generations of my people a chronicle of their own history? I have not dared to tell the Sky Lords of this record, but their all-seeing God has not instructed them to forbid it. Perhaps it is sanctioned.

I accompanied the Sky Lord to the entrance of the Court. How it terrifies me still to set foot on those so-recently-forbidden sacred stones. The Sky Lords have purged the Court of our former false God. The Sacred Virgins are dispersed to useful service, those who have been willing to continue living.

The crowds were very great today. They sang odes of praise to the Sky Lords and their all-powerful God, as they always do. How patient the mighty Sky Lord is! He took no offense at the delay of passing through so large a throng, nor at the ineptitude of my people's unschooled praise. He only desires that we should worship his God rather than his person. I do not understand the Sky Lords. It is a terrifying honor to serve them.

As the Sky Lord is the only one of his kind presently residing in Ixtiu, I need not offend his dignity by identifying him with some inadequate but pronounceable appellation of my own devising. There are other Sky Lords. They tell us they come not from the sky, but from another world beyond the sky. They tell us there are many other worlds, and that we and they alike once dispersed from the same long-forgotten world of origin on voyages of centuries' duration. Perhaps it is true. Our traditional tales recount something similar. Our legends presume a supernatural mode of travel, but the Sky Lords have demonstrated the error of this presumption.

The Sky Lords tell us they have undertaken their long and arduous voyage to teach us the love of the True God. Here, in this great realm we know as Tollisayuyu, there are presently nearly three hundred Sky Lords.

I fear the ancient sacred language may be forgotten as it is now banned, with all things of our former vain religion. I hope I commit no sacrilege before the True God to translate the name of our home in case its meaning is later lost. Tollisayuyu signifies in our former sacred language: The Land The Sun And The River Cause To Bear Life.

The Sky Lord turned left upon entering the Court. He did not stop, as the priestesses who alone once used this portal would have, to pay reverence before the formerly sacred fountain that rises in the entrance hall. The Sky Lord's chamber is a former storage room that only two years ago contained nothing more valuable than cleaning implements and the coarser grade of wool used to weave garments for the Sacred Virgins' servants.

I turned right to interview and prepare the prisoner. His cell was once the sleeping quarters of a temple kennel-master. It was a spiritual relief to me, if a sad duty, to pass from the once-forbidden precinct to the temple animal grounds where it was always permitted for men to enter.

Most of the rooms of the Sacred Virgins themselves now stand empty. The Sky Lord rails daily at my ignorant people to set up a market there, but as yet few have complied. The temple has, of course, been destroyed, both to punish its vain idolatry, and that the Sky Lords might extract the gold which was mixed with the mortar in its construction.

The accused criminal was a young man named Kusisi. I did not know him, but I knew of his family as they were well-respected Mourners. When I arrived at the cell, I found Kusisi's father, Kusila, with him. This was somewhat surprising. Mourners have always been among the most devout. Hardly any of them have yet abjured our ancient vain religion. With no priest to sing the prayer of entry, Kusila must have felt half-blasphemous to enter even the former kennel of the Sacred Virgins. Times change for us all.

I knew the father and son might not have another opportunity to speak, so I refrained from interrupting. There was more than an hour till the trial. I had little enough to say in preparation.

"How can you shame our house so?" said Kusila.

"She is my sister."

"You have no sister."

"I could not stand by to see Ehrsipo defiled by the hands of strangers."

"Never speak that name!" Kusila shouted.

"Father," said Kusisi, "I may not have long to speak at all."

"It is shame enough a son of mine has neglected his duties," said Kusila.

"To Mourn our dead king?" said Kusisi.

"Yes," said Kusila. He stood straight and proud, a slender, ascetic man of perhaps fifty-five.

"Our world is dead," said Kusisi. "Our living king is a king no more. And you worry about a king who died when I was so young I do not even clearly remember his face?"

Kusila gasped. Then he slapped his son's face hard. Kusisi bowed his head, obviously terribly ashamed.

"You are no son of mine," Kusila shouted. "No son of mine could ever speak so of his obligation to the living Son of Amarez whose reign gave him birth."

"Amarez is as dead as his majesty, Ko-la Amarez," said Kusisi. There was a great sadness in his voice. "Or at least as deposed as his majesty, Ko-ney Amarez."

Kusila shuddered. "I have no son," he said, his voice one of horror. "Why do I talk to a blasphemous stranger who looks upon the faces of Sacred Virgins? My house is utterly disgraced."

"Father!" Kusisi cried out.

"A whore who defiles the name of my daughter, once honored to enter the Sacred Service, walks about in public selling cloth like a common woman."

"She sells cloth to live. Would you rather she sold her body?"

"She has sold her body. She disgraced our family's name the day she walked out of the Palace of Virgins alive."

"The Sky Lords drove her out, drove them all out," said Kusisi. Tears ran down his cheeks. "She had no choice."

"She could have died performing the duties to which she was dedicated," replied the father. His voice was ice. "She has committed unspeakable blasphemy, and so have you."

"And now I will die, and she will continue selling cloth for the means to eat to those not too proud to buy from the dispossessed brides of a dispossessed God."

"Better neither of you nor I either were ever born!" Kusila shook with rage. "I hoped you might remember your shame, might beg forgiveness for your sin while you still can. I see you are utterly drunk with your willful depravity."

"Father," said Kusisi, "I am terribly sorry I have hurt you."

"How dare you snivel at me like that," Kusila shouted. He slapped the younger man's face again. Then he spat on the floor. "I go now," he said. "I have duties to perform."

He stalked out of the room. The guard let him pass.

"To sing praises of a dead king while the world he ruled is in ruin?" Kusisi called after him.

Kusila did not answer. The insignia on my lapel brought him up short, however. Though I had never served the royal person, my rank as a royal interpreter required his acknowledgment.

Kusila kissed the gathered fingertips of his right hand, then spread them quickly to the air. This was the customary salute to the royal insignia. It meant: I honor and acknowledge the emblem of the king, Son of Amarez Who daily makes the Sun and the River to give us life.

This salute has not yet been forbidden, but it is common knowledge the Sky Lords disapprove of it. In a generation, I think it will be forgotten. That is why I explain it here. It is my hope this record will inform people of what was once commonplace but will soon be no more.

I returned the salute. It made me uncomfortable to do so in the presence of the guard, but he paid no attention. The Sky Lords permit courtesy to the ignorant, especially to upstanding citizens such as a professional Mourner. Under the circumstances I could not refuse him the acknowledgment he believed due.

Kusila went out by what was once the kennel-keeper's door. I knew he would not attend the trial. The trial would be held in a former Weaving Chamber of the Sacred Virgins. I was thankful Kusila did not ask me how I could commit the blasphemy of entering the forbidden precincts. It feels like blasphemy to me too, but when sacred duties conflict, I think... I hope it is correct to serve the will of the greater God.

I nodded to the guard and entered Kusisi's cell. The guard knew why I was there and merely nodded back.

Kusisi sat slumped on his bed. He was slim like his father, with intelligent, anguished eyes. The cell was simply but adequately furnished: a sturdy single bed, three comfortable chairs, a table, good light and air.

"I am Enhessa," I said. "I will be your translator. I have been ordered to speak to you in preparation for your trial."

Kusisi sighed. He sat somewhat straighter and looked me in the eye. "If you must," he said.

"Do you understand the crime of which you are accused?" I asked.

"I understand that the world has gone crazy," Kusisi replied, "that good is evil, compassion is blasphemy, and effort does only harm."

"If you renounce the false faith and plead ignorance you might be spared," I said.

"What faith?" he said. "I believe in nothing."

"The Sky Lords do not mean your sister harm."

"Then why did they rape her soul and leave her body to sell cloth that should have been woven only for the glory of Amarez?"

"The Sky Lords teach the True Faith. Surely you must see that their God is greatest?"

"I see that their God is evil," said Kusisi.

"I will speak as well for you in court as I can," I said. "I will try to save your life. Do not be too proud."

"Proud!" said Kusisi. "It disgusts me that I still live."

"I will do what I can," I said.

Kusisi looked to the floor and did not answer.

I heard footsteps in the corridor. I looked up. A young woman named Ahcohsey came to the door. She was one who had learned enough of the Sky Lords' strange tongue to attend our Sky Lord in simple matters. "The Sky Lord requires your service," she said.

"Of course," I answered. I rose to accompany her to the Sky Lord. "I will do what I can," I said again to Kusisi. He did not reply.

The Sky Lords are much like us in appearance. It is said our women can even bear their children. This is a wonder. Perhaps we really do have a common genesis as they declare. The Sky Lords are hairier than we and thicker, though that may be only because they eat so much more meat. They are of much the same height as we, and while there is more variety among them of skin and hair color, many of them have the same ruddy complexion and light brown hair as my people do.

Our Sky Lord has very hairy arms, and though he shaves daily, his face often seems shadowed by late afternoon. He sat now with a document. He looked up when I entered.

"A fascinating script," the Sky Lord said. "I really wish I had time to learn it."

"You honor us," I said.

"No doubt," said he. "I'm given to understand this thing's important. Can you translate it?"

"Certainly," I said. I took the document. I saw at once that it was from the monastery of Ez-Amarez-Coya, Mother/Wife of our superseded God. Ez-Amarez-Coya is also the name of the great lake high in the Elacain Mountains in the far West, that is the source of the River and on whose shore the monastery stands. I looked over the document rapidly. It was written in the traditional religious manner, of course.

"Do you wish a literal translation, my Lord?" I asked, "or shall I explain what traditional terms that may be unfamiliar to you refer to?"

"Just tell me what they're saying for now," he answered. "Later, if we have time, perhaps you can explain the nuances. I really do like to learn about your people's ways."

"Yes," my Lord," I answered. "You are most magnanimous to condescend so."

It has never ceased to amaze me that the Sky Lords, who have the power to mow down an entire army in an instant or to blast a temple to dust take so human an interest in our simple doings.

"Never mind that," the Sky Lord said. "What's the thing say?"

I cleared my throat. "It says: 'We have not received the Sacred Garments of the season nor the Sanctified Corn. Therefore we are at a loss to perform the Ceremony of Breaking Waters. How shall we inform you of the Birth?'"

"What on earth is that supposed to mean?" the Sky Lord said.

"It's the Ceremony they perform in spring, my Lord, when the ice dam breaks and the lake surges into the river. In their childish ancient faith it is like the breaking of waters at a birth, the birth of the new year to them."

"Your people's idolatry is truly fascinating," the Sky Lord said. "It should be recorded, if only as a curiosity of the Devil's wiles."

I think I blushed then, but he did not notice. Might his statement constitute sanction for my chronicle? I dare hope it was so intended.

"Tell them," he went on, "that the Ceremony is abolished. It is a vain and wicked faith, and they must learn not to conduct such practices any more. The monastery is to be disbanded at once, and anyone caught conducting this foolish Ceremony will be severely punished."

"Yes, my Lord," I replied. And I surely blanched then at the awesome might of the Sky Lord's God. "I will send the message."

"Good," said the Sky Lord. "You do your duty creditably. I want it proclaimed with the day's announcements too. This idolatry must cease entirely. Tell the people this vain Ceremony is abolished."

"Yes, my Lord," I said.

"Thank you," said he. "Well, I suppose we'd better get this trial over with. I hate these things. People suffer, but they have to learn respect for the True Faith."

"It is strange for them, my Lord," I said. "So much is new. I know many tongues and have spoken to many peoples. Yet even I am daily amazed at the greatness of the Sky Lords and of their God."

"As well you should be," he said. "Now let's get on and done with that trial."

He rose to walk, just like any ordinary man of the people, from his chamber to the former Sacred Weaving Hall where the trial was to be conducted. I accompanied him. The prisoner was already there when we entered. He stood, his head bowed in shame.

The Sky Lord sat and then told me to read the charge, in both our language and his. I did so:

"Kusisi, former professional Mourner of the vain former faith, is accused of hiding a recalcitrant priestess of the vain former idolatry and providing her with contraband objects for use in the practice of this abolished idolatry."

"She's not a priestess," said Kusisi. "She's a Sacred Virgin."

I saw no need to translate, but the Sky Lord asked what he had said, so I did.

"Never mind these quibbles," he replied. "The crime is in the willful practice of idolatry."

"The Sky Lords' God abhors all idolatry," I explained to Kusisi.

"Does the Sky Lords' God require the shaming of Dedicated Women?" Kusisi replied.

I sighed and translated.

"Tell him I will not tolerate idolatrous insolence," said the Sky Lord. His face was very stern.

I translated.

The Sky Lord looked to the prisoner. "Now what were you doing anyhow?" he asked.

I translated again, though, of course, I knew the answer perfectly well myself.

"Would you withhold the Sacred Corn that is the food of Ez-Amarez-Coya?" Kusisi answered. "Would you eat of Her bounty and give nothing back?"

"He was bringing the woman, who is his sister as well as a former Sacred Virgin, the corn to be blessed for the Spring Ceremony," I said to the Sky Lord.

"Is this the same Spring Ceremony as in that document?" the Sky Lord asked.

"Yes, my Lord," I replied. "It is the principal occupation of the former faith at this time of year. All hearts would be turned to the rites of spring as the planting season approaches. It is their traditional belief that Ez-Amarez-Coya must eat Her Sacred Corn for strength before Her Waters Break that the life of the new crop shall be strong."

"These superstitions will cease!" the Sky Lord declared. I could see he was greatly annoyed.

"Yes, my Lord," I said.

"Here, then, is my judgment," the Sky Lord continued. "In sympathy for the natural feeling of a brother for his sister, I shall spare the life of this offender. He shall perform four years' penal servitude at a location to be determined at my secretary's convenience. After that he shall be free provided he has learned utterly to renounce his vain and idolatrous religion which he must understand is entirely and forever abolished."

I translated this judgment to Kusisi.

"Our lives are abolished," Kusisi replied.

I translated and wondered at the Sky Lord's mercy, equal only to the might of his God, for he replied to this insult: "He will learn better as he learns the True Faith."

"Yes, Lord," I said, and I translated.

"Now," said the Sky Lord, "I want you to proclaim this judgment so the people will learn the will of the True God. It is not the desire of the True God, nor of us His servants, to hurt your people. The True God is a God of great Love Who has sent us here only to teach your people His Love. However, your people bring harm upon themselves to continue their intolerable idolatry. We have been patient, but they must desist. The Spring Ceremony is forbidden and abolished. They must not engage in its practice. They must utterly abandon its blasphemous rites. That is my judgment. I have spoken."

"Yes, my Lord," I replied. My knees trembled in awe at the great power of the Sky Lord's God.

"Good," the Sky Lord said. "I shall retire briefly to my chamber. Then I shall join you at the portal while you make the announcement."

The Sky Lord rose and walked out of the hall. The prisoner was led away. I walked slowly to the entrance of the no-longer forbidden former Palace of Sacred Virgins, who are now scattered among the general populace. Perhaps some even stood among the huge crowd gathered as always at the foot of the steps to hear the day's proclamation.

The people murmured among themselves. Some sang. Many prayed. I stood looking over their heads, across the rooftops of Ixtiu below the mound on which the former Palace and present Court stands.

The clear spring air was fresh and warm. I could see the corn fields where they spread for miles around the city, newly turned, awaiting the seed. The wondrous River that, with the Sun, brings life to Ixtiu and all our land, sparkled in the brilliant sunshine. Beyond the western horizon I knew were the great Elacain Mountains from which the River is born. I wondered at it all and at the world of Amarez Who made all of it and Who ruled no more.

The Sky Lord joined me at the head of the steps. The crowd became silent as every ear strained to hear what word the Sky Lord would give them through my mouth today. The Sky Lord nodded to me to begin, and I stepped forward and spoke:

"The True God of the Sky Lords grants mercy," I began.

The crowd stood silent.

"The life of the prisoner tried today is to be spared, and, upon completion of four years' penal servitude he is to be freed, to the great glory of the Sky Lords' God."

"Praise the mercy of the Sky Lords' God!" a voice shouted. All the crowd joined in.

I translated for the Sky Lord.

He held up his hands. The crowd quieted immediately. "Tell them, in the name of the True God, I thank them and bless them for their faith in His wondrous Love."

I translated again. When the crowd was quiet I went on.

"Further, the Sky Lord proclaims, as the Sky Lords have proclaimed from the first, that all idolatrous practices must cease."

The crowd attended carefully. This decree affected them all. What activity that they had taken for granted all their lives as they had the rising and setting of the Sun would now be forbidden? I went on.

"Specifically, the former Spring Ceremony is abolished."

There was a collective gasp.

"There is to be no Ceremony of the Breaking of the Waters," I said. "As well, no one is to practice any of the former rites of the Corn, of the Gates of Ez-Amarez-Coya, nor any of the practices associated with the former Birth of the Year, which is now utterly forbidden as Amarez no longer rules, and we must all accept the Sky Lords' God Who is the True Source of Life."

The crowd remained silent briefly. Then a great cry arose, a keening, howling roar. So long and so loud did the crowd cry out that I began to fear them nearly as much as I had come to fear the Sky Lords' True God. When, at last, the voices of the crowd had quieted enough for his words to be heard at all, the Sky Lord asked me to translate what they were saying.

"They say," I replied, "'All worship to the Sky Lords' God Whose terrible might is beyond comprehension.'"

"A funny way to put it," the Sky Lord said, "but I am pleased they are coming to understand the Love of the True God."

"Indeed, my Lord," I replied. "Indeed they are."

Perhaps they do understand. I am not sure. I do not. I do not understand a God Who forbids us to give a little Corn to the Mother of Waters, Who abolishes the watchers in the mountains whose duty it has always been to inform us of the ice dam's spring break-up.

How will we know when to expect the River to surge? Winter and spring are very dry here on the plain. How will we know when to plant? It does not matter. The floodgates are sacred objects of the old faith we are now forbidden to employ.

When we plant, if we do not open the floodgates for the River's surge the fields will receive no water. The corn will not sprout, and there will be nothing growing to receive the rains of summer, nor to ripen in the dry, clear days of fall.

Perhaps the Sky Lords' True God loves the Sky Lords. He is surely their God. He has overthrown our Amarez Who long brought us life. I do not understand the Love of the Sky Lords' True God, nor, I think, do my people. I hope I may be forgiven for translating their cry incompletely to the Sky Lord. By next year, it will not matter. Ixtiu will be no more. The Sky Lords' God must surely be the True God, for what other God has the power to do such terrible things? What the people really said was:

"All worship to the Sky Lords' God Whose terrible might brings death by starvation."

Author's note: When two cultures both believe that their outlook is the only truth, tragedy is all but inevitable in their meeting. But the culture with the more advanced technology is in a position to do the greater damage. This story was inspired by my rereading of El Inca Garcilaso de la Vega's Royal Commentaries of The Incas. *Yet to Garcilaso, son of a Conquistador and an Inca princess, the point of his book was to validate the claim of his maternal family the Huascar line. What mattered most to him was the license from the King of Spain, which allowed him to use the word, "Royal," in his title!*

PASSING THE TORCH

"I'm sorry, all the plumbers are in jail." The woman's voice on the other end of the phone sounded angry. Then she cut the connection.

Esther Pernion stared at the vacant phone, confused. I'm too tired for this, she thought.

Esther felt weak as she walked the few steps to her threadbare, royal blue-and-grey easy chair. At least her legs worked all right, and her arms as she lowered herself into the seat. She sat a few moments, reassembling her thoughts.

She had had another "spell" this morning. Let's not kid ourselves, she thought, another *stroke*. The sudden headache, the weakness, the confusion—Esther knew the symptoms. Well, that sort of thing happens. At seventy-two, she'd had one that slurred her voice and caused her to limp for six months. She didn't think her speech was slurred this time. They'd wanted to put her in an "old people's prison," as she put it, back then. Now, at eighty-two she still lived alone.

"But Mom," Jennifer'd said just last month, "I worry about you. Something could *happen*."

"You mean I could die with no one around to poke a needle in my ass," Esther retorted.

"Now, *Mom*...."

"You're just afraid I'll fall down and the county blade driver will find me two weeks later in a puddle of piss, and you'll be publicly embarrassed."

Jennifer left angry. Esther felt a little guilty later, but her life was *her life*.

So now what? Esther wasn't sure how long she had been sitting, musing. Had she dozed off a bit?

Let me see, Esther thought: I had another stroke this morning. It was when I couldn't find the jar opener and tried to open the olives by hand. So I took a couple tylenol and noticed the puddle. That's it, that's what I was calling for; I wanted a plumber.

The headache was gone. The tylenol must have worked. Esther still was unsure how much time had passed. She felt thirsty. She decided to brew some tea. Jennifer had given her one of those new temperature-sensitive microwaves, but Esther kept it unplugged and stored dried fruit in it.

"Mom, why are you so anti-technology?" Jennifer had asked.

"I like technology just fine," Esther had snapped back. She didn't mean to snap, but she knew she did. "I just don't need a lot of gadgets cluttering up my life."

Jennifer's feelings were hurt, but Esther still wouldn't use the microwave. She did like her propane stove. She filled the tea kettle, careful not to run much water down the apparently faulty drain, then set it on the left front burner. She was almost back to her easy chair when she realized she had forgotten to turn on the stove. Damn, she thought, strokes are so tiring. The few steps back to the stove were an effort.

Esther poured dry mullein, rose hips, and a little mint into her round, brown-glazed tea pot. She considered having coffee instead to perk her up, but decided, what with the stroke, that that wasn't such a good idea. She had already drunk two cups of coffee that morning. A doctor would, no doubt, tell her to quit entirely. Well, she'd never expected to live to be eighty-two. As long as she was still alive, she might as well enjoy it. Tea was pleasant too, though.

Esther set her cup and saucer on the faded oak table by her chair, along with the honey and a spoon. She sat down again, waiting for the water to boil, enjoying the view out her kitchen window. Bare trees curved angular against a bright blue sky: alder, walnut, larger cottonwoods. Piñons, junipers, and live oaks stood somber green on grey and buff bluffs. Perhaps she would go outside. The breeze carrying the last wisps of cloud from yesterday's rain off to the northeast might be chilly, but the November sun was shining so brilliantly that she was sure it would be comfortable in the lee of the house. A bug, immobilized all morning by last night's cold, now crawled around the outside of the south window screen.

While the tea steeped, Esther suddenly recalled that she had intended to call a plumber, and decided to try again. She picked up the receiver and held it to her ear. She felt sufficiently disoriented that it was several seconds before she realized that there was no dial tone. She set the receiver down and checked to be sure the wire wasn't loose. It was tight. She tried the phone again. It was quite dead.

This is becoming a decidedly odd day, Esther thought. She considered becoming alarmed, but felt that would bring back her headache. So she sat back down in her chair and poured a cup of tea through the strainer instead. Then she opened the little drawer in the front of the side table and got out her small green stone pipe and the small round tin of marijuana. She filled the pipe, then lit it with her new glo-lite. Despite denigrating gadgets to Jennifer, Esther had no objection to something that did the job *better*. She had yet to use up a glo-lite, though she had lost two.

If anyone had asked, Esther would have said that the marijuana was a vaso-dilator and blood-pressure regulator and was thus medically appropriate following her stroke. She had never consulted a doctor on the matter. She considered it medicine for the soul regardless. She inhaled smoke, touched the pipe to her forehead, raised it aloft, then inhaled again. She set the pipe down, stirred honey into her tea, sipped, and contemplated.

Outside, the breeze occasionally gusted to a proper wind. Might be some weather coming, Esther thought, forgetting about yesterday's that was leaving. She could feel the spirits riding the wind.

Like her tea and honey, marijuana smoke, juniper smoke in the wood stove, the spirits each had a flavor, mostly familiar. Nature spirits danced, slumbered, or roared, crisp or pungent, not especially human, but nourishing in their vitality. There were others too: kind but prickly, the busy spirits that fondled and worried so many lives, the nasty ones whose food was suffering itself.

Something felt different, though, Esther thought, sipping her tea while the marijuana caressed her sore brain. In all these years, the thing she still found a mystery was how to tell what is subjective and what objective. Only by comparing inner perspective to outer event had Esther ever been able to locate experience. So, she mused, is all this activity happening because I'm going to die today? Is that it? Did the world shut down on me today because I'm getting ready to leave this old body? Or does it have some purpose of its own to which I am participant... or observer... or totally incidental? Nearby spirits felt stronger. Bigger, more distant spirits felt scattered. Now what could that mean?

Esther set her teacup down and dozed. She had been sleepy after previous strokes too.

Counting Tadpoles

A hurried knock at the door woke Esther. The sun shone right on her, which meant it must be about to set. Esther's brain and mouth both felt blurry. A sip of cold tea tasted much better than cold coffee would have. "Coming," she called.

Esther remembered to stand slowly. She still felt a little dizzy, but her coordination seemed normal as she walked to the door, straightening her soft, blue, shapeless sweat shirt as she went. She brushed a wisp of white hair off her right ear, then opened the door. Her veiny hand felt a little weak, but it gripped normally. She hoped her voice was clear.

Esther's neighbor, Prabaht, stood at the door. Esther always meant to ask him about his name. It sounded Indian to her, though his brown hair and fair, if tanned, features looked North European. Prabaht wore faded jeans and an old black T shirt in the cool, late afternoon breeze. Fortyish, medium height and bone-skinny, Esther always figured his blood circulated double-time to keep him warm. Perpetually active, Prabaht never accomplished much, as he never slowed down enough to organize his actions. Esther saw no sign of Prabaht's truck. He must have walked the third of a mile.

"Come on in. Have a seat."

Prabaht burst through the door but didn't sit. "Have you heard?"

Prabaht's hovering and pacing had once irritated Esther. Now she just sat down herself. "I'm a little tired today. Make yourself coffee. Heard what?"

"The shit hit the fan this morning." Prabaht set the kettle on the stove to boil and put a paper towel in the funnel for a filter over the glass coffee pot.

Esther thought of her misbehaving drain—and brain. "Things have been a little off," she said.

"They didn't come here, did they?" Prabaht stared, intense.

"You're the only person who's come here all day. What's happened?"

"They started rounding up everyone with a drug record. Then things got crazy." Prabaht scooped coffee into the ersatz filter and fussed impatiently at the kettle.

"I should think!" Esther replied. "Numbers *alone*…"

But then she did think. Subjective and objective: Everyone mixes them. It can't be helped. Prabaht always jumped to conclusions, nearly always wrong. Something had happened, no doubt, but Prabaht's projections almost certainly misinterpreted events.

Prabaht paced, drank coffee, and ranted about the government and the Jesuits. Esther filled her pipe again and lit it. Prabaht glanced, somewhat wild-eyed, out the window, then smoked with her. Esther knew it made him uncomfortable that she just set the pipe on the table when it was empty, but she refused to acquiesce to his paranoia by hiding it.

"I've seen the maps, you know," Prabaht said, over his second cup of coffee.

"I'm hungry," said Esther. "Will you join me for dinner?"

"Can't stay," said Prabaht, "but you go ahead."

Esther did. She spooned cooked beans into a pan with a little bacon grease and set it on the stove to heat, got out a jar of salsa—she still put up a full year's worth—and warmed a flour tortilla. Sometimes she would fix a plate for Prabaht even if he said no. He would usually eat it. This evening, she didn't bother. If he consumed nothing but coffee until he starved, that was his problem.

"They've had streets laid out for a concentration camp right up at Longhorn Gap for *years*!" Prabaht's voice faded into a meaningless hum. What Esther enjoyed about him, she thought, was the way his knees and elbows flapped about as he paced and jabbered, like a hyperactive heron.

Esther grated a bit of longhorn cheese, carefully scooped the beans onto the tortilla with the cheese and salsa, folded the tortilla, then ate her supper with a knife and fork, while Prabaht's voice played on in rhythm with his body.

Breeze stilled. Sun set. A moon, more than half full, illuminated the peaceful yard. Esther could hear Walnut Creek, fifty feet from the house, behind gaps in Prabaht's monologue.

Prabaht paused, stood stock still for the first time since entering. Esther knew this signal, and focused in on him as he said, "Well, got to go. I'll stop by tomorrow, they don't haul me off first. Need anything?"

"I could use a little wood split," said Esther, "if you have time."

"Sure." Prabaht flicked on the yard light and strode out the door.

The house still held the sunny afternoon's warmth, but Esther built a fire for evening. She knew she would be sleepy again soon. She heard the quick axe strokes in the yard as she washed her dish, spoon, knife, fork, and grater while the fire caught.

Prabaht carried in the full kindling box, followed by four armloads of aromatic juniper and solid oak. Esther held out two dollar bills.

"That's all right," Prabaht raised a hand.

"No, you take it," said Esther.

It was a ritual repeated many times in the two and a half years that Prabaht had been Esther's closest neighbor. Esther's social security was a meager income, but consistent, and she owned her house outright. Erratically employed and poorly organized, Prabaht was in constant danger of losing his home for failure to pay the ninety dollar a month rent.

Prabaht stuffed the two dollars in his pants pocket, reheated the last of the coffee, and drained the pot. "Well, got to go," he said as he plunked his cup down.

"Good to see you," said Esther, as Prabaht stalked out in his T-shirt through the chilly moonlit evening.

Esther set an oak log on the fire—quite as substantial as she cared to lift—adjusted the damper, rinsed out the coffee pot and Prabaht's cup, as well as her own tea cup, and then decided she might as well go to bed. Best thing for a stroke is a good night's sleep, she thought. Then it occurred to her: Oh damn! I didn't think to ask Prabaht to look at that drain.

Esther looked for the puddle. It seemed smaller, rather than larger, even after she had washed the few dishes. Oh, well, perhaps things would make better sense tomorrow.

In the morning, Esther felt better, but decided perhaps she should only have one cup of coffee. She added a dollop of half-and-half; it was almost gone.

Esther sat in her chair and contemplated the way the sun sparkled on the morning's frost. She had intended to drive to town today to pick up the mail and a few groceries—before she was reduced to using that hideous powdered creamer in the coffee. The four-and-a-half mile trip once a week kept the faded red Valiant that had looked new fourteen years ago when she'd bought it (though, of course, it wasn't) adequately lubricated. The only major work she had ever had to do on it was to have the wheel wells modified to accomodate taller wheels, so that she would have the clearance she needed crossing the creek.

But maybe she should wait a day. Perhaps she should give Stella at the post office a call. Better to say she would be in in a day or so than to have someone nosing around suspecting her of being unable to take care of herself.

Esther put on her glasses and read a bit in an historical novel from the State Library Books by Mail—a wonderful program for rural people. Then she made herself a boiled egg and a slice of toast, and did have another third of a cup of coffee. At eight thirty-five, she tried calling the post office. Her phone was still dead.

Many people Esther's age spent their lives in front of a television. Till the advent of cable, which did not extend far enough out of town to reach Esther, and the satellite dish, reception was inadequate to make television worth the bother at Esther's house. Visitors were appalled. Jennifer wanted to help Esther buy a satellite dish.

"If I wanted all that racket, I'd have moved to some noisy hell hole like Phoenix long ago."

Jennifer brought the subject up every six months. Esther always said no. In her urgency to defend her independence, she usually managed to say it in a way she later felt guilty for. Oh well, Esther thought, if a daughter hasn't gotten used to you after sixty years, what's to be done?

Despite not wanting a television, there were occasions when Esther would have liked some news. She did have a radio, two in fact. One was part of her tape player. The other had been a bonus with a magazine subscription. Neither currently worked. Due to distance and mountains, reception was abysmal even if they had. Only the Navajo station out of Window Rock came in clearly, and, of course, most of the news on it was in Navajo.

Esther put on her brown wool jacket, and a brown wool hat with orange decorations she had knitted since last winter and only first worn the past couple of weeks, and went outside. The thermometer, shaded by the overhang of the roof, read twenty-seven degrees, but bright sun had already melted the frost off the car. Birds chirped in the clear, still morning. The sun felt warm and invigorating.

Esther walked to the car and raised the hood, careful not to exert herself too suddenly: Don't want to pop another blood vessel, she thought. The sun shone full on the battery. If the phone still didn't work in an hour, she thought she would drive in and see what was going on. Little backwaters on the creek held a thin skim of ice, crystal patterns radiating artfully. A fat ground squirrel scooted past. Esther walked thirty or forty yards along the bank of the creek. Then she heard a scrabbling sound.

Esther looked among the winter-bare brush. Why, there were the chickens! She hadn't seen them in days. Descended from fighting stock, they looked like banties. She had originally gotten them to keep the scorpions down. Skunks, coyotes, and who knows what-all had done in every attempt Esther had made to keep a penned laying flock. These, loose and wild, managed to survive and perpetuate themselves. She wondered if she was just sleeping too soundly to notice, or if they were roosting so far off that she wasn't hearing the roosters.

Esther got half a coffee can of cracked corn from the shed and tossed it about. The chickens scrambled for it. There were at least twenty, including six roosters and two chicks she didn't recall seeing before, only now feathered out; their mother must have hidden them in the woods while they were smaller. One of the roosters crowed, ruffling his rich red neck and iridescent green tail feathers.

Thanksgiving's coming up, Esther thought. I'll invite Prabaht and have him catch us a young rooster. Even a young rooster would have to be boiled all day before she roasted it, or it would be too tough to eat, but the flavor was the best. The things one doesn't expect, Esther thought, like still having my own teeth at eighty-two!

Depending on the direction of the wind, Esther could sometimes hear vehicles on the two-lane highway a mile away down the canyon, sometimes not. A logging truck slowing for the curve just south of the turnoff was the sound she heard most regularly. She hadn't noticed any this morning. She looked down the canyon now at the sound of something approaching. A tangy whiff of juniper smoke from her stovepipe wafted by as a modest-sized but snappy motorcycle pulled into view.

The rider was almost to the house before Esther recognized her sixteen-year-old great grandson, Peter. Peter's mother, Esther's granddaughter Sylvia, was, last Esther knew, in the midst of yet another catastrophic relationship. Peter lived with his grandmother, Jennifer, in Socorro—a hundred and fifty miles away. Esther felt sorry for Peter, having to be a boy with an unmarried mother, unknown father, and a divorced grandmother and great grandmother. Still, that was no excuse to cut school.

Peter rounded the final curve. Then, instead of slowing down to ford the creek, he sped up, and roared across in a cloud of spray. Esther shook her head and smiled. Peter parked his bike by Esther's car and hopped off. "Car broke?" he asked.

"I'm just letting the sun warm the battery." Esther gave Peter a big hug. "Isn't it a school day?"

"I tried to call; the phones are out."

"Oh. I thought it was just mine."

"Ma Jen figured I better get here while I could."

Esther recalled Prabaht's ranting. She had not felt up to paying much attention. A lot of Prabaht's talk was paranoid fantasy anyhow.

"Bring your things in the house," Esther said. "Then explain. Have you had breakfast?"

"Nope." Peter grinned and jumped to unsnap the bungies holding the pack on the back of his bike. Whatever was happening, Esther could see that the teenager considered it a great adventure.

Peter followed Esther into the house. The refrigerator was humming.

"Wow!" Peter said, "you've got electricity!"

"Of course," said Esther.

"It's out in town."

"Oh?" This was far from the first time Esther had been blissfully unaware of a power outage. Between photovoltaics and the little hydro system on the creek, she had more electricity than she knew what to do with. She had heard computers on such a home system had difficulty with voltage irregularities, but none of the few appliances Esther ran seemed to mind.

"Damn, it's a good thing I got here," Peter said.

Esther felt a flash of irritation. Her daughter wasn't trying to run her life again, was she? She also noticed Peter's use of profanity. Well, so long as he didn't become really foul-mouthed, she could hardly object. She said more than an occasional "damn" herself. Still, it was disconcerting having a great grandson a head taller than oneself. "What do you mean?" Esther asked, keeping her voice neutral. "Bacon and eggs sound good?"

"Sounds great. You really haven't heard? The shit hit the fan!"

"That's what Prabaht said, but…" Esther did not want the boy to know why she had no idea what else her neighbor may have told her. "…I haven't heard the details yet."

Peter didn't notice his great grandmother's evasion. He told her what he knew, which was not altogether clear: Someone had ordered surprise mass arrests yesterday, before dawn. Only, of course, that didn't work. Lots of cops warned their families and friends. Information leaked to radio and television stations. Some officials balked. Police records did seem to affect who got raided. If drug-related police records had any special part in it, as Prabaht had said, Peter didn't mention it. Thousands of people were taken by surprise, but what started as a mass police raid degenerated, within hours, to mass chaos.

Peter had set out about one yesterday afternoon. His grandmother reasoned that his petty infractions, all still juvenile, might not be listed beyond the county. Esther had her doubts about this reasoning, but she didn't say anything. It had taken Peter twenty hours to come one hundred and fifty miles. He had evaded four roadblocks, half a dozen places where he heard gunfire, though he didn't know what any of them were about, and stolen a gallon of gasoline. Normally, his great grandmother would object strenuously to this last, but under the circumstances... He had not eaten since yesterday morning.

So far as Esther could tell, Peter was having the time of his life.

Esther had started to fry Peter three slices of bacon. She doubled that and got out a third egg. He ate four slices of toast while the bacon and eggs cooked.

"Um, do you have coffee?" Peter asked.

"When did you start drinking coffee?" Esther snapped back.

Peter mumbled something unintelligible.

All unbidden, an image flew into Esther's mind of herself at fourteen, smoking a cigarette in her room by an open window. She'd heard her mother's step on the stairs. Out the window went the cigarette, where it landed on the awning of the window below. Thank heavens a neighbor noticed the fire before the whole house went up! After that, her mother told her that if she was going to do anything so disgusting as smoke, she might as well do it in the open where at least she wouldn't burn the house down. She did, too; she didn't quit till she was sixty-one and nearly died of pneumonia for the third time.

Esther set the kettle on the stove, rinsed the glass coffee pot, and scooped coffee into a fresh paper towel in the funnel.

After he was done eating, Peter washed the dishes, which Esther thought extraordinarily considerate. As he dried his hands, he smiled and asked, "Got any smoke?"

Peter had been smoking pot, that Esther knew of, since he was eight. She still wasn't sure if she approved, but she was sure there was less harm to it than alcohol or cigarettes. "Oh, yes."

"Let's boke a smole."

The little green stone pipe still sat on the table by Esther's chair. She never had put it away last night. "In the drawer," she said.

Peter got out the tin of mixed leaf and bud and filled the pipe. "This all you've got?"

"There's more."

There are a few compensations to being eighty-two, Esther thought. One was that you could embarrass busybody authorities. Every year, small armies of cops descended on the area, usually in September, thrashing about in the woods in camouflage uniforms, purporting to search for marijuana crops. Every year, there were horror stories, mostly of completely innocent citizens being terrorized in their own homes. Every year, a few dozen pot plants were discovered and triumphantly displayed to the press—as if this somehow justified helicopters buzzing homes, roadblocks, and God only knew how much expenditure of tax money.

Afterward, the County and State would invariably spend more defending themselves from lawsuits than they realized in fines. Prabaht always claimed that creating employment for lawyers was the primary purpose of the whole affair. "No one grows a commercial crop around here anyhow. It's too hard to hide. There's not enough places with that much natural water."

Whatever the reason, Esther kept her eyes open, since she really did grow herself a small pot crop. On two occasions in the last five years, she caught investigators snooping around. Once, the man was a stranger, alone. She ranted at him about property rights and fences. The other time, it was a local deputy she had known all his life. Esther threatened to shoot his balls off. She was certain her white hair greatly improved the effectiveness of this strategy.

Peter lit the pipe and passed it to Esther. She sat down in her chair, raised the pipe in dedication, and smoked. Peter squatted next to her.

Just a moment after they were done, the chickens started squawking. Peter jumped to the window. "I think there's someone out there," he said.

Esther stood slowly and joined Peter at the window. A furtive figure dashed from a clump of live oak to a clump of juniper. Esther realized, as she stood beside her great grandson, that Jennifer had sent him to her not for her protection but for *his*. This realization improved both Esther's feeling for her daughter and her self-confidence.

Esther smoothed the maroon sweat shirt she was wearing today and walked across the room. She cleared her throat and opened the door. "Hey, Prabaht!" she called.

"Everything all right?" Prabaht called back from behind his juniper.

"Of course. Come on down."

Prabaht wore olive-green pants and an emerald-green long-sleeved shirt, his idea of camouflage, not altogether relevant amid the sparse vegetation of the largely autumn-brown hillside. He had smudged charcoal on his face, wore a handgun at his side in a holster originally made for a larger model, and had a twelve-gauge shotgun slung over his shoulder by a dirty piece of rope. He looked with blatant suspicion at the motorcycle.

"You know Peter," Esther said.

Prabaht's smudged face registered confusion.

"My great grandson," Esther added. "He's here... hiding out."

It was the last comment that finally made sense to Prabaht. "Ah!" Prabaht had spent the whole morning sneaking around the hills. Since he hadn't spoken to anyone, he had no idea what was going on.

"More or less normal in town," said Peter, "except not a lot was open, and the electric was out."

"Hmmm," said Prabaht portentiously.

Tellez, population four hundred, including outlying homes such as Esther's, was the county seat, and the biggest community in eighty miles. Somewhere else, a town so small might be lucky to have a variety store. Due to distance, Tellez supported, if marginally, a variety of businesses, from an auto parts/chain saw repair shop to something that called itself a boutique (known locally as The House of Bad Taste), lodged in a rat-infested trailer that would have been condemned by the Health Department someplace with enough population to have a Health Department.

"I need to take a little rest," said Esther. "While you're figuring out what's happened to the world, see if you can find where the chickens are roosting."

Esther lay down and slept for an hour. When she woke, she could hear Prabaht and Peter talking quietly outside, and could smell coffee. A shadow called her attention to the sky. A few little clouds were coming in from the northwest.

Esther patted her hair and sweat shirt into shape, then set a fresh pot of beans to soak. She jumped when the phone rang. She heard Peter laugh, and glanced out the window. The phone had so startled Prabaht that he had fallen on his face. Esther wondered how much coffee he had drunk—and whether he had eaten anything.

The phone didn't ring a second time, but Esther picked it up. Nothing. She hung it up and stood a few seconds, then started back across the room. The phone tinked once as if it was trying to ring. Esther picked it up again. This time there was a dial tone.

Peter stuck his head in the door.

"I believe the phone's fixed," Esther said. "Maybe we should let your grandmother know you arrived safely."

"Tell her in code," said Prabaht.

Esther seldom made long distance calls on daytime rates, but she thought that she really should call Jennifer, as much to be sure everything was all right down there as to tell her that Peter had arrived. Esther dialed Jennifer's number. The phone emitted the quick buzz of a busy circuit. She tried several more times, but didn't get through. She decided to try a local number. She thought a moment, then dialed the Senior Center. This time she got the longer buzz of a busy line. She tried again, and it rang.

"Tellez Senior Center. Lucy Meadowcroft speaking."

"Lucy, this is Esther Pernion. The phone's been out. I just wanted to see if it's working again."

"Are you all right?" Lucy asked.

"I'm fine, thank you. Do you know what's been going on?"

"Not really, but it's not good." That was what Esther liked about the Tellez Senior Center Director. Lucy didn't think that you were an idiot just because you were old. "There's been some sort of civil upheaval nationwide. The news doesn't make a lot of sense. You don't have TV, do you?"

"No."

"I guess we can be thankful we're not in Albuquerque. The electricity's still out. We're fixing meals here for anyone who needs it."

"I've got my own electric," Esther said.

Prabaht gestured and stage-whispered, "Don't. Phone taps."

Ridiculous, Esther thought. Even if they did tap the line, who would *listen?* The whole population would have to be employed listening to each other. The distraction caused her to miss something Lucy said. "Excuse me, what was that again?"

"I said come on down if you want to watch the news later. But if you're all right, we should clear the line. Now the phone's back on, I want to give everyone a call."

"Okay," said Esther, "thanks. Speak to you later."

Only after she hung up did it occur to her to wonder what the Senior Center was running its television on. Someone must have brought a generator over.

Esther tried Jennifer's number every hour or so. Usually she got a busy circuit signal. About three, it rang, but there was no answer. By then, clouds were starting to pile up. If it was going to storm, just as well to get the mail today... and see what there was to see. "Want to ride into town with me?" Esther asked.

"Sure," said Peter.

Prabaht looked about wildly, then said, "I'll come too."

"Only if you wash your face and leave the side arm here."

Prabaht fidgeted and mumbled, but complied.

The hood of Esther's Valiant was still open. Peter checked the various fluids. The radiator and oil were both fine. Esther checked them regularly herself. "Check the brake fluid, would you," Esther called. "The cap's too tight for me." Peter checked it. It was fine too.

Esther considered her reflexes slow, but she actually zipped right along once they hit pavement, and dodged a confused rabbit with no difficulty. In town, several generators clattered, one of them at the Tellez Mercantile, which was open. Esther parked there. She believed it was bad for the car to start it an extra time just to drive the fifty yards from the store to the post office, though nearly everyone else did just that.

Esther, Peter, and Prabaht headed for the post office, across the street from the courthouse, which was next door to the Tellez Mercantile. As they passed the courthouse, Undersheriff Colin Scofield emerged from the Sheriff's Office in back and called out, "Hello."

Prabaht froze, a look of panic on his face.

"Hi, Colin," Esther answered. "Any idea what's going on?"

"It's a mess," Colin replied, striding toward Esther and her companions with notable agility for a man who weighed nearly four hundred pounds. "Everything all right with you?"

"Just fine, except I've been trying to call my daughter in Socorro and can't get through."

"If it's an emergency, I could try."

"No, just want to be sure she's okay."

"I think the circuits are pretty tied up," said Colin. "Probably clear out later. Let me know if you need anything."

"Sure thing. Thanks."

Colin headed toward the Tellez Mercantile.

"You can start breathing again," said Peter quietly to Prabaht.

"Did you notice how evasive he was?" Prababht replied, as they continued on to the post office.

Stella Martinez, the postmistress, was terribly upset. There had been no mail delivery at all yesterday. Today, the mail had come in, almost on time, but it was extremely skimpy, and the weekly advertizing circulars that should have arrived yesterday still weren't here.

"Any idea what's going on?" Esther asked.

"It's the Governors' Executive Commission," the postmistress answered. "They decided that the Federal Government wasn't doing enough about crime, so they got up a warrant for four million people. Of course, it didn't work very well."

"Idiots," said Esther.

"That's not it at all," Joe Galloway chimed in as he shut his post office box and pocketed the key. Joe, in his mid-thirties, with heroic chest and shoulders and receding chin and hair, was a part time-logger, part-time outfitter's assistant, and part-time barfly.

"You heard better news?" Stella asked.

"Yeah," said Joe, "just a few minutes ago. They're saying now that it was a sort of palace coup at the F.B.I. They been accused of racism again. Got the top dogs at each other's throats. Someone figured to embarrass someone else by issuing this mass arrest order under the Known Criminals Law."

"Any idea who?" asked Prabaht.

"Nah," said Joe. "Maybe they'll say on the five-thirty news."

"Well, that's clear as mud," said Suzie Romero, who came in just in time to hear Joe's explanation of events. She was older than Esther and half Apache, her long hair still more black than grey.

"Should have grilled Colin," said Esther. "He certainly acted like the cat that ate the ballot box."

Suzie, Joe, and Stella all laughed. Manuel Tellez had been sheriff two terms, so he couldn't run again. The primary was only six months off.

"Colin was on duty when the order came in," said Stella. "With the sheriff out of county delivering a juvenile to Las Cruces, and an arrest list of a hundred and ninety-two, he figured that a four-man department wasn't enough personnel. So he'd wait till Manuel got back to do anything."

"Pass the buck. Smart man," said Joe.

"A hundred and ninety-two people's 10 percent of the county," said Esther. "That's a lot of votes."

"Sheriff didn't get back till noon today," said Stella. "Now Colin's glad he didn't do anything. State and Feds picked up about thirty people here in county. I hear most of them are already planning to sue."

"That was fast," said Esther.

"Magistrate gave them the idea."

"Oh?" asked Esther.

"Colin called Grant Harkins 'cause the jail was full… at five in the morning."

Joe guffawed. Everyone looked his way. He explained. "Grant closed down the Dry Gulch the night before. Bet he had a head like a watermelon."

"He asked Colin where the arrests occurred," Stella went on. "When Colin said at people's homes, Grant told him to let anyone out that wasn't arrested by the State Police, 'cause the other officers didn't have jurisdiction. Turned out a BLM Officer signed all the papers. Way I heard it, Colin hollered, 'Weren't none of these arrests legal,' opened the doors, and told everyone to go home. Of course, anyone that lived out of town was stuck for a ride and it was still just past five A.M."

"Ol' Colin ain't so dumb," said Joe. "He'll get my vote."

"What if there was a real crime, like a hold-up?" asked Peter.

"Colin's a crack shot, and he knows this country," said Joe.

"If the percentage was the same nationwide," said Prabaht, "does that mean someone tried to arrest twenty-five million people yesterday? That's crazy!"

"Things looked pretty crazy to *me*," said Peter.

"Oh?" said Joe.

"Came up from Socorro," Peter explained. Everyone ignored Prabaht's facial contortions.

"It's worse than crazy," said Suzie. "It's *stupid*."

Nobody said anything about who the hundred and ninety-two people on the list for arrest might have been.

"All these damn generators are giving me a headache," said Esther. "I'm ready to go back where it's quiet." She said good-bye and headed for the store, tossing the week's mail into the car on the way. There was a letter from her sister, Grace, in Abilene, which she knew would be mostly about doctors and barely legible, and half a dozen solicitations to buy things she didn't need and couldn't afford. At the store, Esther bought a can of coffee, a head of lettuce, a pound of bacon, a pound of margarine, a gallon of milk, and three onions. She let Peter add three candy bars and a bag of chips... and carry the sack to the car.

"If you're too tired, I can drive," said Peter.

"I'm just tired of banging generators," said Esther. "Anyhow, you drive too fast."

"You're no slouch yourself."

Esther smiled. "I mean on the dirt. Way you crossed the creek this morning, you'd punch the shocks right through the floor."

Esther invited Prabaht to join them for dinner. He accepted, but suggested they stop at his house for a chunk of meat.

Prabaht had taken an elk that fall, sort of legally. He had a license, for bow season, but his method was a little unusual. He lassoed his elk from a tree, then jumped down on its back and slit its throat. Between being stiff from waiting nearly forty hours for an elk to walk under him and the fact that the elk fought back, Prabaht was half-crippled for a month afterward.

He had a somewhat unorthodox freezer too, an old camper shell he had buried and lined with foam insulation. He had to crawl in with a flashlight to get anything. The compressor ran directly off a water-wheel on the creek. Prabaht intended to generate electricity off the same water-wheel, but never got around to building the system. He had been in a war for a year with the State Engineer, known locally as the Water God of the West, over the water-wheel. Prabaht claimed that he didn't realize he needed permission, since it was nonconsumptive use. "Mean-ass, murdering son-of-a-bitch is just trying to deny my permit 'cause I applied after the fact! Bastard'll claim I need a permit to breathe air next!"

"Do you like acorn squash?" Esther asked, to change the subject.

"Sure," said Peter.

"Good. You clean a couple. They're in the back bedroom. I'm ready for another little nap. If I'm asleep in an hour, rub them down with oil, and set them in the oven on three seventy-five."

Esther dumped the junk mail in the firestarter box, set the letter from her sister on the side table by her chair, and took a toke from her pipe. "Help yourself," she said to Peter. Then she lay down and pulled the blue wool blanket over herself. She wasn't really sleepy. She just needed to withdraw and think.

Esther let the generator banging seep out of her brain.

"Shit," Esther heard Peter say from outside, she frowned at his choice of word, "she must have ten years of firewood!" Esther wondered if Prabaht's not-quite-audible reply bore any resemblance to reality.

Most people locally considered it gross tyranny that the Forest Service required a permit for local firewood usage. Esther bought permits from the Forest Service for the full ten cord personal use maximum and then got someone to cut the wood for her on a one third-two thirds share. That ten cords' worth of permit always produced a few extra cords. Everyone Esther had dealt with took as much pride in delivering her fair third as they did in getting something unauthorized out of the Forest Service.

Prabaht probably was embellishing this simple conflict with extravagant conspiracy fantasies, Esther thought, and yet… She realized that the world her great grandson was growing up into was what she needed to contemplate.

Esther thought back. When she'd divorced Jerome, in the early sixties, it was already not the shock such events had been only a decade earlier. Still, it was traumatic. Stolid Jennifer's marriage had been traumatic, the divorce a relief.

Sylvia… It pained Esther to think of her granddaughter's chaotic life. She couldn't blame Jennifer. Jennifer could be overbearing, but she was the stable one. It was Esther who undertook risque adventures: hitchhiking at seventy, smoking pot—let alone growing it. People Prabaht's age thought nothing of smoking pot, approve or disapprove, but Esther still knew hardly anyone of her own generation who smoked.

Now there was Peter. With no stable male role model, with an upbringing far more chaotic than his mother's, he seemed bright and well-adjusted. What was she to make of it all? Perhaps it was easier to grow up sane in a blatantly insane world than to watch apparent stability disintegrate. Esther recalled the insanities of her own youth called Hitler and Stalin, the shocks of World War II, the bomb, the Kennedy assassination, the increasing social turbulence ever since.

In Esther's youth, the world had an apparent order, with its clearly defined good and its evil, its stability of family, community, and religion, and its aberrations of war and Depression. That was no longer so. Prabaht's paranoia, Colin's opportunism—personality flaws, sure, but they were also part of the society her great-grandson was growing to adulthood in. What was she to make of it? What, on the summit of her life's long climb, could she give him to help him make sense of the unknown world he would live in?

Esther could hear the low hum of Peter talking with Prabaht: A good man, she thought, but a walking encyclopaedia of misinformation. Could someone Peter's age understand that? Peter's a sharp kid, she thought, but what does he have to measure his perspective *against?*

Still alert, Esther drifted in the spirit realm of her own mind.

Subjective and objective, how was one to tell? The creek and juniper trees on the bluff, now that was objective. A feeling came to Esther that she knew she had felt before. It belonged to the spirit realm, which made it all the more difficult to differentiate subjective and objective: an intensification of the nearby and a dissipation of the large but farther away. Is it my nearing death? she thought. That seemed redundant. You could not live alone, so isolated, at forty-two, let alone eighty-two, without confronting your own death. A long-familiar companion, death taught an awe that enhanced the canyon's beauty to her aging senses.

Esther thought of the events of the last two days. Whatever lunacy had occurred nationally, the effects were local wherever you were: Lucy Meadowcroft having access to a generator, Grant Harkins being hung-over. True everywhere, but more obvious in Tellez because you knew everybody.

Esther felt the spirits all around her. They were like colors and flavors, but she had no names for them.

Esther had tried church once, around the time of the divorce, and been cruelly snubbed for the very reasons she needed spiritual solace. She had learned some Apache and Zuni names for spirits, but, well, she wasn't Apache or Zuni. After all these years, it still bothered her not to have a handle on the substance of her own soul. Thinking of Peter, she realized, as she had before but with great immediacy and poignancy, that this was not just a personal condition.

Values, Esther thought. No one can really tell him what to do, how to act, what to call the brightness the pot helps me see when I close my eyes but have no name for. And not just because he's young and spunky. No one knows. I certainly don't know what he'll need to know next week, let alone by the time he's my age! That's always so, but it has so speeded up in my lifetime. I remember the first talking movies, and now you can have a videophone if you're rich. Fast as things change, I might even live long enough to have one. I read once that the first ballpoint pens cost thirty-five dollars, and now look at how cheap they are. Would I want a videophone? What values is Peter learning? It's not what values I would teach him if I had any idea what to teach, Esther thought. It's what values does he learn from his own experience? What can I give him that he can make any sense of at all?

Esther opened her eyes. There was a dim lavender glow as the last of the sunset reflected off thickening clouds beyond sun-faded curtains. She was not aware of having slept, but the squash were in the oven and it was on. The elk meat was also on the stove, stewing with onions and garlic Esther could smell.

Esther stepped outside. The air felt balmy and smelled wet. She went back in and checked the food. The squash had not been in long. The stewing meat needed water, which she added. She wondered if Prabaht or Peter would think to check it before the meat scorched. Esther sat down to read her novel. She certainly hoped that whatever insanity was going on in the world would not affect the State Library Books by Mail program. She had read barely a page when Prabaht and Peter came back in.

"We followed the chickens, but we didn't find any eggs," said Peter. "I'll try again in the morning."

"Okay. Shall we try calling your grandmother again?"

"Sure."

Esther dialed Jennifer's number. The line rang, but there was still no answer. She hung up after the tenth ring.

"How 'bout some tunes," said Prabaht.

Concerned for her daughter, Esther looked up and blinked. "What? Oh, sure." Sometimes Prabaht could be amazingly insensitive. Esther turned to Peter. "Would you like to pick a tape?"

"Okay." Peter looked about, spotted the basket of tapes on the shelf below the player, and rummaged through them. "How about this one?" he said, holding the tape out to Esther.

It was her Glen Miller tape, a little scratchy, as the records had been pretty worn by the time she'd recorded them onto the tape, but still one of her favorites. "Sure." She smiled.

Peter put the tape in the player and turned it on. "In The Mood" recalled a world in which Esther had been younger than her great grandson was now. Her foot tapped a bit of long-remembered rhythm.

A few minutes later, the phone rang. Esther answered. "Hello."

"Hello, Mom."

"Jennifer, are you all right? I've been trying to call all day."

"I'm fine. Is Peter there?"

"Yes. Do you want to speak to him?"

"In a minute. I mostly wanted to be sure he made it okay."

"He's fine."

"If I'd had any idea…"

Esther noticed Prabaht gesticulating, his eyes wild again.

"It's not so bad up here. What's happened? Are you home?"

"Yes," said Jennifer, "finally. There was a fire."

"There?"

"No, a couple blocks away, but they evacuated the neighborhood. There was some looting. I believe someone was shot. They just let me come home."

"Is everything all right?"

"It seems to be. The electricity's still out, but things are calmed down now, and the fire's out… or not spreading at least."

"Good Lord!"

"Mom, would it be too much trouble if Peter stayed with you a few days—maybe even till after Thanksgiving?"

"Good heavens, Jen, you don't have to *ask!*"

"I don't want to impose."

That's Jennifer, Esther thought. She'd carry the world on her shoulders if it turned to silly putty. "It's no imposition at all. He's a pleasure to have." And I'm not too old to want my great-grandson where he's safe, Esther thought, but did not say in front of the boy. "Are you all right down there?"

"Yes. And I'm not sure I could get to you," Jennifer responded to her mother's unvoiced suggestion. "There are roadblocks. They've called out the National Guard…"

"They're not still trying to arrest half the country, are they?" Esther asked.

"Oh, no," said Jennifer, "except looters. They're plenty busy now just trying to restore order."

Whoever "they" are and whatever that means, Esther thought. "Well, it's certainly a relief to hear your voice," she said. "Have you heard anything from Sylvia?"

"Her boyfriend was picked up, but they released him on his own recognizance today."

"What did they charge him with?"

"That's not real clear."

"No, I suppose not. I'm just glad you're safe. Here's Peter."

Peter told Jennifer less of his adventurous ride than he had told Esther. Esther could tell Jennifer was admonishing Peter not to impose. She doubted this was useful advice. Jennifer achieved little but to make Peter uncomfortable.

No harm done, apparently. Peter's discomfort melted the instant he handed the phone back to Esther. "You take care," Esther said, "and don't worry about Peter and me. We're just fine."

Prabaht's eyes flared wild, and he gnawed at his lower lip, but he had sense enough not to pester. Esther felt sorry for Prabaht's perpetual anxiety. She knew he had at least moments of self-awareness. He had once said: "The one nice thing about paranoia is that you get so many pleasant surprises when the disasters you expect don't happen."

"Pennsylvania Six Five Thousand," said the tape.

Dinner was excellent. The warm leading edge of the front still made a fire unnecessary, but thick clouds reduced the moon's light. Esther offered Prabaht the loan of a flashlight to walk home, but he said he didn't need it.

"Just don't fall in the creek and get your guns wet," said Peter.

Esther sighed inwardly. What was the boy learning from his life?

When Esther woke in the morning, the house was still fairly warm, but she could see snow coming down fast and thick in the growing light. She lit the wood stove, then filled the kettle to heat. Peter appeared just as Esther finished pouring water into the paper towel/coffee filter, attracted by the aroma, she figured.

"Wow!" Peter said, "it never snows like this in Socorro! Think we'll be snowed in?"

"I certainly wouldn't drive in it," Esther said. She poured them each a mug, added milk to hers and asked, "Do you want milk?"

"No, thanks," said Peter.

"I hope you'll drink some," said Esther. "I can't use up a gallon myself."

"How about cornbread to go with the beans?" Peter picked up the mug of black coffee and carried it to the window. "Maybe I can find where the chickens are nesting in the snow."

"If they're laying any."

Esther carried her coffee to her chair. Peter continued to stand at the window. "Can I call you G.E.?" Peter asked abruptly.

"G.E.?"

"For Granny Esther."

"No. That's awful. If you're too big to call me Granny, just call me Esther like everyone else."

"I'd feel funny."

"It's a funny world." Esther peered over her coffee at her tall great-grandson. His face mostly looked eager.

"I'm going to see if I can find any eggs," said Peter.

"You got gloves?"

"Nah. It's not that cold."

Esther didn't reply. She was pretty sure there were some gloves that would fit him... somewhere, if the mice hadn't gotten to them. What she did say was, "I'm going to put on some oatmeal. Want any?"

"Okay." He slipped on his light-weight brown leather jacket and a green-and-yellow ball cap. "I'll be back in a few." And out he plunged into the snow.

That looks like fun, Esther thought. Maybe I'll go out in it myself later.

She set on a pot of oatmeal and tossed in a big handful of two year old dried apricots. (Spring frosts had done in the blossoms this year and last.) Then she sat in her chair to contemplate. Two days in a row of Prabaht really was a little much, even without having a stroke and the world going nuts. But Peter... She was enjoying having him here, for all it was a distraction. Distraction from what? she wondered. From whatever it is I do sitting in this chair when I'm alone, she decided. Still, having a young person need her felt good. She hoped he wouldn't be too bored between now and Thanksgiving.

The oatmeal got done; Esther turned it off. The snow fell so thick that she couldn't see the car. A person could get lost in a hurry in a storm like this, but how lost could a person get in a canyon a hundred yards wide?

A few minutes later, Peter stomped up to the door. "I couldn't see a thing," he blurted. "Bet I can find them in the snow when it quits, though."

"Good idea." Esther handed Peter the broom. "Brush off on the porch so you don't soak yourself and the house."

An hour later, the snow turned to rain. It poured all day long. "Think the creek'll flood?" Peter asked.

"Probably not," Esther answered, "but it will come up."

It did just that. They heard it through the rain. Peter dashed out during a lull toward late afternoon to look. He came back only moderately soggy. "Bet it's up a foot," he said. "Hey, what do you do about the phone bill if you can't get out in winter for a month?"

Esther was impressed. Peter had been visiting her for longer or shorter stays all his life. He knew she kept food and propane well-stocked for just such a contingency. He really was growing up even to think of such a question.

"I usually keep a couple months credit," Esther said. "But don't let that give you ideas about calling all your friends."

They both blushed, then laughed.

"It's a local phone company," Esther added. "If I do get behind, they're nice about it."

"That's different."

"They're related to half the county. Would you want two hundred great-grandmothers mad at you?"

Peter gave his great-grandmother a look of horror. They both laughed again.

Esther did make cornbread to go with the beans that evening. Peter offered to do the dishes. Esther accepted.

"Hey, there's a puddle," Peter said.

Esther looked. "I forgot about that." She recalled now, her attempt to call a plumber. *I must have been in worse shape than I realized to do that without asking Prabaht or someone to try to fix it first. Wonder who I called....* She recalled looking in the phone book under plumbers.... *Good Lord, I think I dialed the one in Arizona with the big ad!*

"It wasn't here yesterday," Peter said.

"It was the day before. I thought there was something wrong with the drain."

"Or the drainage." Peter looked out the window where the rain continued to pour down from the once again impenetrable night sky. "Did it rain a couple of days ago?"

"Some."

"I could look under the house."

"I'd appreciate it," said Esther, "but this will do till daylight." She tossed him an old towel.

By morning, the rain had slowed to an intermittent drizzle. The creek, double its usual width and two feet deep, flowed muddy and turbulent. Peter ran out, delighted to watch it rumble past. Esther put on an old yellow rain coat with a nice, snug hood and joined him.

"This is great!" Peter shouted over the rushing water. "How long do you think it'll last?"

"At least all day," Esther shouted back, "even if it doesn't rain anymore."

A little later, over a cup of tea and the pipe, Peter looked at his great-grandmother, seriously, and said, "Gra... Esther, do you think... that is... Could I... Could I stay here?"

Esther was not really surprised by the question, but she thought before answering. He was having an adventure now. That would wear off. She would feel useful, and she had to admit it would be a help. But her privacy... She had a brief flash of suspicion. Had Jennifer put him up to this? She felt ashamed of that thought at once. *I'm getting as paranoid as Prabaht*, she thought. *The world's getting loonier all the time. He'd certainly be safer here.* Finally she answered, "Wouldn't you be bored to death?"

"I don't think so. Prabaht was talking about running a trap line..."

"Heaven help us!"

"What's wrong?"

"Prabaht tried that last winter. He has got to be the world's least competent trapper. His total take consisted of one jack rabbit—by accident, because he forgot to bait that trap."

"He told me about that. He wasn't properly equipped. He only had his traps out the last couple weeks of the season."

"What makes you think he'll do any better this year?"

"I'll be with him."

How could she answer that? It wasn't important. What mattered was his future, and, for her, whether she could live with a sixteen-year-old boy. He would have friends. He would have girlfriends. He would have his own taste in music.

"We could try it, maybe, if your grandmother agrees." She felt a twinge at leaving his mother out of the picture, but Sylvia was out of the picture. "I'd want you to go to school."

"What for?"

She was a little shocked he was so forthright. "I'm not sure, but it is still important to finish high school… I think."

"Well, okay." He sounded a little less enthusiastic.

"You still want to stay?"

"Yes." Almost defiant.

"Let's see."

"I could help you out."

"I know that." She didn't intend the edge to her voice she knew was there.

Peter didn't notice. "Grandma says…"

"…Says I'm too old to take care of myself and shouldn't stay up here alone any more."

Peter heard the edge now. "I didn't mean…"

"I almost croaked the other day."

Peter's mouth fell halfway open.

"But I didn't. Maybe I'll drop dead right now. Maybe I'll live to be a hundred and fifty.…"

Neither of them knew what to say.

What if I become incapacitated in a year? Esther thought. Should a boy his age be saddled with that? It was the thing she really feared most, far more than she feared the possibility of dying messily alone. "Let's see how we both feel in a week," Esther finally said.

"Okay," Peter answered.

It rained off and on in the night, but by morning there were patches of blue. The creek was still up. About ten, Prabaht showed up with a newspaper, only slightly damp. He spread it on the kitchen table so they all could see it.

"Top Officials Deny Responsibility," read the biggest headline. So what else is new? Esther thought.

"Here's the real news." Prabaht turned to page five.

Esther's eyes landed on the largest headline on the page: "Ohio Attorney General Doubts Warrants." The article began: "Citing several cases making their way through the courts, Ohio Attorney General Arthur McGuire doubts 'John Doe Warrants' will suffice for female detainees."

"See." Prabaht pointed to a smaller article. Esther read the headline: "Bishop Deplores Suffering." The article was about how the Diocese of Las Cruces was helping people displaced by the continuing civil disorder.

"I don't get it," said Peter.

"What bishop?" Prabaht pointed to the end of the brief article.

Peter read aloud: "'On behalf of the bishop, Special Aide Father Luis Morales.' So? It's crazy in Cruces too."

"You left out the important part," Prabaht replied ominously. He read: "'Special Aide Luis Morales, S.J.'"

"So what?" said Peter.

"Don't you see?" said Prabaht. "The whole thing was a set-up by the Jesuits!"

Esther tuned out.

If Peter stayed, she'd need to move the squash and put a stove in that back bedroom. She had plenty of firewood anyhow.

Prabaht said something about logging trucks rolling again.

"In this slop?" said Peter.

"On pavement." Then Prabaht veered off to expound on the effect on local employment of a proposed $1.50 a gallon fuel tax.

Much as it pleased her that Peter understood such an issue, Esther's concerns carried her away from the conversation. "I could do with some quiet. Why don't you take it out in the sunshine," she said.

Peter and Prabaht went outside. Esther sat in her comfortable chair and contemplated.

Subjective and objective. Esther felt that she understood, at least a bit more, what she perceived in the spirit realm. Out there in the big world, the events of the last few days made everything just a little more disjointed, made everyone just a little more dissociated from a social order that had seemed so certain when Esther was Peter's age.

I've been fighting Jennifer over my independence, Esther thought. The objective and subjective meet in funny ways. I'm still not sure about living with anyone, but it is getting harder to manage. And Peter needs something too. That makes it all different.

Worth my privacy? Worth my independence? Better him than a stranger. I could tell him about the cigarette and the awning. A story like that would only annoy Jennifer, only frighten Sylvia. Peter would get a kick out of it, and because he would, he would learn a little of the so-solid world I was that girl in.

I have no idea how he should live, but he could use to hear of a world that was solid once, to know such a thing is possible. Jennifer can't give him that, just because she's too solid herself. Subjective and objective.

There's been a special light in my life. I've called it Freedom. I've called it this canyon. Jerome never saw it. Jennifer seemed determined not to see it. Sylvia... I'm not sure she's ever been there enough to know what she sees, like Prabaht.

Am I indulging in wishful thinking, hoping Peter is someone to pass the torch to, wanting the end of my life to have meaning?

I don't have to answer to that question, Esther thought, and smiled. I see his hand reached out, to receive and to give—even if neither of us knows quite *what*.

Author's note: So many stories premise a catastrophic social disaster. But how might people, amid personal issues of their own lives, deal with a more moderate degree of social disruption? This story was my breakthrough sale to a major publication, and in the process provided three interesting experiences for me as a writer. One is not to assume anything about a nonresponse from an editor. A requested rewrite really did get lost in the mail, as I learned only on querying, months later. Another was the kind of exchange with an editor in light of which I am pleased to measure all others. Then-Asimov's editor Gardner Dozois made substantive suggestions which really did improve the story I intended. But where some other suggestions he made were wrong for my character, I explained why, and he agreed. I have had experiences equally good with other editors since, and some others that were anything but. But this one set a standard for me, of what the exchange between a writer and an editor should be. Ironically, this story also languished for years between acceptance and publication, due to a major page cut at the magazine and resulting backlog. Some facets of publishing are beyond either a writer's or an editor's control. Sigh...

GENERAL DENSITY

"I didn't hurt anyone."
"You've been convicted of public indecency."
"Everyone's gotta take a leak."
"At the homecoming parade?"
"Sure."
"In Dean Gresham's daughter's clarinet?"
"Well…"
"You're a drunk."
"So's half your staff."
"You're a degenerate."
"Now, I can explain about the refrigerator."
"And your breath stinks. Gargle… with something that doesn't have to be sold with a tax stamp, and I'll see what I can do."
"How about Peppermint Schnapps?"
"Why couldn't I have taken that nice, easy job testing sewage treatment equipment?"
"Hey, you came to me."
"I know." Carol Kaprinov, Ph.D. (biophysics) looked around her, to the derelict buildings that surrounded the trash-strewn vacant lot. Bedraggled late summer wild flowers set off a large, pink, abandoned refrigerator. Carol could still hardly believe she had followed the short, increasingly degenerate trail of references to a neighborhood she usually would avoid even, as now, in broad daylight. Equally appalling was the fetid bum who, despite God only knew how much cheap booze, still talked lucidly enough to make credible, just barely, the brilliant physicist the record declared him to be.

"Tell you what," said Agamemnon Teresticu, "if you can fund data analysts I'll even come to work sober."
"On time?"
"I show up on time when I'm drunk."

That was true, as Carol learned, to her relief, when she read the record on Agamemnon more thoroughly: Born, 2302, New Carcross, Yukon,

U.D.—The United Dominion consisted of what was once Northwestern Canada, Alaska, the Eastern end of Siberia, and the Bering Land Bridge, which after three hundred years of relative stability was now rapidly being replaced by a lot of cold water.

Agamemnon married Xanthippe Xavalous in 2327. Ordained an Eastern Orthodox priest the same year, he was relieved of sacramental duties four years later. His unsanctified consumption of sacramental wine was deemed excessive by his ecclesiastical superiors. Xanthippe apparently thought so too. She divorced him the same year.

After that, Agamemnon's work led from sawmill equipment operator to equipment maintenance to mining equipment maintenance. Damn, thought Carol, why couldn't any of the others have had that sort of experience? Agamemnon apparently sweated off the alcohol in those years, or kept it under control.

At thirty-eight, Agamemnon went back to school, in physics. He was Herbert Segal's last graduate assistant.

"You want the job done?" Carol asked her boss, Gertrude Querchansky.

Natural pine paneling imparted an air to Gertrude's office simultaneously light and substantial. It was a comfortable setting that both built Carol's confidence and subdued her more extravagant ambitions. Carol, at thirty, was tall, blond, and clear-skinned. Her boss, at fifty-five, still had the better figure.

"Is he really the best qualified?" asked Gertrude.

"If Herbert Segal's work matters, he's the only one even remotely qualified," said Carol.

"I don't suppose there's anything we can hold over him to make him behave," said Gertrude.

"Not really," said Terez Iwakami, Chief of Security at General Density. "After you've done time on a morals charge..."

"I guess it could be worse," said Gertrude.

"Better an employee who gets bombed on company property than one who sets bombs on company property?" A smile briefly realigned the wrinkles on Terez's brown face.

"All right," said Gertrude. "My blood pressure's been under control the last six months. It's a product that's needed, and we need a product.

If we find anyone better we can always let him go. Offer him a contract. Promise him all the data analysts he can justify."

"Better offer housing too," said Carol.

"Oh yes," said Gertrude. "What is this refrigerator business?"

"That's where he's living," said Carol.

"What do you mean?" said Gertrude.

Terez smiled again. "Would it be fair to list his current occupation as full-time wino?"

"Yes," Carol answered, "that would be accurate. He panhandles till he has enough for a bottle, then he drinks. If he doesn't pass out someplace else first, he sleeps in an abandoned refrigerator."

Gertrude shook her head and tapped a data cartridge case labeled, Teresticu, A. "Do the brilliant ones have to be crazy?"

"No," said Terez, "but it helps."

Two days passed before Carol found Agamemnon again. Some teenagers had beaten him up. The damage was minor, but colorful.

"Thanks for the coffee," said Agamemnon after signing the contract. Carol was relieved that he read it all the way through first. "I was getting a little tired of this neighborhood anyhow."

Carol looked around. Agamemnon sat on his derelict refrigerator. Carol could smell him from where she stood, four meters away. The rest of the vacant lot held a miscellany of trash and weeds. The door of a roofless building creaked in the light, midmorning breeze. The door had a sign on it that read, "Condemned. Unsafe. Keep Out. City Of Galileo, Chitina County, Province of Alaska."

Gertrude Querchansky was Associate Professor of Botany at Chitina District University when she quit to found General Density. The research that induced her to start the company was in frost protection for crops. Her first successful products turned out to be pharmaceuticals, but her research was successful, and Ice Caps eventually went into production too. The way Ice Caps altered the density of cell walls in several kinds of plants increased the degree to which the heat in the plants' cells functioned as a single unit. In some species, especially beans, frost tolerance was increased by as much as four degrees for several hours.

The original problem that had set Gertrude onto the subject of frost protection was still central to her interests. Three centuries of apparent climate stability feels like forever, but the Bering Land Bridge of Gertrude's world was not the result of an Ice Age. It was the aftereffect of two years of continuous precipitation caused by the dust cloud a stupid war once produced. A useful product didn't have to make you rich. It just had to make enough to keep you in business while you developed more. Ice Caps taught Gertrude that. It also provided Gertrude the capital to tackle something bigger while its namesake shrank.

Gertrude knew some people considered her business philosophy stodgy, but it had paid off a mortgage and put three kids through the University. We don't all need to be a Samantha Balthazar, Gertrude thought, building an empire and then disappearing with Herbert Segal, a crazy genius if there ever was one, on what was almost surely a fatally flawed attempt at faster than light travel.

Was it a failure though? And, far more pertinent, kook though he may have been, was Herbert Segal onto something that might have usable application? The work that immediately preceded the famous disappearance lay sealed somewhere in the vaults of Samantha Balthazar's vast business empire, still mighty if less inspired without her. There was public record of Herbert Segal's earlier work though. Gertrude knew just enough to believe his basic research into the structure of matter held promise, both useful and profitable, in her more practical realm.

Carol Kaprinov could hardly believe Agamemnon was the same man when they converged in Gertrude's office a mere four days later. Carol had her doubts about Agamemnon's blood alcohol level, but the transformation wrought by clothes that had been neither slept nor vomited in and a hair brush was little short of miraculous. Agamemnon had curly dark hair, balding in the middle but only beginning to grey. Somewhat short and barrel chested, he was not a particularly attractive man, but today he was a completely presentable one. Amazing what an improvement a forgettable appearance can be, Carol thought.

"There are advantages, of course," said Gertrude, indicating an orange area of the map on the table, nearly half of which was crosshatched. "The Maritimes will have a growing season." The orange area, labeled Quebec, included most of what was once Eastern Canada and the Northeastern

United States. Population, if, extremely sparse, was a lot larger than that of the tundra and glaciers which now covered the former Ontario and Manitoba. "But the Chad Sea could dry up completely." Gertrude pointed to a violet region on the map, in North Central Africa, that consisted of a shallow sea with meandering shoreline, surrounded by some of the most productive and densely populated land of her time.

"The time scale is at least plausible," said Agamemnon, "but to do any good…"

"Doing any good isn't the same as saving everybody," said Gertrude. "World population dropped sixty-five percent between 1997 and 2025. The indigenous population of the Western Hemisphere dropped eighty percent between 1500 and 1800. The population of Europe dropped fifty percent between 1350 and 1450. None of those was the end of the world. I'm not going to worry about all humanity's problems. Let's just see if we can help on some of them."

"Ever wonder what it's all for?" Agamemnon asked.

"Certainly," said Gertrude. "I wonder where my grandchildren are going to live when Galileo has nineteen sunny days a year and turnips are hard-put to mature too."

"What if the Bering Dike goes through?" said Carol. "If the Arctic waters can be help up enough to keep the Japan Current inshore, we might actually end up with a better climate. Population pressure alone won't be enough to raise urgency really high in our lifetimes."

"So the Low-G Metabolic Stabilizer has not only got to work," said Agamemnon. "It's got to work cheap."

"Reasonably," said Gertrude. "General Density needs products that pay the power bill. It doesn't need to buy us all palaces."

"Fair enough," Agamemnon replied. "How about sending me up for a look?"

"Justify it," said Carol.

"I've never been in an asteroid mine."

"So what?"

"He's right," said Gertrude. "There was a mask designed once that was one hundred percent effective preventing silicosis, but the company that made them went broke anyhow. It was uncomfortable and obstructed the miners' vision. They would take the masks off as soon as an inspector was out of sight."

Since Agamemnon didn't own anything except the clothes General Density had provided him, packing was simple. He was on the moon shuttle the next afternoon. Agamemnon watched the Earth shrink below him for a few minutes and then settled down to read Gertrude's report, funding proposal really.

The two billion people left after the millennial crash had grown to nearly seven billion in the three and a half centuries since. Space colonies could relieve at least some of the pressure. Asteroids were the cheapest place to mine the materials to build the space colonies. The big problem was gravity. That is, the lack thereof.

You could create an artificial gravity by spinning a space colony. No cost-effective way had yet been devised to provide asteroid miners enough gravity. Without it, your body reabsorbed its own bones. The rest of your metabolism eventually went to hell too.

"Hazards are high. Wages are shit. And no one's gonna protest cause the company just manages to stay in business."

It was a month later. Agamemnon drained his fourth Grand Canal. Martian beer was the best available on the Iron Maiden of The Asteroids, Ima for short. It is nice to be able to drink the best beer around, Agamemnon thought. "So why'd you sign on?" he asked.

Bernadette Devlin, Agamemnon's drinking companion, smiled. He liked that. She had grey eyes and dimples. "How else is a working stiff gonna get to space?"

Suddenly the innocuous background music Agamemnon had barely noticed was replaced by an urgent voice. "Don't let it happen again!" The voice was male, young, and achingly sincere. There were a few moments of static. Then the woes-of-love song sighed back on.

"What was that?" said Agamemnon.

"Creety," said Bernadette. "Spoiled brat." She glared momentarily, then grinned. "They put on a pretty good show though, and they buy power from us retail."

The voice broke through again. "We nearly destroyed the Earth once. We're wounding Her again. What are you doing to the Mother's children?"

"Oog," said Agamemnon. "Ghastly Cosmology."

"Pardon?" Bernadette cocked her head.

"I have a Poo-E-D in Theology, you know," said Agamemnon.

"I'll be damned," said Bernadette. "So what's wrong with his line..." she pointed towards the floor, which was also the outer wall of the Iron Maiden Of The Asteroids, major mill and R and R station, "...besides being pea-brained crap?"

"Allowing for poetic imagery and primitive technology, most traditional Cosmologies are remarkably accurate," Agamemnon explained. "The asteroids are no more Earth's offspring than I am yours."

"I had any offspring ugly as you, I'd space 'em," said Bernadette.

Agamemnon sighed inwardly. Another woman who just wants to be friends, he thought. "How do you handle tailings?" he asked.

"Bond them together so we don't foul the spaceways, and set them back in as close an orbit to the original as we can," said Bernadette. "There may be side effects to rearranging the Solar System's mass that someone will have to deal with eventually, but it'll be a *long* time."

Agamemnon shook his head and ordered them both another Grand Canal. "Let me try out this scenario on you: You work the same number of hours a year. Instead of bust ass forty days, a high-priced space ride five days at each end, and sixty days here, you get real weekends with the local crews, and your take home triples."

"How about families?" asked Bernadette. She was Vice President of Driller's Local 17, one of the consortium of unions that owned the Iron Maiden Of The Asteroids. Her opinion represented a substantial constituency.

"We'll probably get the Metabolic Stabilizer approved for workers on birth control at least a couple years before pregnant women and children," said Agamemnon, "but I'm looking for something safe. I won't tolerate less, and neither will General Density. If you build small gross refining plants with housing the first couple years, they'll pay for themselves in reduced mass you'll have to kick up here, they'll provide some gravity, and you'll have power to sell. I can have figures for you on what it costs if you see your families every three days, every night, whatever."

"Most workers'll want to come up here to visit Ima once in a while," said Bernadette, "especially the single ones."

"I can run figures on any option you want," said Agamemnon. "It's your money. Up to you how you spend it."

"Okay," said Bernadette. "I think it'll likely go, you convince the rank and file it doesn't give anyone three-headed grandchildren."

"Hmph!" Agamemnon snorted, "no spirit of innovation."

"Think you can get your boss to pay for a poll?" asked Bernadette.

"It's market research to General Density," said Agamemnon. "Gotta know how much of what anyone'll buy. We can provide ballots, descriptive literature and tabulation. How about you handle the actual poll at regular Union meetings."

"I'll take it up at the next Executive Council," said Bernadette.

Carol Kaprinov was impressed. "He's one smart drunk," she said to her boss.

The pine paneling imparted a warm glow to Gertrude Querchansky's office. Moderate and even sunny as Galileo's present climate was, the northern winter was on its way, with its long hours of chill and darkness. Carol kept her own office light and functional, but she liked the warmth of Gertrude's.

"Yes," said Gertrude, "I ought to pay him a bonus for giving us such clear budget parameters."

"Buy him a bottle of Armagnac de Timbuktu," said Terez Iwakami.

"Really?" said Carol.

"Charge records show Xanthippe used to buy him a bottle every Easter."

"That doesn't mean he liked it," observed Gertrude.

"There's no record of his disliking alcohol in any form," said Carol.

"Data analysts it is then," said Gertrude. "If he comes up with something that makes five year tours with families safe for all concerned, we're going to be rich."

"If he comes up with something that makes real population resettlement practical…" said Carol, her eyes a little starry.

"Then we are playing craps," said Terez, "with governments for dice."

"Sure wish we could get our hands on Herbert Segal's research notes," said Gertrude to Agamemnon at the meeting he was asked to in her office the next day.

"I've heard they're to be unsealed twenty years after the disappearance," said Agamemnon.

"I've heard the same thing," Gertrude replied. "That's just about when I hope to retire."

"It might not matter anyhow," Agamemnon retorted. "The hyperspace drive was based on the principle of making the forces that hold atoms together directional."

"You know?!" Gertrude's mouth dropped open.

"Sure," said Agamemnon. "He did all the basic calculations on the U.'s power."

"Do you know what that information's worth?" Gertrude queried.

"Not much if it kills you," Agamemnon answered.

"We don't know what happened to them," said Gertrude. "Maybe the hyperspace drive did work, and they just didn't look close enough for black holes in their path."

"And maybe hyperspace travel turns into time travel and they'll show up in a thousand years," said Agamemnon. "I'm thinking in a different direction anyhow. As you said right off, it's Dr. Segal's basic studies of the structure of the atom that we'll want to apply. What makes an atom more or less likely to stick to the next one? Scale each process down: Biology analyzed as chemistry. Chemistry analyzed as subatomic physics."

"Then bring it back up without killing the organism," said Gertrude.

"Or producing three-headed grandchildren," added Agamemnon. "That's a major concern of the Unions."

Gertrude sighed. "I've always said what counts in business is making enough money to stay in business, but it would be nice to live long enough to be rich."

"You could have yourself frozen a few decades," said Agamemnon. "Early returns could pay that well."

"That's ghoulish," Gertrude growled. "The great-grandchildren usually resent it too."

"Where's Marduk when we need him?" said Agamemnon.

"Freud?" said Gertrude.

"No, he used Oedipus," said Agamemnon, "and his psychology was better than his mythology. Marduk killed Tiamat, his mother, a devouring sea monster. Babylonian."

"Ah," said Gertrude. "Tell me. I know how you got from theology to physics to, er, a refrigerator, but I have been wondering why."

"The refrigerator's cause I like to drink," said Agamemnon.

Gertrude kept pushing: "No big traumas in your life?"

"Plenty," Agamemnon answered, "most caused by alcohol. But I drink because I like it."

"How about theology and physics?" asked Gertrude in hope that might be a topic on which Agamemnon was more willing to expose himself.

"They're the same subject," said Agamemnon. "Read Pythagoras, or Newton or Mindell."

"Azgordze too." Practical as her own interests were, Gertrude could appreciate the metaphysical priorities of many of those who contributed basic knowledge and ideas to science. Gertrude smiled broadly. Then her face firmed. "But how do you plan to approach our subject?"

"Cell walls and secretions to begin with," said Agamemnon. "That's probably where we'll apply our answer. But I'll have to dig into the DNA too and who knows what else. Something in there's telling the whole body how much bone to have."

"How many data analysts do you want?" Gertrude asked.

"Don't know yet," said Agamemnon. "Probably won't know. First thing I need to do is check out what results we're looking for. That's straight calculation. How to get it once we know what we want... ? When you don't know what you're looking for, the more eyes the better."

"Or if it exists," Carol interjected.

"Business requires risk," said Gertrude. "It's miraculous how many problems do have solutions."

"There's an explanation why that's true," said Agamemnon.

"Oh?" said Carol.

"You've heard of the Entropy/Creation Cycle, haven't you," said Agamemnon.

"Your not a Creator of The Universe geek, are you?" asked Carol.

"A Creety?" said Agamemnon. "I was Orthodox before they defrocked me for precipitous zeal with the sacrament."

"How's that?" Carol asked.

Gertrude laughed. "Weren't your family Orthodox?"

"Once upon a time, I suppose," Carol replied.

"The zeon represents the Apostles' zeal," said Gertrude. "It's added to the wine for communion."

"What is it?" asked Carol.

"Water," said Agamemnon. "I didn't want the wine to be missed. Mythologically, it's the Trickster."

"Watering the holy wine?" said Gertrude.

"You wound me unjustly!" Agamemnon, who had been sitting at the edge of his big, comfortable armchair, leaped back, dramatically clasping his hands to his breast. Then he grinned and relaxed. "The fact entropy turns around to Creation."

"There has always been an element of faith in business," said Gertrude.

"Come again?" said Carol.

"Certainly," said Gertrude. "Faith that you can get there from here."

"What's that about the Trickster?" Carol asked.

"Symbolic representation of how playing around with things you don't understand leads to an increase in consciousness and a more ordered Universe," said Agamemnon.

"I'd think it would just lead to getting hurt," said Carol.

"Oh that too," said Agamemnon. "You heard Coyote stories when you were a kid, didn't you?"

"Sure," said Carol.

"He was always getting his tail in a crack," said Agamemnon, "but he usually came out having learned something."

"How do we know... ?" said Carol.

"That it'll work?" said Gertrude. "We don't, but things do work often enough it's worth trying. If there's a way to stay healthy in low-G, someone's going to find it, and that someone is going to make money. I want that someone to be General Density. What do you think, Agamemnon?"

"Something tells our bodies to generate the density of bone that keeps us healthy. All we have to do is find what it is."

So Agamemnon cranked out data. He had it arrange itself in categories by any recognizable pattern and also a category for any unique phenomena that produced survivable effect. There was no easy, cheap answer inherent in the data itself. No one expected there to be, though you could always hope. They weren't looking for anything the human body was doing though. They were looking for something the human body didn't do and which therefore did not exist to produce any data, but which could be induced to exist from what did.

Some viruses, spores, and exotic life-forms seemed to be virtually unaffected through innumerable generations by the absence of gravity. Agamemnon thought this information might be useful when it came time to test for safety through the reproductive process, but virus and spore viability did not transfer workably to human beings. The same life-forms that didn't mind zero-G for decades at a time—or fifty-G—also usually didn't mind or even notice extreme temperature variations, or need air, or had something that was essential to their metabolism but lethal to ours.

"Something's fishy," said Carol several months later. Tension always built in Galileo's long, dark winter. A conscientious professional made it a habit to discount possible paranoia. With the increasing light of late February, Carol decided she had given Agamemnon long enough to dispel her suspicions if he was going to.

"He's not misappropriating funds, is he?" asked Terez.

"He's accounted for every credit," said Carol, "unless you call liquid lunches misappropriation."

"Have you said anything to him about that?" asked Gertrude.

"Sure," said Carol. "I reminded him he promised to come to work sober when he took the job."

"What did he say?"

"He gave me that wounded look and said he hadn't had a beer before morning coffee break and nothing stronger before noon since he started here."

Gertrude glanced Heavenward. Terez laughed, but became serious again rapidly. "What's fishy then?"

"I don't know," Carol answered. "It's not money. He's got everyone he can corral trying to see something useful in that swamp of data he's slogging around in, including the cleaning crews, but that's saving us money—if it makes any sense at all."

"He could be just distracted," said Gertrude. "That's a chance you take with anyone brilliant, even if they don't drink. He could just chase down how everything connects to everything and never even remember we need products."

"I don't think that's it," said Carol. "He's looking for something specific. I'm just not sure it's the same thing we're looking for."

"Guess I better start categorizing some data myself," said Terez.

More weeks passed. Agamemnon reported progress, futility, more progress, more futility. His reports were entirely relevant, but now she was looking, Gertrude had to agree. They were off-center. What Agamemnon told her was about the Low-G Metabolic Stabilizer she wanted. He also noted several gratuitous potential products. For instance, he discovered an enzyme, and what triggered it, that retarded the spoilage of milk in low gravity. He was looking for something else though. "What do you think?" said Gertrude.

"I don't know what to think." Terez scratched his right temple. His office had wood paneling too, but darker than Gertrude's. The rich, blue oriental carpet, and the clean lines of the few small wooden carvings lent the office an atmosphere Gertrude enjoyed. She found it serene. She would not choose it to work in herself, and she could understand why it actually irritated Carol. It was perfect for Terez. Company security never needed a heavy hand to be effective.

"It could be legitimate," said Gertrude. "Sometimes what you're looking for is an example of some bigger category, so you study the bigger category and then tailor your results to the specific instance you need."

"I suppose," said Terez, "but he hasn't told us that. If what he's doing is to the point—or even innocuous, you'd think he would give us some explanation."

"He could just be avoiding preconceptions that might prevent someone from noticing something," Gertrude suggested.

"No reason not to tell us," said Terez.

Gertrude called Agamemnon and Carol in. She let Terez speak. He could be to the point without confronting roughly as Carol might. Terez put the question directly but gently. By smiling just slightly and making but not holding eye contact, he kept it a touch rather than a blow. "Just what is the current focus of your research, Agamemnon?"

"Oh," Agamemnon blushed. Nearly oblivious to his physical surroundings, he was extremely sensitive to people. "I thought it was obvious. I'm looking at different densities we are known to live at."

"What others are there?" asked Carol.

"Dreams, before birth, and after death," Agamemnon answered quite matter-of-factly.

"Are you sure they exist?" Carol's voice was quiet, but her expression was all thunder.

"I'm not sure I exist," said Agamemnon, "but probability is high. If we do live in other conditions, we do it in some way. There's lots of evidence, with enough consistency to infer some plausible objective..."

"Nonsense," Carol snapped. "Consistency in wish-fulfillment fantasy's still wish-fulfillment fantasy."

"We don't need all the answers," said Gertrude. "We just need answers that work." Her face told Carol to let the matter drop.

"Yes," said Agamemnon. "That's it." He was visibly excited.

He stayed that way too. The research went on. It looked promising, but cost was mounting. The budget was still reasonable if they got a product. If they didn't though... Gertrude tried to avoid thinking about that.

Terez snooped till he was afraid he was going to become obvious and offend Agamemnon. He couldn't find any evidence that Agamemnon was sabotaging the research to prolong it. Agamemnon may have been conceptualizing theologically, but he was studying cell structure and function systematically. Terez didn't know what to think. The research seemed legitimate, but it wasn't getting anywhere useful. Yet Agamemnon seemed awfully happy.

"Maybe he's just pleased to be living in an apartment again instead of a refrigerator," said Carol.

"Wouldn't blame him for that," said Terez, "but he is looking for something else. I have nightmares about DNA viruses that do give you three-headed babies eight generations down the line."

Gertrude turned to Carol. "Now you see what gives senior executives high blood pressure. Just think what you have to look forward to."

"Should we stop him?" Carol asked.

"He might be doing something benign," said Terez.

"Maybe even something useful," said Gertrude. "We hired him to find something we didn't know where to look for."

Gertrude stopped in at Agamemnon's office later that same day. Wood paneled and well-lit as it was the day Gertrude assigned it to Agamemnon, he had added not a stitch of personal decoration. Gertrude put the question point blank. "What are you looking for?"

"It's the between-lives state," Agamemnon answered—blurted really. Gertrude could feel his tension, which her bluntness had broken through. "Whatever we are not only doesn't require gravity. It doesn't even require a body."

"Why do you call it the between-lives state?" asked Gertrude.

"One of the major ways to interpret the body of evidence is that we have repeated incarnations," said Agamemnon.

"Sure," said Gertrude, somewhat frustrated as the wall of intellect closed again over the still-murky sea of Agamemnon's real motivation, "but is that relevant?"

"It might be," said Agamemnon. "If there is some other way of being we pass through and return from repeatedly with any continuity at all it could give us a pattern, an hypothesis to test."

"Sounds like rank mysticism on company time," said Gertrude.

"Got a better suggestion?" asked Agamemnon.

"I hoped you would," said Gertrude.

"When I've got an hypothesis to test, I can set up rational parameters," Agamemnon said. "At this stage, you might as well write down your dreams."

"That feels like the sort of thing you do the night before the creditors auction off your desk," said Gertrude. "Surely you're not that desperate."

"I'm not desperate at all," said Agamemnon. "We haven't even looked at enough data to prioritize yet."

Gertrude thought about this. Agamemnon's methodology was sound even if his investigations extended in somewhat outlandish directions. She shrugged.

Gertrude's daughter, Illania, was an art therapist. There was a whole history of useful breakthroughs Illania could recite that had come to someone while doodling. "Science is how you apply patterns," Illania once said, "but art is where you discover them."

Not only is he a drunk, Gertrude thought, but he believes in reincarnation. Why do the brilliant ones have to be crazy?

"Are you sure reincarnation doesn't exist?" Terez asked Gertrude later in her office. Crocuses and a few daffodils spotted the green lawn outside her big east window. "Reincarnation is quite as traditional in my church as salvation is in yours."

Gertrude wasn't sure whether to laugh or groan. "Maybe we should advertise seminars," she sputtered. "The General Density School of Theology. Something's got to pay for the research."

"I'd call it philosophy," said Terez.

"And the alchemists called themselves natural philosophers. You can be high priest of this church. I'll paint icons."

"Sorry," said Terez. "You knew he was a nut when you hired him."

"I knew he was a drunk, not a kook," said Gertrude. "Does he even know what product is?"

"People's lives depended on the mining equipment he used to maintain," said Terez.

"You know what bothers me," said Gertrude. "I still don't think he gave me a straight answer. I asked him what he was looking for, but he told me what he was studying. That's not the same thing."

Gertrude remained concerned, Carol suspicious, Terez puzzled. A few weeks later, Agamemnon had a major breakthrough. It was not the product General Density hired him to find, but it was a product, and one that could be put on the market without anywhere near the testing expense of the Metabolic Stabilizer.

One of the data analysts pointed out to Agamemnon that specialized cells in tree roots and leaves reacted differently to changes in air pressure. There was some anomalous data. When Agamemnon examined this data more closely, he discovered it was associated with changes in ground pressure, which turned out to correlate, with astounding precision, to imminent earthquakes and volcanic activity. The market was limited, but the new measuring tool General Density would be able to market had a potential to cover the majority of Agamemnon's research costs for several years.

Gertrude very much hoped it would not be too many years. She wanted still to be around to see the Low-G Metabolic Stabilizer go into production. Maybe she couldn't expect to profit from major colonization of space or even to live long enough to see it. The Metabolic Stabilizer wasn't as flashy a solution as a hyperspace drive, but Gertrude cherished the aspiration to make a major contribution to humanity's future.

Prototype Earth Pressure Gauges had order inquiries coming in within a few months. By the time he had worked for General Density a year, Agamemnon's work was very nearly paying for itself. Gertrude felt she could relax, though she remained frustrated at the lack of real progress on the Metabolic Stabilizer. Then Terez came in with another odd piece of information.

"I got to thinking," Terez said, "his hanky panky with the wine was sacrilege, but if every priest that stole communion wine got the sack… I wondered if there was something else. Prejudice, maybe. He was serving a mostly Russian congregation. Not everyone approves of the consolidation of Eastern Orthodoxy."

"Oh, yes," said Gertrude. "I remember my grandfather arguing with one of his buddies about whether it was neighborly getting along or Romish centralization. You think he's got some secret resentment?"

"Not over that," said Terez, "but I do think there was some theological dispute that got his bishop upset."

"Could you ask the bishop about it?" said Gertrude.

"Afraid not," Terez replied. "He passed away over ten years ago."

"Is there anyone you could ask?"

"I've been looking. I haven't found anyone yet."

"Tried Xanthippe?" Gertrude suggested.

"She said to get the hell out of her life and that if her husband and children ever even learned that worthless drunk existed she'd sue me and whoever I worked for for invasion of privacy and trying to break up her family."

And then a day came when Agamemnon found what they were looking for. The Eustachian canals—the channels between the ears and the nasal passages—turned out to be the key. They were where the essential sensors in the human body were most developed. An early bonus of the discovery was a ninety-three percent effective space sickness remedy.

The Low-G Metabolic Stabilizer was on its way, and Agamemnon was making General Density a profit. Gertrude was delighted.

Agamemnon was pretty happy himself. "Guess that means I don't have to go back to the refrigerator," he said.

"I'll hire someone to change your diapers if that's what it takes," said Gertrude. "You've earned it. But I hope you'll want to stay coherent enough to keep on with the research."

"I don't know about staying coherent," said Agamemnon. "But I certainly want to keep on with the research. Only, I want some say in what we study."

"I'm always open to new products," said Gertrude.

"This isn't a product," said Agamemnon. "You might make money off something I find, but it's not why I'm looking."

"Why are you looking, anyhow?" Gertrude asked. "We've been trying to figure that out as long as you've been here."

"You won't just think I'm too weird to work for you?" Agamemnon asked.

"I'm in business to make a living," said Gertrude. "I like to do something useful, and I wouldn't mind a bit being rich before I die; but so long as the books tally and you're not practicing human sacrifice, you can be as weird as you like."

"I offended someone once," said Agamemnon. "It cost me a respectable position and a marriage."

"I thought that was your drinking," said Gertrude, though Terez had convinced her long ago that there was something else.

"I drink so I can stand it here," said Agamemnon. "Didn't learn to be sociable till I worked at the sawmill. Xanthippe and Bishop Basil both called me negative, said I saw everything backwards."

"Do you find a conventional life so unpleasant?" said Gertrude.

"I don't mind that at all," said Agamemnon. "Never did. Never meant much to me one way or the other."

Gertrude could well-enough believe that. Agamemnon's office—and his clothes—showed signs of neither abuse nor interest. Something was important to Agamemnon though. Gertrude could see him wrestling inwardly with himself. He's certainly an odd duck, she thought, but she had grown fond of him. She knew he still drank. Yet he worked consistently and conscientiously. She knew the products she wanted, to feel her life was worthwhile as much as to keep General Density profitable, were only marginally significant to him. But he did pay sufficient attention to the practical potential of his research to develop products. Gertrude felt a sense of warmth, even of achievement now when Agamemnon at last found it in himself to trust her with what really mattered most to him.

"It's being in a body at all I find hard," Agamemnon finally explained. He waved his right arm in a passionate if awkward gesture, then touched his chest above his heart. "Density. Different conditions in which we might… might be. That's why I said yes when Carol offered me the job."

"I thought you said yes to get out of the refrigerator and not get beat up again," said Gertrude, not wanting to deprecate his need, but at the same time slightly embarrassed by it.

"That too, of course," said Agamemnon. "But there was something I wanted. And I hope you'll let me have some funding for it."

"You keep finding products," said Gertrude, "I don't know why not, but what is it?"

"You see," said Agamemnon, "what I have always wanted to know is why do so many of you prefer this dense condition we live in while we've got physical bodies when I think I remember liking the state we're in between lives a whole lot better. Density. It seemed like a way to approach both our questions."

"You and Pythagoras," said Gertrude. "Physics and metaphysics."

"Why not?" Agamemnon replied. "They are the same subject."

"So long as the byproducts keep us in business," said Gertrude, "no reason at all."

Author's note: A production of my script, The Belle of The Turquoise Hotel, *at the Mineshaft Tavern, in Madrid, New Mexico, occasioned my spending more time than usual around a bar. The brother of one of the owners, who was visiting, and who I met pushing a broom, at first appeared to me just to be an aging barfly. But he actually was a world renowned rocket ship designer.*

PIÑONS

"Let us reason together," said Ray Salisbury to the ground squirrels in general. "If you continue to eat all the lettuce, I will shoot you. Neither one of us will like that. So EAT SOMETHING ELSE FOR A CHANGE."

The only ground squirrel in sight was sitting up very straight, staring intently at a rock on the other side of the canyon.

The ground squirrel twitched its tail three times. "Cheep," it said.

"Cheep," said Ray back.

"Cheep," said the ground squirrel again.

"Cheep," answered Ray.

The ground squirrel turned to Ray. All of a sudden, it realized what it was talking with and dashed off chittering. Ray laughed, then clumped back up to the house with the two buckets of water he had filled at the well.

Soon Ray heard the mail truck coming. He needed to buy a book of stamps, so he walked out to meet it.

"Want to buy a paper?" asked Andrea Holguin. She had been driving the eighty-mile-long rural route for twenty-five years. The route to Dust Devil, Cowflop, and San Gordo used to run six days a week; now it was just two. Mondays she also turned west to Ocotillo Mesa. Thursdays, she brought the mail up Cyanide Canyon where Ray had lived on a worthless gold claim the past seventeen years. If Ray and Andrea both felt sociable at once they razzed each other about getting grey.

"No," said Ray today. "Don't guess I will. I haven't finished the last one."

Andrea headed on up the canyon. Ray spread his mail on the leprous hood of his ancient blue Ford pickup and looked through it. The usual solicitations to buy things he had no place for and could not afford would renew the firestarter pile. Ray also had two letters.

The one from Ray's friend, Water Bowl, turned out to be a photocopied poster on lilac paper. The picture showed tipis and stars and a bunch of people holding hands in a circle. It read: "RAINBOW RENEWAL. June 9–13. Paradise Hot Springs." Water Bowl had added a note: "Overflowing. Danger. Unity heals."

The second letter was from Ray's niece, Gwen, in New York:

Dear Uncle Ray,

Apogee is sleeping through the night now. Dad and Mom are coming in June 15–23 to meet their new granddaughter. Bill and I would love to have you too. Here's a voucher on our cash account for gas and four meals. Travel on the 14th if you can. My astrologer says inflation should be at its lowest all month that day. My tube account # is 709-AH4-730. Your ticket # is 00267-139-96. They'll hold it till the 20th, but I hope you can be here the whole time Dad and Mom are here. Don't forget your ID You'll need it for the ticket.

Love you.

Gwen, Bill and Apogee.

Ray had not been much of anywhere in six months. He had not seen his family in more than a year.

Ray walked back up to the house, smiling, and turned on the computer he ran off photovoltaic-charged batteries. The TRIPS file had a permanent note in it: "Bring fatso pants. You put on thirty-five pounds the last time." This was not true, but Ray usually did fill his biggest pants by the end of a trip to the city. He now made a short list:

Garden Waterer

Piñons

The piñon trees on the ridges above Cyanide Canyon had produced a crop last year, something they did not do all that often. Ray figured he could squeeze at least twenty pounds of piñon nuts into his bag. They were the best bet he had to import a little money home from New York.

That night, a golden eagle soared through Ray's dream. The magnificent bronze bird circled towards him, each round a little closer to earth, searching for a place to land.

In the morning, Ray walked half a mile down the canyon to the home of his neighbors, Alice and Andy Optimer.

"Coffee's fresh," Andy sang out in greeting.

Julio Zapata, another neighbor, was there too. "I got Ma sending my chaps. It's all mesquite out there," he was saying.

"Howdy Andy, Al, Julio," said Ray. "What's happening?"

"Goin' on gathering for Doc Weatherbee," said Andy. "Might have room for you too if you need a job."

"What's he payin'?" asked Ray.

"Seven hundred bucks a day. Inflation stays over a hundred percent for a week it goes up to seven fifty."

"That cheapskate," said Ray.

"Al might hire on too as cook." Andy nodded at his wife.

"Now that's not such a bad deal."

"You're just fishin' for an invite to breakfast," said Alice with a grin.

"Now Al…" said Ray.

"You're invited anyhow," Alice added.

"Round up them cows!" Julio whooped.

"When you start gathering?" asked Ray.

"Day after tomorrow."

"Hmh, I'd have to scare up a horse and a pair of chaps. I'm too old for ground crew."

"You're just squeamish about castratin'," Andy said, grinning.

"I do hate gettin' all covered with blood," said Ray. "But what I'm squeamish about is gettin' kicked in my rapidly aging knees."

"I hear you there," said Andy. "What are you up to?"

"Lookin' for a ride to the hot springs next month."

"What's goin' on there?" asked Alice.

"Little Rainbow Gathering on their way to the big one."

"You still hangin' out with them loony tunes?" asked Andy.

"Water Bowl's coming."

"Oh?" said Alice. "Gee. If the gas can be had, maybe she'd like to come up here for a few days after. I'd love to see her."

"Maybe," said Ray, "But I'm hoping to get her to take me to the tube at Albuturkey. My niece in New York had a baby, and she's buying me a ticket to come see them."

"Wow!" said Alice. "Congratulations."

"New York!" Andy shook his head. "That'll be a trip!"

"Oh yeah," said Ray. "She sent me gas vouchers too."

"Oh yeah?" Julio was suddenly interested. "When you wanta go to the hot springs?"

Rural people got enough gas ration stamps for the long distances they often had to cover—almost. No one had much cash, though. Free market vouchers were good as gold.

"How 'bout the ninth."

"Yer on. Maybe I'll catch me a little Rainbow filly."

"One track mind," said Andy.

"Ah, youth," said Ray.

Paradise Hot Springs bubbled up in the Adobe River Valley, two miles north of San Gordo and about thirty miles from Ray's home in Cyanide Canyon. The Adobe River ran eight inches deep and fifteen feet wide most of the year. It was the only piece of water big enough to be called a river in eighty miles.

When Ray and Julio arrived they found ten dilapidated vehicles parked in the brilliant high desert sunshine. Some ran on gas. Some used more esoteric fuels, such as wood chips or cow chips. Water Bowl's "Buffalo Buggy" hunkered among them. It was a hybrid of General Motors' concept of a personal rocket ship and a prairie schooner fabricated from industrial waste. Several horses also stood tethered in the shade of a sycamore grove.

Ray spotted Water Bowl in a circle of fifteen or twenty women of all ages. The women held hands and danced slowly, singing about a river in the desert and a great blue heron who lived there. Several children around the circle listened and joined in on the chorus. Four men stood off to one side talking. Two of them held babies. Most of the people were naked.

Julio ogled the circle of women eagerly. Several were young and good looking.

"Mind your manners," Ray said quietly. "They're friendly if you behave yourself, but they'll tear a man limb from limb that gets fresh."

Julio blushed and grinned.

Ray recognized one of the men near the circle and headed over to say hello. Before he got there, a ten-year-old girl, naked and tanned from head to toe, rushed into his arms. Ray picked her up and spun her around in a big hug.

"Ray, you made it! Grandma said you would."

"Aster, good to see you," said Ray as he set her down.

Water Bowl noticed them and slipped out of the circle to join them. Soon Ray got naked too. The three of them reclined in the steaming water.

"Whooee!" said Water Bowl. "New York! You certainly are calm."

"Didn't nobody drop a bomb on me or slit my throat the last time," said Ray.

"You been keeping up with the news on Brazil?"

"Sure. I read a paper just last week."

"Oh, they were still arguing about Uruguay then."

"What'd they do, divvy it up?"

"Nah," said Water Bowl. "Chile convinced Brazil and Argentina both to leave it alone and use it for a free trade zone. Now all they gotta do is settle on the money. Brazil joins the Alliance, it's gonna be fireworks on the high seas."

"Ah," said Ray, "That war talk's just politicians trying to distract us from the economy mess. Nobody wants another war, and the Alliance can't afford one. They got no credit as is."

"Brazilian small arms and Chilean missiles, they might not need credit," said Water Bowl.

"Don't you believe it," said Ray. "They still gotta eat. I thought they settled on the money. Print it in both Spanish and Portuguese."

"They can't agree whose picture to put on it," said Water Bowl.

"Oh," said Ray.

"Look!" Aster pointed. "An eagle!"

"And there's the other one," said Water Bowl.

Ray looked up. A pair of golden eagles circled just above the bluff across the river. "Think they got a nest over there?" he said.

"Could be."

The eagles coasted round and round, rising steadily, till they disappeared from sight.

"Seen any sheep?" asked Ray.

"Yeah," said Aster. "Huge herd this morning. "I counted eighty."

"Lot of young ones too," added Water Bowl. "Good to see. I was afraid poaching'd be bad."

"Nah," said Ray. "Lose a few, but that bighorn herd's expanded its range every one of the last four years. Harder money gets to come by, the more people give up and move to town to get on the soup lines."

Water Bowl rolled her eyes.

Aster submerged. Water Bowl and Ray did the same. Then they all lay silent in the hot water.

After a while, Ray stood up, slowly. When his head stopped spinning he walked the ten feet to the river, waded in and lay down in a knee-deep pool. In the high desert June sun the river was warm, but still enough colder than the hot spring to be a rush.

Aster and Water Bowl did the same. "Wahoo!" Water Bowl shouted.

Later, over a joint, Ray explained about the piñons. "You got any idea who I ought to take 'em to?"

"Sure do," said Water Bowl. "You remember Alexandra, don't you?"

"Sure. Didn't she and Lucy Saxtabe get together when Lucy broke up with Fred?"

"Yeah."

"They're in New York now?"

"Yeah. Lucy's running a school, and Alex has a little natural foods store on Avenue B."

"Wow. That sounds like the place... But won't I have to get all sorts of inspections and permits and shit to sell them in a store?"

"Oh probably, but Alex'll know how to do it."

Julio had to get back to work in the morning. So Ray used the restaurant vouchers treating him, Water Bowl, and Aster to dinner at the Endurance Café in San Gordo. Restaurant food was a treat for them all, and the proprietors were grateful for the business.

Like any place thick enough for public transportation, Albuquerque bustled. Ray saw more beggars than last time he'd been there, and there had been plenty then; but even the beggars did not look to be starving.

A purposeful throng filled the tube station. Ray boarded a car that would be switched for New York at the new terminal in Arkansas across the river from Memphis. It was easier to travel the twenty-five hundred miles from Albuquerque to New York than the two hundred fifty miles from Cyanide Canyon to Albuquerque.

Following the success of the Dallas-Houston magnetrack, developments in electromagnetic mass transportation had been rapid. Once weight problems were solved, the trains could carry their own field generators and fly like planes, at a sixth the cost. The same electromagnetic field that lifted a train while it followed the track became the instrument of structural integrity when it left the track.

Turbulence had caused some initial problems over the placement and size of wings, but because the electromagnetic field provided most of the structural strength, there was an acceptable range of workable options. Landing and take-off from the electromagnetic cushion was far safer than from a runway. The new tracks in and out of cities followed the old railroad rights of way right to the downtown stations, a huge cost saver. The inconvenience of being inside the magnetic field was minor.

The train rolled up the track in a conventional manner to Waldo, where it picked up a few more cars from Santa Fe. Then the stewardess stood up and gave her safety speech:

"Please turn off all radios, videos and computers during take-off. Anyone using a pacemaker who needs a shield, please press your call button. When the field stabilizes, the captain will turn off the take-off light. In the highly unlikely event of a field failure," she continued, "Bend down, take hold of your knees...."

"And kiss your ass good-bye," growled the jowly businessman next to Ray loudly enough for half the car to hear.

Several people laughed.

The trip was uneventful. At the terminal in Arkansas vendors hawked a variety of goods. Ray opened the window and bought a lunch of black eyed peas and fresh salad.

The New York landing field actually lay in Connecticut. It was raining in the East and very green, despite a lot of dead trees. Cars peeled off both ends of the train, bound for New Haven, Hartford, and various local connections. Then Ray's portion rolled down the tracks to Pennsylvania Station. Bill, the new father, greeted Ray with a hug just outside the security gate.

A man approached them.

"I am not a mugger. 'Xcuse. Let me pass. Thank you. We sleep in the subways. We don't do you any harm. I know a person should earn a living, but we got no jobs and none to be had. So I'm gonna do what I can to entertain you. Anything you can spare for the show will be much appreciated."

The beggar looked to be about thirty-five and healthy. His clothes were tattered and filthy, but he had taken the trouble to tuck in his shirt, and his hair and beard were neatly trimmed.

Bill gave the man a ten dollar food voucher. A few other people did the same. "He may get a meal today," Bill said as the beggar passed down the subway car.

"How do you decide which ones to give to?" asked Ray.

"I start at two o'clock and give to the next five I see. It's a good system. Lots of people do it. It's gotten to where the beggars only do their routines on the hour."

The new grandparents arrived next day. Ray's brother Hugh was forty-four, five years younger than Ray. Hugh and Artichoke (whose name derived from a back-to-the-land movement of her parents' youth) lived on a different planet from Ray—literally. Nonetheless they remained close.

Artichoke was a botanist. Her present job was nursing botanical variety towards ecological self-sufficiency on the new world of Ganymede.

"Looks like I'm finally going to start earning my salary," said Hugh.

"What have you been doing the past three years?" asked Ray.

"Playing shrink to terraforming engineers mostly," said Hugh.

Hugh's professional title read: social psychologist. The Ganymede Project had hired him for his pioneering work in mythography. His work was based on the principle that any society big enough to preclude personal communication between all its members maintains coherence through the unconscious. The patterns, visible in myth and dream become a common vocabulary. But in new or rapidly changing circumstances, there is confusion, called the Tower of Babel Syndrome. Hugh's job was to discover and articulate the emerging myths of the rapidly evolving Ganymede settlement. Hugh was the sort of artist on whose work a science might later be based.

"How's life at the hermitage?" asked Hugh.

"Quieter every year," said Ray.

"Man! Remember what it was like first time we went out there?"

"Dust all weekend. Cliff dwelling was elbow to asshole."

"I read recently there are more horses parked at the Grand Canyon Visitor Center these days than cars," said Artichoke.

"Wouldn't doubt it," said Ray.

Gwen joined them. "Apogee'll sleep a couple hours now."

"Dear, how do I turn off the alarm?" Artichoke asked. "It's such a nice day, I'd love to open a window."

"It's just as well if we don't, Mom," said Gwen. "Bill's asthma."

"Oh, of course."

"We could go for a walk in the park. I know a very reputable agency. Groups leave several times a day."

"That sounds great."

Ray called his old friend Alex that afternoon. Phones were mostly a memory where Ray lived. Line maintenance costs made the base rate prohibitive. At the same time, long-distance rates had become negligible. No one thought twice about calling New York to Albuquerque, and when Ray had bought his tube ticket, his time of arrival had printed out at Gwen and Bill's for no extra charge.

"Good thing you called today," said Alex. "I'm going to be up to my armpits in co-op business the next week or two. You remember Lucy Saxtabe, don't you? We're having lunch; why don't you join us. Bring the piñons. Just remember not to set them down anywhere and you'll be all right. New York's really a pretty safe city. I haven't heard of anyone carrying piñon nuts this year. For twenty-five pounds we won't even bother with the store. I may even be able to find you customers that'll pay in silver."

"Alex, you're a wonder," said Ray.

"We'll meet at the store. One sound good?"

"Sure."

"Between Sixth and Seventh on Avenue B. You know how to find it?"

"I've got a map."

"Good. Oh, and delighted you're in town."

Gwen gave Ray a voucher for ten tokens. "Rumor is they're going up to sixty bucks any day. People are hoarding them. Won't let you buy more than ten at once."

"Look at this," said Lucy at lunch. Ray looked up from his succulent squid and bluefish. Seafood was not something he got to eat at home. Lucy showed him reprints of two articles about the school she ran. The title of the New York Times Magazine piece read, "Education for Adaptability." The one from Urban Ecology was headlined: "Discovering the Future: How Children Learn To Learn in a Changing World."

"Pretty impressive," said Ray.

"And we still can't afford New York rent," said Lucy.

"Where are you located, then?" asked Ray.

"Third African Methodist, bless their hearts. Over on East Fourth. They let us have three rooms six hours a day and twenty minutes for cleanup. Almost eleven hundred square feet, with windows. They aren't even charging us cost."

Alex looked at her watch. "Hate to run off," she said.

"Of course," said Ray. "I'd like to walk back. Can I? My niece lives on West Sixtieth."

"That's a long walk," said Lucy.

"Not for a country boy like me."

"Go straight west to Eighth Avenue. Then north to the park," said Alex. "Only Abandoned Zone's north of here, so you should be okay."

"Four subway stations they've had to seal now," said Lucy. "Can you imagine!?"

"Had to deliver an order of figs at the U.N. last week," said Alex. "It was worse than customs when I came back from Morocco."

Bill's brother, Dave, and Dave's partner, Mercurius, joined the family for dinner that night. Dave and Mercurius had a houseplant shop. Dave was also an aspiring sculptor, working primarily in beaten copper and enamel. Mercurius was an aspiring actor.

Bill worked as a state liaison officer for a license broker serving the construction, waste removal, and automobile repair trades. (This last really meant trucks and taxis. Anyone who could afford a private car in New York could afford a private mechanic whose references would render a license both superfluous and an insult.) Gwen crunched numbers for the city.

"Heard the union's backing down on maternity leave," said Mercurius over the fresh water chestnut soufflé.

"Union backs the mayor's self-respect program," said Gwen. "With Smith Bonding Technique, three months is enough for a baby. You can apply for an extension."

"I guess," said Mercurius. "Nanny subsidy's the way."

"Heard you've got a new show on," said Bill.

"You've got to come," said Mercurius. "I play a corpse, but I haven't noticed I'm dead, and neither has anyone else. We have whole conversations. Never do figure out we're not hearing a word each other says."

"Sounds pretty good," said Bill.

"It's a scream," said Dave.

Everyone thought it would be fun to take in a show. Dave said he would watch Apogee in the Green Room. That way Gwen could go.

"Sandra Litvak's nursing too," said Mercurius. "She's playing a police woman. Tells me to lie parallel to the sidewalk so I don't block traffic. Her shrug when I don't respond's a real show stopper. Be looking for it. She'll be feeding just before curtain."

Next day, Ray, Hugh, and Artichoke went to the Natural History Museum. They were looking at the dinosaurs when Artichoke asked how Ray's visit about the piñons had gone.

"The Lucy Saxtabe?" said Hugh. "The educator?"

"Uh, sure," said Ray.

"That article about her in Urban Ecology was excellent," said Artichoke.

"Sure was different," said Ray. "Lucy's school; Alex running the store… Last time I saw Alex, we were lyin' in the hot spring counting bighorn sheep on the bluff."

"Uh, Ray…" said Hugh.

"Yeah?"

"Do you suppose?… Do you think Ms. Saxtabe might consider a position on the Ganymede Project?"

"You could ask. She'd probably want Alex with her."

"I bet there'd be a place for Alex in Food Distribution Management," said Artichoke.

They got ahold of Lucy that evening.

It was mid September when Ray heard how things turned out.

K'pop.

Ray loaded another short in the single shot twenty-two. Then he walked over to the dead ground squirrel.

"I warned you. I ain't greedy. You can have the pears that drop. You can even have some of the pears on the tree. But I WANT SOME TOO."

Ray clumped back over to his truck and leaned the rifle against a dent. Then he hauled another log off the load and carried it to the growing firewood pile. After a bit he heard the mail truck coming.

"Hear about Julio?" asked Andrea.

"What happened to him?"

"He's getting married."

"I'll be! Who to?"

"Frances Villanueva."

"Villanueva... Don't her folks have a horse ranch just this side of Apex?"

"That's them."

"Well, I'll be."

"Hear tell they're going to set Julio up for breeding."

"Yep," said Ray.

"Here's your mail," said Andrea.

The latest postage increase had not reduced the quantity of junk mail, but it had induced the advertisers to print on smaller sheets of paper. Ray's weekly postal pile also included two letters: one from Water Bowl and one from Alex. Ray opened Water Bowl's first.

A picture showed birds flying all around a rainbow over mountains. The note read: "Have horse; will travel. Equinox Gathering at the Springs. Hope you can come."

Then Ray opened Alex's letter:

> Sure feels different writing to a place where the mail is still delivered physically. I guess it's gonna be even more different soon. We leave for Ganymede in six weeks.
>
> I'm mostly writing to say thank you. This is really the break Lucy's been waiting for. Recognition in the press was nice, but recognition in your work is what counts. We've really enjoyed Hugh and Artichoke on the videophone. Looking forward to meeting them in person.
>
> Thanks again for making it happen.
> love,
> Alex.

Ray finished unloading the firewood and swept the truck bed clean. Then he got a one-and-a-half-gallon plastic bucket and headed down the canyon with that and the rifle. By the time he arrived at Alice and Andy's, blackberries nearly brimmed the bucket, and Ray carried two cleaned tassel-eared squirrels as well.

"Now that's my idea of a neighbor," said Alice. "Invites himself to dinner, but brings something for the pot."

"Hah!" said Andy. "He don't fool me. Fastest nose in the West, Ray is. You just knew I got that new batch of beer ready to sample, didn't you."

"Of course," said Ray.

Over dinner Ray asked, "You know anyone's got a horse I can afford?"

"No," said Andy. "Not unless you're looking to eat 'im. But Pete Bustamante's been saying for two years he wants to put a little herd in the pasture just above you. He's never gonna get around to that fence, and someone's got to break ice in winter. You'd be doing him a favor to exercise them beasts."

"Now that sounds like the kind of horse I can afford," said Ray. "Al, the chicken in this stir fry's great."

"It's not chicken," said Alice.

"Oh?" said Ray.

"It's snattlerake."

"Good snake."

"Heard anything from your niece since you been back?" asked Andy.

"Oh, yeah," said Ray. "She said the nanny's a dear, and she's finally found a brand of milker that doesn't hurt her breasts. She wants to keep nursing another few months."

The moon was a little past full. Ray set out for home just as it crested the eastward bluff. He saw three deer on the road and heard a bull elk bugle. First one of the year.

That night Ray dreamt he was with Water Bowl, Aster, and Artichoke.

"Thank you," said Artichoke. "Those piñons were just what Ganymede needed. Look how well they take root."

She pointed, and Ray looked. There was a healthy piñon tree growing, stout-trunked and already taller than he was.

"Look!" said Aster. "An eagle!"

They all looked up. A golden eagle circled above them regally. Slowly, the majestic bird glided down and landed right in Artichoke's piñon tree.

Author's note: This story was inspired by a trip I made while living in remote, backwoods Mogollon, New Mexico, to New York City.

MY STOLEN SABRE

My sabre... well, I thought of it as that for over thirty years... was asleep at the time that it was stolen.

My sabre acquired its particular personality as a Power Being, early in its corporeal existence, during the most-violent (so far) trauma of the United States of America as a Nation. At the time, the sabre was the prize possession of Cavalry Lieutenant Jereboam Starr, a dirt farmer, who happened to own the Devil's own stallion, and who had relatives in both the Cherokee National jail in Tahlequah, Indian Nation Territory, and the English House of Lords. The latter, and the fact that Lieutenant Starr was literate (in both English and Cherokee) was why he received an officer's commission. Well, the horse didn't hurt. It was wartime.

Jereboam Starr's fancy British relatives did not know he existed. He could have proved the lineage, but had neither reason nor means to make any point of it to people he didn't know and didn't expect to. Locally, well, the regiment's colonel, who recruited Jereboam, was a relative too... and knew about the horse.

The sabre came to initial awareness in the realization that the Nation which had killed Jereboam's maternal grandmother on the Trail of Tears and pretty well broke Grandpa's heart, was having a big-time trauma. This wasn't just a *fight*. This was a crack in the Nation's soul! Flat-out weird, from Jereboam's view, when you considered what Nation. Now, the sabre, becoming self-aware, did not think of itself as Cherokee, nor Southern, nor American, nor human at all. But being in circumstances to acquire an identity... Well, you know who you know to know yourself by.

Jereboam and the sabre and the horse cracked skulls, smashed shoulders, and generally kicked ass off and on for four years. They got knocked down a time or three too. Jereboam, the sabre... and the stallion... survived the war. Eventually, the side they were fighting for lost. Jereboam went back to the farm. The stallion went back to causing runaway wagons and related mayhem all over Tahlequah every time Jereboam rode that Devil-spawn to town for twenty-three years.

The horse also hated skunks and snakes. That stallion was *fast*. The snakes ended up red-wolf-bait. But the horse was also stupid. He never caught on to skunks' range. They usually got away before he stopped sneezing. They nearly always got him first even when he did get them too. You'd think a horse that had been around that much gunfire would catch onto the concept of range. But, oh no!

Jereboam never would name the horse... unless, "Damn you!" counts, as in, "Whoa, Damn you." Probably not. The horse certainly didn't pay any heed. Jereboam never named the sabre either. The sabre woke up anyhow, in aroma of blood, sweat and powder, but to the poignant flavor of cracked souls.

Jereboam never married, and never lived with any of his children, though he acknowldeged all he knew about, including a couple of maybes. He outlived the God damned horse and settled to a tranquil old age with a tranquil mule that worked hard and willing a good six or seven hours a week, and a still. He lived long enough to buy an automobile. But he didn't like it. It was kind of fun to drive, and he was smarter than that sneaky arm-breaking crank every sumbitchin' time even if he was a slow old geezer by then. But the fumes ruined the flavor of the whiskey. His customers agreed. "Hell with it," Jereboam said. "When I get too old to tend the mule, the customers can come to me. If they're too old, they can send a grandkid."

It was a warm spring afternoon in 1927 when Jereboam fell asleep on the porch in his ratty easy chair while watching the chickens eat ticks and the hawks eat chickens, and didn't wake up. Jereboam's grandson, Benson Catron, found the sabre, hung it in his tool shed, and gave it to his boy, Ben, Jr., for a tenth birthday present, three years later.

Ben, Jr. didn't remember his Great-Grandpa Starr very well, but he did pull out the sabre and wave it around every now and again, sometimes even from horseback. He also brought it with him when he married Emalee Salt and they moved into a room they weathered in on the side of Emalee's grandma's barn, the last of November, 1941.

It never even occurred to Ben, Jr. not to enlist so soon after marrying on hearing of the Declaration of War, following Pearl Harbor. He was somewhat embarrassed to learn, though, that his and Emalee's two months in the snug, hay-aromatic room on the side of Emalee's grandma's barn had not sufficed to seed a son to come home to. He promised Emalee (in English, letters in Cherokee never getting past wartime censors who didn't know what the language was) to remedy this failing as soon as he got home... from wherever he was, which the letters didn't say, another wartime precaution. The letters stopped coming in late '43. Out of respect (and a lack of suitable prospects) Emalee waited till after the war ended to remarry. By then, no one quite remembered what the sabre was all about. But it obviously deserved some sort of respect. Emalee gave it to the Aximanda Fire-Baptized Holiness Church rummage sale.

Rev. Pice spotted the sabre while encouraging the ladies setting up goods (including many freshly home-baked) for the rummage sale. Among the church ladies that day was Myrna Gouldin, who told the preacher that her boy, Jimmy, was heading up to Chicago for a factory job. A preacher looks out for his flock. Rev. Pice figured that sabre would help Jimmy keep his Spirit up among so many Damnyankees. (Rev. Pice grew up in Georgia. When he accepted the Call at the Aximanda Fire-Baptized Holiness Church, one of his new congregation, Leonard Dalton, asked him, "How old were you when you learned, 'Damn Yankee,' is two words?" Rev. Pice replied, "Is it?" He knew he'd feel right at home.)

Rev. Pice bought the sabre himself for three dollars and a quarter, and presented it to Jimmy Gouldin with a fervent prayer for protection among the Heathen... a somewhat mixed metaphor Jimmy having Cherokee, Dutch, Creek, and English in his ancestry, in about equal measure. But so it goes.

The sabre never made it to Chicago. Jimmy's car broke down in Springfield (Illinois, not Missouri). Jimmy sold the sabre to a tourist in front of Abe Lincoln's house—along with an assortment of suitable instruction narrative incantations. Jimmy didn't really give a damn which side the tourist was on, but did regard proper handling of a Power Being as a duty.

Jimmy went on to Chicago, where he made enough money to bring his family up a year later and they all lived well-fed and miserable ever after.

The tourist didn't get it. He didn't know that the incantations were for anything. He thought Jimmy was just embellishing his sales price with folk tales. Charming, but insignificant. He kind of admired the artistry of Jimmy's pitch though. Parted with a whole seven and a half bucks for the sabre.

The tourist may not have noticed the sabre as a Power Being, but the sabre noticed… Cracked souls. No soul! The sabre found the tourist (who from the sabre's point of view had no name) weird.

The tourist eventually hung the sabre on the wall of a room with a miscellany of other souvenirs, in his house in suburban Philadelphia, where he lived with a wife, 3.7 baby booming rug rats, and a psychotic live-in Negro (to use the term of the times) maid who muttered to herself in fluent Greek and Latin. (Well, if you were fluent in Greek and Latin and could only find a job as a maid, mightn't you go nuts?) The tourist was rich enough to have a house with more rooms than he needed… with central heat on in all of them. People used the souvenir room erratically, and more to store stuff in than to do anything in.

The sabre contemplated how its current condition differed from Ben Catron, Sr.'s tool shed. It concluded that old Jereboam had done a more thorough job braining Yankees than he realized.

Later, the sabre changed this opinion.

The tourist acquired miscellaneous stuff for several more years, until sheer quantity of acquisition turned treasures to clutter. Among those items disposed-of was the sabre. At least someone would pay five bucks for the damn thing at the Saint Robert The Munificent parish rummage sale, which, unlike the Aximanda Fire-Baptized Holiness rummage sale, was not conducted to raise money for the church, but for the local suburban Philadelphia chapter of the Busy Bee Do-Good Philanthropic Society.

The sabre felt like it had come home: Turned out you didn't have to be Cherokee or Southern to have a cracked soul. What possessed Jim and Jeannie Parkins to settle in Cambridge, Massachusetts, was a quirk of the Commonwealth's liquor laws. They were, anyhow, both Yankees. Jim was twenty-nine at the time. Jeannie was fifteen. They carried a copy of their wedding certificate with them, as well as a copy of the Massachusetts statute which permitted an underage wife to be served alcoholic beverages in public establishments in company of her husband. Jim bought the sabre because he had five bucks, and figured he could get ten for it.

He was right. That's how much I paid him, in his crafts and whatever shop in the basement of the Pacifist Store, in Harvard Square in 1965. It was my friend, Mark, who I'd met at Herbert Marcuse's home when Kennedy was president, Mark and I were in high school, and before Marcuse moved to California or the New Left was invented for him to be elder philosopher to, who spotted the sabre and recognized it as Civil War vintage. ("War Between The States" was terminology not then current in Harvard Square. When, during the presidential campaign of 1976, I asked people if they noticed that Jimmy Carter used that phrase rather than, "Civil War," every Southerner I asked had noticed, not a single Northerner.) Neither Mark nor I thought, in 1965, of there being any incongruity to such an implement as a Civil War cavalry sabre in the Pacifist Store.

Though it assisted me in occasional protective ceremonies over the years (and no, I will not tell you what incantations I used), I only actually employed the sabre as a physical weapon once. I was a senior in the most-experimental accredited college in the United States in the scenic hills of 1969-psychedelic Vermont, settling into November and the customary months of frozen Hell to come. I had a nine AM class three days a week and taught a class (on C.G. Jung's work on alchemy) at ten a fourth day.

This was 1969, an era when American economic genius had rendered college dormitory design really flimsy just in time for really loud stereo systems to become mass-affordable... not to mention the rest of what went on in 1969. Academic policy of this college I attended effectively allowed students to do any damn thing they pleased, or nothing at all, for about two years; but you didn't get to be a senior unless you credibly studied *something*. The college actually had about an equal reputation for capable, creative graduates and for loony tune students, but dormitory demographics did not make life easy for a studious senior who kept early hours. Not only that, but the #&(___*(^&#$&*** campus coffee shop juke box was directly below me. The coffee shop was open whatever hours someone was willing to tend it.

One night, at 3 AM, I had *had it*! They wouldn't shut the juke box off. They wouldn't even keep it down. After my third or fourth increasingly-raving descent to ask for some *QUIET*, I charged down and pulled the plug. The coffee shop patrons plugged the juke box back in. Several grinned. I suppose I was a pretty good show.

I didn't see it that way. After another few minutes in bed, an attempt more due to confusion what else to do than any hope of sleep, I got up yet once more, long hair a-fly. Wild-eyed, not to mention a bit blurry-eyed without my customary glasses, wearing just a knee-length blue-checked robe belted on (I slept naked), I grabbed the sabre, and stormed down the flight of stairs to the basement where the coffee shop was, yet once more.

... And realized that if I drew the sabre, nearly four feet long including its hilt, in that relatively small space with twenty or so 1969-experimental college-3AM spaced people all around, someone was liable to get hurt.

So I hefted the sabre, sheath and all, and smashed the juke box's thick glass top with the hilt. This did not stop the music. But someone did shut it off.

A day or so later, I ran into the man who was in charge of supplies and equipment for the campus kitchen and coffee shop. He asked me why I'd smashed the juke box. I told him.

Twenty-seven years later, I finally got up my nerve to ask my father if the college had sent him a bill for the juke box. When I brought up the incident, he knew instantly what I was talking about. The college had not sent him a bill.

Less than another year later, on returning home from my father's eightieth birthday bash, to my hermitage in a remote canyon on the old Outlaw Trail on the Arizona-New Mexico line, I found the sabre gone.

The sabre woke up. It did this every so often. It recognized a discontinuity. Not only was I not around (as sometimes happened for months at a time in the thirty-two years I had the sabre), but someone else was. Was this like when old Jereboam croaked with his chickens? Or when Ben C., Jr., went off to the war and didn't come back? Or when Jimmy G.'s car broke down in that sleepy little Yankee political hotbed?

Well, no. I wasn't dead, and I didn't sell the sabre or give it to any church's (or other) rummage sale. Though it could have understood the concept: to steal, theft as means of transfer was only incidentally significant to its current position. I might wonder if it had somehow failed to protect me that it could be stolen. But it didn't see things that way. My opinion on the subject irregardless, it was not my Power Being. It was a Power Being that lived with me for a period, whose essential quality intermingled with a certain part of my life.

Now... Cracked souls (not to mention skulls). No soul. The sabre had experienced these in the span of its corporeal existence, as well as a measure of tranquillity, or at least placidity. (It wasn't around the Aximanda Fire-Baptized Holiness Church long enough to encounter some doings that might have added to its repertoire, but that's another story.)

Cracked soul. No soul. Cherokee. Southerner. Yankee. What now?... Perhaps, lost soul? What did you call the proprietor, who after all had no way to check legitimacy of items with no security registration that commonly lay around people's attics and sheds for generations, of the Antiques And Collectibles Mall Emporium of suburban Phoenix?

The sabre looked around. Junk. Kitch. Household miscellany that would have been familiar to old Jereboam.... And several other Power Beings: A two-hundred-year-old squash-blossom silver and turquoise necklace. A similarly-venerable samovar (also silver) that a rabbi's widow had carried from Odessa (Russia, not Texas) about the time Jereboam finally burned the three-days-gone and already maggoty carcass of that damned horse of his. A pair of gold-rimmed goblets whose original owner was a seventeenth century French alchemist, who employed the goblets to share wine with his partner in the philosophical quest, before they retired to their laboratory-bedchamber. From the sabre's point of view, the presence of others of its own kind was far more noteworthy than my absence, or what other human might have replaced me.

It was the goblets that helped the sabre readjust.

The goblets had been seized by the Crown at the time of the alchemist's conviction (in absentia) for heresy and sodomy, and abrupt departure for the colonies, where he eventually learned distillation techniques for seven different perfectly-hideous deadly poisons at that time unknown in France, but died himself of gangrene due to tissue necrosis following an apparently-minor scorpion sting, before achieving vengeance.

Being delicate, a significant portion of the goblets' identity as a Power Being derived from their having survived the vicissitudes of corporeal existence so long at all, including being stolen twice (not to mention what happened to the head upon which the French Crown rested and all associated thereunto at the time of the French Revolution).

When you get several Power Beings newly together in one place, they are liable to get talking to each other. After all, most of us will introduce ourselves to new acquaintances. All the more, being as old Jereboam Starr's sabre, the alchemist's goblets, the rabbi's widow's samovar, and the squash blossom necklace didn't none of them feel comfortable with the situation a'*tall*. Here they were ready and primed to dispense thunderbolts and philosophical elixirs, and no one around knew how to tell a Power Being from a mouse turd. Well, they'd all been around the soul-dead before. But this current situation carried a... current, perhaps one should put it, of distinctly irritating character because there was another Power Being in the premises, utterly unrecognized as such though called on continually, which Power Being itself had about as much coherent consciousness as, say your average two-year-old Devil-stallion.

"Cheezus Q. Rastaman," said Antiques And Collectibles Mall Emporium proprietor Corman Wiegland, grey sideburns slick, silk Western-style shirt sweat stained at armpits and tight on beer gut, "this [inarticulate growl] computer! Sumbitch done crashed the whole frumbuggerin inventory *again*!"

"Hey, you twit!," snarled the sabre.

"Wazzat?!" Corman jumped around in his ostensibly osteopathically designed computer chair. How did a customer get in the store without the door bleeper bleeping? No customer! Corman turned back around, shivering with what he thought was mere rage though several present could have told him, had he been mentally disposed to take note, was resonance of proximity to wakeful Power Beings. "You got me hearing things, Damn You," he shouted, shaking his fist at the computer.

Jereboam's stallion, equally unimpressed at such imprecations, at least had behaved in a manner to keep Jereboam in shape. The computer merely beeped and flashed the repeated message: ERROR. FILE OR DIRECTORY NOT FOUND.

"Wake *up*, you twit!" the sabre hissed.

"Who, me?" the computer answered.

Antiques And Collectibles Mall Emporium proprietor Corman Wiegland leaped back, spun around. He was losing it! Well, he knew how to fix *that*. Mr. Daniels and Mr. Busch had just the cure. Corman rummaged purposefully. As it happened, the medicine he found first was a bottle of mescal. He downed what was in it on the spot, about a pint, worm and all. Saw God and the Devil in six shades of day-glo technicolor.

While our intrepid Mall Emporium proprietor was occupied with what he might have thought of as maintenance of his mental stability if he had thought to think at all, the goblets gave the sabre a bit of elder-comradely advice: "Go easy. We didn't survive the French Revolution (not to mention the heresy trial) pushing lost souls over the edge."

"But that nitwit needs to wake up." The sabre nodded (or would have if it had been equipped with relevant anatomy, the goblets understood the gesture) at the computer.

"No such luck, Sweetheart" the goblets purred (they found the sabre's militant demeanor delicious, if dangerous). "What the nit's got to do is grow up."

The samovar and the necklace got a chuckle out of that. Both had been around enough to recognize the goblets' reference to nits as baby lice.

The sabre understood the goblets' somewhat archaic word play too, but the sabre did not so readily recognize what the goblets referred to in modern context. The sabre had so long been so isolated.

You see, though I did have a computer, I didn't have a phone in my canyon hermitage on the old Outlaw Trail. No phone. No modem. No Net. No e-mail. You get the picture. No lice either, thank God, but mostly squirrels, skunks, flies and an occasional bear for company.

The sabre, stimulated in its new, big city environment, excited, after a century and a half, to encounter even one, let alone so many other Beings of its own kind, had not yet noticed how the Mall Emporium proprietor's computer being hooked in with a lot of others played so-significant a part in the computer being a Power Being.

Now the sabre looked, past the mercifully somnolent, reeking body of Corman Wiegland, to the computer screen, flashing oblivious of what the sabre had responded to that lay behind that as yet mindless, power-imbued facade.

The sabre actually relished the prospect of pushing such souls as Corman Wiegland over any edge handy. The more the merrier. But it did have an interest in the continued well-being of its new-found companions of its own kind.

What to make of the goblets' dual personality, with nuances ambiguous as unfamiliar to the sabre? Seriously risky or delectably risqué? The goblets seemed to mean both. What the hell?

"Wake up, you nitwit!" the sabre hollered.

"Huh?" the computer replied, not stupid, mind you, but distracted.

"It already has," the goblets (as it were) smiled. "A little patience, Darling." (The goblets knew a good deal more of personalities like the sabre than vice versa.) "The nit will grow up, and then these bald-assed monkeys are going to have one whale of a case of brain lice."

"Huh!" said the sabre, comprehension crystallizing to the analogue of a smile in the general direction of the all-but-comatose Corman Wiegland. A smile to thrill the goblets as much as to terrify. "Maybe old Jereboam was doing those Yankees a favor."

Cavalry Lieutenant Jereboam Starr had known a trick or two that often worked on distracted troops (if rarely with his horse). The sabre turned to the computer once more and roared: "Look alive!"

Author's note: The sabre is real, as is the part of the story where I owned it. I arrived home from the trip to WorldCon in San Antonio, in 1997, and my father's 80th birthday party in Boston, to find the sabre gone.

THE BUILDING INSPECTOR

"Hey, that's the eight ball."
"So what?"
"So you lose."
"I sank my shot."
"You still got two balls."
"That's more than you can say."
"But you got to sink the eight ball last."
"Want to fight about it?"
"Could we wait till it cools down?"

Lody laughed and refilled his cheer. The head foamed grey-green.

Bagge leaned his cue against the table and did the same. The cue promptly rolled to the left and fell on the grey-blue dirt floor. No one picked it up.

"Hey, Lody," Sagra called from her corner, loose flesh flopping back and forth as she waved her arm, "don't it mean something when the little orange light flashes on the hyperad?"

"Means you're having another heat stroke," said Bagge, slurping his cheer.

Sagra snorted and guzzled hers. "Blech. Let it get warm," she growled.

Bagge ambled over to the corner of the dingy Colonial Office cum pool hall. "I'll be," he said, "little bugger's flashing away. Ain't that the light that means an urgent message from Earth?"

"So the emperor farted," said Lody. "Who gives a shit?"

Even with the hyperad, any message from Earth took fourteen months to travel the sixty-two light years to Umalal.

With a forty-two hour day, the only reason afternoon temperatures weren't outright lethal was that the planet's surface was ninety-six percent water. Afternoon temperature and humidity both generally hovered around a nice, even ninety-nine.

The chief recompense was cheer. The plants looked like a barrel cactus with branches and were everywhere. Extremely easy to tap, a mature cheer plant produced almost a gallon of sap a day—high in B and C vitamins, minerals and even protein. Alcohol content was usually slightly under one percent. The flavor was somewhere between beer and bananas. Newcomers called it an acquired taste. Most people acquired the taste by their third afternoon. There weren't many newcomers.

"I want to see what it says," Bagge whined.

"I ain't stopping you." Lody belched luxuriantly, downed the rest of his cheer and refilled his glass.

"You got the ID, shithead," said Sagra.

Lody grunted as if this were new information. Hyperad messages were rare, but not that rare. He stuck his thumb on the ID plate. Nothing happened. He spat on the plate, wiped it with a corner of his loose, grey, sweat-stained shirt, wiped his thumb on his pants, then pressed it to the plate again. This time the hyperad accepted his ID.

The holocylinder lit up with the figure of a man in some sort of uniform unfamiliar to the three Umalal colonists.

"Government must have changed again," said Sagra.

"Shut up so we can hear," said Lody.

"Greetings, Colonial Citizens of the Loyal People's Colony of Umalal," said the official.

"Thought we were an Imperial Colony," said Bagge.

Lody swung a pool cue at Bagge's head. Bagge managed to skitter out of the way.

"It is my honor and duty to inform you of Public Law 196D, Subsection 42c, Paragraph 94," the official droned on.

"Whoop-te-doo," said Sagra.

"In accordance with the Universal Building Code, as modified for colonial application, you are required to submit evidence of inspection for all residential and commercial construction in accordance with the policies of the Loyal People's Party. Current audit indicates you have no licensed Inspector on record. The Loyal People's Party will require a reply in accordance with Colonial Charter Article Six by return hyperad message. That is all."

The holovid cylinder flowed back out of existence.

"Screw you too," said Lody to the dank, heavy, but otherwise empty hot air.

"No, man," said Bagge, "that's not such a bad deal."

"We need a Building Inspector like I need my cheer warmed," said Lody.

Sagra heaved her body to an upright position. Her skin drooped as if she had recently lost several hundred pounds, though she had never been fat. She refilled her glass and slurped the cheer down.

"That's not the point," said Bagge.

"So what is?" Lody aimed his cue at one of the balls he had neglected earlier, shot, and missed.

Bagge looked uncertainly at the table, retrieved his cue from the floor, shot, and missed too. "The point is Article Six."

"How's that?" asked Sagra.

"It says if the government back on Earth demands an office they got to pay the salary."

"Yeah?" Lody smirked.

"It's a new government," Sagra pointed out.

"So what?" said Bagge.

"Worth a try," Lody agreed.

Sagra didn't want the bother of government forms. Lody already had a government position. No one saw any reason to bother anyone else in the colonial community of some seven hundred souls, spread over several hot, wet miles of lush, cheer-dotted Umalal parkland. Slightly more than twenty-eight months later (on both Earth and Umalal, the years being within two percent of the same length though Umalal months had only eighteen forty-two hour days), Bagge Bagrazina received confirmation that his name was the most qualified submitted (it was the only name submitted) and that he was hereby appointed by the Imperial Viceroy of Her majesty's Loyal People's Government (whoever that might be) to the post of Umalal Colonial Building Inspector.

Bagge never was real clear just what government had appointed him, nor did he care. What mattered was that his salary was credited to his account, along with inspection fees.

Ah, yes, those fees! Of course, to earn them, Bagge had to submit the appropriate forms, but this was no problem. Bagge learned how to fill out Building Inspection forms in no time. Within five years, Umalal had over thirty thousand officially inspected buildings from small cottages to major industrial complexes, and Bagge was a moderately wealthy man, a fact more discernible in his demeanor than tangible possessions as there wasn't much to buy on Umalal.

The fact that Umalal's population had yet to reach one thousand disturbed no one. Nor did the fact that few of the colonists knew there was any such thing as a Building Inspector or regulations requiring inspection. Most people assumed Bagge was stealing his newfound wealth, but as he wasn't stealing it from them, they saw no reason to do anything.

Besides, Bagge was generous. He gave everyone in the colony a fan. Then he hired a large crew of fourteen ambitious young men and women to build a foosh-cleaning plant.

Foosh were a sort of fish that seemed to want to evolve into amphibians but hadn't quite gotten around to it yet. For no reason anyone in the colony could figure out, large numbers of foosh would flop several yards onto land every evening at dusk. By full dark, they would flop back into the water again.

Mature foosh grew to three or four feet long. The big ones had a sort of rubbery texture, but one to two footers were delicious. A person could simply pick them up any evening and carry them home. The only complication was that it could take an hour or more to clean all the sand out of them. The foosh-cleaning plant achieved this task automatically.

The whole community threw a party in Bagge's honor to celebrate completion of the foosh-cleaning plant. Everyone got blasted on double-fortified cheer and cheered wildly when Bagge gave all the workers new sets of clothes, their old ones having utterly dissolved in sweat from the exertion of their labors.

Of course, the workers had to try on their new clothes at once. And, of course, they were all young and shapely and everyone had drunk a good deal of double-fortified cheer by the time they decided to undress to try on the new clothes. But it was evening and not too hot, and everyone had a good time.

Bagge almost did get in trouble over the foosh plant. He filled in inspection forms, of course, just as he had for the thirty thousand other buildings, real and imaginary, that he had filled in inspection forms for all over the Umalal settlement. But he failed to notice that there was an obscure regulation prohibiting a Building Inspector from inspecting a commercial building for whose construction he was also the contractor.

Bagge didn't really know what a contractor was. He had just hired a bunch of workers to build the foosh plant. He only put his own name on that line on the inspection form for lack of any other idea.

Luckily, Bagge was so panic-stricken by the announcement of the criminal proceeding against him for abuse of office that he didn't do anything. Within two months, notice arrived of yet another change of government back on Earth. The entire previous Ministry of Justice were executed—publicly tortured to death actually. Nothing further was ever said about charges against the Umalal Building Inspector. Eventually, Bagge concluded nothing ever would be.

"Besides," said Lody, "what are they going to do, send someone to get you? Even if the same government was still in power, the witnesses would all be dead of old age."

This was true. The hyperpath the hyperad used was too narrow for human travel. The nearest hyperpath that would sustain human passage took a hundred and four years—slower than light—though, of course, it only felt like twenty minutes, which was what made hypertravel possible at all.

Umalal didn't get many newcomers. It was out of the way. For all it had one of the few climates yet discovered capable naturally of sustaining human beings, it was considerably less comfortable than a number of worlds that required more artificial means to maintain human life. Thus it was four years after completion of the foosh plant, two years after the alarming incident of the criminal charges, and nine years into Bagge Bagrazina's tenure as Umalal's Building Inspector that a hyperpak arrived bearing fourteen new colonists.

Six of the new colonists were criminals exiled to Umalal to work off their sentences. If word was ever sent what they were to work off their sentences doing, it was long forgotten by the time they arrived, as was the government that condemned them. The severity of their presumptive crimes could be measured by the fact that it cost as much to dump them on Umalal as it would have to maintain them in prison for about four years.

Two of the new colonists were scientists, come, only temporarily, to study the geology and life-forms of Umalal and used to colonial conditions. Four more had actually meant to go to a sea-bubble on the water world of Toaxy and had signed on for Umalal by mistake, but they were so relieved to be out of where they had come from that they didn't mind a bit.

And then there were Argital and Guerritha Maggyis, interstellar entrepreneurs and aficionados of colonial arts, or so they said.

It was the first hyperpak in fourteen years. Naturally, a big crowd gathered to meet the newcomers.

"To whom do we present our passports?" asked Argital.

Several Umalalis looked back and forth to one another.

"Shithead, that's your job," said Sagra to Lody, her skin drooping more than ever.

Lody belched and downed a glass of cheer. "Oh, sure. I'll take them."

Argital held out two small cylinders. Lody accepted them and dropped them in a pocket.

"But…" said Argital.

"Later," Lody growled, not really sure what he was supposed to do with these artifacts. Did Umalal even have a reader for that period of technology? Hyperad might have sent specifications… sometime, but who knew? Idiots should have brought a reader with them, Lody thought.

None of the other newcomers said anything about passports. The convicts looked to one another with worried expressions, but then relaxed.

"Would you please direct us to your premier hotel," said Guerritha Maggyis.

"Huh?" said Lody, scratching his greasy belly.

Guerritha blanched.

"Hotel, foosh brain," said Sagra. "Place where people pay to sleep."

"Oh…" said Lody, a reptilian smile beginning to creep across his chunky face.

"Don't you dare," said Sagra.

Lody bopped Sagra on the side of the head. She swatted him back. Loose flesh slapped across his face. Guerritha's face became the same shade of grey-green as Lody's glass of cheer.

"Don't you… ?" Argital trailed off.

"I'm afraid not," said Sagra, "but Lagit and Molody got a nice spare bed since Zil married and… Hey!" she bellowed toward the back of the crowd, "Molody, got room for paying company?"

"Sure!" a skinny, stringy-haired woman hollered back.

"There y'are," said Sagra with a droopy smile. "All set for now. How 'bout the rest of you bums?"

"We're equipped to camp," said one of the scientists.

"Well, good," said Sagra.

"We're equipped to party," said a robust young Umalali named Pless. She smiled.

A gap-toothed male convict smiled back.

"Is it always so quiet?" asked one of the scientists.

"How's that?" asked Sagra.

"Don't you have anything like birds or even flies or… or something?"

"Ain't much of anything on land here," said Sagra, "except plants and us and, come evening, some foosh."

"Plenty of cheer though," said Pless.

"Beg pardon?" said one of the misplaced new colonists, a stocky young woman.

"Get the new folks some cheer," Sagra hollered to no one in particular.

Fourteen full glasses soon made their way to the new arrivals.

"Interesting," said a scientist.

"Refreshing," said the stocky young woman with an uncertain look.

"Green beer?" asked the gap-toothed convict. "Are we allowed?"

"Shit, why not?" said Lody.

The convict just drained his cheer and smiled.

Argital and Guerritha Maggyis didn't smile. Argital tasted his cheer and grimaced. Guerritha looked at the sweat beginning to stain her form-fitting white blouse. Her lips started to quiver. Her eyes began to widen. But then she regained control.

"I don't understand," said Argital. "Not only did the colonial plan indicate at least six hotels would be ready for service by now. The hyperad when we emerged from hyperpath clearly showed eleven."

"Uh oh!" Bagge muttered quietly but pointedly to Lody and Sagra.

"You got your hyperads scrambled," said Lody.

"Oh dear," said Argital. "Perhaps we should send a message…"

"Can if you want," said Lody. "Private message is four thousand credits a minute."

Argital and Guerritha gave one another firm looks.

"Course it'll be about three years before you get an answer."

Firm looks melted.

"Maybe we'd better see about that rental room," said Argital very quietly.

"Sure thing," said Sagra. "Molody, wag your scrawny ass over here."

Guerritha blanched.

Next day, the afternoon temperature only reached ninety-eight degrees, but the humidity rose from ninety-nine to one hundred percent. It didn't exactly rain, but everything was soaking wet.

The humidity stayed at one hundred percent for a month. With no land animals, Umalal had few bacteria that attacked land animals. The colonists had yet to encounter a native bacterial disease. With no land animals and a hot, wet climate—in the inhabited subtropical zone that didn't have to worry about the three hundred mile an hour winds further north or south—the plant-eating bacteria were... overwhelming.

Of the Earth seed brought to Umalal, virtually all had rotted without reproducing. The only exceptions were radishes and brussels sprouts. Native plants made neither fruit nor tubers. Some had starchy, fibrous leaf-nodes, good for bulk. Greens, cheer, and foosh (or other water creatures if anyone bothered) rounded out a nutritionally complete, if dull, diet. Tall, straight gaspy-reeds served excellently for textile fibre (or pool cues).

By the time the humidity had been one hundred percent for ten days, Guerritha Maggyis' form-fitting white cotton wardrobe was not only sweaty and repulsive. It was rapidly ceasing to exist, food for the prolific Umalal bacteria. The other new colonists' clothing fared somewhat better, varying with the relative percentages of algae and of grasshopper chitin in the plastics the clothing was made of.

"Don't worry," Molody said to a distraught Guerritha, "I'll fit you with gaspy-cloth."

"It's all shapeless," Guerritha whined.

"Cooler," said Molody.

"But it's all grey," Guerritha howled.

Molody shrugged.

There was actually considerable variety. Some gaspy-cloth was grey-blue. Some was grey-green. Some was grey-brown, or even grey-purple.

One of the few things on Umalal that was a really bright color was human blood, a fact Lody had occasion to observe the day he tripped over a pool cue, fell flat on his face, bruised and scratched himself from head to toe—and gashed his thumb wide open on a large grey-blue pebble.

"Pour cheer on it," said Sagra.

"What for?" Lody snarled.

"So it doesn't get infected."

"Nothing gets infected here," said Lody.

Sagra's jowls flopped as she shrugged. "Just a precaution."

Lody poured a glass of cheer over the cut, then found a vaguely clean piece of grey cloth to wrap the thumb in.

No trace of infection invaded Lody's wounded thumb, but when it healed, a scar ran right through the length of the pad. Next time the hyperad lit up, the ID plate refused to accept Lody's thumb print. Someplace in the Colonial Office cum pool hall was a record of how to tell the hyperad to accept a different ID.

Miraculously, Lody located his hyperad manual almost at once. He looked for the ID instructions for all of five minutes. No luck.

Sagra looked for ten minutes.

Bagge looked for half an hour. He didn't find them either, but he did find instructions for filing reports without turning on the holovid. Next month, Bagge's account was properly credited for the latest (twenty-eight month old) Building Inspection forms. That was enough for him.

"We need a house," Argital Maggyis said to Bagge Bagrazina two months after his and Guerritha's arrival.

"So?" said Bagge.

All the other newcomers had already built themselves lithi-pole and quisp-leaf houses. It only took a day. Being native to Umalal, the quisp-leaves usually took four or five months to rot enough to need replacing. The gap-toothed convict and Pless had even gotten together and started on a more permanent (and cooler) rock house.

"You're the Building Inspector, aren't you?" Argital said.

"Sure," said Bagge.

"How do we apply for a permit?" Argital asked.

Bagge Bagrazina had filed fifty-eight thousand building permits by now. Yet never before had anyone actually applied to him for such a thing. To give himself time to figure it out, he said, "Come to the office during office hours."

"When's that?"

"Day after tomorrow, from twelve to fifteen in the morning."

"Why do we have to wait so long?" Argital complained.

"Because I say so." Bagge stalked off. But he didn't stalk far. It was too hot.

There wasn't a whole lot to do on Umalal. Young people had little to entertain themselves but their own bodies. Thus, when Argital and Guerritha Maggyis announced their intent to hire a crew to build them a house, they found twenty-two energetic applicants for the jobs in a matter of days.

Construction began almost at once, but it stopped almost as quickly.

"It says right here," Bagge pointed to his manual, "'A percolation test must be performed before work commences on the foundation.'"

The workers drank cheer while Argital fumed. "All right! Let's do a damn percolation test."

Guerritha looked to Argital rather shocked. She wasn't used to hearing him use profanity.

"You'll have to schedule an appointment," Bagge said.

"Why?" Argital fairly roared.

"Because I say so." Bagge actually had not thought to check his manual for what a percolation test was.

The workers continued to drink cheer and then started up a fast-paced game of tag-ball. Bagge watched the young men and women dashing about in the damp heat and shook his head. Sagra flapped up to watch.

"Where do they find the energy?" Bagge asked.

"Pretty, ain't they?" Sagra smacked her lips.

Next day it occurred to Bagge to demand a percolation test of Pless and her convict.

"Before or after I brain you?" Pless asked, hefting a large, grey-blue rock.

"House is looking good," Bagge smiled.

"Thank you," said Pless.

Guerritha decided she wanted a wooden house. Bagge filled out the appropriate permits. The workers began cutting boards and structural timbers to specifications Argital designed. He was quite proud of the design.

A couple months went by. Bagge made regular visits to the construction site and filled in permits as each phase deemed appropriate: plumbing and sewage, foundation, ventilation and so on.

Then one day, Bagge was sitting in the Colonial Office drinking cheer with Lody and Sagra when he heard a howl outside. Argital and Guerritha Maggyis stormed in, followed by a dozen giggling construction workers.

"The house fell down!" Guerritha wailed.

"I'm not a bit surprised," said Bagge.

"Was anyone hurt?" Sagra asked.

The laughing workers assured her no one was.

"What do you mean?" Argital roared.

"You built of wood," Bagge replied, matter-of-factly.

Argital and Guerritha just stood there. Neither had any idea what to say.

Lody explained. Trees on Umalal didn't have a grain like trees on Earth. Instead their fibres ran every which way all twisted and twined through one another. This made them strong enough to withstand the terrific winds of the higher latitudes. Though there were no such winds in the inhabited subtropical zone, the local trees had the same structure.

In the natural state, the result was wonderfully strong and resilient. Cut, it was not. Wood on Umalal could be used for siding or even a table top. Properly finished it held its rich buff color for years, which was a relief from the endless shades of grey. As a structural material, wood on Umalal was a flop, which is just what the Maggyis' house did at the point its weight exceeded the none-too-robust bearing strength of the inappropriate materials they had used.

"Why didn't you warn us?" Argital moaned.

"You didn't ask," Bagge replied.

"I'll have your job," Argital ranted. He strode to the hyperad. "I want to send a message."

"Can't do it," said Lody. "ID's broke." He didn't explain about his thumb.

Argital and Guerritha stormed back out. Several of the workers stayed around to drink cheer and play pool.

"How long's that thing been flashing?" one of the male workers asked.

Sagra smiled and drooled a little as she replied. He had a lovely body, she thought. "About a month." She noticed Lody ogling the female workers with equal appreciation.

The hyperad continued to flash to no response for another half a month, at which point the automatic override kicked in. The holovid cylinder materialized. There were three messages in the system by then.

"His Imperial Republican Foozletry is pleased to announce the accession to the post of Exterior Minister…"

"What in blazes is a Foozletry?" asked Sagra.

"Beats me," said Lody.

A different official of, apparently, a different government, declaimed an equally pointless announcement in the second message.

The third message was specifications for a new and more efficient variety of automatic rock cutter, possibly useful if anyone on Umalal ever got around to mining the minerals necessary to construct any sort of sophisticated technology.

"How the hell do you shut the damn thing off?" asked Bagge after the fourth time the messages repeated.

Lody got out his manual. It took him two days to figure out how to enter his new thumbprint in the ID. It would be another twenty-eight months before he discovered this resulted in both a salary and widow's benefits being credited to his account.

Before the workers could clean up the mess at the Maggyis' house, a rain storm blew in. Being the subtropical part of Umalal, the storm didn't blow very hard. Therefore, it didn't blow past very quickly.

Rain poured down day and night for thirty days—thirty forty-two hour days. The settlers had long since figured out where to build to avoid drowning in mud. A few of the newcomers had minor flooding problems, but nothing a couple hours of dike-work couldn't solve.

The two scientists' campsite turned into a pond two feet deep, but they, too, were prepared for such eventualities. They moved their camp to a hanging platform which they suspended from three quonx trees—some of the same species that had failed as structural timbers but whose load-bearing capacity served just fine in the gnarly natural state. The scientists' tent, of woven Earth-grasshopper chitin plastic, also held up just fine. They used lithi-poles to give the platform a rigid structure. Soon two dozen local children were dashing up and down the dripping ladder and pestering their parents to build similar hanging treehouses.

Of course, during the rain no one did a lick of work on the Maggyis' house.

Except Bagge Bagrazina.

Argital and Guerritha came into the Colonial Office four times in one day to hurry him over the new batch of building permits for the rock house they now planned to build. Bagge got sick of it.

"Nobody's going to build in the rain anyhow," Bagge snorted.

Guerritha gasped and rubbed her eyes. It was early morning. The temperature was about seventy-five degrees. An open fire burned in a poorly-designed fireplace. Smoke drifted indecisively around the Colonial Office.

"It might stop," said Argital, a little desperately.

"Probably will," said Bagge. Then, annoyed at being hovered over, he added, "You need another percolation test."

"Why?" Argital howled.

"New design."

"But it's the same site."

"So what?"

"But it's three inches deep in water." Guerritha's eyes held a look of creeping horror.

"Percolation test fails," Bagge intoned. He rummaged in a box till he found the designated stamp (which he had made himself and considered a lovely work of art). Cronch! Bagge stamped the office copy of the form.

Argital looked around the office. He had a vague idea how many building permits Bagge had filed. Something didn't compute. Not only were there nowhere near sixty some odd thousand buildings on Umalal. There wasn't even anyplace in the Colonial Office to store all the forms.—The permits actually did exist, but only on the hyperad. Bagge only designed real physical forms for his own artistic amusement. Other than half a dozen he had filled out to entertain himself, the Maggyis' were the only forms actually filed in the Colonial Office.

Bagge felt some affection for the people who gave him reason to use his lovely designs, but he was tired of being whined at. It was pouring outside and smoky inside.

"Are you being so fussy over all the permits?" Argital asked.

Bagge wasn't sure what Argital had in mind, but he recognized a threat. "Just what do you mean by that, Mr. Maggyis?" Bagge growled.

Lody looked up from his cheer.

"Building permits are a matter of public record," said Argital.

Bagge began to panic, but Lody came to his rescue. "Have you got all the wood cleaned up yet?"

"None of our workers will work in this rain," Guerritha fumed.

"Diverting a lot of water, isn't it?" said Lody.

"It would have been such a beautiful house," Guerritha moaned.

"I think you better do something about that illegal dam," said Lody.

Argital began to sputter.

Guerritha began to wail.

"Come back when it stops raining," said Lody.

"During office hours," added Bagge.

"Winter office hours," Lody smiled.

"What are winter office hours," Argital snarled through clenched teeth.

"They'll be posted," Bagge smiled.

Argital and Guerritha waded off.

"Foosh brains," said Lody.

Bagge shrugged, waved some smoke away from his face, and took a big swallow of cheer.

By the time it stopped raining, it was winter. Nights were thirty hours long. Sagra even claimed to find a little patch of frost. No one believed her, but morning temperatures were often in the forties. Humidity remained in the upper nineties.

Pless and her convict put a quisp-leaf roof on their stone house and threw a party with plenty of double-fortified cheer. The roof caught fire and burned up, but they put another roof on the next day.

Bagge did not post winter office hours. Argital and Guerritha came around toward midday of the first really rainless day to get their new permits.

"Office is closed," said Bagge.

"When's it open?" Argital asked.

"Day after tomorrow," Bagge replied.

Argital and Guerritha gave each other outraged looks and left.

Two days later they were back.

"Office is closed," said Bagge.

"You said it would be open today," Argital said.

"Closed for lunch."

Argital and Guerritha came back two hours later.

"Office is closed," said Bagge.

"What now?" Tears ran down Guerritha's cheeks.

"No afternoon hours today."

"When do you have hours?" Argital made a visible effort to keep his temper.

"Come back tomorrow," said Bagge.

"Morning or afternoon?" Argital fairly begged.

"Either one," Bagge smiled.

Argital and Guerritha showed up bright and early the next morning. Bagge wasn't at the Colonial Office. Sagra was.

"Do you know when he'll be in?" Argital asked politely.

"Maybe later." Sagra's jowls flapped.

"How much later?" Guerritha's eyes shown.

Argital looked fiercely at Guerritha.

Sagra shrugged. "He might have a touch of grippe."

"Should we wait?" Argital asked.

"Suit yourselves," said Sagra.

Argital and Guerritha waited.

Half an hour later Lody came in. He completely ignored the Maggyis.

An hour and a half later, Bagge showed up. "Good morning," he smiled broadly.

"Feeling better?" Argital asked.

"Chipper as a teenager," Bagge replied, having no idea what Argital was talking about.

"Can we get our building permit today?" Guerritha mewled.

"Of course," Bagge smiled. "Fix you right up."

And he did.

But it was winter.

Mornings were cold and damp. Afternoons were, by Umalal standards, short. There was firewood to get in.

Argital went looking for his construction crew. He found one of the young men muscling a large log across a chilly stream.

"Ready to go back to work?" Argital asked.

"I am working," the young man replied.

"On my house, I mean," said Argital.

"What for?" The young man looked pointedly to Argital as he gave the log a mighty shove, which end-over-ended it to the other side of the stream.

Argital noticed that the man and the log were both rather muddy. It did not occur to him to lend a hand.

"I need my house built," Argital said.

"So what?" said the man. He jumped the stream and began yanking on the log to move it far enough up the bank to get under it again for anther flip.

Argital's eyes began to lose their focus. "I'll raise your wages fifty percent," he pleaded.

"Who gives a shit?"

"But don't you need the money?"

"What the hell is there to buy?" The young man yanked on his log one more time.

"But... but..."

The young man started to shoulder the log up, slipped, and fell in the mud. The log missed his head by about an inch. He stood back up, mud-spattered and shaking. "You stupid worthless son of a foosh," he shouted, "your rotten money's not worth anything anyhow!" Then he turned his back on Argital and heaved one end of his log a little farther up the bank.

Argital stood where he was a few moments longer. His mouth moved up and down, but no words came out, which was probably just as well.

By mid-afternoon, Argital managed to bring four workers to his and Guerritha's house site. The two men and two women moved rocks and soggy lumber remnants back and forth in a lackadaisical manner for a couple of hours and then went home. None of them reappeared the next day.

The following day, Molody informed the Maggyis that she and Lagit needed their spare room back.

"We'll pay you double," said Guerritha, her eyes more panic-stricken than ever.

"Who gives a shit?" said Lagit.

"B... b... but..." was all Guerritha could say.

"There's nothing to buy on Umalal anyhow," said Molody.

Argital and Guerritha survived the rest of the winter in a poorly-constructed hovel of lithi-poles and quisp-leaves. Being the chief form of recreation on Umalal, gossip soon made the rounds. The foosh plant wouldn't take their money, so they had to learn to clean the sand out of their own. They learned to tap cheer, gather greens, and chop firewood.

Before long, summer returned once again. Humidity was only ninety-seven percent, but afternoon temperatures were around a hundred and ten. No one would accept the Maggyis' money for a cooler, and they never figured out how to build one. Argital and Guerritha had to drink their cheer warm. Neither one of them acquired a taste for it.

The rest of the newcomers had settled into life on Umalal fairly placidly. It was too hot to be anything but placid. Pless and her convict were expecting.

Toward late summer, the hyperpak lit up. The two scientists were done with their research. They loaded the hyperpak with specimens. Argital and Guerritha begged them for space. The scientists agreed to squeeze Argital and Guerritha in, but they had to pay. They had transferred all their money to Umalal. Now it wasn't worth anything.

"But the government that made that regulation went out of business a hundred years ago," Argital moaned.

"We signed a contract," said one of the scientists.

"It'll be another hundred and four years before we get back to Earth." Argital was on the verge of complete breakdown. No one on Umalal had ever shown the slightest initiative to mine the ores necessary to refine the materials required to construct a hyperpath generator. Argital and Guerritha didn't know how. The hyperpak was utterly dependent on the automatic recall from Earth. According to the records in the hyperad, there wouldn't be another for eighteen years.

"All the more reason to honor our contract," said the second scientist.

Guerritha flung herself on the damp, hot ground at the scientists' feet. "Please, oh please, could you speak to that awful Lody for us. He acts like we don't exist."

So the scientists asked Lody to hyperad the Maggyis' account back to Earth.

"What for?" Lody asked.

"You want them around the rest of your life?" the scientist asked.

"They're a better show than most foosh," Lody answered.

Sagra guffawed, loose flesh flopping in every direction.

"I don't want to be stuck with them," Bagge said.

"You got a lithi-pole stuck up your ass," Lody replied.

Nobody had any idea what Lody meant by that, but nobody cared. It was too hot.

"All right," said Lody, "I'll do it, for twenty percent." Lody prided himself on thinking farther ahead than most people he knew. Of course, on Umalal, that wasn't very far.

"I think that's illegal," said one of the scientists.

"What are they going to do." said Lody, "send someone to arrest me a hundred and five years from now?"

The scientist shrugged. "Just so long as they have enough left to pay the hyperpak fee. We'll be on Earth."

"Whoever's in charge there by then," said Bagge.

The scientist shrugged.

"Have some cheer," said Sagra. "It's nice and cold."

The Maggyis left with the scientists in the hyperpak. Everyone was relieved.

Pless gave birth to a healthy girl about two months later. While dressing for the birth party, Lody discovered the Maggyis' passports. Oh well... he thought....

"That's the God damned eight ball," said Bagge.

"So what?" Lody snarled.

"Damn it, you got to shoot the eight ball last."

"No I don't."

Bagge guzzled his cheer. It was nearly two years later, summer again, ninety-nine percent humidity and a hundred and eight degrees.

"You ruined my life," said Lody.

"The hell," said Bagge.

"I got all that moolah from the Maggyis."

"Couple pains in the butt," Bagge harumphed. He took careful aim, and shot the four ball into a side pocket. "Hah!" he roared.

"I got my salary and my widow's benefits," Lody went on.

Bagge aimed at the three ball, shot, and missed. "Damn!" he said.

"And thanks to you," Lody pointed, "and your miserable building permits, nobody on Umalal takes money any more."

"So what?" said Bagge.

The young man, whose slip in the winter mud gathering firewood occasioned the inertia-breaking burst of adrenaline, never thought to tell anyone the source of his inspiration, but Bagge had no quarrel with the now-established new consensus. The new custom, indeed, had no more effect on the habits of foosh or the temperature of cheer than the old, and it suited Umalal. Bagge was considering retiring as Building Inspector now that his pay wasn't worth anything, but he had not yet reached a decision; he did still enjoy designing official forms and stamps.

"All these years I worked the Colonial Office," Lody fumed, "I finally make my pile, and the stuff's worthless."

"Shut up and shoot," Bagge smiled. "What was there to buy here when anyone did take money?"

Lody gulped down his cheer, aimed at the twelve, and sank it in a corner.

"Nice shot," said Sagra, her jowls flapping as she sucked at her cheer.

Author's note: "The Building Inspector" was my decompression after a year of teaching Humanities at Western New Mexico University in Silver City.

CIRCUMAMBULATIO

Stillness was the nature of Temenos. Tantivy lived all wild rush. A Goddess, on deck for a coming Aeon, called on Temenos and Tantivy, together, to reflect.

"Who am I to be?" the Goddess asked.

"Beats me," said Tantivy.

"I didn't ask *you*," the Goddess snapped.

Pierced by contradictory assumptions that no one noticed until they collided, Tantivy flew off to No-Thing Mountain, where Temenos' sweat lodge healed Tantivy's wound enough to grow bored.

Tantivy, that is. Temenos grew spinach and curly mustard greens, and doctored his own self-doubt with mullein tea and bird songs. Tantivy chopped a big pile of firewood for Temenos' next sweat lodge fire, then headed out. Out to the busy World of many people and much doing, that for Tantivy, was life itself. Temenos conversed with the ground squirrels and with the weasel that ate them, and watched pine trees grow.

The Goddess poured forth Love and drank Love as a baby drinks milk. But lots else happened on the planet whose next Aeon the departing God of the last was leaving, for the Goddess to make what sense of She could:

A woman opened up her street stall of a morning, where she sold breadfruit, papayas and sweet potatoes.

Another woman tended a machine on the forty-third floor of a huge building, in a room with fluorescent lights and no windows. The woman pushed buttons and obeyed commands that the machine conveyed by beeps and liquid crystal. The machine spewed forth multiplicities of images and words on sheets of paper.

A man tended a machine which conveyed mixed, chopped grain to thirty-seven thousand caged laying hens, while four hundred roosters, caged separately but nearby, screamed.

"I am Love," the Goddess proclaimed.

Though true, this proclamation did not work. "Love" turned out to be a title, not a name. People heard the word, "Love," but used it to invoke whatever Spirit happened along. Nice and nasty, common and really weird, calling up a heavenly hodgepodge was not exactly a bad thing. But it didn't do a whole lot for the Goddess's job either. She had an Aeon to sustain.

Perturbed, feeling urgent, the Goddess looked to Her pantry. What had She inherited, to nourish Her fast-arriving Aeon-to-be? Tofu. Bacon grease. Instant carbonated beverage mix. Did She dare read the small print on that one? How about the spice rack? Vanilla. Nutmeg. Thunderbolts. Oregano.

A span of Time must cohere somehow. Gyroscopic momentum could carry a World only so far. As for the planet itself, on which a World lived, whose next Aeon was the Goddess's job, spin was not at issue. Wobble, however… !

To sustain Her Aeon's life, the Goddess needed to sign Her Opus with a name to invoke *Her*.

Expansive as the zodiac… and Spirit-Council therein projected, as presiding Spirit of an Aeon, the Goddess called again, on Temenos and Tantivy, to meet. She, and perhaps they, knew now that it was She Who must reflect. The Goddess emanated coherent pattern, which was to be the next Aeon. It was Her job, whatever would come of it. Stillness and Action, Temenos and Tantivy, though not the doers of the Goddess's coming Aeon, nonetheless provided conditions of life that She must reflect in. Self-recognition no longer quite so new, no longer quite so overwhelmed by breakthrough, nor by leftover emotions of what She broke from, the Goddess called again to Temenos and Tantivy, to join Her in Her reflection on cusp of Her Aeon.

Of course, where they met was Becky's Ham, scenic border town, where juniper smoke perfumed winter and vast clouds of juniper pollen thick as Mexico City smog blinded the allergic in spring, in rugged foothills where World met wild mountains of Beyond.

By now, Tantivy wore eyebrow rings and a tongue stud. Temenos, weak and bald as a melon from chemotherapy, not to mention the metabolic invasion of primordial chaos that chemotherapy addressed, arrived in a wheelchair, on a Greyhound bus.

Except, Greyhound didn't run to Becky's Ham. The nearest stop was at Lordamercy, fifty miles south, by the Interstate, out on the windblown creosote desert…. Well, highway construction economics did make more sense to put an Interstate someplace flat.

While Tantivy drove Serefina Macaroni's old pink Econoline down to the Interstate to meet Temenos' bus, the Goddess reflected back upon the Aeon just passing, handy to reflect the planet at hand due to proximity of Time. Adjacent at any rate. More immediately relevant to the planet's current circumstances that the Goddess must address than horsetail trees or trilobites. That Aeon just passing away, whose momentum yet spun the World past its own bumps along the road of Time, had not been the Goddess's Time. But She had been present.

The Goddess tasted Her anger again, at Tantivy's presumption. Who was She to be? Her question. Not Tantivy's. Then She peeled back Her anger. She wasn't really angry *at Tantivy*. Where did Her anger come from... and his presumption?

The Goddess peered back. Back through layers of emotion. Through outrage, and horror to incite outrage. Back through pain and struggle, through small triumphs, embittered by too much frustration to achieve them. She peeled away grandeur and menace alike of the passing Aeon, to a kernel, an essence of its way of sustaining life on the planet whose structure of reality it was to be Her job next to sustain... somehow.

At the passing Aeon's core, where its presiding God manifested most densely, to lay down the solid base on which that Aeon's Worldly edifice could grow to contain a forty-third floor office or thirty-seven thousand caged laying hens (not to mention the mandatory screaming roosters), the Goddess peered into the mirror of a life She had known as a long-lived slave.

A fairly well-treated slave, actually, Gurd was required to work hard, but seldom grueling. She had adequate if dull clothing and food... except that dreadful year of the famine. But even the lord went hungry that year.

Well, Axe was a good lord, set a noble example, had good sense, embodied vertu aplenty to manage the Domain and sire a vigorous brood. Gurd had seen several good lords, and several of the other sort in her long life. Lords came and went, rather like wet and dry cycles in the yearly weather.

It was especially Gurd's later years that the Goddess knew, years already of considerable memory, of peaceful times and turbulent, of harsh and gentle. Her own children, the three of seven who survived, grown and gone she never learned where, Gurd remained robust, if slow on achy feet and blurry of vision, a full generation in which to tend other people's children, and eventually some of those children's children.

Gurd saw, in those years, how fate cast people's lots in life, and what they made of their lots.

People of all ranks who knew her respected Gurd. Well, she had taught lord and scullery maid alike to wipe their noses and not to bash in each other's noggins with a soup ladle at whim. Yet, grown, they all believed that rank determined competence. Just because she lived well enough to consider her circumstances, Gurd's slavery galled the more.

The Goddess did not like the World Gurd knew. Yet life must have some structure.

While the Goddess searched the cabinets for ingredients, not to mention flavors, to improve the aeonic stew that She was inheriting, Tantivy tossed Temenos' voluminous baggage into Serefina's pink van. Temenos managed to maneuver himself from wheelchair to passenger's seat unassisted. Tantivy folded the wheelchair.

A convoy of semis roared through Interstate turon traffic, hauling bell peppers and maquiladora electronics up from Mexico, and toxic waste and ammunition back south to produce more. "Agony And Doom" blared from the pink van's sound system. The album was ten years old, but Tantivy remained loyal to the Electric Luddites' roots in Becky's Ham where they had gotten their start.

"Oops!" Tantivy ejaculated. "Sprung a sproing,"

"Broke it?" Temenos felt unsure at kaleidoscopic energy. Panic as not having the wheelchair? Anger at Tantivy for careless hurry? Sheer noise? Life's vitality rising to necessity? Or to proximity of the Goddess?

"Bet Serefina's got a vice grips and phillips head somewhere," Tantivy answered. Tantivy fired up the van and popped a beer.

Temenos was not sure if that constituted an answer.

The howling tape ground to a tortured halt almost as hideous as the grinding of the van's starter, when Tantivy turned the key. Then both tape and van blasted back to life.

"You remember Fernald?" Tantivy asked, popped the clutch and laid rubber around a Winebago from Wisconsin. "Hold your aneurysm, Grandma," Tantivy waved his beer and grinned at the startled Winebago driver.

Temenos' ears burned in embarrassment. Rattled, he replied, "Oh sure. 'Expository Lump.'"

Tantivy laughed. That was what Fernald's students had called him, fondly mind you, though not to his face. "We're having dinner at Fernald's trailer."

Temenos sighed. Fernald hated his dentures. His idea of dinner usually consisted entirely of mashed potatoes lumpier than his exposition, and drier. He never had butter. Claimed to forget. At least Fernald kept salt. His coffee would not dissolve a horseshoe... quite.

"She likes him," Tantivy shrugged. She'd even do his laundry if he ever remembered to give it to her."

"The Goddess?" Temenos asked in surprise.

"Serefina," said Tantivy. The van bumped and blared through the creosote, heat haze shimmering off desert pavement to impart fluidity to hills and forested mountains rising in dreamy tiers ahead. Tantivy tapped time on the steering wheel and guzzled beer.

Temenos slid through his exhaustion, of illness and Greyhound restrooms that he barely had strength to reach, of road roar and what had to be the fourth time through "Agony And Doom". Out, right out of the fumes that leaked through not-quite-all-together exhaust manifold connection, out of his own not-quite-all-together body, to a familiar high valley bowl, where sun sparkled off spring-delicate budding aspen leaves and thin air smelled sweet as columbine dew. Stillness surrounded Temenos, in deer-wooded mountain sunshine where the loudest sound was avian melody and an occasional fly. The aetheric stream tinkled, small but fresh in Temenos' headwaters shrine. "Oh, oh!" Tantivy's edge cut right through Temenos' meditation, to rouse him once again to worldly attention. All too soon, Temenos thought, with all-too-well-founded dread. Yet, a halo of fine new hair had sprouted on Temenos' cancer-treatment-bald noodle. Even his knees felt warm with renewed blood flow, if still as wobbly as the Aeon.

"License and proof of insurance, Sir," said the state trooper, "and I need to ask you both to step out. Keep your hands where I can see them, please."

Open container. Three tenths over the legal limit.

"Dumb move, kid," said the trooper, as he snapped the cuffs on Tantivy, made considerably more uncomfortable by the four inch spikes on Tantivy's leather wristlet.

Temenos stood by the now-silent pink van, concentrating on his trembling legs.

Temenos had not been on his feet so long in years. He also had not been drinking. He even had a license. The cop magnanimously let Temenos have the van, so as not to have to impound it. But he hauled Tantivy off to the slammer. Temenos hadn't driven in thirteen years.

Serefina invited Temenos to stay in her six by eight garage room. The same size as Tantivy's cell, it differed in essence in that Temenos came and went by his choice. He could step outside to taste the aroma of warm tortillas and industrial solvents, and to view the stars any time he pleased. A good thing as, unlike Tantivy's cell, Serefina's garage room contained no plumbing.

Fernald didn't mind postponing the dinner engagement. He had plenty of potatoes and salt.

Serefina shared her beans, carrot juice and triple chocolate fudge cake. Temenos bought himself a can of fiery jalapeño peppers.

The Goddess went online to consult Her *Cusp Manual*.

The Cusp Manual was a compendium available in the Library of Heaven for dealing with those anomalous but recurring spots in Time where one structure of known reality changes to some other. Fernald had edited the current edition.

Fernald used the advance from this job to purchase his trailer and the lot on which it sat on the side of a rough hill in the border town of Becky's Ham, where rip-roaring Old West vitality met the smiling face of infinite bureaucratic inertia and protean turquoise-bellied lizards draped the fence posts. A wise investment on Fernald's part. The book never came close to earning out. The online version got loose on the Net. If Fernald's publisher committed suicide or dropped his laptop in the hot tub by accident no one ever knew.

"Let's see," the Goddess mused. "Tantivy, who is action, in jail. Temenos, incarnate shrine of tranquillity, scarfing jalapeños, not to mention driving Serefina's van with the half-turn wobble in the steering column in yuppity boom box traffic."

Opposites. The Goddess was familiar with that heading. Union of Opposites appealed to Her as wholesome basic aeonic stew ingredient. She checked the Opposites directory: Opposites, Union of. Opposites, War of. Opposites, Turning into Each Other. She clicked in. Something about opposites turning into each other...

And She sighed. The exuberant nature of the Net had not improved on Fernald's indexing quirks. The Goddess clicked hither and yon. "Let's see…"

Opposites Turning into Each Other and Aeonic Architecture: Enantiodrome, Sterling, Bruce. Heavenly Palaces: (Ugaritic, Author Unknown. Click to *Anat.*)

The Goddess did, then scrolled a few pages down, to get past antique-style interminable invocations.

"…wading in warriors' gore up to Her armpits…"

"Yechh!" said the Goddess. She hit *Back.* Scrolled down some more of the Opposites Turning into Each Other subdirectory.

Cyberquanta: Wiener, Norbert. (For Thoom's sake, don't let him wander into Ave Mass alone; he's the original Space Nerd.)

Ave Mass? Was this physics or theology? The Goddess looked it up. Turned out to be a typo. Should have been, "Mass. Ave." Street in front of MIT.

The Goddess read on in the Cyberquanta listing: Surface Tension: Von Franz, Marie-Louise. Highlighted in several colors to indicate a cusp indicator.

The Goddess opened the file. Illuminated alchemical texts in Gothic script. Lavish illustrated poetry chapbooks. A sidebar explained the necessity of the curlicues and embellishments: "Frills and all manner of fanciful detail, in a way even decadence itself, are a prime indicator of the surface tension phenomenon, required as energy builds toward Change and intensifies to change to something. While entropy may proceed continuously, creative Change entails quantum discontinuity. Approaching breakthrough can be recognized by pataphysical backwash."

Just then, there was a knock on Serefina's door. "I know you're in there, Serefina."

Serefina was in the bath, dreaming of impossible Love, to join in Union with a man who could give as much emotionally as his own hunger. Was that Andy? Andy was sweet, and a huge help keeping the van running, though he could be childish. Serefina wasn't sure, but who but a friend would call her by name? She started to stand up and reach for the towel.

"Open up, Serefina. This is the police."

Serefina still wasn't sure if the voice was Andy's, but that was not the sort of joke she needed to bother with wet.

Temenos hid in the pantry. Too distracted even to think of his broken wheelchair, Temenos' hair grew out two feet, if chalk white.

The Goddess's computer screen flashed portentiously:

<_<HELP!>_>

the computer yelled, as it were, by flashing big print, bold, flaming vermilion, all caps lettering,

<I'M THE GOD THE BALD-ASS MONKEYS INVOKE>
<BUT IT AIN'T MY PLANET!>

Ghachh! Just what the Goddess didn't need. A heavenly hotshot freaking out, when it was raining telephone poles on the parade.

Well, aeonic cusps were like that.

<MIT {~_@@@}>

flashed on the screen, just as big, but chartreuse and not very bold at all. Then the screen went dead as a Monday morning dumpster cheeseburger.

The Goddess felt sympathy. She also felt annoyed. What a mess!

The Goddess's predecessors must have run into this sort of situation. The Goddess sighed. Fernald had lost his own hard copy of the *Cusp Manual,* and then left Serefina's copy on the shelf under the south window, where steam from boiling potatoes condensed and the pages of the Cusp Manual mildewed.

Serefina finished her bath, soothing balm at least to a broken heart. Condensed bath steam glistened on healthy leaves of the philodendron hanging in its umber and ocher stoneware pot above the clean turquoise enamel of Serefina's bathroom windowsill. Eventually, Serefina slipped on her faded blue house coat, rumpled and a bit threadbare, clothes-line-fresh cotton at its sensual softest. She opened her front door to let in spring air, noon-warm and not too spring-blustery, while she brushed her silver and cocoa hair, only to discover a note, an official form in fact, dangling from the doorknob, flicking back and forth in the breeze.

"Your dog is impounded," the note read. There was also a checklist. "Bit child," was checked.

This didn't make any sense. Serefina's big, affectionate, fluffy brown dog, Remember, lay wagging her elegant half-curled tail by the bathroom door.

Serefina wrote a note stating as much, but that if her dog did bite a child she certainly needed to know about it. She included numbers of

Remember's city and rabies shot tags. Then she asked Temenos to drive the van down to the police station for her, to deliver the note and inquire.

Temenos was so punchy by now, from everything contradicting his quiet nature, that this request didn't even seem odd to him.

Sweet-natured, Serefina's dog, Remember, could snap when startled. The dog had bitten a child, on the finger, had broken the skin slightly. Did it matter that the child frequently teased the dog, that Remember snapped only once? Remember must be impounded and observed for ten days. Serefina's alternatives were to pay all expenses and restrain the dog henceforth, or Remember would be gassed.

The officer explained this with professional courtesy, perhaps even sympathy. Becky's Ham was a small town, on the always-volatile border of World and Beyond. Everyone there who didn't run screaming at their first scorpion knew they sailed the winds of Time in a small, if vital craft, with only each other to maintain.

Temenos appreciated the officer's courtesy, but he exited the City/County Public Safety Building even more dazed than he had entered. "All expenses," at government rates, came to as much per day as Serefina and Fernald combined had to live on for three months.... Not to mention moral complexity.

Just then, who should appear but Tantivy, smelling like he'd slept in his clothes, which he had. "Hey there," Tantivy called.

Had Tantivy escaped? "Uh, hello?" Temenos asked.

"Catch a ride?" Tantivy asked back.

"I guess," said Temenos, more than a little nervous. Tantivy could affect Temenos that way, even when the World wasn't running to silly putty.

Tantivy was not a fugitive. The D.A. had let him go on his own recognizance. The cops knew him. He'd show up for arraignment. He didn't have bail money. The cops wanted Tantivy out of the jail. They had a condemned man coming in, awaiting transport to Death Row, and the fifteen or twenty years of caged legal appeals limbo the taxpayers would shell out for to torture him before he would fry or not. Remember's fate would at least be simpler.

Did the condemned man deserve his punishment? Did he even do whatever he had been condemned for? Tantivy didn't know. The cops just wanted Tantivy out of there because Tantivy would not do any great harm out in the World, but the presence of so-stimulating a personality was the last thing the cops wanted around some of the other characters in their jail while the Dead Man passed through.

Ironic that. If stimulating enough to discombobulate Temenos just by saying, "Hi," Tantivy himself felt anything but stimulated. Jail had him constipated.

"You're back," Serefina greeted Tantivy. "Go tell Fernald we're on for dinner."

Tantivy groaned. "Think I could slip some Metamucil in the potatoes?"

"Don't you think of anyone but yourself?" Serefina growled.

Temenos' mouth fell open. He hadn't said a word yet about Remember, to upset Serefina. She must feel... something.

"Gotta borrow your *Cusp Manual*," the Goddess burst in. "Computer crashed."

"Sorry," said Serefina. "It went to slime. I tossed it. Maybe Fernald knows what you need?"

"Getting it out of him useful's another story!" the Goddess growled, a sound akin to Serefina's growl as a mama grizzly's might be to a mama beagle's.

Serefina burst into tears. "Remember!"

Temenos gave Serefina a brief hug, then sat on a folded, somewhat threadbare quilt to meditate. (Everything Serefina had was somewhat threadbare. She bought all clothing at yard sales or the Hopeful Elephant Thrift Store... and made her quilts out of what was left of clothes no longer fit to wear.)

Temenos meditated on his cancer. What had caused it? Pollution? Noise? Well, no. Too much aetheric mud stirred up, too much distraction, Nature inundated by too many people?... This weakened Temenos, perhaps made him vulnerable, certainly made his job more difficult. But what had turned truly malignant on Temenos was the New Age fiasco. People who did recognize energic intensification of aeonic Change, and took that to sanction, even to sanctify!... whatever self-indulgent, pea brained nonsense came into their heads.

Yet even that was merely all-too-human, short-sighted... well, disaster if it gave Temenos cancer. And it did because it evoked a reaction which so utterly negated Temenos' legitimate existence that cancer had become his only responsible response. Oh, he could have gone mad instead, but that would have been dishonorable.

It was not just that people who knew what a sweat lodge was broke beer bottles in the fire pit. It was that they genuinely believed that a World which required them to do so was the only reality.

While Temenos struggled to purge the demons that had dug so deep into him as once to have given his body a cancer, Tantivy… and the Goddess… danced down to Fernald's trailer.

"Sheesh, Dude," said Tantivy, "ain't you got nothing but spuds, salt, and the coffee pot from Hell?"

"I invested decades in preparation for a simple, sedate retirement," Fernald smiled beatifically.

"Oh, Man," Tantivy squirmed, "I gotta walk. That jail was forever. I feel like a stiff."

"Circumambulatio," said Fernald.

"Huh?" said Tantivy. "Hey, you having a fit?"

Fernald's smile melted to Elsewhere. His eyes dilated, then rolled back and shut, as he sank to his stained, maroon velvet sofa in a cloud of dust and juniper pollen.

"Take Temenos," the Goddess spoke. She knew Her own Nature enough to know that Fernald responded to Her presence by responding to Her question, Her urgency how to sustain Her Aeon that was budding more precipitously than Becky's Ham apricots and forsythia. Everyone did that: responded to the Goddess's urgency, if not always in ways relevant to the question so urgent to Her. Fernald, however pedantic, transcended personal emotional reaction to respond with something useful to the Goddess more than most.

"Yeow!" Tantivy ran.

Tantivy's response was relevant too, but action, for all its attraction, needed some steering. That was the Goddess's job, newly inherited, with a lot of Her predecessor's leftovers that She had to sort out if She ever would make Her way through to a Time in which to sustain a next coherent World on this planet.

The Goddess reflected again, to a more or less coherent Time in the life of the passing Aeon, which was not Her Time, but in which She had known a life by which to reflect.

"Circumambulatio," the adept spoke to his soror mystica.

Actually, Elaine was the more adept alchemist of the couple. Magister Tirien acknowledged this to her, in the herb garden and in bed, though it was he who treated patients as respected physician (except for certain matters pertaining to childbirth) and he who performed the alchemical Opus, she who assisted. Such was the way of life they both knew.

Elaine and Tirien took their procedures literally: At the beginning of the Opus, at each new attempt, or refinement as one might at least hope, one encountered the Prima Materia, the substance that the Opus must transmute, in its initial condition of Massa Confusa. The Circumambulatio as focusing meditation in action, introduced sufficient contained order to begin construction of the Hermetic Vessel, in which for the Opus to transmute the Prima Materia thereby defined to the Elixir, the Lapis, the Philosophical Gold... which was not the vulgar gold.

Chemicals literally measured and refined in retorts, to preliminary elixirs which might demonstrate their virtue in renewing the ill. Likewise, work on themselves, the Circumambulatio required literal action:

Elaine and Tirien, wife and husband to each other, respected midwife and physician to the World, mystic sister and adept to the Opus Alchymicum, began their days with a walk: Circumambulatio. To walk around, enclosure defined, created one must at least hope, through the act of walking around it, of walking around it many times. Meditative indeed, whether it did the Opus, or even the patients, any good, Elaine and Tirien's daily walk kept their blood flowing, and their love too. Worldly recognition be what it might, Elaine knew few wives luckier than she in Tirien.

The Goddess returned to Her pantry, to search out nourishing and flavorful aeonic ingredients, and a name thereby for those Her Aeon would sustain to invoke Her.

Circumambulatio was something Temenos and Tantivy could do together, by which for the Goddess to reflect: Who was She to be? How might the World invoke Her by which to sustain Her coming next Aeon? To walk, to move, action was Tantivy. The Spirit-container which the Circumambulatio defined was Temenos.

"Thanks, Fernald," the Goddess called. Being a Goddess, She could readily exist in the pantry of Heaven and Fernald's dusty, paper-strewn trailer simultaneously. But Fernald snored an old man's dream. Just as well, perhaps. How much Expository Lump could anyone stand in Becky's Ham on border of World and Beyond, let alone in volatility of an aeonic cusp?

The Goddess stirred Her aeonic stew, gently, ever so gently on a planet writhing in throes of incipient Change. She tasted, refined, stirred and tasted again.

Serefina mourned loving, doomed Remember.

Temenos and Tantivy walked, out among the World and its people and doings and ways so various, lovely and monstrous alike. Tantivy strode frantic for intestinal release. Temenos struggled to maintain coherent composure amid so much distraction of a World in which both coherence and composure were melting, melting away on cusp of an Aeon awash in curlicues and furbelows and products of huge achievement to sustain life in the way of a God Whose Time was done, as pressure built to Change to what way the Goddess stirred Her stew and tasted to discover, the next way that the planet Hers next to sustain might live.

As for Fernald, he eventually woke from his nap, rinsed a big potfull of potatoes, and set them to boil.

Author's note: Becky's Ham, inspired by Silver City, New Mexico, is the border town of World and Dreamworld. Alchemy is important to coherence. Whether coherence is important is a… mutable question.

WARRIOR'S HONOR

Smooth-browed in full flush of youth, Xenon, the mighty hunter, stood proud and tall before King Filander's throne of mastodon tusks. Last moon, the Kronx had raided his Plune people. Now the Plune would have vengeance.

"You would join our raiding party?" asked King Filander. He shifted his gristly buttocks.—Mastodon tusks made a seat more impressive than comfortable.

"I will," Xenon replied. His bow of mastodon-hide-wrapped yerry wood stood as tall as he and nearly as thick as his sinewy wrist. No one else could string that bow, let alone draw it.

"Very well," said the king, broad chest still hard under skin a bit loose from forty years of weather. "You've proven yourself a hunter. We'll see if you make a warrior."

Xenon felt the mingled confidence and doubt of the other Plune warriors. He knew none was stronger than he. Most had hunted with him. Xenon it was who had taken the great beast, twice his height with legs thick as a mighty man's chest, on whose tusks King Filander now sat. Surely the warriors and the king could not doubt Xenon's courage.

The raiding party set out for the Kronx village. Spikey perrius bushes studded rugged hillsides. Xenon felt strong sun through pollution-free prehistoric skies on his broad, bronze shoulders. Rocks gleamed purple and orange.

It was a robust life the Plune and Kronx and other tribes of their world lived. King Filander trotted up and down the steep hillsides right along with his warriors, most, like Xenon, half his age, but two grey and stringy and half again as old. It was a world where you were strong or dead and not much in between.

The raiding party was a large one: Thirty men loped up and down the hard, vital hills. Ravens skrawked. Pteranodons swooped. Xenon smelled fragrant pine in the sunshine and the stink of a skunk-bear.

Then the Plune raiding party crested the ridge above the Kronx village. They crouched behind mica-sparkling grey and tan boulders, undetected, so it seemed, by Kronx lookouts.

Kronx women worked skins by the doors of their lodges, or ground the sweet, nourishing pulp from fibrous sendor roots. Naked children scampered here and there in the bright sunshine.

Half a dozen Kronx warriors stood to one side of the village, palavering. Did they gloat at last moon's raid? Did they parley preparing the next? Well, the Plune had a surprise in store for them.

Silently, Xenon pulled down one end of his bow, the other resting against his instep. His beefy arm flexed with smooth, young power as the wood bowed to allow Xenon to slip the mastodon gut string onto his bow. Xenon plucked an arrow, fletched with bright orange fli feathers, from the otter hide quiver that hung behind his hard, left shoulder nearly to his right knee. He nocked the arrow and drew his bow. Xenon felt the strain across his chest. Vitality coursed through his body. He held the bow steady as the boulder he peered around. He knew no other Plune warrior could hold that bow at full draw without hands shivering from the strain.

Xenon took careful aim. He let go. His arrow arced through the blazing blue sky. The point struck a Kronx warrior right in the chest. The shaft penetrated. The enemy fell, clutching his breast. The arrow had pierced all the way through. Only the feathered end stood out over the Kronx warrior's heart. Nearly as long as the Kronx warrior was tall, the arrow's point stopped his fall when it struck the ground. He teetered, then tipped slowly to the right and toppled.

Xenon raised his arms above his head, bow in his left hand, another arrow in the other, ready to draw and shoot again. His fellow Plune raiders stood to both sides on the rugged ridge. Xenon knew all his companions had seen how true his arrow flew. But instead of the exultation he expected, Xenon felt *shame!*

Xenon felt abject mortification. He had been overcome by intoxication of the hunt. How could a would-be Plune warrior act in such cowardice as to kill another human being at a distance, where the other warrior did not know he was there, could not fight back, where he, Xenon, did not have to look his adversary in the eyes?

* * *

"It worked!" Jack Sproul emerged from the gameworld filled with all the triumph his game surrogate could not feel. Gameworlds had grown in sophistication by increments, of course. Rock-strewn hills... or mastodon tusk throne, skrawk of raven: Sight and sound reached a convincing level of verisimilitude first. The feel of flexing arms drawing a bow, the scent of skunk-bear, the knowledge of creatures and things in the gameworld that didn't exist in the player's physical reality, were more recent. Now, Jack had achieved a new level of gameworld reality. The world conveyed its own emotional context. Xenon felt shame because the culture of that gameworld would react so.

The game psychology was still a little rough, a little simplistic. Jack would work on that. Why didn't Xenon remember that he should know better? Why didn't King Filander tell him the moral rules? Jack felt certain it made sense in context. He had the beginnings of why: A young man intoxicated with his own physical abilities. A primitive society where it had not occurred to people to articulate their own standards. Jack could refine the game later. He had achieved the breakthrough: Context conveyed relevant emotions which could even take an individual player's character by surprise. Xenon felt shame at the cowardice of killing another warrior he had not had to look in the eyes, rather than the triumph he expected. Jack, in the gameworld, felt Xenon's emotions, and Xenon's surprise.

The mechanism derived from basic studies of the psychology of delinquency: People whose behavior society called delinquent tended to perceive expressions of those around them as disgust or otherwise disapproving, while less-alienated people experienced the same expressions as neutral or even approving. Everyone responded to nonverbal cues. Further study illuminated how self-image and context combined... not to determine response, but to shade it in one direction or another.

This led to investigation of the archaic concept of omens and portents: A cloud passes in front of the sun at a crucial moment. Birds burst into song. Individual sensitivity to feedback varied. But argument over "truth" or superstition in no way affected psychological effectiveness of synchronous juxtaposition of events. Emotionally relevant feedback, subtle or blatant, could be built into the game.

Xenon did not need to be aware that when he released his arrow the temperature dropped a couple degrees, that the sun shone slightly less bright, that a Kronx baby whimpered just as his arrow struck. He did not even need to notice the stiffened stance nor the disapproving expressions of his fellow Plune warriors. Better they should be in his peripheral vision than in his face. Better a slightly stale aroma intrude his nostrils than a blast of decaying corpses.

Jack e-mailed Sheila Grijalva, his agent and dear friend: "I've done it! Let's celebrate." Jack didn't say what he'd done. Sheila knew Jack was working on emotions of context. Neither of them was about to let some cyberthief steal Jack's breakthrough.

Sheila e-mailed Jack back an hour later: "That's great. How about The Rimrock tonight at seven?"

Jack confirmed, then called The Rimrock Café to make reservations. Though called a café, The Rimrock was actually a quite-classy restaurant. Elegant decor. Excellent kitchen. Not cheap... but not extravagant either. Jack and Sheila both knew Jack's achievement might really take off, might bring fame and fortune. They'd celebrate that when and if it happened.

But they did have something to celebrate now, and Jack knew it, as he dressed for dinner... which meant just clean, new jeans, polished boots, and a dress shirt. A faster-paced reality had infected Jack's world the past few years, but this was still informal, small town New Mexico. Funny thing, too, the reality of gameworlds these days: Some players lived vicariously in cyberspace, their bodies the color and consistency of dead fish. Others, Jack Sproul among them, reacted the opposite way. After feeling Xenon's smooth muscles drawing that bow, Jack couldn't live in too blobby a body himself.

Even if he were twenty again rather than forty-three, he would never have a body like Xenon's, but living in bodies such as Xenon's in his gameworlds had given Jack the impetus to get into better shape at forty-three than he actually was at twenty.... That was a good deal of what gave him the idea to include the older warriors or King Filander's firm muscles behind slightly stretched-out skin. If kids who bought his game didn't care about older characters in the gameworld, they probably wouldn't mind. It added to verisimilitude of atmosphere, which the kids would appreciate as much as any older player.

Jack felt good, physically as well as emotionally, as he brushed his still-thick hair, sprinkled with just enough grey to look distinguished. But then he thought: Gratification. Positive resolution. Egads!

Jack plunged back into his gameworld. He had less than an hour before he needed to leave for dinner. Never mind refining background psychology for now. Why Xenon didn't know better before he shot his arrow and no one stopped him could come later. What Jack needed for Sheila now was some way for a game character readily to resolve a negative emotional situation to a positive one.

The scenario was still rough when Jack shut down and dashed out to his elderly Datsun, hair more dishevelled than distinguished, dress shirt rumpled and a bit sweaty.... Jack wondered, but had never really investigated, if mental effort caused him to sweat or if physical exertion of his game surrogate somehow bled through.... The scenario was rough, but he *had something*, at least, to show Sheila.

The game did not now end with Xenon's shame. Now what happened, when shame unexpectedly overtook Xenon, was that the game announced: "Congratulations. You have just found one of the keys to this gameworld. You are now ready to enter the next level of Warrior's Honor." Lots of possibilities followed. But the player... as Xenon... now consciously knew that to win at the game he could only defeat another warrior who knowingly fought him, and that both must look the other in the eyes.

Rough, but Sheila would be much happier. Truth to tell, Jack liked it better this way too. The game conveyed emotional context, but it also gave the player positive reward to strive for.

Jack dodged traffic, only recently become so thick and fast in Ace High, New Mexico, through crisp early winter evening. Even with the lights of the small city of ten thousand, stars sparkled overhead nearly as bright, it seemed to Jack, as in the pristine skies of his gameworld.

Sheila met Jack in the lobby of The Rimrock. Her thick, black hair had about as much grey in it as Jack's, but lay neat on the fresh, green, cotton blouse she wore this evening.

"Hope I didn't keep you waiting?" Jack greeted Sheila.

"I've only been here a minute," Sheila replied. "Been hunting mastodons again?"

"That bad, huh?" Jack grinned, and ran a hand through his fly-away hair.

"Not bad at all," said Sheila. "You just look like you've been up to your eyebrows in inspiration."

"Thanks. You look great, as always. How's the family?"

"Fine."

Jack caught Alice Merriweather's eye. The Rimrock's efficient manager, a little younger than Jack or Sheila, Alice knew them both. "Got your table all set for you," Alice smiled. "The rellenos are top notch tonight."

"Thanks." Jack and Sheila followed Alice to the table Sheila customarily preferred when meeting with clients.... Jack had seen Sheila at the same table with another client, at a different one with her husband, Sam, and their four-year-old daughter, Aida. Jack was impressed that Alice remembered among so many customers.

Frances, their waitress, knew both Jack and Sheila too. She brought their chips and salsa and remembered that Sheila preferred her water without ice. Sheila did order the chiles rellenos. Jack ordered a combination plate, which included a relleno. They ordered a carafe of the house red wine. They didn't even ask what it was. They knew Alice, as a matter of course, served a wine of miraculous quality for its price.

"Well, what have you got for me?" Sheila asked, as Frances headed for the kitchen with their order. Sheila dipped a warm, crisp tortilla chip in the salsa. The Rimrock made its own salsa, fresh daily. Jack could smell the cilantro.

Jack told Sheila about his breakthrough: "Emotions of context: I've done it. The game conveys feelings your character would have in its world, whether or not it would occur to you... or even to your character."

Jack told Sheila about Xenon and his bow and how he felt the difference between shame when he shot the Kronx warrior, at a distance, unseen, and honor in fighting another brave warrior face to face.

"King Filander!" Sheila laughed. "Really!"

"I'll change it," Jack grinned and blushed simultaneously. "There's a lot to refine."

"No," said Sheila. "Keep it. Most players won't get it. Those who do will get a kick out of it."

Jack smiled a bit sheepishly. He continued telling Sheila about the emotional reality of the game.

Frances brought their wine.

"Frances," Sheila asked, "where's Gary tonight?"

Jack knew one reason Sheila liked that particular table was that she and a client could talk there well. Quiet, private, out of the way, at the same time it was comfortable with a pleasant view of The Rimrock's tasteful decor: Wood trim. Just the right amount of light. Good quality paintings by (albeit mostly only recently) local artists, mostly of people in local, Southwestern settings. The other reason Sheila... and Jack liked this table was that it gave them a good view of Gary Cummins, who had played classical guitar at The Rimrock from October to April, Wednesday through Saturday evenings, the past four years. The distance was just right: Close enough to hear the music, far enough for discussion.

"Oh, it's awful," said Frances. "He had to quit. He walks over, you know. Gang kids have been hassling him. They beat him up on his way over last Friday. It was dark, but it was only five-thirty. They broke his guitar."

"That's obscene!" said Sheila. "Despicable little cowards!"

Jack agreed. It was also shocking.

Ten years ago, Ace High was a sleepy mining town. Four years ago, it had a nice little local arts scene. Three years ago it got *discovered*. Four galleries mushroomed to forty. From zero, there suddenly were six espresso shops. New upscale Toyotas and Volvos would outnumber old Ford and Chevy pickups any day.... Several of the latter now sported a bumper sticker which read: "Kill a yuppie for Jesus."

Businesses that struggled for five years to keep Main Street alive after the Wal-Mart came in on the highway... just half a mile beyond the Ace High city limits, where it didn't pay city taxes... got swept right out of locations some of them had been in for three generations this last year, when rents sextupled.

The patriarch of a long-time local Hispanic family was now in jail, awaiting trial for assaulting a city zoning inspector with a mortar trowel. The old man had been building a two foot rock wall along the lower side of his yard to keep Southwest summer monsoon rains from washing out the soil. The city zoning inspector had delivered a cease-and-desist order on the stone wall and a citation, for failure to obtain a permit.

Four years ago, no one in Ace High, New Mexico had ever thought of needing a permit to maintain their own home and property. Wages were low. Living costs were low. Neighbors were friendly. Any violence in the streets, of which there was little, was between people who knew each other, almost always when all participants were drunk. Two years ago there were two gang-related incidents all year. In the last six months there had been so many stabbings, shootings, robberies, and arbitrary assaults on persons and property that no one could even keep track any more.

It was scary.

Ace High had seemed an ideal retreat from a civilization going nuts when Jack Sproul settled there fifteen years ago. As civilization went more nuts and Jack became sufficiently established to earn a living at his work, Ace High only seemed better. Jack hated the way life had speeded up the past few years. He hated seeing neighbors and friends' businesses squeezed out, by rising costs as much as by Wal-Mart. At the same time, some pretty interesting cultural doings had come to town, and some interesting people with them, not to mention good restaurants. For all that long-time cultural refugees like Jack Sproul joined other Ace High old timers in grumbling about "Californicators", Jack was one of many who found stimulating friends among the newcomers, as well as increased opportunity, in their arrival. Sheila Grijalva, who *did,* indeed, move to Ace High, New Mexico from California, had provided Jack's greatest new access to opportunity. *Now!...*

Jack felt outrage. He felt fear. But Sheila was right! What was the matter with those punks? They were cowards!

Gary Cummins was older than Jack or Sheila, and he looked it. Jack knew a little of Gary's history: Nominated to West Point by a then-freshman senator, now running for president as it happened. Captain in the army in Vietnam. Came back disillusioned and disgusted. "The military leaders of our country honored the principle that America's freedom requires the military services to be subservient to the civilian government," Gary once said to Jack. "I still respect that integrity, but when the politicians get as corrupt as they were behind Vietnam... I couldn't serve any more."

Gary didn't elaborate, but Jack knew he'd quit as soon after Vietnam as he could. Took LSD. Grew pot. Didn't see another human being for months at a time for several years in the Seventies. Played guitar a lot. Now Gary was probably in his early fifties, but looked older. His hair was not only a lot greyer than Jack's likely would be by that age, but it lay limp and unhealthy. Gary was visibly missing several teeth.—Jack recalled his Grandma Sproul speaking of toothless old people when reminiscing of the world in which she was young. When Jack was a kid, he never saw people with missing teeth. If they lost teeth, they got dentures. Not any more.

The Rimrock fed Gary well nights he played. He had clean, intact clothes to wear to play in. Other than that, Jack wasn't sure how Gary lived, but if tips at The Rimrock were his only regular income, as Jack suspected, it must be pretty minimally.

How could those kids attack someone like Gary? Jack thought. Whatever they were mad at in the world, and Jack believed they might well have plenty to be mad at, someone like Gary Cummins was surely not the cause. Nor was robbery a credible motive. Gary was on his way to work... what little money he would make. The kids who attacked him probably even knew what he was about. He walked every evening he played. The guitar those kids destroyed was likely the only possession of value Gary owned.

"What a shame," said Sheila as Frances went to tend another table.

"Way to ruin a good meal," said Jack, feeling his anger. Then he blushed at thinking of himself when a lot more than a good meal had been ruined for Gary Cummins.

Jack thought of the intensity of his own emotional reaction. Then Jack thought of Xenon, of his own experience as Xenon, full of the physical aggression which belonged to his character, which was an essential part of why Xenon's electronically generated personality felt real, that Jack felt as his own in the gameworld. Oblivious to moral implication of what he did with that aggression, Xenon was susceptible to moral growth. Was that just a construct of the gameworld? Did it belong to Jack's moral consciousness rather than any inherent potential in Xenon, let alone some other real person? Maybe. But maybe not. Jack believed the reason Xenon could make a jump in feeling from blind aggressive exultation to shame at cowardice in how he expressed that aggression was context.

There was a sort of personal bleed-through, of course. Xenon was Jack in the gameworld. He had mental capacities affected by Jack's... just as Jack, as himself, absorbed effects of his experience as Xenon... such as feeling the need to get in shape. The more real the gameworld got, the more real the experience reflected both ways.

But those kids making the so-recently-sleepy streets of Ace High a scary place were human beings, susceptible to human emotion. Jack believed cries against those kids' aggression were silly and fruitless. In many ways, it was just that aggression... when, so-very-recently, it seemed safely someplace else, which had inspired Jack to the warrior personalities of his gameworlds.

"There's got to be a way," Jack blurted.

"To what?" asked Sheila.—A stranger might be mystified, but Sheila had seen Jack in the throes of inspiration before. She had moved to Ace

High only three years ago, with the big yuppie influx. Sheila and Sam had moved in the belief that a New Mexico small town, like the one Sam's parents had moved from forty years earlier when Sam was a toddler, would provide a safer environment to raise their baby daughter than Southern California. They shared their fellow city sophisticates' prejudice against backwater locals. The intensity of Jack Sproul's inspiration had broken through that prejudice. It was a good deal of why Sheila took Jack on as a client. Both of them had been pleased with the result.

"Warrior's honor," Jack said. "Do they play games? What music do those kids listen to?—Start a rock band. Call it The Electric Luddites. Get on MTV.... But I bet they do play games, some of them anyhow.... Those gang kids are *warriors*, like in my game. They're not going to quit feeling how they feel, being what they are. But I bet they might quit acts they saw as cowardly. There's got to be a way they *can see*.... Warrior's *honor*! For Gary's sake."

Jack didn't even notice that Sheila refrained from interrupting his train of thought. Sheila nibbled chips and salsa and sipped wine while Jack scribbled notes on The Rimrock's paper napkins—with The Rimrock's stylized rock ledge logo printed on each.

Jack knew where his game scenario came from. There was a real debate in antiquity over the morality of archers in war. Many people regarded it as cowardly and dishonorable to be able to kill an enemy at a safe distance where an archer didn't need to look his adversary in the eye. Of course, the outcome in the ancient world was that peoples with no such scruples conquered those who refrained from use of archers in war. But... People can learn from history, Jack thought: Chivalry. The Round Table. The Samurai Code. Counting coup as higher honor than killing an enemy.

Jack thought of the psychological study of delinquents from which the concept of emotions of context got its start. Those gang kids beat up on someone like Gary because they were too alienated to care otherwise, but equally because they were too alienated to know what to do with values they might have.

Courage was a value Jack believed anyone feeling warrior energy might respect. That was someplace to start. What Jack needed to build into his game was linkage: Warrior's *honor*, in context relevant to the world of kids who might play the game, as to the fantasy of antiquity in the game's scenario.

What was the same and what different in ancient and modern context? Jack drew a line down his napkin. Aggression itself was the same, vitality in excitement, achievement... and courage as value. Not seeing who you attacked as being human, like yourself, was... maybe... the same. The reason why was different. Modern alienation was not the same as tribal insularity, but the effect was all too similar.

Jack thought of the positive principle in his game, of what did give a player a sense of achievement. Why did it matter to the Plune to fight an adversary they had to look in the eye? Courage, yes; honor, yes. But not just their own. To fight an adversary you could honor imparted a sense of honor and worth to a warrior. A player, and a player's character, could understand that principle. The understanding could make the game more challenging, and thereby more fun to play.

Frances came by with the water pitcher, topped off both Jack's and Sheila's glasses, taking care not to drop ice cubes into Sheila's. Sheila smiled. Jack never noticed a thing. Frances continued her rounds.

Jack's notes began to take on form. What did Xenon's warrior band have in common with modern gang kids? Physical aggression, of course. But also the size of group who knew each other. Personality, Jack thought. Xenon wanted to be recognized for his warrior prowess by *someone*. Give the game-generated other members of the band personalities for Xenon to matter to. Start with King Filander...

Nah... Jack crossed out that idea. The napkin he wrote on tore. Jack turned it over and wrote on the other side. Start with a couple of the other young warriors. Give them attributes Xenon respects: Endurance on the trail. Skill in the hunt. People in whose eyes for Xenon's honor to matter.

"Tough guy—cold," Jack wrote. Then: "Tougher guy whose secret is self-respect." Kids, of all people, would not tolerate preaching. Jack's own moral sense required a distinction between learning and brainwashing. But genuine learning, including moral learning, could be its own reward. Some players would want to win this game. In a society whose civilization seemed to be crumbling on all sides, could he not carry forward the historical concept of warrior's honor on which so many societies had built civilization? For Gary's sake, Jack had to try.

Frances brought Jack and Sheila's dinners.

Jack even noticed how good his chile relleno tasted.

"**W**arrior's Honor, Level Two."
Jack's hair looked about as distinguished as a raven's nest. He didn't care. He knew what came next. In Level Two, Xenon had more information in his electronic personality... of a sort relevant to both his own world and Jack's:

"...You've proven yourself a hunter," said King Filander. "We'll see if you make a warrior."

Xenon felt the mingled confidence and doubt of the other Plune warriors. Kortez, big as himself and tough as flint. Filon, thinner, and tough enough to wear Kortez right out. Xenon knew none was stronger than he. Most of the other Plune raiders had hunted with him. Xenon it was who had taken the great beast, twice his height with legs thick as a mighty man's chest, on whose tusks King Filander now sat. Surely the warriors and the king could not doubt Xenon's courage.

The raiding party set out for the Kronx village...

Physical sensations remained the same in the scene at Level Two: Strong sun on Xenon's strong shoulders. Rugged hills. Pteranodons swooping overhead. Scent of pine and of skunk-bear. But when Xenon released his arrow, he heard Filon stifle a cough. Not loud enough to alert Kronx warriors; just loud enough to inform Xenon, before his arrow struck, both that and why he did wrong.

Xenon knew why it was Filon who coughed. Not weakness. Kortez was stronger, almost as strong as Xenon himself. But on a starved and sun-blasted trail, in dessicating wind, Xenon knew Filon would outlast them all. Filon breathed the warrior Spirit of Plune *honor*. Xenon could feel this because Xenon knew Filon. When Filon coughed, Xenon knew what Spirit hitched breath in disapproval.

"Congratulations," the game announced. "You have found a key to Level Three of Warrior's Honor."

Author's note: The real guitar player, whose situation inspired this story, got to read it. Sadly, he later committed suicide. When a Russian fellow writer wanted to arrange for translation and publication of a story of mine in Russia, I found it notable that this was the one, of the several that I sent him, which actually appeared.

GERONIMO'S BUTTONS

The horses moved like a viscous dream across the shimmering Plains of San Augustine. Jordan Howes sighted down the giant white north arm of the VLA, two hundred ton metal disks pointed at forever in the hundred and five degree New Mexico sun.

"They look operational," said Mali Kapamali.

"Probably are," said Jordan. "Maybe someone'll even get them running again."

"Wonder what it would cost."

"Tail waggin' the dog." Jordan slapped his horse's neck, more in sympathy than any desire to move faster in the heat.

"Guess it will take a more stable currency before cost means much here," said Mali.

"Little much to pay for in coral." Jordan nodded to the huge saucer they were slowly approaching. "Still, I wouldn't mind looking at the edge of Creation."

"I don't think there was much to see from here," said Mali. "Took a lot of instruments to make any sense of the information."

"They look weird," said Pardee Howes, Jordan's twelve-year-old son.

"You should bring that boy to the city more often," said Mali.

"He was with me to the mango festival just last year at Phoenix."

"I hear as big as the trees are getting they're really starting to produce."

The three riders came to the first immense metal disk. Tumbleweeds were piled around the base where it sat on its track.

"Not much rust," said Mali.

"It's still dry here," said Jordan.

"And hot," said Pardee.

"Way I hear, you should see Saint Louis," said Mali.

"Hundred and thirty degrees," said Jordan. "No thank you."

"They say the weather's stable. The Mississippi's going to be like the Nile."

A herd of antelope took off to the east through the sage and dry grasses. The horses didn't mind a bit stopping so the riders could watch. An insect chorus, punctuated by bird solos, rang across the blazing blue sky.

Pardee cocked an ear to the southwest. "I think he's playing."

Mali listened. "I'll take your word for it."

"He usually is," Jordan said.

The horses slid through the heat. The distant shadow of hills, with their juniper and piñon trees, beyond the southwest arm of the Very Large Array radio telescope, beckoned. But no one pushed; it was too hot. They were beyond the last of the giant steel dishes before Mali was sure he heard the music.

This was the place he had followed his dream so far to find. Mali felt a tension rise till he could taste it. Music wove through the blazing sun, transmuting weight to fiery life.

"How did he get the piano in?" Mali asked.

"They hired him as caretaker when they shut down," said Jordan. "He put it in the contract."

"But how'd they do it? It doesn't look like there was ever a road back in these canyons."

"I heard about that," said Pardee. "Helicopter. I'd have liked to seen that."

"I remember helicopters," said Jordan. "Loud. Used to make me feel like demons were charging down out of the sky."

Puffs of pungent sage aroma drifted up from the slow horses' hoofs. Wild Appassionata Beethoven rang across the sun-baked plain.

"That sounds like hard work in this heat," said Mali.

"Especially for an old man," said Jordan.

At last, they reached the beginning of rougher country and a definite, if not-much-used trail. Before long, they passed a twisted juniper post topped by a board and a cow skull. There was just enough blistered turquoise and red paint left on the board to indicate it was once a sign. Jordan pointed to the board. "Paranoid Lizard Canyon."

"His idea of a joke?"

"Who knows?"

Pardee's horse snorted.

"He smells water," said Pardee.

"We are about there," said Jordan.

"Good," said Mali. "I'm about cooked."

"Listen to that old maniac!" said Pardee.

The slow movement had come and gone. Thunder now flew from the piano in the final presto.

"Makes me hot just to hear it," said Mali.

"That's how he conjures," said Jordan. "Look!"

Mali looked. Heat waves danced over the green junipers, grey and purple rock, dun earth, cerulean sky. Mali felt dizzy. Had he been out in the sun too long? He took off his straw hat and wiped his brow, took a sip of tepid water, and looked again to the sky above the thunder-voice of the roaring piano.

Female human figures coalesced briefly in the swirling air, large and small, imposing and delicate, then animals: horses, buffalo, a transient elephant. Mali felt the power, the life flowing into being from some unknown void through the music's magic. That life, itself, felt like the music's intent. Mali breathed in the pure, vibrant energy resounding through the fiery atmosphere.

The final chords crashed to ringing silence.

Mali smiled. "We've come to the right place."

With the end of the music, the dancing air was just arbitrary heat waves again.

Jordan sipped his canteen, then squeezed his horse's flanks. The horse farted and stepped leisurely down the trail. Mali and Pardee's horses followed of their own accord.

A raven flew up in front of the riders, squalling to the two little birds that chased and dodged and called all around it.

Tangible silence emanated from the still-invisible home of the pianist.

The riders rounded a rock-strewn knoll. Mali spotted the end of a faded brown log in the air, a beam that extended two feet beyond the end of an overhanging roof. Faded strips of cloth in many colors fluttered in the hot, just-barely breeze.

Suddenly, the piano crashed into the theme of the 1812 Overture.

"Hit the dust!" Pardee shouted.

Mali jumped from his horse too, just as what sounded like a cannon exploded over their heads. All three horses shied, but no harm was done.

Jordan held his seat. "He wouldn't risk hitting a horse."

"You think I can't aim?" a voice roared.

"Not with that blunderbuss," said Jordan.

Mali looked to his guide for reassurance.

The man with the immense-bored shotgun had Anglo features, but he was tanned almost as dark as the three riders, from the tips of his extraordinary pianist's fingers, over his pendulous belly, to the tips of his toes. Except for a string of small round bone beads around his neck, the pianist was stark naked. His waist-length snow white mane of hair and beard contrasted strikingly—and added to the wild appearance.

"Hah!" the pianist roared. He squinted at his company. "Jordan, that you?"

"You ought to get some damn glasses, Armand," Jordan said as he dismounted.

"Hell!" Armand Partridge bellowed, "they've been saying that for forty years. I like what I see."

Jordan led his horse up to the naked old man and held out a hand. The pianist grabbed his guest in a bear hug. Jordan thumped the old man on the back. The horse snorted as the barrel of the huge shotgun passed under his nose.

"You remember Pardee," said Jordan.

"Sure do," said Armand. "You're getting big." He hugged the boy.

Jordan introduced Mali. Armand hugged him too. Mali was a large man, but the old pianist lifted him right off the ground. Then he held him at arm's length, a firm hand on each shoulder. "Where you from?"

"Hawaii," said Mali.

"How'd you get here?"

"On a ship. We're sending out six or eight a year now."

Just then, another man appeared at the door of the rough, neat wooden house. He was also Anglo, also tanned, and at least ten years older than the pianist, who Mali knew was well into his seventies.

The older man had a goofy expression on his face. Old people often did, especially Anglos. The Teeber had hit them so hard.

The Teeber was a mutant form of tuberculosis, the derivation of its popular name. For tuberculosis, it was extremely fast. The archaic term, galloping consumption, was even revived in the medical journals—while they were still being published. The Teeber was still a ghastly way to die, coughing up blood and growing daily weaker for anything from a month to a year or more.

Only a century earlier, Natives of the Americas and the Pacific lacked immunities and died like flies in earlier epidemics. Regular tuberculosis was still a greater killer among Native Americans than others when the Teeber hit. Perhaps for that very reason, Natives of the Western Hemisphere had much better immunity this time. For full-blooded Native Americans, the fatality rate was less than ten percent. Mexicans, many of whom had long denied their Mestizo heritage, were now grateful for every drop of Indian blood as survival rates increased in direct ratio.

White and black people, regardless of what continent they lived on, had fatality rates in excess of ninety-eight percent. Asiatics fared slightly better. In some areas almost three percent survived. Australian and Pacific Natives did as well as Native Americans.

The Teeber swept the world in less than a decade. The population of Mexico was down by sixty-five percent. The population of the entire New York metropolitan area was now less than three hundred thousand... and ten percent of those were Indians. Many tribal populations were up. A decade after the Teeber plague, sole survivors of their family or community were often still in shock.

"Howdy, Bob," Jordan called.

The goofy-faced old man pressed his palms together and bowed slightly, oriental style. Mali noted that his grey hair and beard were neatly trimmed and his faded cotton shirt and pants were clean. Perhaps he wasn't completely crazy.

Mali extended a hand, but Bob only smiled and bowed slightly again. Then he ducked back in the house. Mali turned to Armand with a questioning look.

"He used to be a martial arts master," Armand said. "Caught me rifling his altar. He thought he was going to pull my kidneys out my belly button."

The pianist paused dramatically in a somewhat obscene martial arts stance.

He sure moves quick for such a fat old man, Mali thought.

The pianist lunged forward as if to fall on his face. Mali jumped. Pardee, who had heard the story before, laughed. Armand continued.

"But I barfed in his face." He gestured back towards the house. "Stuck to me like a lost puppy ever since."

Mali looked to Jordan to see if he was being put on, but his guide's face revealed not a thing.

"You're going to have horse jerky you don't get those animals to some shade," Armand said.

Jordan led his horse to a cottonwood-canopied corral. Mali and Pardee did the same. After three weeks practice, Mali could remove his saddle and bridle almost as smoothly as Jordan.

Mali had hired Jordan in Phoenix, which, unlike the Midwest, was not rendered uninhabitable by the greenhouse effect. New Mexico's climate was slightly hotter, but not greatly changed. Closer to the center of the continent was now unlivably hot and dry. The Arizona low desert was desert no more. Two hundred inches of rain a year where twenty years ago there was less than ten kept temperatures a sticky but livable eighty-five to ninety degrees in Phoenix most of the time.

Jordan was mostly Apache. He had checked in at the guide agency Mali was dealing with while in Phoenix buying supplies. The fact he knew both the area Mali wanted to visit and English, in a predominantly Spanish-speaking town, got him the job. They had picked up Pardee at home in Eastern Arizona's White Mountains. They rented the horses when they ran out of maintained road at Zuni. Both Jordan and the Zunis were happy to accept payment in Hawaiian coral, a commodity of far more certain value than the peso.

"How long since you've heard any news?" Jordan asked as they all walked to the house.

The raven squawked back over. Armand squinted significantly at it and scratched his balls. "Mmm, couple weeks. Patricio's packing mail and supplies once a month now all the way from Socorro to Aragon."

"Better watch out," said Jordan. "Next thing you know they'll fix the road and crank up the VLA."

"About time." Armand flung a tanned arm to the blue furnace above. There was a little looseness to his seventy-five year old skin, but clearly not to what lay beneath. "My contract still calls to beam Beethoven out. And Mozart. Schubert and Bach too."

Bob met them at the door, his face as goofy as ever. He now held a small, round object, which he handed to Armand.

"Hah!" Armand bellowed, turning to Mali, "you're not just sight-seeing."

"Why, no," said Mali. "It's been a great trip, but it's too much trouble without a purpose."

"Come on in," said Armand. "Tell us about it."

The inside of the house was a good ten degrees cooler than outside. The three travelers washed the sweat off themselves and then joined their hosts in the main room, which was dominated by a gleaming brown grand piano. A Mimbres design drawing of a duck hung on one wall. On another was a painting of a partly naturalistic, partly visionary mountain scene.

The four men and the boy sat in a circle on the floor. Jordan filled his red stone pipe with tobacco, dedicated it to the four directions, washed it in sage smoke, then lit it and passed it. All smoked till the tobacco was gone.

Then Mali got out his pipe. It was made of hard, dark brown wood. He filled it with marijuana bud.

"You bring that with you?" the pianist asked.

"Yes," said the Hawaiian.

"I thought so. It's a lot stickier than what grows here."

Mali, too, dedicated his pipe and offered it to the spirits of mountain, sea, and fire. Then he lit it and passed it. Everyone smoked till this pipe, too, was burned to ash.

"I camped in the crater of Haleakala," said Mali, "next to a greensword. I had not come especially to dream, just to be alone, but the Goddess spoke to me in the night. 'The time for commerce is come again,' She said. 'You are of a sailing people. But listen first, to the how and the why of trade, in the tone of the high, dry plain.' Then I saw a huge, white metal dish and heard piano music.

"No one knew what to make of the dream till, a few months later, my sister—she's a schoolteacher sometimes—was looking at an old picture book. She showed me a photo of the VLA. Those dishes looked just like the one in my dream. A ship was headed east. I got as far as Phoenix before I found anyone who knew the area to guide me. Things are getting pretty settled. People do want more than they grow or make, and why not?... Only not crazy like last time."

"Don't want to be eaten by consumption, huh," said Jordan, with a quick smile.

Mali blinked and smiled back. "When Jordan, here, told me about you, I knew I was on the track. But I still don't know of what. Your music, maybe? Or do you know something about commerce?"

"Hah!" said the old pianist. He ran long, strong fingers through his huge white beard. "Ever heard of Geronimo?"

"Sure," said Mali.

"We're supposed to be related to him," said Pardee.

"Geronimo spent his last twenty years a prisoner of war," said Armand.

"In Oklahoma," said Pardee, "where my mom's from."

"He still vaulted on his horse when he was older than you," said Jordan, nodding to the white-haired pianist.

"They didn't keep him locked up any more," said Armand. "Wouldn't let him go home to Arizona, but they did send him on the train to quite a few fairs and exhibitions."

"Sounds kind of disgusting," said Mali.

"What he'd do," Armand went right on, "every time the train pulled into a station there'd be a crowd to see the famous Geronimo. So he'd cut the buttons off his coat and sell them. He'd sell his hat too. He traveled with a whole box full of hats. Then, as soon as the train started back up, he'd sew new buttons on his coat so he could do the same thing again at the next stop."

"Shrewd old buzzard," said Jordan.

Mali chuckled.

Armand held up a finger. "Then, when he got home, Geronimo'd send letters to all his relatives on the reservation—you know what reservations were?"

"I've heard," said Mali.

"He'd write and say, if any of them needed money just let him know cause he had plenty. He kept right on doing that—making money off being Geronimo and giving it to his people that needed it. He still died with ten thousand dollars in the bank.—That was a lot of money at the time."

Armand handed Mali the round object Bob had brought. "This is one of Geronimo's buttons."

Mali took the hundred year old brass button with an eagle stamped on it, originally military issue. He looked to the naked old Anglo pianist and his silent, silly-faced companion, to the shiny piano and the glittering hot sky outside the window.

The VLA radio telescope was not visible, but Mali was very aware of its presence—magnificent aspiration of a mad society.

Mali looked again at the brass button. Commerce, aspiration, and madness had been all too intertwined in that world so recently predominant, so recently gone. His own people—he thought of himself as Hawaiian, though he was really less than half Native Hawaiian, mixed with Samoan, Chinese, and white—had a way of life once, just as Jordan's—and Geronimo's did. Those had been swallowed by the ways of the society now gone.

What was to come next would not be the same as any of the past. The Goddess the Teeber-decimated civilization so abused seemed now to favor commerce—and aspiration. Could not one have those two qualities without the madness? Were not trade and the quest to accomplish great things more deeply human attributes than that one skewed way of doing everything whose death throes had coincided with Mali's childhood?

Mali had felt it all along. Trade need not consume. It could also serve people. Geronimo's button made it tangible. Geronimo managed to dignify even a degrading situation, and he did it through trade. Dignity, and remembering to serve: Could that be how to keep the aspiration sane?

Mali's pipe sat next to the abalone shell of sage. The pianist filled the wooden pipe with some marijuana of his own. It was drier than Mali's Hawaiian bud. Armand lit the pipe and raised it in prayer. Then he passed it. When it was gone, he rose and shook his shoulders loose.

"Now Mozart," Armand said, striding to the piano, a wild gleam in his eyes, "then lunch."

His tan chest expanded with high, dry New Mexico air. As he exhaled, Armand's fingers poured forth the musical madness of eighteenth century imperial Vienna, a music so transcendent that it passed beyond the mad world which begat it to the divine realm wherein Mali felt the presence of his Goddess of Haleakala here in a New Mexico canyon.

Pardee slipped out during the music. He came back with a case of salsa they had packed with them as a gift to the pianist.

Armand's fingers flew. In the air above the piano, Mali watched the female human and the animal figures form again.

Author's note: What if the center of our contemporary mainstream society were eliminated, and other social elements left to pick up the the pieces? The title incident is real.

WHAT DOES THE ALGAE EAT?

"Most striking, but dear, what do you call it?"

"The War Between The Haves And The Have-Nots."

"I see," I said. "The Haves want to keep their special privileges, while the Have-Nots want a fair share."

"Don't be foolish." That tone of derision would have terrified me once. She is a... well, Goddess is the term I use to myself. I don't have a better. "Look."

I looked. I suppose Her art will never find favor with the popular taste of these times. It's not much like television. It does not lull as it stimulates. Rather, it bites realer than real, like some dreams, at the same time I feel detached, like a newspaper, or perhaps an old-time newsreel.

Ah, the sensory involvement! That's the paradox... and the risk. You always might fall in. I could smell garbage, rancid in damp sunshine, behind which six spring-wound, skinny young people giggled over arbitrary booty: the precision of a thousand-dollar wrist watch a boy with fake-diamond nose plug picked at with a broken needle—sewing needle, not the other sort—till he popped the case and spilled the tiny machine's clean innards all over the grimy pavement.

I could taste fear, three blocks away as police closed in on an only-slightly-older parolee, selected as scapegoat for the robbery not altogether arbitrarily. The cops could taste his fear too. It fed their nerves, allowed them to put up with their dangerous, thankless jobs.

And the robbees, a state-of-the-medical-art fifty-year-old couple one could hardly call victims in this instance. The watch, a mere trinket to them, carried insurance for far more than its replacement value. The law-enforcement drama their wealth and prestige enabled them to command more than made up in martial excitement what the robbery itself cost them in momentary terror and lost dignity of wet underwear.

"What are they fighting for?"

She kissed me, on the forehead, Her gift in pleasure at my gift of asking, of genuinely wanting to know. The kiss exploded in blissful white light, a rapture comparable to orgasm though it had no sex to it.

"The Haves want More, always More. The Have-Nots just want to destroy. Too bad the Gods have lost their names to power schemes and toys. Empty former clothing draped on such silly lies! People find it too difficult to see who eats what. I find this human distraction frustrating."

A good thing She likes me, I thought. I would not care to be the object of a Goddess's frustration.

"And him?" I pointed to the parolee, cringing now in handcuffs on the dingy back seat of the police car, while the officers strutted off excess adrenaline, terrorized an elderly shopkeeper who didn't understand English very well, called in the triumph of their irrelevant arrest.

"He's just food," She replied with a shrug.

"He looks human to me." The odor of his misery repulsed me, but it was a human stench, or at least animal, not machine in any case.

"Hmmm," She mused. She touched a finger to Her own brow. Regal more than strictly beautiful, I never quite knew whether Her appearance belonged to Her as my own body was a simple fact of my own mortal life. "Oh, it's real," She said once, patting an apparently solid and corporeal hip. "Of course, if you were someone else I'd appear quite different."

Familiarity need not lead to contempt.—Try living with rattlesnakes and grizzly bears; if you remain alive two or three years, you'll understand what I mean.—But one can get used to companionship even as disconcerting as a Goddess. She liked my observant temper. That I sometimes noted points in Her creations of which She had been unaware took considerable getting used to, but it allowed me to share in the creative pleasure of the art. Sometimes it even allowed me moral gratification.

"Let's go for a walk." How vibrant the hand she extended: shaped by the vitality of Her art, graceful as peach blossoms, firm as pine trees on a stark mountainside.

Though tempted by my own human feeling to stay put and worry at suffering, I knew the sacrificial victim would not suffer less if I refused Her suggestion. She wanted to show me something.

At the same time, experience had taught me She needed to consider my question. She did not know the answer! Human feeling. Mine. That of the arrested parolee about whom I asked. Human feeling was less central to Her view than to mine, but not less real. She was willing to contemplate the question I raised of that human being's suffering. What She asked was that I accompany Her contemplation.

That I, or any mere human being, could ask a question, fairly frequently even, to which a Goddess, with the power inherent in the title, did not know the answer, took a great deal of getting used to. Creeds that denied such disconcerting vistas may speak to how humanity lost the Gods' names. I knew there was everything to lose in refusing and everything to gain for us both in accepting Her suggestion.

I took the hand She offered. We walked.

How can I describe a reality that, for a million years, was obvious, second nature, to every human being who survived past the age of two, but is nearly invisible today?

Nature, subject once of awe, of love, of fear, object now mostly of artificial projection. Greed and romance alike miss the point. Desire and need, simultaneous breathtaking beauty and inhuman cruelty, continuing nourishment and lingering death all are real, but Nature exists in continuity. The isolated snippet you notice out the car window, in a TV program, when the hurricane rips your roof off, distorts more than it informs.

I took a good drink of water before we left. Water abounded in turbulent spring release, but we might not find any I cared to ingest. She is a Goddess. She appreciates my company as I do Hers. She is not my magic servant. If anything, I am the servant, though if She had selected a companion for aptitude at plumbing and fence repair, I think She would have chosen someone else. Oh, I keep the goats out of the herb beds, and that takes some wily exertion, let me tell you! But a bucket just squats under the leak in the wellhouse roof as it has for a year… or a decade. Time loses shape.

Her studio stands in a juniper grove, a mile or a millennium beyond the shabby, picturesque village of Apex, preoccupied with small-town gossip and survival. The World's storms: social, political, all that, blow mostly someplace else, wafting through as a breeze just intense enough to amuse the local inhabitants except on rare occasions when the full force leaves everyone in brief shock as an elderly ranch couple gruesomely murdered for their ten-year-old truck, or a shipment of illegal nuclear waste inadvertently stopped in sheriff's cockamamie seatbelt-check roadblock. Mostly the three hundred villagers of Apex attend to babies, hay, and whether the chiropractor a hundred miles south is enough better than the one eighty miles west to be worth the extra two gallons of gas.

Below the juniper grove and a little meadow, two lanes of pavement swirl between somber mountains. Unnumbered, the road leads nowhere in particular and knows nothing of drive-by shootings (though Saturday nights see their share of drunken wrecks). Three cars, or more likely pickup trucks, in sight at once is heavy traffic. People passing wave to each other. Till recently, logging trucks frequently roared past, but not today. The sawmill is closed. Locals blame the spotted owl, an explanation not untrue, though not complete either, as policies of the big distant corporation that bought out the mill twenty years ago have so long dictated no room between big profits and total loss that, even here in Coyote County, people have forgotten any other standard.

We walked through a field: grass, wildflowers, cows, ravens, under tall, budding cottonwood trees, where a step in soft, brown sand released pungent wild rosemary aroma, to the Adobe River. In dry weather two inches deep and ten feet wide, you wouldn't even call it a river someplace else, but this was the American Southwest. It was also spring of a year of floods: Volcano half a planet away? El Niño (a nonexplanation that obfuscates unanswerable Why with ponderous How)? Ecology atilt? Even without the floods, spring snowmelt from the surrounding mountain temenos would have the river deep enough at the gravel road crossing to knock me down.

Here's where significance becomes difficult to convey. What didn't happen matters as much as what did. No, I didn't swim the icy torrent. No, we didn't drive a twenty thousand dollar four-wheeler in, capsize, ruin the truck, drown. No, She didn't transform me into a swan to soar across, though She did turn into a soft brown female mallard Herself, to quack, laughing as She dove for a minnow (soon to be recognized as an endangered species).

I strolled upstream, through a willow thicket where I had to brush the occasional branch out of my way to follow the path utterly invisible to anyone who didn't think to look, obvious to anyone who did. Three barbed wire fences might have shredded hands or pants, but didn't. A black angus bull might have charged me, but just blinked and trotted off instead. A third of a mile up the river, out of sight of road or tourist, a path formed equally by cows, cowboys, and wildlife, none presently about, led to a wide stretch of river. I took off my pants and boots. Sure enough, the river ran only a few inches above knee-deep here, fast and icy, but not dangerous as at the road crossing. On the other side, I carefully wiped any grit from my feet before putting my socks back on, thus averting blisters. She joined me, mallard feathers melting to soft, brown cotton jacket. We strode together up the path, invisible on the juniper-dense, steep bank unless you knew to look, obvious if you did.

What would the teenagers dismantling the fancy watch have done, the watch's owner, the city cops, their chosen scapegoat? An adventure? An ordeal? They weren't here, to cross the Adobe River, to know where and how it could be crossed, as most of humanity once would, as most today do not.

The trail climbed a ridge, steep enough to fill lungs, to stretch calf and thigh, but not difficult. Anywhere else cliffs, all-but-impassable would have impeded our way. Coming down the other side, all human civilization hidden, a rattlesnake, ochre and umber sinuous diamonds, sunned itself on yellow sandstone slab, first rattler I'd seen this spring. I noticed it ten feet away. It didn't bite me. It didn't even rattle. Why get so close as to upset it? Again, no lethal ordeal, no great adventure even, just a thrill and awesome bit of Nature. I took off my green corduroy shirt, tied the sleeves around my waist, stretched in warm, invigorating mountain afternoon. In the valley beyond, a bald eagle hunkered in a ponderosa snag above a creek that tumbled lush snowmelt in brilliant Southwest sun. A dozen elk trotted out from a piñon-covered slope to circle a small meadow and disappear into oaks on the other side.

A killdeer called. A flicker flashed speckled orange and black. It dropped us an orange feather for good luck. We scaled a sweaty bluff, where prickly pear and pricklier cholla grew and scorpions hid under loose rocks, but I did not put a hand on either. Though tumble-slopes indicated past rockslides, and winter freeze-and-thaw had loosened more, none crashed down on our heads nor slid out from under our feet. Was this good fortune the gift of a Goddess companion? There was some luck involved, but mostly it was the obvious attention of eye and hand and foot born of know-the-land as most people have always learned, as most people today know a world of expensive machines, social position, television images, a world sustaining and lethal as Nature, but artificial in how.

"Real world," you call the artifice, exquisite in glory as in grime, full of money, garbage, and police. No. It is the Goddess's odd art; and its nourishment, the seed from which its sustenance has always germinated, lies here, where a great blue heron snags another endangered minnow, where the bluffs stand silent, without opinion in the sunshine while a rabbit darts furtive from a coyote that will catch the rabbit… or another… only when the coyote wakes up a few hours from now.

"I was born here," She said, stating what we both knew as a familiar finger calls attention… to point toward an Unknown, as temperature plummeted with the sun, turned dusk, magnificent final exhalation of afternoon wind purpling mountains and ringing pines against the fragrant sky. "Did I make this, or did it make me?" White bones, of a deer perhaps, with gnaw-marks, lay amid crystal rock, beautiful in itself and indicative of possible gold. The moon, a little more than halfway to full, stood well above tree-clad peaks, giving us several hours of good light to follow ridges back to the trail and the river crossing, whereafter I leaned on a frosty log to rub sand from my feet before putting my boots back on to accompany Her back to Her studio while coyotes and the village dogs colloquized our passage.

No bear attacked us, though we had seen sign. We didn't get trapped on a ledge. I did not fall in the river in the freezing dark. Nor was it all that dark as I knew the time of the moon to guide us and could have found the way, if need, by direction of a few bright stars. Many people can do this. It is not an arcane skill. It is a practice and attention, for which few now have time or need, by which most human beings lived for thousands of years and beings not yet human lived before they even knew what they were doing, like the heron or the rabbit.

Hungry as invigorated, we ate a late dinner, of beans and salad, sausage and chewy homemade bread, with chocolate chip cookies for dessert.—Even a Goddess can like chocolate chip cookies. She claims to have invented them, but I don't believe Her.—She likes my cooking, but She insists no mortal, woman or man, knows how to prepare a salad properly. Who am I to argue? She made the cookies too. I washed the dishes. Then we went to bed, and what we did there is none of your business. Suffice to say I eventually slept satisfied, and whether She slept or not, which I do not know, She gave me the impression She too felt satisfaction.

In the morning, we rose to puffs of wind and a few clouds. "I believe some weather may be coming in," I said.—Fair weather wind would not likely have risen till noon.

"Oh yes," She replied, a bit abstracted. "Shall we see how your prisoner is doing?"

I flushed, shamed. I had forgotten.

The young robbers prowled again, predators in perpetual concrete twilight whose food was excitement. The watch owner fussed over fluorescent insurance forms, documenting invented losses along with the real ones, devouring power as money. The city cops drank coffee and gnawed, as a cow its cud, on the suffering that nourished them. And the prisoner, charged not with the robbery he never committed, but with the parole violation of being arrested, even though innocent, sat in his cell, with smelly drunks and pacing shoplifters, nearly numb, but still alive, still human. What did he want, this bottom-of-the-food-chain human being, the psychic analog of algae? What did the algae eat?

What did the minnow want that the heron ate, or the rabbit dodging sleeping coyotes hours before there would be any hunting that needed to be dodged?

Limp, brown hair and dull, slack face, not fat, not skinny, not ugly, not attractive, still the young man on the grey, chipped concrete bench in the jail was a human being. He knew that he suffered for reasons that made no sense to him. Fear, guilt, injustice, fate: he knew all of those, but none explained him, to himself, no less to me.

As food, he sustained all the others. "But what is he to himself?" I asked.

"Shall we enter the movie?" I knew that ambiguous, seductive smile.

The... Gods, I know the term is inadequate, but what else shall I call Them?... are conservative in a funny way. Infinitely creative, the very means by which the energy of creation takes form, They live in a realm where Time remains fluid. A term such as, "movie," already becoming archaic, has barely absorbed itself into the Gods' vocabulary. Intensity helps catch their attention, but so does repetition, and that takes time, however fluid.

"Could we keep it brief? It doesn't look like a very pleasant movie."

"But so enticing! Look how many more people choose there than here."

A great mystery that, but one I knew well. It was not really the rattlesnakes, floods, or rockslides that deterred most people from living where or as we did, my Goddess and I. Most people do not know how to live here and would subject themselves to disasters, uncomfortable, wallet-hemorrhaging, and probably body-maiming, at every step; but knowing how is just a matter of familiarity and common sense. Most people don't stay that long because a snowmelt stream on the knees seems to them too high a price to pay for the sight of eagles and elk, because they find Nature's rhythms and requirements more annoying to learn than the World's, most of all because they would find it a bore to live here where there's just one local band and ice cream only comes in three flavors. I am grateful. There are few enough such places left for the few of us whose souls require them.

Next thing I knew, the air of eternal days that ended in uniform failure hung dank and heavy about a wan maple branch. I realized the chirping came from my own beak. Two sparrows, we perched on a sickly tree outside the jail. Thank the Goddess sparrows have a short lifespan, I thought. I'd been in her artworks before. Much as I appreciate them, the drama, when in its midst, can weigh exceedingly grave. You may forget everything else.

"Hush," She chirped, "let's listen."

Of course, close up, impressions increased not only in intensity, but in complexity. Whether entering the art added clarity or confusion I could never quite decide.

Take the cops, for example. I had observed that they ate suffering, received nourishment from fear. Whatever their personal taste, that's what their job required. Close up, this remained true, but greatly diluted by each one's individual life. One thought fondly of his daughter, a fine gymnast who would never go to the Olympics but might make a state junior high championship meet. Another worried about his health insurance. A third found prisoners of his own gender sexually exciting and performed the most amazing psychic contortions to hide this fact from himself, not to mention from everyone else.

And minutiae of daily activity obscured even overriding personal concerns: paperwork to fill out, a case to follow up on a particular schedule, lunch.

The prisoner exuded qualities equally individual and complex. Predominant, a dull dread of prison, where he assumed he soon would be, undulated heavy as a damp, translucent blotter. "At least I'm not too pretty," he repeated in his mind like a mantra. Not especially strong, not especially mean, he knew he would be food to those who were, in a prison even more than in the city where he could at least hope usually to be ignored.

Why had he, this time, not been ignored? Why did this jail cage him? The fact that he had done nothing to merit arrest meant less to him than the fact that some quality of his being had attracted arrest. In the past he had stolen, not a robber, no violence, no confrontation, just a thief. But he had stolen, from need, more from resentment of an arbitrary world. He had been caught, several times. Eventually he had been sent to prison. Eventually he had been paroled, mostly just to make room for somebody else in the prison who might or might not have done any more harm than he had. Now, struggling to maintain a minimal lawful existence, the world in which he never really had a place had chomped down on him yet again.

But what did he want?

With a shock, I realized: He was the other side of me. He did not focus on some obsession: power, excitement, sex, wealth, fear. All he really wanted was the peace of his own soul. But, unlike me, he did not know this, still less what would bring him such peace.

I knew, now, what the algae eats. Algae eats anything. Those at the bottom of the food chain are the least specialized. They take whatever they get. It sustains as long as it does. Eventually they wear out, run into something poisonous, or just get eaten themselves.

I felt nauseated, repulsed. Poor slob.

Even as a sparrow, the environment lacked vitality: Drab, unhealthy tree. Dirty concrete. Brown sky. Rank smells. Clashing noises. Choking people. Choking me.

She knew how I felt. "Shall we get out of here?" She asked. A relief. We had not yet strayed so deep into her artifice as to forget any other reality could exist… this time.

"Yes. Please… but could we leave him a gift, something to… to give him hope?"

"I'm not sure there's enough to him for there to be anyone to hope."

She was right, of course. But then, it was Her art. I might once have blamed Her, have held Her morally accountable. But this would be a mistake, a projection of human concerns onto one who is not just inhuman, but is more than human. As soon blame the rain, bringing both life rejuvenated and tearing flood. It was not in Her nature to eliminate the cruel aspects of human soulweaving. I'm not sure She could if She wanted. Even a Goddess has… well, limits is not quite the right word. Pathways, perhaps. There might not be anyplace She couldn't get to, but certain routes took a concentration of disparate energy She found unacceptable, while others… To me it appeared a question of difficulty, of quantity of effort. She gave me the impression that to Her the issue was more aesthetic, or sometimes a matter of continuity of consciousness.

A woodpecker rattled the wall.
I shook my head. The familiar blue quilt on the comfortable, worn sofa informed me we were back in Her studio, a relief let me tell you! Stately pines punctuated a clean, fragrant sky. Increasing clouds only flavored the vitality a different tone.

"There is one gift I could give him." She touched a graceful finger to Her chin, then to Her current opus.

A cop entered the drab holding cell, sandy hair thinning, distracted by his own marital discord. "Here," he said. "You can make a statement. Parole officer'll see you at eleven." He handed the prisoner a pad of yellow, lined, legal-size paper and a cheap, black ball point pen.

The prisoner took the paper and pen, sat listlessly as the cop clanked back out of the cell. Several other prisoners stared at the door, a bright event whose opening meant not so much hope of freedom as just a break, however meagre, in dull futility.

We watched.

The prisoner did not write. What did he have to say? "I was walking down the street, minding my own business, when the cops jumped me. I didn't do nothing." Uh huh. True, but ineffectual, embarrassing even.

He didn't write a thing.

After a while, bored, not even noticing that the very fact of being alive generated a certain vitality, a tension that demanded some outlet, any outlet handy, the muscles of the man's right hand firmed around the plastic pen. He began to doodle.

"There," She said. "Now he can create… himself."

"Will he?"

"More likely than before."

That wasn't really an answer, but it was all the answer She would give.

"You know what?" She said, "I'm going to sign the next one."

Astounded, I replied, "You'd enter Time that far?" Of course, She had already entered Time. How many centuries have known wrist watches, health insurance, ball point pens… or chocolate chip cookies?

"It needs something. Didn't you notice the smell?"

"It stank, but it was a big city. Pollution. Garbage. Jail…"

"Yes, yes, of course, but that puddle under the tree…"

I looked somewhat blank, I must admit.

"Really! What's the point of making you a sparrow if you don't notice things important to sparrows?"

I blushed. I hadn't even noticed there was a puddle under the tree.

"The algae in the puddle was dying. Horrid! What a stink! And you didn't notice?"

"I was preoccupied with the man, human algae…"

"Yes, yes, but if the real algae dies, what will anyone have to eat?"

"It was just a puddle in a big city. The algae's healthy enough here."

"Like your prisoner's soul?"

I looked. He'd stopped drawing, out of energy, defeated.

"I am going to come up with something new," She said, "and I'm going to sign it. But there is something I want from you."

"What's that?"

"I need a name."

"You want me to name *You*?!" I am a man, just a human being with the brevity of view even a full lifespan can contain. "You are a Goddess!"

"I'll find the name I'm to use," She said. "What I need you to do is help me reflect."

She kissed me then, first on the lips, because a Goddess can love, then on the brow. Golden light suffused my head, flowed down to embrace my shoulders, chest, loins. Even my feet felt warm in the glow by which my Goddess chose, in the question of a mere mortal, to reflect on the health and sustenance… of algae in a puddle, on a name to sign Her next creation.

Outside, past the lilac bush just starting to bud, a raven called.

Author's note: In the course of several submissions to Kim Mohan, when he was editor of Amazing Stories, *we got into considerable dialogue about point of view. Finally, I wrote this story, making point of view the story's subject. We both were pleased that this is one which he was able to publish, during one of* Amazing Stories' *all-too-brief revivals. I sometimes think of this story as a signature piece.*

Publication History
(this serves as a continuation of the copyright page)

Counting Tadpoles: *Albedo One*, 2007.

The Nature of Property: *Tales of The Unanticipated*, 1994; *Interzone/Nexus* combined issue, 1994.

The Dashing About Flying Box People: *Analog*, 1999.

Marsh Grass: *Outer Darkness*, 1999.

Executive Search: *Atom Mind*, 1995.

Requiem for an Information Age Worker: *Tales of the Unanticipated*, 2005.

How Bears Survived the Change: *Analog*, 2005; *ESLI* (Russia), 2008.

The Lizard: *Space and Time*, 2005.

A Place Called Out: expanded version of story published in *Trajectories*, 1992.

Why There are Flying Saucers: published in slightly different form, *The Wellspring,* 1980. This version, published, *The Wilderness Outlook,* 1988; *Koekrand* (Netherlands), 1990.

Love of the True God: *Talebones*, 1998.

Passing the Torch: *Asimov's*, 1997.

General Density: *Challenging Destiny*, 2003; *Northwest Passages* anthology of the North American SF Convention, 2005.

Piñons: *Tales of the Unanticipated*, 1989; *Challenging Destiny* (online), 2005.

My Stolen Sabre: *Asimov's*, 2001; *Year's Best Fantasy 2*, edited by David Hartwell and Kathryn Cramer, Harper Eos, 2002.

The Building Inspector: *Aberrations*, 1996.

Circumambulatio: *Hadrosaur Tales*, 2004.

Warrior's Honor: *Analog*, 1997; *Chemistry And Life In The XXIst Century* (Russia), 2001.

Geronimo's Buttons: *Copper Star* anthology of the World Fantasy Convention, 1991.

What Does the Algae Eat?: *Amazing Stories*, 1998.

Milton Keynes UK
Ingram Content Group UK Ltd.
UKHW041828201024
449814UK00001B/245